HARLEM
RHAPSODY

HARLEM
RHAPSODY

HARLEM RHAPSODY

VICTORIA CHRISTOPHER MURRAY

BERKLEY
NEW YORK

BERKLEY
An imprint of Penguin Random House LLC
1745 Broadway, New York, NY 10019
penguinrandomhouse.com

Copyright © 2025 by Victoria Christopher Murray
Penguin Random House values and supports copyright. Copyright fuels creativity, encourages
diverse voices, promotes free speech, and creates a vibrant culture. Thank you for buying an
authorized edition of this book and for complying with copyright laws by not reproducing, scanning,
or distributing any part of it in any form without permission. You are supporting writers and
allowing Penguin Random House to continue to publish books for every reader. Please note that
no part of this book may be used or reproduced in any manner for the purpose of training
artificial intelligence technologies or systems.

BERKLEY and the BERKLEY & B colophon are registered trademarks of
Penguin Random House LLC.

Book design by George Towne
Interior art: Elegant Wallpaper Pattern © Omeris / Shutterstock

Export edition ISBN: 9780593954140

Library of Congress Cataloging-in-Publication Data

Names: Murray, Victoria Christopher, author.
Title: Harlem rhapsody / Victoria Christopher Murray.
Description: New York: Berkley, 2025.
Identifiers: LCCN 2024022679 (print) | LCCN 2024022680 (ebook) |
ISBN 9780593638484 (hardcover) | ISBN 9780593638491 (ebook)
Subjects: LCSH: Fauset, Jessie Redmon—Fiction. |
Harlem Renaissance—Fiction. | Harlem (New York, N.Y.)—Fiction. |
New York (N.Y.)—History—20th century—Fiction. |
LCGFT: Biographical fiction. | Historical fiction. | Novels.
Classification: LCC PS3563.U795 J37 2025 (print) |
LCC PS3563.U795 (ebook) | DDC 813/.54—dc23/eng/20240613
LC record available at https://lccn.loc.gov/2024022679
LC ebook record available at https://lccn.loc.gov/2024022680

Printed in the United States of America
3rd Printing

The authorized representative in the EU for product safety and compliance
is Penguin Random House Ireland, Morrison Chambers, 32 Nassau Street,
Dublin D02 YH68, Ireland. https://eu-contact.penguin.ie

To Jessie Redmon Fauset,
upon whose shoulders I,
and thousands of other writers,
proudly stand

HARLEM RHAPSODY

CHAPTER 1

SUNDAY, OCTOBER 19, 1919

thrust open the taxicab's door, and the moment my T-strap heels hit the pavement, a cacophony of city sounds welcomes me. The music enraptures me first.

I can't sleep at night . . . I can't eat a bite . . .

From a Victrola perched near an opened window, the lyrics from "Harlem Blues" float down, and then Mamie Smith's contralto drifts into the breeze. The joyous sound of two giggling girls skipping past draws me from the song.

"You're just bumping your gums," a man shouts, and uproarious laughter rises from the circle of men dawdling in front of the barbershop a few doors away.

I stand, absorbing it all: the patter of a thousand footsteps of men and ladies and kiddies rushing past . . . motorcars chugging and clanking and clicking behind me . . . honking horns squealing into the air.

'Cause the man I love . . . he don't treat me right . . .

It isn't a cacophony, it's a rhapsody, and my heart races to match its beat.

"Jessie!"

I face my mother and am surprised to see her brown eyes framed by a frown. She points to my valise on the sidewalk next to hers. "Are you expecting me to carry both?"

"Oh." I laugh, and a smile fills her face. "Apologies, Maman. But we're in New York." I twirl in front of her, and my wrap coat billows at my ankles.

"We are." She gives me a short nod. "You're behaving as if you've never lived in a big city."

"You can't compare Philadelphia and Washington, DC, to this. New York is everything. It's music and theater and . . . come on, Maman." Carrying my valise, I rush toward the sienna-brick brownstone.

At the first step, I glance over my shoulder. My mother stands in the same spot. In her pale gold overcoat and matching cloche, she is as fashionable as any New Yorker. But her eyes are as wide as mine as she soaks in the city's vivacity.

My heart swells for the woman who didn't birth me but who, for the last twenty-five years, has nurtured me with love. "You were born from my heart," she's told me since I was twelve.

Over the city's music, I call out, *"Allez, Maman!"* in the same tone she'd used with me moments before.

At the front door, my hand trembles with excitement as I try to steady the key. We step into the vestibule and then through another door before we enter the hallway and I move to the only door on the first floor. But before I insert the key, the door swings open.

"Will!"

"Welcome to New York!"

I study the man I'd first contacted when I was a student at Cornell University, some sixteen years ago. His mustache has been trimmed since I last saw him in August. And there is a bit more silver blending with the jet-black hair of his beard. As always, he's dressed impeccably in one of his brown three-piece, wide-lapel suits. Tonight, though, he wears a more formal bow tie rather than the neckties I know he prefers.

The twinkle in his eyes and his wide smile draw me closer. However, just as I reach for him, I remember. My mother. How had I forgotten her so quickly?

That is the effect of W. E. B. Du Bois. His mere presence emits a magnetic force that is difficult to deny or resist.

This is a reminder that now, living in New York, I must be measured in my actions. This will be different from seeing Will on his occasional stopovers in Washington, DC.

I shift so my mother can enter our new apartment, but she doesn't take a single step. She expects an introduction. "Maman, allow me to present Dr. William Du Bois."

"Mrs. Fauset, it is my absolute pleasure to finally make your acquaintance." He takes her valise.

My mother's smile has vanished. She steps over the threshold and greets Will with a curt "Good afternoon."

My mother strolls around the parlor, taking in the regal Victorian-style room decorated in crimson and gold, and runs her hands over the oak edge of the sofa, then the matching damask-upholstered wingback chairs.

"This is a nice apartment." I hope my mother agrees. I turn to the bay windows facing Seventh Avenue. "But look at this, Maman. This . . . will be my favorite place."

The windows jut out of the brownstone like a pair of owl's eyes keeping watch over the neighborhood.

Will says, "This is the largest apartment, the only one in the building that hasn't been split."

"What do you mean?" My eyes are once again on my mother as she rounds the room.

"With so many people flocking to New York from the South, landlords are reconstructing the spaces, dividing apartments in half, then doubling the rent," Will explains. "I know the owner of this brownstone, so I secured one of the best furnished spaces in Harlem for you."

My mother's steps are silent against the Oriental area rug as she saunters toward the back.

"Some of the gals from the office prepared the apartment. Then, of course, Helen," he says, referring to my sister. "We wanted to make certain you had everything you'd need until your belongings arrive."

My mother pauses where the parlor spills into the kitchen. Even with the icebox, stove, and sink, there is space for a hutch and a small dining table.

"Would you like me to show you the two bedrooms and the water closet, Mrs. Fauset?"

"No." She waves her hand. "I'm certain those rooms are sufficient."

I nod, Will nods, and my mother says nothing as she lowers herself onto the sofa. She sits—back straight, shoulders squared, her coat still buttoned—as if she hasn't determined whether she'll stay.

After a moment, I sit in one chair and Will in the other. Maman speaks first: "Dr. Du Bois, thank you for not only finding us this home, but for securing this job with *The Crisis* magazine for my daughter."

"No thanks is necessary. I wanted to make certain you would be comfortable, and Jessie . . . I mean, Miss Fauset has earned this position as the literary editor. I expect that section of *The Crisis* to thrive under her leadership."

"I agree; my daughter will be a credit to your magazine. Jessie has always been a writer, and has been educated well. She's not only a Phi Beta Kappa graduate, but she's proficient in several languages. And in her teaching career, she has already—"

"Maman," I interrupt, dismayed. My glance shifts between her and Will. "I'm certain Dr. Du Bois doesn't desire a recapitulation of my credentials."

"Yes, I was quite impressed with your daughter when I interviewed her for this position."

"Is that when you first became"—she pauses—"impressed?" Another pause. "With my daughter?"

If Will hears my mother's derision, he gives no indication. "I was very impressed. Beyond Miss Fauset's writings is her understanding that literature is a venue that must be utilized to display the best of the Negro race."

"On that, we can agree, Dr. Du Bois. Literature can be useful in this fight for equality. That's what I tell my daughter. She can change this world with words."

My mother's sentiments are no surprise to Will. I've shared her background, especially the two factors of most interest to me when my widower father, the Reverend Redmon Fauset, introduced Bella Huff as the woman he was going to marry. Bella, herself a widow, was Jewish and a staunch integrationist.

At twelve, I understood Judaism, but had no understanding of an "integrationist." I came to understand the term more by my stepmother's actions than by explanation. She supported the complete social integration of the races, something she spoke about often in my father's church, after she converted to Christianity, and at local NAACP meetings. But she didn't just speak her belief, she lived it. Bella had married a Negro—twice—and in those unions, she'd birthed six mixed-race children.

Will's voice draws me back. "I'm excited for Miss Fauset to be with us at this propitious time, Mrs. Fauset. The war is over, the world is changing, and we not only need to be part of that change, but must also facilitate that change. This is the time for the new Negro, and literature must play its role. At its best, literature is a useful form of propaganda."

My mother tilts her head. "That's an interesting concept."

Will says, "I am not interested in any kind of literature that isn't propaganda. Any art by Negroes must serve one purpose alone—to uplift the race and present Negroes in a way white folks have never seen. Art must serve to change more than minds, art must change hearts. Through literature, stories can be shared that recognize the contributions colored folks have made in just fifty years, post-emancipation. The written word can be more powerful than any speech I can deliver."

"I hear your passion, Dr. Du Bois, and I am inspired by your words."

I release my apprehension about Maman and Will finally meeting. Here, the two can agree. William Du Bois and Bella Fauset possess the same fervor for equality.

But then my mother abruptly says, "How old are you, Dr. Du Bois?"

"Maman!"

Will sits up straighter. "I am fifty-one," he proclaims, with a bit of grandiosity. I do not fault him for this. In his fifty-one years, there are few—colored or white—who can match the accomplishments of W. E. B. Du Bois, the professor and civil rights leader. From his two college degrees, to being the first Negro to receive a PhD from Harvard, along with all of his teaching and writing and speaking, his achievements precede him.

My mother knows this. Yet when he tells her his age, she hums and smirks, and I am at once embarrassed. She says, "It seems you are closer to my age than my daughter's."

Inside I pray to the almighty God above to open the floorboards below and swallow me whole. But it appears I am the only one perturbed.

"What you say may be true, Mrs. Fauset." He responds with an innocence that makes me question how he'd missed the edge in my mother's tone. "That is one thing I admire about your daughter. Her youthful exuberance."

"At thirty-seven, I'm hardly youthful." I laugh through my jitters.

"Perhaps then I'm the exuberant one. Mrs. Fauset, the poetry, essays, and even the book reviews your daughter has contributed to *The Crisis* are some of the best writing we've published. She will bring that excellence to the magazine."

My mother's smile returns. "You have chosen well, Dr. Du Bois. I understand why you are impressed with my daughter."

Again, my mother and Will have reached a respite . . . until: "Dr. Du Bois, I'm certain you're a busy man."

Will nods. "My schedule is quite full."

"Which is why I'm surprised you're here. You knew my daughter had the keys. I understand you'd personally delivered them to her weeks ago. Although, I cannot conjure up a single reason as to why you'd make a trip all the way to Washington, DC, just to give my daughter . . . the keys."

Heat warms my cheeks, and I make a mental note to give Arthur quite a talking-to. I am certain it is my younger brother who shared those details with our mother, since he was visiting when Will came to Washington.

"Yes." Will's eyes are wide. My mother has finally surprised him, and he scrambles for an explanation. "I wanted to make certain, in case I was not available, you would have access to the apartment, as I knew Helen and her husband would be away. However, when my schedule opened up, I thought it best to greet you myself."

My mother asks, "Do you live in Harlem, Dr. Du Bois?"

"Yes. I love it here. This part of New York isn't just a neighborhood. Harlem is a character, with its own personality. I plan to make this place my permanent home."

"Do you and your wife live close by?"

I wince. Will stiffens. "Yes. About a mile away."

"So close," she says, then adds, "It won't take you very long to get home." My mother stands, and Will does the same. "I'm going to look at the bedrooms while Jessie shows you out, Dr. Du Bois."

When she disappears into the hallway, I am both astonished and mortified.

I whisper to Will, "I'm so sorry."

His volume matches mine. "She doesn't like me."

"That's not true," I deny and lie. "She doesn't know you."

He chuckles. "It seems your brother has shared some stories about us."

"No." I shake my head emphatically. "Arthur would never discuss such things, and besides, what does he know? Anything he's heard about us is merely rumor."

"*Ma chérie,*" Will begins, making me smile, "every rumor about us is true." He reaches for my hand, and although I should pull away, I don't. Weeks have passed since I've felt his touch, and I want to slow time.

"I'm so glad you're finally here, Jess." His voice remains low. "This is quite an endeavor. I've built *The Crisis* into the most important periodical for Negroes, and now, with you, it will become the preeminent magazine for Negro writers. Everyone with a poem or a story will want their name inside these pages."

"I'm looking forward to it all."

His voice is thick when he adds, "I'm looking forward to the magazine . . . and much more."

I want to draw closer, but we aren't at the Whitelaw Hotel in Washington, DC, and my mother is not even a stone's throw away.

When I hear my mother's footsteps, Will and I move apart. He takes an envelope from his jacket. "Here is the address and directions to the office. Everyone on staff is looking forward to meeting you."

There is so much more that I want to say and know and ask. But I feel the heat of my mother's stare, so I only thank Will before he exits.

If Maman hadn't been standing so close, I would have rushed to the window to watch him. Instead, I paste on a smile and face her.

She says, "So, that is your Dr. Du Bois."

Her statement is designed to set a snare, so I press my lips together and say nothing.

"He's not at all what I expected."

I am unable to resist. "What do you mean, Maman?"

"He has the reputation of being such an important and grand man." A beat. "And yet, he's rather short."

CHAPTER 2

MONDAY, OCTOBER 20, 1919

I stand transfixed in front of the alabaster-colored brick building. Behind me, the trolley car creaks and whistles. Around me, people hasten to their jobs.

Yet I scarcely hear a sound. I just stare at the twelve-story structure at 70 Fifth Avenue. Five floors up are the offices of the National Association for the Advancement of Colored People—and where I'll be working, as *The Crisis* magazine is the NAACP's premier publication.

Although I've written for *The Crisis* since I submitted my first What to Read column in 1912, I have never visited the headquarters. In the ten years since its founding with the aim of combating the savagery of lynching, the NAACP has taken legal battles to the Supreme Court, fought against President Wilson's resegregation of federal agencies, and even organized the Silent Parade two years ago, the largest mass protest by Negroes in this country.

When I enter the lobby, the elevator operator nods his greeting. I step into the cage, and he drags the wrought iron gate until it clinks shut.

"Fifth floor, please."

The chamber creaks and groans on its ascent until it shudders to a stop. In front of the fifth-floor office with the letters NAACP stenciled onto the frosted glass panel of the door, I take a second to appreciate this moment.

Inside, the space is charged with energy. The large room is abuzz with clacking typewriters, clicking adding machines, and the rhythmic tapping from an incoming telegraph.

A young woman, perhaps eighteen, stands from her desk. She wears a simple white lace-collared blouse atop a black skirt. Her striking straight black hair is pulled into a single braid draped down her back. "May I help you?"

"My name is Jessie Fauset and I'm here to see—"

"Oh, Miss Fauset. I'm Pocahontas Foster, Dr. Du Bois's stenographer. He said I'm to show you to your office."

She leads me around the perimeter, and we stop outside a small room with sufficient space for a desk, two chairs, and an empty bookcase.

"Dr. Du Bois is in a meeting. He'll be with you shortly." I thank her and she turns away, but in an instant, spins around to face me once again. "Miss Fauset, I hope I'm not being too forward, but all of us girls are so excited. It's remarkable that a Negro woman will have such an important position at *The Crisis*." She beams when she adds, "We're so proud."

I clasp my hands together. "Thank you, Miss Foster." When I'm alone, I remove my coat and settle behind the desk. The room is bright, the light filtering in from the huge window across from me. This is *my* office.

I sit, and try to picture the days, months, and years ahead, before I reach for my canvas bag and my small Bible inside. My father had given me this when I was just seven. I close my eyes and recall his words:

I may not always be by your side, little lamb, but as you carry this holy book, always remember that my love for you is everlasting and my belief in you is resolute.

Papa's belief in me is why I believe in myself. Just as I tuck the Bible into the top desk drawer, Miss Foster taps on my door.

"Miss Fauset," she says, "we just received this for you." Her tone is suffused with awe. "We've never had flowers delivered here." She hands me the vase with three roses. "I asked the messenger, but there isn't an accompanying card."

"Thank you," I say before Miss Foster exits once again.

I inhale the flowers' fragrance, and at once, I'm taken back to the only other time I received flowers as a gift—a single rose. From Will.

Just then, a rather short man with broad-set eyes and a wide smile peeks into my office. "Miss Fauset, I'm Augustus Granville Dill, and it is a pleasure to meet the woman who has honored *The Crisis* with some of the finest poetry and prose I've ever read."

"That is quite the welcome, Mr. Dill." I laugh.

He sits in the chair beside my desk. "I've been reading your writing for years, and it makes sense to have you join us."

"Dr. Du Bois," I begin, remembering to speak of Will properly, "has told me you've been an asset to *The Crisis*. No organization is successful without a competent business manager."

For a few minutes, we chitchat. I tell Mr. Dill about my time in Washington teaching Latin and French at Dunbar High School, and he shares how he and Will met at Harvard and have been working together at *The Crisis* since 1913.

"I hope you're prepared for this, Miss Fauset," he says. "We're a lean staff."

It hadn't occurred to me to ask Will about the people I'd work with. "How many work for *The Crisis*?"

"Well"—his brow furrows—"there's W. E. B. and me. And now you." He grins.

I wait for him to continue, and when he doesn't, I ask, "Just the three of us?"

He nods. "Of course, the stenographers assist, and even board members and others will help when needed. And we work with outside operators like the printer, who assists with everything from the layout to the printing, and then the distributor."

The three of us? Has Will been publishing the magazine for the last almost ten years with no assistance?

Mr. Dill glances at his wristwatch. "I've been asked to give you an office tour."

"I'd like that." I follow Mr. Dill to the threshold of my door.

From where I stand, I can see the entire expansive space. It feels cramped, but only because of the half dozen escritoires and other desks. The telegraph machine is in one corner, and in the other, a multigraph printing machine.

Mr. Dill says, "From here, you can see everything. This area is what some of us call the bullpen; it's the heartbeat of the NAACP." I watch the young men and women scurry about. Even with all the movement, there is order and efficiency to the activity.

"About half of these young people are employees, and the others are volunteers who field calls, help with research and anything we need. Sometimes, the gals will run out and grab sandwiches and Coca-Colas for us." That makes him chuckle. "It sounds mundane, but it's all important work."

I inhale, as if by that gesture, I'll absorb it all.

"The offices on the perimeter"—he motions to the doors, each with frosted glass panels, surrounding the bullpen—"are for the officers of the NAACP. It isn't very big, but you don't need much space in the struggle."

When Mr. Dill spins to the left, I do the same. Without saying a word, he steps inside the corner office. However, I freeze and stare at the five faces surrounding the table.

"Miss Fauset." Will, who is sitting on the other side, stands. "Welcome." His smile calms me. "I was hoping you would arrive before we concluded." Will rounds the table until he's by my side. "You're here on the rare occasion when several of our esteemed members are in New York. Everyone, I'd like to introduce Miss Jessie Redmon Fauset, the new literary editor for *The Crisis*." Turning to me, he says, "And Miss Fauset, this is—"

Will begins what feels like a roll call, but introductions aren't necessary.

Although we've never met, their reputations as founders and staff of the NAACP precede them. On one side—Moorfield Storey, the seventyish Boston-born attorney and current president; and the much younger Joel Spingarn, the treasurer and a member of the family that funds the Spingarn Medal, the prestigious annual award presented to Negroes for outstanding achievement. And finally, Mary White Ovington, whom I am most delighted to meet. Not only is she the chair of the board, but I admire her. Years ago, I reviewed her open letter she'd written for *The Century* magazine titled "On the New-Time Negro," and I appreciated her audacity, as a white woman, to broach the subject of how colored men had changed from enslavement to the present.

Finally, Will turns to the only other Negro around the table, and the only man who stands to greet me. "Miss Fauset, I don't know if you've ever met Mr. James Weldon Johnson, the field secretary for the NAACP."

"Mr. Johnson, it is certainly an honor." I hope I conceal my excitement. Mr. Johnson is a hero to colored folks. I'm giddy, standing before the man who, almost twenty years ago, penned a poem that turned into a hymn and had just, this year, been declared the Negro national anthem. "I do have to say, Mr. Johnson, every time I sing 'Lift Every Voice and Sing,' I'm inspired."

While the gentlemen smile and proffer greetings, Miss Ovington bids me no words of welcome. Instead, she turns to Will. "You said she will be the literary editor?"

My inclination is to step forward and speak for myself, but I defer to Will. I must be careful on this, my first day, my first meeting, my first impression.

Miss Ovington's eyes narrow. "I wasn't aware we needed another editor."

"I brought this before the board, Miss Ovington," Will says with a patience in his tone that lets me know he's accustomed to repeating himself to her. Then, turning to Mr. Dill, he says, "Would you mind giving Miss Fauset the papers we discussed?"

I make certain to smile at everyone, even as Miss Ovington turns away. When Mr. Dill and I step outside, I whisper, "What should I know about Miss Ovington?"

He waves his hand. "She's very protective of the NAACP and every-thing that comes with it, including W. E. B." At my office, he pauses. "I'll be right back."

As I wait, I start to replay my exchange with Miss Ovington; how-ever, all thoughts of her are abandoned when Mr. Dill returns, carrying two boxes stacked so high, I can't see his eyes. He dumps the cartons onto my desk.

"What is this?"

"A gift from W. E. B." He chuckles. "He said you would take charge of this."

I shift through the mountain of paper: letters to the editor, poetry and short story submissions, advertising requests. The correspondence isn't limited to *The Crisis* business alone. There are letters from colleges, inquiries for appearances, and letters referring to the subject of a Pan-African Congress. Most are dated from months before.

When I glance up, Mr. Dill grins down. "W. E. B. said you were an organizer. We need a system to keep up with all of this."

"What has been your system up to now?"

He points to the boxes.

I shake my head. This isn't my responsibility. "Mr. Dill, I'm not . . ."

I pause. Refusing this request on my first day wouldn't be the most prudent course. Especially after learning there is such a thin staff. Start-ing over, I say, "I'm not . . . certain where I'll begin. However, I'll get right to work."

"Great." He hastens from the room.

I sigh. This is quite disorganized, but it won't take much time to devise some structure for the contents of these two boxes. As I settle into that thought, Mr. Dill returns with two more cartons. Then two more, until a dozen overflowing boxes are lined against the wall. "That's all of it," Mr. Dill says, just as there is another tap on my door.

"Ah, Miss Fauset." Will steps inside. "I see Augustus is helping you become acclimated."

I hear the challenge in his tone, and I match it. "Although this isn't quite what I expected, I'm certain you put me in charge of this project because you know I'm capable."

"You are quite capable, and this will benefit both of us. By the time you complete this, my files and correspondence will be organized, and you'll be fully versed in the business of *The Crisis.*" His glance wanders to the roses on my desk. When he returns his gaze to me, I nod my gratitude and he smiles.

Will says, "I have several meetings this morning, but we should have lunch, Miss Fauset. In the interim, Augustus, do you have a moment?"

Before he answers, there is another knock. Miss Ovington steps inside and snatches my smile away. "Dr. Du Bois, I need a moment with you . . ." Her eyes center on me. "Miss . . ." She pauses as if my name escapes her.

"Fauset," I say, quite certain she remembers.

She gazes at me as if my mere presence is a personal affront. "I must have a better understanding of your position here before I can agree to such a hire."

"Miss Ovington," Will begins, "Miss Fauset has already been hired, but you said you need a moment with me?"

"Oh yes." She pivots, and I'm completely forgotten.

Will gives me a reassuring nod before he and Mr. Dill follow Miss Ovington.

For heaven's sake. What a way to begin.

CHAPTER 3

MONDAY, OCTOBER 20, 1919

Will and I step into the Civic Club, and a wave of awe washes over me. The entrance is grand: a vaulted ceiling adorned with intricate golden designs soars above us, while the white marble floor gleams beneath our feet. Chandeliers, resplendent with hundreds of glittering crystals, cast a dazzling light across the space. This is the epitome of opulence and grace.

"Good afternoon, Dr. Du Bois." A gentleman with a stiff-collared white shirt and black tails greets us. "Shall I have your coats checked?"

"Thank you," Will says, and the gentleman nods to a young colored man hovering nearby.

As the maître d' leads us to the dining room, a man and woman, somewhere in their twenties, stop us.

"Dr. Du Bois." The woman, whose blue eyes shine bright, says, "It is an honor to meet you. I started my new job today at the Women's Peace Party."

"I'm very familiar with the WPP, and the good work being done there. Congratulations."

"Well." She glances at the young man, and when he says nothing, she continues, "It was a pleasure." The two scurry away, chattering with excitement.

Finally, Will and I settle at our table. With its gold candelabras and ashtrays atop white-linen-draped tables, the dining room is even more elegant than the entrance. The three gilded mirrored walls create the illusion of grandeur, reflecting the dozens of tables and making it appear as if there are hundreds in this room.

Waiters angle throughout, serving men dressed in three-piece suits and women draped down in smart day dresses. Here, the faces are more racially variegated than I've seen since my arrival in New York. Colored and white mix together, some even sharing a meal at the same table, exactly the way the founders of this Greenwich Village club—many of whom were members of the NAACP—wanted it to be.

When I turn back to Will, his grin meets my smile. "What?" He laughs, and I say, "I love this place, I love New York. I love everything in and about this city."

"You love New York over Paris?"

"I adored my summer in Paris, but this"—I hold out my arms—"the world is the body, and New York is its heartbeat. Now I'm a New Yorker, and I hope to live here forever."

He nods. "After living so many places, New York, especially Harlem, feels like my North Star. But it's not because of the city alone. The NAACP and specifically *The Crisis* . . . that's what makes my heart beat. That"—he leans closer, covering my hand with his—"and you. Now that you're here, I hope you'll be in New York forever, too."

He caresses my hand, and I can scarcely breathe. I command myself to pull away, but I feel utterly defenseless against the power and the pull that have always drawn me to this man. The attraction overwhelms my good sense. I am lost until . . .

"Dr. Du Bois."

At the sound of the man's voice, I snatch my hand away and Will stands.

"Dr. Imes." He greets the gentleman.

I hesitate to glance up, but once I do, I take in the tall, fair-complexioned man, wearing round wire-rim spectacles. The woman next to him could have been his sister, except for the way she clings to his arm.

"It is good to see you, Dr. Du Bois," Dr. Imes says. "I'd like to introduce my wife, Mrs. Nella Larsen Imes."

Will nods at the woman, then says, "And I'd like to introduce Miss Jessie Redmon Fauset. Miss Fauset is the new literary editor for *The Crisis*."

"My word!" Dr. Imes exclaims. "*You're* the new editor?"

"The literary editor," Will hastily corrects.

"Congratulations! And please excuse my husband," Mrs. Imes says as she playfully yanks his arm. "I, for one, am very excited to see a woman in one of the top positions at *The Crisis*."

Dr. Imes flashes a bashful grin. "My apologies," he says. "My only excuse is that I must become accustomed to women in such positions. Please allow me to add my congratulations to my wife's."

I thank Dr. Imes, and he adds, "This meeting is indeed serendipitous. Just this morning, I was again encouraging my wife to follow her passion—she's a writer as well."

"Are you?" Will says, and now we all face Mrs. Imes.

She raises her eyes to the heavens, but her smile signals she is pleased by her husband's mention. "Yes, although I haven't completed anything."

"Perhaps you will now," the doctor says to her. Then he explains, "My wife is a nurse by education and training; however, she was just hired as a junior assistant at the 135th Street library." Dr. Imes's chest swells with his words.

"Now we must say congratulations," Will says, and I nod. "I love that Miss Ernestine Rose has started to integrate her staff."

"Yes," Dr. Imes says. "My wife is only the second Negro to be hired."

"Impressive," Will says. "I'll have to send Miss Rose my congratulations."

As Will and the doctor chitchat, Mrs. Imes stands and I sit silently, although we exchange glances and smiles every few seconds.

"I believe our table is ready," Dr. Imes says as he nods toward the maître d'.

After we say our goodbyes, Will returns to his chair. "I *really* like Dr. Imes. He's only the second Negro to receive a PhD in physics. I'd like to get the Imeses more involved in the NAACP. Perhaps it will do us well if you were to invite Mrs. Imes to lunch."

"I'll do that."

My motivation differs from Will's. The moment he'd mentioned the doctor's credentials, I knew the Imeses were his kind of people. I, on the other hand, have a single reason why I'd love to dine with Mrs. Imes— to gain a new friend in this new city. Perhaps she'll consider submitting a piece for *The Crisis*.

A young waiter steps close, and when Will glances up, his smile is instant. "Patrick, I was hoping I'd see you today. I want you to meet my guest, Miss Jessie Fauset." To me, he says, "Patrick Jackson is a student at Columbia University."

"Oh, what are you studying?"

His lips spread into the widest smile. "Languages."

"That was my concentration."

Before I can say more, Will interjects, "Miss Fauset has a degree from Cornell, she just received her master's from the University of Pennsylvania, and she's the first Negro woman to graduate Phi Beta Kappa."

"That's astonishing."

"She also studied at the Sorbonne." There is a shade of pride in his tone, as if he is a proud father . . . or lover.

Will beams as he says, "I invite Patrick to our offices often because this young man is our future."

The young man stands straighter, as if he wants to be worthy of Will's extolment. "Dr. Du Bois, will you be having your usual for lunch?"

Will nods, then says to me, "Everything here is good."

I peruse the bill of fare quickly and choose the clam broth and pork chops.

When Patrick steps away, Will wags his finger in his direction. "We must do all we can to raise more young men like that who are educated and proud of their heritage. They will rise up to lead our race into greatness. I can envisage a world where, one day, a young Negro man such as Patrick is president of the United States." I laugh, but even when he does not, Will isn't offended. "Jess, look at what we've achieved in just two generations post-emancipation. To me, that vision is clear. That is why I fight so hard, for a future that is not only possible but essential."

"I may not be able to see what you see, but I can certainly pray for such a day."

We pause as our soups are served, and Will waits as I bow my head and say grace. Then he continues, "To have that kind of future, we need more young men like Patrick. But those young men are not born, they're raised. Our community must construct a world where we're educating and providing the tools for them to become leaders. Currently, we're not doing enough to build that world for our children."

"*Pas assez?* That's poppycock, Will. What about the children's edition?" I ask, referring to the annual issue of *The Crisis* dedicated to young readers. "Inside those pages, you are creating that world."

"The children's edition is only a single annual issue, and the positive messages to our children must be more consistent. There is only one way to accomplish that—through a monthly magazine for colored children."

"In the last issue of *The Crisis*, I noticed the announcement, but you never mentioned it to me."

"I've been awaiting your arrival. This is one of my dreams, Jess, but I'll need you to help me bring it to fruition."

I smile. "I'm intrigued."

With the same passion in his voice every time he speaks about uplifting Negroes, he says, "In a country where white supremacy reigns, how can we raise leaders who feel themselves worthy, when they're being told they're no more than pickaninnies or are called niggers, like in that children's poem that's been published everywhere?"

Those words stop my heart, which is exactly what happened when I first read that poem. I couldn't continue beyond the first line:

Ten little nigger boys went out to dine; one choked his
little self . . .

Through my haunting thoughts, Will keeps on. "That poem . . . that
is why we must do this. We must imbue our children with messages that
override what they're being told by America. And we can do this through
a magazine where the children of the sun are educated in everything
that is beautiful about being a Negro. I want them to read about colored
doctors, and attorneys and engineers, and teachers and writers. I want
them to read about Negro men who—"

"And women," I interrupt.

At first Will frowns, then he smiles. "Negro men *and* women who've
already set the path and shown the way. Through the pages of this magazine, we will nurture the next generation of the talented tenth."

Ah, yes. The talented tenth. A perpetual thought and constant consideration of W. E. B. Du Bois. A notion that Will first conceptualized
in 1903, in an essay that sent Negroes throughout the country into a
fervor.

Will had declared that the betterment of the Negro race rested upon
colored men earning college degrees, rather than the vocational and
industrial training that others, like Booker T. Washington, espoused.
Then, the best of the best—ten percent—would set aside their own aspirations and become race leaders, examples for the ninety percent to
follow.

"I already have a name for the magazine, the *Brownies' Book*, and
Augustus and I started a publishing company—Du Bois and Dill."

I tilt my head. "It won't be published by the NAACP?"

"No, there's no need. *The Crisis* is self-sustaining through subscriptions, and this magazine will be as well. I have spoken to several board
members who think this is a splendid idea."

Splendid indeed! How thrilling it will be to act as a guiding force
in shaping how Negro children are seen, especially through their own
eyes.

I lean toward him. "Let's do this. Ideas are already spinning in my mind. I'll handle the initial planning and whatever research you need for us to move forward."

"Excellent," Will says. "And inside some of those boxes, you may find submissions."

"Already?"

He nods. "Since I made the announcement, we've been inundated. Jess, perhaps you haven't yet grasped the profound influence of *The Crisis*. If colored writers want to see their words in print, the largest Negro publication is their best, and most times only, opportunity. With the *Brownies' Book*, we'll open that door even wider."

"Then I'm ready," I say, just as our main courses are set before us. "Do you have a timetable?"

He grins and whispers, "The first of the year."

My fork clinks against the china. "The first of this coming year? Nineteen twenty? In less than three months?"

He shrugs. "I think we can do it."

I take a deep breath—*The Crisis*, the organization of the magazine's files . . . and now the *Brownies' Book*. I exhale. "Yes, we can do it."

Then we veer away from business, chitchatting about Congress passing the Volstead Act and whether President Wilson is well or concealing a serious illness, and when I tell him that I'm currently reading *The Wages of Men and Women: Should They Be Equal?*, he says, "I think I'll join you in reading that. I envisage we'll have quite a discussion."

"Oh yes, we will," I say, always loving when Will and I read books together and the animated discussions that follow.

Finally, we push aside our plates, and as a busboy clears them away, Patrick steps up to Will. "Dr. Du Bois, are you ready for your package?"

"Yes, thank you." Will taps a cigarette from his case, then lights a Benson & Hedges. Within seconds, Patrick returns and places a plain white gift box in front of me.

I stare at the package, then turn to Will. "What is this?"

He shrugs. "You'll have to open it and see."

While the package is simple, what's inside is not. I gasp as I hold the gold-buckled double-strapped brown leather satchel.

"Will," I whisper as I caress the soft leather. "It looks just like . . ."

"It is," he says before I can finish.

When Will traveled to Washington in August, we'd spent the day strolling along Seventh Street, stopping in Hecht's, a rare haven for Negro shoppers. Inside, amid the glass and mahogany display cases, I'd admired this leather satchel, the price far beyond my means.

"Look inside."

I unbuckle the straps, and my heart leaps again. Now I hold a leather journal whose cover matches the satchel. And inside the front cover is an inscription:

J:

From the day you first shared the story you want to write, I have been anticipating your great American novel. I know you can do it. I will always believe in you.

W.

I swallow the tide of my rising emotions. "I don't know what to say," I whisper.

"Just say you're finally going to complete your novel." Holding his cigarette aloft, he edges closer. "You have such a gift, and while I know you'll be occupied with your responsibilities at *The Crisis*, I want to see your dream come to fruition, too." With his free hand, he grasps mine. "What can I do to help you, Jess? What can I do to help you achieve your dream?"

CHAPTER 4

MONDAY, OCTOBER 20, 1919

A s I pay the cabbie, a tap on the car's window startles me. My sister presses her face against the glass, and I slide out and into the arms of Helen, or Mary-Helen to me. Once my sister married, she dropped the Mary, but I still address her by her childhood name.

"I'm so glad to see you, Sissy." She speaks with such glee that anyone passing would believe I'm returning home from war. "Goodness gracious, it is almost midnight."

After a long embrace, I step back. "Midnight? It's just after nine."

With a wave of her hand, she dismisses my words. "It's dark! Darkness, midnight. Come inside," she says, as if she's inviting me into her home instead of mine.

We loop our arms together, and I'm reminded of our earliest days. When my sister, seven years older, would leave her high school classes to meet me so I wouldn't walk home alone.

Inside, I greet our mother with a kiss. "Bonsoir, Maman."

"Bonsoir. Did you have a good day?"

"I did. It was long and exhausting and one of the best days of my life." I slip my coat over my shoulders, keeping the satchel from my mother's view. There is no need for that discussion this evening.

Mary-Helen says, "You must tell us everything about your first day in such an auspicious position." She sweeps her arm through the air, then bows at the waist.

I laugh. Although my sister is a teacher, the stage seems more apt for her talents.

"I want to hear everything," my mother says, though she sounds weary. I reach for her hand.

"Are you well, Maman? What did Mary-Helen have you doing today?"

Mary-Helen answers for her. "Bella and I had a marvelous time."

Twenty-five years have passed, yet I've never become accustomed to the way Mary-Helen addresses Maman. The first time I'd heard her call our stepmother by her given name, I'd held my breath, waiting for Papa to dispense swift punishment for her insolence.

Our father, however, hadn't winced. I realized that at nineteen, Mary-Helen could indulge in behavior that I would never be able to at the age of twelve.

Maman says, "We had a delightful day. First, our trunks arrived this morning and Helen helped me unpack. Yours is in your bedroom."

"Unpacking alone wouldn't have you so tired."

"We strolled through the neighborhood, and then Helen took me to the 135th Street library."

"It's one of my favorite places. And today, there was an art exhibit of the work of James Van Der Zee."

"Oh, I would have enjoyed that," I say of the work of the colored photographer who is swiftly rising to prominence in the city.

Maman says, "It was an exhibit of the pictures he took of the Harlem Hellfighters when he photographed their victory parade earlier this year."

"Sissy," Mary-Helen says, "the pictures were amazing. But it wasn't just the exhibit that was wonderful. Bella has already made a friend."

My eyebrows rise as my mother explains, "We met a lovely lady. Ernestine Rose, the branch librarian."

"Miss Rose and Bella have much in common. She's a writer like you two, and she's doing incredible things at the library. Her library is the first integrated branch in the city."

"I met one of the young ladies Miss Rose hired," I say, "Nella Larsen Imes. She's a writer as well."

"Is everyone in this city a writer?" My sister shakes her head. "You met her at the office?"

I hesitate, then say, "Something like that," not wanting to explain my lunch with Will. "It's exciting to have Negroes working in the library."

"As it should be," my mother says. "Harlem is becoming colored and—"

"Becoming?" Mary-Helen shoots straight up in her chair. "Haven't you heard, Bella? Harlem *is* the colored capital of the world. The food, the music, the people." She prattles on with an enthusiasm for the city that matches mine. "I cannot wait to show you everything."

Maman chuckles. "I want to see it all; however, first"—she turns to me—"tell me, did you meet any poets today?"

Exhaustion peppers her tone, yet there is a fervent light in her eyes. She shines that way whenever we speak about my writing.

Our love of reading and passion for writing has been our connection from the day we met. It was Maman who'd introduced me to authors like Conan Doyle and H. G. Wells, books like *Les Misérables* and *The Picture of Dorian Gray*, and magazines like *McCall's* and *Redbook*.

And it was Maman who encouraged me to study languages at Cornell and spend a summer in Paris at the Sorbonne. She believed all of that would help me become a better writer . . . a desire she's harbored since her own childhood.

"Not today. However, I met several members of the NAACP board and staff, and I learned of my responsibilities. And Will"—I quickly correct—"Dr. Du Bois and I discussed publishing a children's magazine."

"In addition to *The Crisis*?" Mary-Helen asks.

I nod.

"That sounds like so much. *Ma chérie*"—Maman's tone is stern—"what about *your* writing?"

"I'll be writing even more than before for the magazine."

"And your novel?" she questions. There is a longing in her voice when she adds, "You must have time to work on the novel you've dreamed of writing."

My dream has become Maman's as well. "There is a lot before me, but I will write my novel."

She gives me a satisfied smile. "I think I'll retire now." She presses her palm against my cheek. "I'm so very proud of you."

She hugs Mary-Helen, and my sister and I stay silent until her footsteps fade behind her bedroom door. Then Mary-Helen hops up and in two steps flops onto the sofa beside me. "I want to hear everything you didn't tell Bella."

"C'était incroyable."

"Speak English!" Mary-Helen waves her hand. "No more Latin."

I laugh. "Not Latin, French."

"It's not English. A summer in France and now you're a Frenchwoman."

"Oh, I wish I were. I speak in English, but I *dream* in French."

"Enough dreaming. Tell me more."

"Every hour was astounding. From the office to lunch at the Civic Club to—"

"Stop!" Mary-Helen holds up her hand. "The Civic Club? That must have been divine."

I sound breathless when I lean back and say, "It was the best part of my day."

My sister's eyes narrow, and the joy vanishes from her voice. "Were you with Dr. Du Bois?"

"Yes, we had a business lunch . . ."

"Um-hmm."

"To review my responsibilities." My sister hums again. "There was much for us to discuss. *The Crisis*, the children's magazine, and I'm organizing all of the publication's files."

"Sounds like Dr. Du Bois will benefit greatly from your presence."

"Absolument!" Sitting up, I twist to face my sister. "I'm so happy right now, Mary-Helen."

"Happy because of your close proximity to Dr. Du Bois?"

I glance toward my mother's bedroom. "Perhaps we shouldn't discuss this right now."

"Do you believe Bella doesn't know about the two of you? Everyone knows."

"No one knows," I whisper. "You're the only person I've ever told." I give her a sideward glance. "Any rumor would have come through you."

"Perhaps I'm the only one you've told, but anyone who has eyes can see."

"Will and I have been very careful."

"'Careful' is not a word you can use with a married man." She lowers her voice when she adds, "Jessie, he's married," as if I'd missed her point.

Her words are colder than a bucket of ice water, dousing me in the truth. For five years, those words—*he's married*—have been my sister's mantra to me. For five years, those same words have echoed incessantly in my mind.

When I say nothing, Mary-Helen continues, "Before, I only feared for the whispers about you and Dr. Du Bois. But I confess that, while I'm thrilled you're here, I'm consumed with worry. His wife and daughter have returned from Europe, and now all of you will be living right here in Harlem."

I sigh. "When I asked Will for assistance in finding a place to live, I never considered he'd choose an apartment so close to his home."

"So very close," Mary-Helen says. "That means you'll soon find yourself in the very same spaces as his wife. In the same stores, sharing the same aisles, visiting the same salons, and even mingling at dinner parties. How on earth will you navigate crossing paths with her on Lenox Avenue?"

Her question is sobering. "Has there ever been a force in your life that brought you an equal measure of joy and sorrow?" I don't pause for my sister's response. "When I received Will's letter offering me this position, I was stunned that he'd create a role for me at his magazine.

"But then, quickly I questioned, why would he make this offer knowing I'd have to relocate to New York? We wouldn't be able to carry on while living in the same city. I considered that perhaps Will was asking *me* to make a choice. To remain in Washington, where everything would stay the same between us, or to come to New York, where everything in my life would change. He wanted me to decide whether I wanted to be with him or become the literary editor."

Mary-Helen's eyebrows rise, my words astonishing her. "Is that what Dr. Du Bois said?"

"This was my assumption, and surprisingly, my choice wasn't difficult. I wanted the position more than I wanted him."

My sister's eyes narrow. "So . . . are you saying . . . that you and Dr. Du Bois are no longer—"

I shake my head. "When we spoke, Will made it clear that was not his intent."

My sister moans. "Of course it wasn't. Why would he want to end it with you when now he can have you and his wife so close to him?" She clicks her tongue, the echo of her disapproval resounding throughout the parlor. "Why shouldn't he set you up here?"

"This isn't a setup, Mary-Helen," I snap. "Will is not financing me, and I've rightfully earned this position. I've been with *The Crisis* for six years." I begin counting off on my fingers. "I've written close to one hundred pieces, I've read and reviewed hundreds of books, my column is among the magazine's most popular, and I've constantly advocated for the inclusion of more poetry and short stories." I cross my arms. "Although this is precisely what I've always desired to do, I never envisaged there would be such a role for me. However, now that Will has created this position, I *should* be the literary editor."

"My apologies, Sissy," she says, and takes my hand. "I certainly wasn't implying that you hadn't earned this. I know how hard you've worked, and I am infinitely proud of you." Now she sighs. "I just wish I understood this attraction you have toward that man."

"It's not physical, although—"

"Stop." My sister holds up her hand. "I don't want to know any more."

When she chuckles, I do the same, and my shoulders sag with just a bit of relief. "With Will, it's everything but the physical. It's our conversations and the way he challenges me to think beyond the four corners of my life. It's what we read together and our discussions afterward. It's what he stands for and how he wants to change the world. It's exciting to stand next to a man who is so . . ."

"Powerful?"

"I was going to say stimulating. But yes. Powerful. And, God help me, power is alluring."

"Dr. Du Bois is a powerful man."

"Who has a wife," I say. "And that's what fills me with such sorrow. If only there was a way to have all of Will without . . . all of him. Do you know how often I've told myself that the last time would truly be the last time? I have such resolve when I'm alone. And then I see him again, and I just can't walk away." My sigh is heavy. "I guess it's hard to let go of the first man . . ." I close my eyes. I don't wish to disclose that fact to my sister. So instead, I say, "The first man who believed in me the way Papa did."

"I often wonder if this is about Papa. And you losing Mama when you were just a baby. And you being the baby of the family."

"I'm hardly a baby now."

"But you've lived such a sheltered life and—"

"Please, Sissy. Don't lecture me on how coddled I've been when it's not true. I traveled across the ocean and spent a summer alone in Europe, for heaven's sake."

Mary-Helen inhales, and I know she's swallowing her words, ones I've often heard. But being born the seventh child thirty-seven years ago is not the source of my failure.

When Mary-Helen asks, "Have you ever thought about courting again?" I sigh. This is another conversation we've had innumerable times. "So many gentlemen would be delighted to call on you."

"All of those men want something from me."

She snickers. "And Dr. Du Bois doesn't?"

"He doesn't want what other men want—he doesn't want to make me his wife."

"You were so young when you first told me that you would never marry," my sister says, recalling the night before her own wedding when I'd made that declaration. "I always harbored hope that you would outgrow such a silly notion."

I shrug. "I don't want to be a wife. Perhaps it's because I never had the opportunity to watch my own mother. And while I adore Maman, by the time she came into our lives, I was old enough to understand how much she'd given up for marriage and to have enough children to fill a choir stall."

"So." Mary-Helen pauses. "You're choosing to be with a man who can never ask for your hand in marriage because he's already married, and you don't want to be married." Her words sound like scattered puzzle pieces that do not fit together.

It takes me a moment to respond. "Am I choosing this? I'm not certain. All I know is that I'm inexplicably drawn to this man. It is truly beyond my understanding." I shake my head. "I once read that there are strict limits to what we can comprehend as humans, and perhaps that's why I have no good explanation for my choices and decisions when it concerns Will."

She whispers, "Are you in love with him?"

Even though I've been in this affair with Will for five years, I do not hesitate. "Yes, but not in the way his wife loves him or you love Nathan. You both see a future with your husbands, while I don't see past next Tuesday with Will. But what I feel is deep enough that I don't want to walk away."

My sister exhales a long breath.

"I know I will walk away one day, but today is not that day." Tears burn behind my eyes. "I'm sorry if I'm disappointing you."

"No, Jessie. Be that as it may, you're still my baby sister, Papa's little lamb." Our smiles mask the turmoil of our emotions when my sister takes my hand and pulls me from the sofa. "This situation is fraught with trouble; how can there possibly be a good ending for you?"

"I'll be fine. Regardless of what occurs, Will will protect me."

Mary-Helen presses her lips together, making me demand, "If you have something to say, please . . ."

She nods. "Remember Dr. Du Bois's first loyalty will always be to his wife." She sighs. "Just know I'll be here for you. Always, Sissy." She kisses my cheek, and then she is gone.

CHAPTER 5

*H*ow can there possibly be a good ending for you?

Mary-Helen departed some time ago, yet her words linger in the darkness. I flip over to the other side of the bed.

Remember Dr. Du Bois's first loyalty will always be to his wife.

Finally, I toss aside the blanket and kneel in front of my trunk. Beneath my clothing, I find the book. Caressing the cover, I recall the day when I first heard the name W. E. B. Du Bois.

J essie," Papa called from the dining room.

I rushed to him, then paused at the entry. This was one of the familiar sights I so missed whenever I was away at college—my father at the table with papers and periodicals scattered before him as he prepared his sermon.

"Yes, Papa."

He glanced up and smiled, his visage a blend of love and pride. "Little lamb," he began, using his nickname for me, "I just finished reading this book, and I want to pass it to you so we can discuss."

Some of my most cherished moments with Papa revolved around

books. On my tenth birthday, he'd given me a copy of *Uncle Tom's Cabin*. From that time until today, our discussions continued. Papa said I was his reader, I was his thinker.

I was certain his affinity for sharing books with me was partly due to my not being sickly, like most of my older siblings. Still, I always wanted to rise to my father's praise.

He handed me the book, and I savored the scent of the printed pages before I read the cover. "*The Souls of Black Folk*?" I frowned. "What an odd title."

"Because of the plurality of the word 'soul'?"

"No, although I am curious as to why the author used that literary device. It's the word 'black.' I assume this author is referring to Negroes, so why call us black? There is nothing black about my skin."

Papa shook his head. "The title is but a mere five words introducing the collection of writings that challenges the reader with the question, What does it mean to be a Negro in America?"

"Can that be answered in a single volume?" I smiled ruefully.

"Perhaps not. However, W. E. B. Du Bois wasn't attempting to answer the question, but rather, he presents the thesis of double consciousness and the daily burden that places on Negro Americans."

"Double consciousness? I've never heard that expression."

"Dr. Du Bois theorizes that while white folks can simply be American, Negroes cannot. Because of the way America treats its Negro citizens, we must live separate as Negroes first, and then as Americans. It is a dual existence. And because the two identities cannot coalesce, we are left to live two lives, have two minds of thought and . . . two souls."

"A double consciousness." I nodded.

"Yes, and with the title, I believe the author is making a distinct contrast between white and black—white folks who will never have to live with this, and black folks who must bear this daily encumbrance."

"It seems rather complicated," I said.

"It is. Read this over the Christmas holidays, my dear, and then we'll discuss the content as well as the title before you return to Cornell."

"I'm eager to begin." I flipped through the two hundred or so pages.

"And I'm eager to hear your analysis." Papa reclined in the chair. "You know, Jessie, I glean so much from you. You have a critical mind, forever challenging me. I'm so very proud of the young woman you've become. The world is your domain, and as you venture forth, always know that I will be by your side, always believing in you."

I rushed across the room and wrapped my arms around him. Papa's unwavering belief in me had always been as palpable as his love.

I almost skipped out of the dining room, looking ahead to the day when Papa and I would have our discussion about *The Souls of Black Folk*.

That discussion never transpired.

Just weeks later, three days after we celebrated the New Year, my beloved father, the Reverend Redmon Fauset, received his just reward and went on to glory.

I shake my head now, not wanting to relive those devastating moments when I heard that my father had joined my mother and five of my siblings in the place he called heaven. I don't want to recall his funeral or the depth of my grief when I asked myself how I was supposed to navigate this world without my Papa. After all, I wasn't yet a toddler when my mother passed away, and by the time I began to grasp the effects of being a motherless child, Maman was there. But as a twenty-year-old, I understood the profoundness of my loss. Who would believe in me now?

With the book in my hand, I slide back into bed, my thoughts still ensconced in the past. I had completed a little more than a third of the book when my father died, and had no intention of ever reading it again.

It was Maman who encouraged me to finish what Papa and I had started. How formidable a task that had been! Yet, I persevered to the end.

I was alone in my room, as I often was in Sage College, when I read the final words. I closed the book and my eyes. *The Souls of Black Folk* had transformed my understanding of how I was affected by the prejudice that pulsed through this country. And that prejudice had created a color line behind which every Negro lived, with a consciousness of our race that we never had the privilege to ignore.

Race determined when we could speak, what we could say, where we could live, how we were educated—race was the burden every Negro bore, and that verity left us with a double consciousness that we had to chart through every minute of each day.

Papa had given me this book because it was requisite reading, in preparation for what I would face once I graduated and ventured into America. I'd already carried the burden of my darker skin when I was denied admission to Bryn Mawr, my college of choice.

My father wanted me to understand that humiliating rejection was the starting line. He was handing me the rules of readiness, written by Dr. Du Bois, or Professor Du Bois, as his biographical information stated.

Professor Du Bois was brilliant, much like Papa.

Was it providential that three days into this year, I'd lost my father, and now three days before this year's end, I finished this book?

Rushing to my desk, I pulled out the Sage College stationery, and without even thinking, I began:

My Dear Professor Du Bois:

Before I introduce myself, I want to say thank you for writing the masterpiece that you so brilliantly titled The Souls of Black Folk . . .

I think now of how this book had been the bridge connecting my father and W. E. B. Du Bois. From the moment of our first correspondence, Will stepped into those spaces left empty by my father's death. Not only had he responded to my letter, but our communication continued. He became a counselor and a mentor, even helping me secure my first teaching assignment, a summer position at Fisk University. His benevolence extended to assisting me with my application to the Sorbonne, and assigning a column for me to write for *The Crisis*.

Then, I'd only mentioned my interest in writing a novel, and once again, Will's support has been unwavering. We discuss the characters, the plot, and how my story will be the first novel of its kind—about college-educated Negroes. Will's persistent exhortation is *This is a story that must be told. How can I help you?*

Hidden on the other side of the trunk are the loose papers of my manuscript. Two years have passed since I typed the opening lines. However, my studies at the University of Pennsylvania and, most recently, my preparations for my move to New York have kept me away from this story.

I skim through the one hundred or so pages, and the characters and their narratives hasten back to me: Joanna, Maggie, and Peter. Childhood friends in Philadelphia. While I'd fallen in love with all three, it is the protagonist, Joanna, whose story I want to tell—the ambitious singer and dancer who refuses to set aside her aspirations for marriage. Instead, she pursues her dreams with an utter disregard for the unyielding societal norms.

I want to do the same. I want to be like Joanna.

I close my eyes and pray that my sister is mistaken. I pray that somehow, some way, this position at *The Crisis* and my position with Will will come to a good end for me.

CHAPTER 6

WEDNESDAY, OCTOBER 29, 1919

I straighten the seams of my stockings, then check my tweed suit in the mirror. Ten days have passed since I arrived in New York, and I have worked in the office on every single one—even Sunday, much to Maman's chagrin. However, this is the first day that I've chosen to wear a suit. Today, my attire will be as important as my words.

I grab my satchel, then step from my bedroom. Like every day since we've arrived, the aroma from Maman's breakfast encircles, then cradles me in an embrace. This morning, it is the scent of cinnamon.

In the kitchen, Maman sits at the table with her well-worn Bible. I'm certain that in the last twenty-five years, she has started every morning this way—with God.

Abruptly, she glances up with a smile that quickly inverts into a frown. "*Ma chérie*, you're dressed? What about breakfast?"

"No time, Maman." I pull a cup and saucer from the cupboard. "Only tea this morning."

"But the porridge is ready."

"I'm sorry. I want to verify one date with Miss Foster before the meeting."

Her brow furrows. "You're prepared, aren't you?"

"Very." I wave my hand as I slide into the chair across from her. "I just want to confirm."

My mother nods her agreement and approval. "Then you must get to the office. But you cannot have this meeting on an empty stomach. I'll toast two slices of bread you can take with you," she says, standing.

Of course, I will not eat buttered toast at my desk. However, I'm not going to wrangle with my mother. She already has the pan atop the stove.

"You arranged to meet Miss Foster early?"

My mother has not visited the NAACP offices, yet she is as familiar with my colleagues as I am. Most evenings, when I return home hours after she's finished her own dinner, Maman prepares my plate, then sits beside me, listening intently as I recount the events of my day.

I speak to her about everything: meeting Walter White, the young Negro investigator whose pale skin, blue eyes, and blond hair allow him to infiltrate racist groups and gather information for the NAACP; the correspondence we received from readers who support the organization's missions and encourage the fight; and the proposal I'm preparing for the *Brownies' Book*.

However, while I share everything, I do not include everyone. My mentions of Will are kept to the barest necessity.

Now I tell my mother, "Miss Foster will be there. Everyone on the staff is excited about the magazine and wants to do whatever is necessary to assist."

As the bread sizzles in the pan, my mother beams. "Every morning I awaken still astonished that you are the literary editor of *The Crisis*."

"Me, too, Maman," I say, and memories sweep me away. Some of my most cherished days were the ones when Papa brought home my favorite magazine, and I'd nestle into a corner of the sofa, poring over the pages of *Ladies' Home Journal*. The stories for girls left me spellbound, and the illustrations fascinated me. Even the advertisements for pocketbooks and corsets filled me with wonder as I dreamed of a world beyond my Philadelphia home.

"It's not as much as I'd want you to have," Maman says, bringing me back to the present. She wraps the two slices of toasted bread in butcher paper, then pauses before she tucks my "breakfast" into my satchel. Settling in her chair, Maman eyes my leather bag.

I'd told my mother the satchel had been a welcome gift from the NAACP. Either she believed me—although I harbor doubts—or she's resolved that she will not engage in conflict over this.

"Thank you for the toast, Maman. You take such good care of me."

"I guess you finally agree I should be here with you."

I shrug nonchalantly. However, my smile reveals I am only joshing. When I told my mother about this opportunity, we'd had quite a debate. Even with Mary-Helen and her husband living nearby, my mother had insisted on accompanying me to New York.

No respectable young woman lives alone.

That discussion had continued for weeks, until I received a telephone call from my youngest sister, Marion.

Mother doesn't want to be here alone, she informed me. *And when I leave for college, there won't be anyone home with her.*

Of course, then I acquiesced.

"I'm glad you're here, but you needn't have come to watch over me. I've been living on my own since my first job."

"Renting rooms from upstanding families isn't living on your own, Jessie."

"Well, I could have lived on my own in Washington, and I certainly can now." As Maman shakes her head, I say, "You must come into these modern times. Haven't you heard? The world is changing for women. We're doing more, working like men, and by this time next year, we'll even have the right to vote."

She remains steadfast and stern. "The world may be changing, but you must always remain respectable." When I part my lips to protest, she holds up her hand. "Yes, women are taking small steps toward equality, and perhaps a few things are advancing for Negroes. But, *ma chérie,* nothing has changed for you." Her joviality is usurped by the caution in her tone. "You're a colored woman who lacks any of the advantages this country treasures. You are neither white nor a man, and so you'll be judged harshly and unfairly, even as you perform well. However, you will be judged doubly, and the consequences will be severe if you falter." She gives me a pointed glance. "Not just professionally. You'll be judged by the company you keep."

After taking such care not to mention Will, it feels as if now he is the center of this conversation.

"Remember how you were raised," Maman continues. "Proper decorum at all times."

Proper decorum. Those words from Maman always strike me as odd. There is nothing decorous about my mother, a white Jewish woman who left her family and faith to marry a Negro. What my mother has done is the opposite of proper; she is the embodiment of rebellion. Yet she fears the same for me.

"Your father had such high expectations for you, as have I, and you have always made us proud. There are few things better than calling you my daughter."

I press my hands over my heart, stand, and kiss my mother's cheek. "*Merci*, Maman. I'll see you tonight."

She grabs my hand. "God has great plans for you. But He cannot give you greater than what you desire for yourself."

I only nod, because I cannot speak as my mother's words settle on my heart.

CHAPTER 7

WEDNESDAY, OCTOBER 29, 1919

The roar of the subway thunders in my ears. But neither the sound nor the speed disturb me. I prefer the IRT to the streetcar. It's faster, less crowded, and gives me time to do what I love—read.

I've had little time for pleasure reading, though. Instead, I remove the proposal from my satchel. I gave Will and Mr. Dill a copy of this last evening, and now I want to set every word to my memory.

After a little more than thirty minutes, the train jerks, then shudders to a halt at the Fourteenth Street station. I line up with other passengers and wait for the conductor to crank open the train's gates.

The moment I ascend the subway stairs, I am swept into the furor of the city, and minutes later, I am inside my office.

"The only items in the timeline that are not definitive," Miss Foster begins in response to my question, "are the dates I appropriated for the illustrators. I wasn't certain how much time or how many illustrations would be needed."

"Thank you. Please tell Dr. Du Bois and Mr. Dill that I'll be waiting in the meeting room. And please make certain they both have their proposals."

This is not my first presentation, of course. How many times have I stood in front of a classroom of twenty students? This will be an audience of only two, although the stakes are much higher.

Inside the meeting room, I pace to quell my jitters. When there is just a minute to spare, I move to the table. I study the chairs, then slide into the one at the head of the table. I plant my feet and wait.

In less than a minute, the door opens. "Good morning," Will says with cheer, and then he pauses. His eyebrow arches as he stares at me.

I sit up straight and rest my arms on the table, letting Will know that I'm sitting where I belong. "Good morning," I greet Will and Mr. Dill with an air of surety.

After a moment, Will lowers himself into a chair on one side of the table and motions for Mr. Dill to sit opposite him.

Will begins, "The first thing I must say is that I never expected you to have this proposal completed so quickly." He flips through his copy. "How long have you been here? Three weeks?"

Mr. Dill chuckles. "Less than two weeks, right?"

"Ten days exactly," I say. "We are bound by a strict timeline if we are to meet your goal of January first. That means the magazines must be ready for shipping December fifteenth. And to the printer three weeks before then. The proposal had to be completed for your approval so I can move forward."

The ends of his lips twitch as if he's struggling to contain his smile. "It seems you're already familiar with the production schedule."

"Mr. Dill assisted me with that." I nod at him. "As you can see on page eleven, I have the complete schedule, followed by the projected monthly budget."

"I read through this last night. Quite impressive. I have questions, but I'd like to hear what you want to share first."

I make certain to look at both of them. "The magazine's mission is to show Negro children that being colored is beautiful. Inside the pages, children will meet accomplished men and"—I pause and emphasize—"*women* who have achieved major feats. We will publish biographical sketches of people like Harriet Tubman, Frederick Douglass, and Phillis Wheatley. However, we should include not only people who have gone on to glory, but also successful Negroes today whom children should know. Of course, you," I say, as not a point of flattery but of fact. "Then others, like Mary McLeod Bethune, the educator who, twenty years ago, started a school for girls that continues to thrive. I'm certain you're familiar with her."

Will gives me a wry smile. "I know Mary."

I realize my error. Of course the two are acquainted, and very likely friends. "Others I'd like to feature: Mary Church Terrell, one of my mentors, and Mary Eliza Mahoney."

"Is there anyone on your list not named Mary?"

He chuckles, and although I know his true question, I tease, "Mary is a popular name."

"I'm talking about men . . . do you have any men to feature?"

"Of course. Richard T. Greener is at the top of my list. He came to my attention when he was featured on the cover of *The Crisis* two years ago. And there are, of course, others."

Will presses his fingertips together, and because I know him well, I know his thoughts. While he most often gazes at me with longing or lust, today his eyes shine with appreciation and approval. My shoulders square. *This* is what I crave most from him.

I continue, "The magazine will also serve to prepare our children for higher education."

Now I read Will's thoughts through the beam in his eyes—the next generation of the talented tenth.

"Beyond history, we will teach mathematics, the sciences, and world geography with a focus on Africa specifically. Children must learn the truth of that continent."

"I love the idea of presenting the beauty of that land. We must be careful, though. I want the *Brownies' Book* to be an enjoyable reading experience."

"It will be. We'll use games and songs and even photographs to teach these lessons."

"Ah." He motions for me to continue.

"And, of course, literature. Short stories and poetry and folklore.

However, what I'm most excited about is having the children participate in the magazine."

He leafs through the pages of the proposal. "Are you talking about the Judge and the Jury?"

I nod, and Will leans forward as I describe those two columns. "I will write the Judge, and teach everyday lessons about friends and family, school and church. Stories about finding the joy, even as they're faced with the conundrums of childhood. The Jury will be letters from the readers. I want the children to have a space to speak."

"I like this," Mr. Dill says. "Where else are colored children encouraged to use their voices?"

I wait for Will to nod before I continue, "When I think about the influence this magazine will have on colored children and how, as we change minds, we can change lives . . ." I pause, my emotions swelling at the potential impact of the *Brownies' Book*. "When we change minds and lives, we will change this country and the world."

Will and Mr. Dill nod, and then I respond to their questions about the specifics of the timeline and securing content for the magazine. We discuss the design for the inaugural cover and make a task list of what must be completed next.

In less than an hour, Will says, "I think we're finished. Do you have anything else, Augustus?"

He shakes his head. "This was most informative and impressive, Miss Fauset. W. E. B."—he turns to Will—"perhaps we need to change the name of our publishing company to Du Bois, Dill, and Fauset."

Mr. Dill and I chuckle; Will does not. He only says, "I think we're ready to proceed." His tone is somber. Had he been offended by Mr. Dill's quip?

"I'll get started," I say, and when Mr. Dill stands, so do I. Will remains seated.

As Mr. Dill turns toward the door, I move to follow him. However, as I do, Will says, "Miss Fauset, there is another matter I'd like to discuss."

"Certainly." I return to my seat and wait for Mr. Dill to close the door.

Will taps his fingers together. What altered his mood? He says, "I'm looking for the right words." A beat and then: "How do you say"—he leans toward me—"in French . . . you were remarkable, you were magnificent. And I am so proud of you."

I smile in relief and pleasure. *"Tu étais remarquable, tu étais magnifique. Et je suis si fier de toi."*

Will attempts to repeat what I said, and I laugh. My laughter turns to giggles when he pulls me from the chair and then twirls me as if we are on the dance floor in a Harlem speakeasy. When he places his arms around my waist and draws me close, the comfort of his embrace is beyond this moment. I've missed him. Since I arrived, I've set aside my desire for his affection, my attention centered on this project.

But now the proposal is complete. And now, God help me, I want him.

"Jess. Do you realize what you've done?" He doesn't give me a moment to respond. "You've breathed life into my idea."

"I'm thrilled to be doing this with you."

"We are quite a pair, aren't we?" he whispers.

Our lips are so close when I say, "Yes, we are."

What happens next is inexplicable. Is it because of the magic of this moment—Will finally beholding his dream while simultaneously giving me the opportunity to achieve mine? Or is it the ever-present frisson between us?

Regardless, our lips inch closer until we're pressed together. It begins so tenderly . . . until a tumult of thoughts rushes through my mind: I'm in the office . . . there are people just feet away . . . Will is married.

I regain my senses and press my hands against his chest, pushing him away. However, it is too late.

"Dr. Du Bois."

The meeting room door has already swung open by the time we leap apart. Miss Ovington stands, with lines carved deep into her forehead, her expression more severe than the scowls she's given me all week. Her glare darts between Will and me.

Will clears his throat. "Miss Ovington, you were looking for me?"

"Miss Foster told me you were having . . . *a meeting* . . . in here." She pauses long enough to turn her glare fully onto me. "I wanted to speak to you, Dr. Du Bois, before your trip."

"Trip? Where are you going?" I sound like a breathless sixteen-year-old.

"To Detroit. For a meeting to discuss the rise in lynchings."

"How long will you be gone?" Miss Ovington and I speak the same words at the same time.

We glance at each other before we face Will, both of us with our arms crossed.

"I'm not certain." He turns to me. "I'm leaving *The Crisis* in your hands."

"Her hands? She hasn't been here a week," Miss Ovington protests.

Ignoring Miss Ovington, I say, "I can manage this."

"I think not!"

"Miss Ovington," Will begins, sounding agitated. "Even with her brief tenure, Miss Fauset has already been managing so much with *The Crisis*, and if she needs anything, Mr. Dill will assist. And you, too, of course. I hope you'll be kind enough to oversee the magazine's operations."

Now I am the one who is appalled. "I don't need supervision."

"I never said you did," Will replies. "If you have any questions, Miss Ovington will support you."

It isn't the idea of supporting me that plasters that grin on her face. "There is one other matter, Dr. Du Bois." Miss Ovington pauses. "May I speak with you in private?"

I gladly gather my notes and rush out. Inside my office, I close the door, and only then do I exhale.

How foolish! Yes, we'd been behind a closed door, but it wasn't locked. And the presence of the frosted glass panel gave us no privacy.

Now Will is leaving me under the dubious eyes of Miss Ovington. I wonder if she, as the chair of the NAACP, can have me removed from this position. And if that is her desire, can Will stop her? Will he protect me?

Then I recall my sister's words: *Remember Dr. Du Bois's first loyalty will always be to his wife.*

CHAPTER 8

WEDNESDAY, OCTOBER 29, 1919

The sun has long ago set, but I've become accustomed to working by the dim glow of my desk lamp. Taking a minute, I massage my temples.

All day, thoughts and tasks collided in my mind: What will Miss Ovington do . . . and addressing the items on my work list. Will Miss Ovington have me terminated . . . and reading through submissions for the *Brownies' Book*. Should I speak to Miss Ovington . . . and should I speak with Will.

I return my attention to the stack of papers piled high on my desk. We've received hundreds of submissions for the *Brownies' Book*, and after hours of reading, I've chosen only a few. From the top of the accepted stack, I once again read the first poem I'd selected: "Recruit" by Georgia Douglas Johnson.

Through the years, I've enjoyed this renowned poet's work and was thrilled that she'd submitted such a timely piece:

> Right shoulder arms, my laddie,
> Step like your soldier-daddy . . .

I continue through the ten lines, and at the end, I love it even more. It is as brilliant as it is simple. With so many men returning from the war, becoming a soldier is on the minds of many little boys.

My first selection—a poem by a woman.

I reach for the next letter from the pile. This isn't a poem or a short story. It's a graduation photograph. I study the picture of quite the handsome young man, with jet-black wavy hair and a wide, welcoming grin. But it's his eyes that draw me. Deep and dark. Penetrating. As if, even at his young age, he is endowed with the wisdom of the elders.

His note reads:

To the editor:

I have heard of your Brownies' Book, and although I don't have a creative piece to submit, I'd like to offer my graduation photograph. I understand the magazine is for kiddies aged six to sixteen, and I myself am seventeen. I hope my graduation picture can be an inspiration for your young readers.

The letter continues with a list of his accomplishments: class poet, author of his high school class song, editor of his school paper.

I hadn't thought of featuring high school graduates for the *Brownies' Book*. But this is an idea worthy of the magazine. These photographs will inspire our young readers.

I read the young man's name. Langston Hughes.

Footsteps outside my door draw my attention away, and Miss Ovington marches past.

Without a thought, I call out, "Miss Ovington. May I have a word with you?"

In the next moment, she's standing before me as rigid as a rod. "Yes, Miss Fauset." Her lips scarcely move.

I hesitate; what am I to say? Still, I tell her, "Dr. Du Bois said you'd be available to answer my questions."

"You have questions?" Her eyes narrow with skepticism. "For me?"

I nod and motion to the chair beside my desk. "I know Dr. Du Bois considers you a valuable adviser. Has he spoken to you about the *Brownies' Book*? I'd love your thoughts," I say in earnest.

Although my words haven't softened her visage at all, I truly wish for a fresh start with Miss Ovington. Not only because I do fear she may hold my fate, but because I've so admired her over the years. At fifty-four years old, she stands as a suffragist, and is the driving force behind the founding of the NAACP.

However, what I've respected most about Miss Ovington is her willingness to set aside marriage and convention to chart her own course, which is what I wish to do.

"How do you think I can help?" Her tone stays sharp.

"I've been reading your work for many years. You may not recall, but your article *On the New-Time Negro* was the first review I submitted to *The Crisis.*"

She sits a little straighter.

"But, pertinent to this discussion, I've read the books you've written for colored children."

Her eyebrows arch higher.

"I particularly enjoyed *Hazel*, of course." This book was the first of its kind, uplifting and absent of the stereotypical pickaninny imagery.

This time, she grants me a sliver of a smile. "Well, Miss Fauset," she says, the edge gone from her tone, "I am proud of those projects. There was so little literature available for colored boys and girls, and I felt it my duty to tell a story for Negro kiddies."

"That's what we want to do with the magazine. Give Negro children a chance to see themselves in a heartening manner. We want to do what you've already done."

"I don't know much about children's magazines, I'm afraid."

"But having traveled and spent time with children, you have an understanding of the writings that will best serve them. Of course, we will have stories, but do you think poetry will work?" I ask as I discreetly set aside Mrs. Johnson's poem.

"Oh yes." She is emphatic. "Colored children should be exposed to all forms of literature, just like white children. And colored children must also read about real issues: racism, discrimination, the struggle toward equality. The children can handle it."

I nod as Miss Ovington continues on about how the publication should expose Negro children to other important social concerns, like interacting with white children. We speak effortlessly, almost like friends, and when Miss Ovington glances at her wristwatch, we are astounded an hour has flown by.

"I can say it has been a pleasure speaking with you, Miss Fauset."

"A pleasure for me as well." Then, after a deep breath, I add, "There is one more thing I'd like to address. Concerning this morning . . ." She stiffens, but I push on. "Dr. Du Bois and I found ourselves swept away by the excitement of this magazine. While it was impulsive, our behavior was unacceptable and regrettable. Nothing like that has ever happened before, and be assured, it will never happen again. Please accept my sincerest apologies."

She stares at me for a moment, then: "It seems to me I am not the one to whom you should be apologizing."

Heat rises beneath my skin, but before I can respond, she holds up her hand.

"However, apology accepted. I understand how a man like Dr. Du Bois is attractive to a young woman like you. A momentary indiscretion is excusable and forgivable."

"Thank you," I breathe with relief.

"As long as it is momentary," she adds before she stands. "Good night, Miss Fauset."

CHAPTER 9

SUNDAY, NOVEMBER 9, 1919

s it too chilly to walk?" my mother asks as she adjusts the feather on her cloche. Once she sets her hat just right, she slips on her gloves.

"It's just a few blocks." When I open the door, a sudden blast of music bursts from the floor above. The scratchy vocals of Irving Berlin blare from a Victrola:

> *You cannot make your shimmy shake on tea*
> *It simply can't be done*
> *You'll find your shaking ain't taking . . .*

As she picks up her Bible, Maman shakes her head. "*That's* what they want to share with their neighbors on a good Sunday morning? 'You Cannot Make Your Shimmy Shake on Tea'?"

I lean away to get a better glimpse of Maman. "How do you know that song?"

She shrugs, smirks, and then struts out of the apartment. I laugh. Less than a month in Harlem and my mother, the reverend's widow, knows the words to one of Mr. Berlin's most popular songs, now a hit in the *Ziegfeld Follies.*

Outside, a fresh melody greets us. I link my arm with Maman's, and we walk to the rhythm of bells tolling as if from a thousand churches. The air is autumn crisp as we hasten along the brownstone-lined street. Just minutes after eight thirty, yet Harlem is as lively as if it were noon.

It is always this way on these streets. Today, however, there is a difference. The men all wear dark overcoats, topped with matching fedoras or homburgs. And the women, whose skirts peek from beneath the hems of their fur-trimmed coats, are a walking rainbow, with wide-brimmed hats and matching gloves, of course. Even the children are dressed in their best, the boys in knickers and caps, while the girls are kiddie versions of their mothers. Today is assuredly a Sunday.

"Am I walking too fast, Maman?"

"No. It's not as cold as I thought it would be."

I'm glad she doesn't want to rush along, because I've scarcely had a moment to take in Harlem this way. Since we arrived, I've spent every day diligently at my desk. The last ten days have been especially taxing while Will has been away.

I enjoy this stroll, having the opportunity to finally take notice of my neighborhood. There are the businesses nestled between the brownstones: Dr. Folks Drugstore, the meat market, Hessen Tailors. Then, newspaper boys on the corner hawking the *New York Times* and *Amsterdam News*. Right next to them are two-wheel carts, manned by vendors selling apples, bananas, and grapefruit.

When we pause for passing cars, Maman says, "I've noticed that while most of Harlem's residents are colored, the store owners are all white."

"Why does that astound you?"

"This is Harlem," she says. "I was hoping."

I sigh. "Race relations are as knotty in New York as they are everywhere."

Silence, then she adds, "Perhaps you should get your Dr. Du Bois working on this."

Will's name has hardly been mentioned between us, and I'm not certain how to respond. So, I say nothing.

At 129th Street, we cross Seventh Avenue, and the crowd is so thick in front of Salem United Methodist Church that the sidewalk is not passable. I am not surprised; Will explained that the church has more than two thousand members. Along with everyone else, we wait and wade forward toward the doors.

The way we're greeted at every turn reminds me of the place that will always be my church home—Athens AME, where Papa was the preacher. We respond to at least a hundred hellos before we make our way through the vestibule. I follow Maman, and as she parades down the center aisle, I'm reminded of the first time she walked through the doors of Papa's church.

I'd sat in the front pew that Sunday morning, watching as my father crossed the threshold with my new stepmother's arm locked around his. As she passed the colored congregants, she smiled and nodded, striding down the aisle not only as if she belonged, but as if she'd always been there.

The mixing of the races crossed in both directions for Maman, an integrationist. She believed whites had a righteous obligation to welcome Negroes into their midst, and she expected the same from colored folks. It was because of that expectation that the members of our congregation embraced her as if she were a favorite auntie returning home from a long visit somewhere down south.

Once we find seats on the third pew, no more than a few minutes pass before the choir enters in cornflower-blue cotton robes. The congregation rises, and when we hear the pipe organ's first musical chords, Maman and I don't even reach for the hymnal.

Blessed assurance, Jesus is mine . . .

Three more songs follow before the Reverend Frederick Cullen saunters to the pulpit in a black robe trimmed in the same blue as the choir robes. I've heard much about this preacher from Will. Reverend Cullen fancies himself an activist preacher. He is not only the president of the Harlem branch of the NAACP, but also one of the organizers of the Silent Parade.

The reverend doesn't speak as he places his Bible onto the lectern. He is silent for so long, I wonder what's wrong. His voice is deep when he finally bellows, "A man was lynched yesterday!"

Maman squeezes my hand as murmurs roll through the congregation.

He waits for the congregants to settle. "Those are the words that will appear on a flag outside of the Fifth Avenue NAACP offices every time a man is lynched in this country!"

The muttering returns. I have not the faintest notion of what the reverend is talking about.

Reverend Cullen says, "Churches throughout New York have been asked to make this statement. The NAACP has announced that a flag with the words 'a man was lynched yesterday' will fly right above Fifth Avenue, the busiest street in the busiest city. It will be so shocking that every white man and woman passing will have to notice it. Every white newspaper will have to report it. And then we'll see if good people can continue their complicity by their silence. Perhaps this flag will move America."

The congregation applauds. Some even stand, as if we're attending a political rally.

When the applause abates, the reverend says, "I am proud that the NAACP has once again found a way to advocate against this abhorrent act, as we all must. They are fighting until not one Negro is ever lynched in America again, as we all must fight."

"Amen!" someone shouts.

"The NAACP is doing God's work." He holds up a very large Bible. "The Lord hates the monstrosity of lynching! Just look in the Good Book, brothers and sisters. Proverbs 6:16."

In mere seconds, Maman has her Bible turned to the scripture.

The reverend reads, "These six things doth the Lord hate: yea, seven are an abomination unto him. A proud look, a lying tongue, and hands that shed innocent blood." He pauses, and the congregation is so silent that when he begins again, he only whispers. He continues reading, until he says, "And a false witness that speaketh lies . . ."

Reverend Cullen slams his Bible shut, startling everyone. "God's word is true. The Lord hates hands that shed innocent blood, and He hates a false witness that speaketh lies."

In just a few minutes, the reverend has me enthralled.

"It's right there in the Word of God, brothers and sisters. Every man who has been lynched was innocent, because he was never afforded the citizen's right of due process. And how many men have been lynched on the word of a liar?"

Closing my eyes, I allow those words to settle in my mind as the reverend continues his sermon. The abomination of lynching was right there in the Bible. How many abominations had been committed in the eyes of God?

I do not have an inkling how long Reverend Cullen has been speaking when he finally says, "It is not because of man alone that this evil must end. It is because lynching is a heinous act that God abhors."

The congregation remains still, even as Reverend Cullen returns to his grand chair on the altar. It is only when the choir begins to sing that the sanctuary stirs. I'm pleased when the song is one I'd learned in Sunday school decades before:

He's got the whole world in his hands . . .

The darkness that has hovered with Reverend Cullen's sermon wanes with this hymn of hope. Maman's shoulder bumps against mine as she sways to the music.

After the offering, the congregation rises for the benediction. This sermon has certainly stirred my soul. And I will not miss another Sunday service at Salem Methodist Church.

The receiving line is long as we wait to pay our respects to the reverend and his wife. When it is finally our turn, Reverend Cullen reaches for Maman's hand.

"It's nice to meet you, Reverend," my mother says. "I'm Mrs. Bella Fauset, and this is my daughter, Miss Jessie Fauset."

He tilts his head as he takes my hand in his. "You're Miss Jessie Fauset?"

"Yes," my mother and I say together, both surprised.

Before I can ask the question, he answers, "Dr. Du Bois told me you'd be joining *The Crisis*. I'm very excited, because my son is a great writer." He raises his hand, calls out, "Countee," and beckons to someone.

A young man with a round face and serious expression rushes toward us.

"Son, I want you to meet the lady I was telling you about. The literary editor of *The Crisis*, Miss Jessie Fauset."

He is a slight young man, with a soft voice. I suspect he's only fifteen, perhaps sixteen. He raises his glance and holds out his hand. "I'm Countee Cullen, and it is my absolute pleasure to meet you." Countee looks at Maman, but only nods at her.

It is Maman who extends her hand to him. She knows this colored boy will never touch her, not even in New York. His eyes widen when she grips his hand. "I'm Mrs. Fauset, Miss Fauset's mother."

"Oh." His already high-pitched voice rises as his gaze shifts between my mother and me.

Reverend Cullen says, "My son is quite the poet. He's been published in the *Modern School Magazine*, and recently won second place in a major poetry contest."

His mother speaks up. "And he's in the honor society at DeWitt Clinton High School."

To Countee, I say, "You have made your parents proud."

He nods and again averts his eyes.

I say, "I'm a poet as well."

"I know, I've read some of your poems in *The Crisis*." Countee speaks so softly, I lean forward to hear him above the din.

When Mrs. Cullen steps away to chitchat with Maman, I take Countee aside. "I'd like to know more about you. Besides all the achievements your parents have already mentioned."

He smiles and looks away. "I like to write. And I read a lot of poetry, too."

"Who are some of your favorites?"

Now he raises his voice. "I love the European poets like William Wordsworth, but my favorite is John Keats."

It is more than his enthusiasm that astounds me. "How old are you?" I hadn't read Keats until I was at Cornell.

"Sixteen."

This young man—his age, his achievements—is very impressive. "I'd love to read some of your poetry." When his eyebrows rise, I say, "You're an award-winning poet."

"I don't know how good I am." His voice is low again.

"You must be good. Your father says you are, and he's the preacher, so he only speaks the truth."

For the first time, the young man smiles. "He's also my father. He's obliged."

I laugh. "Let me tell you a secret. I've been writing since I was your age, and that was a long time ago. Yet I still don't know if I'm good."

His dark eyes widen. "I've read your poetry and stories. You're very good."

"All of us have a few insecurities. That's just the ethos of writers."

A familiar voice interrupts us. "So you two have met."

"Dr. Du Bois!" I exclaim. I am giddy with glee at the sight of him. "What are you doing here?"

"I returned from Detroit last night and thought you might be here this morning. I was hoping you'd had the opportunity to meet Reverend and Mrs. Cullen as well as Countee." He turns his attention to him. "How are you, young man?"

I stand back as Will inquires about his studies and his writings and what he's currently reading.

Finally, Countee turns to me. "It was nice meeting you, Miss Fauset."

"I'd love to read your work. I'm looking for a few good poets to publish in *The Crisis*."

"I think I'm too young to be published in *The Crisis*."

"There are no age restrictions on God-given talent. And, working together, perhaps we can help you to become even better."

Countee grins.

"Come by the office one day after school."

"Yes, ma'am," he says, before he scurries off.

Once alone, Will leans closer to me. "I'm a genius."

I face him with a smirk. "I agree, but why do you say that now?"

"Because I chose you as the literary editor. Writers need someone special by our sides because you know how capricious we can be."

"Is this a moment of introspection, Dr. Du Bois?"

When he shrugs, we laugh. But when Maman steps to my side, we stop abruptly.

"Dr. Du Bois." She greets him with the warmth of an ice storm.

There is nothing but cordiality in his voice when he responds, "It's nice to see you again, Mrs. Fauset. I hope you enjoyed Reverend Cullen."

She almost smiles. "I did. Thank you for recommending this church to my daughter. We will certainly return next Sunday." Then, to me, she says, "Are you ready? Helen and Nathan may already be waiting for us at home."

My mother is standing in a sanctuary on a Sunday morning spinning lies. My sister and brother-in-law won't be arriving for a few more hours.

I explain to Will, "Mary-Helen and her husband are coming to dinner."

"I'm heading in your direction; I'll give you a lift."

Knowing that Maman would rather spend two weeks crawling on hot rocks from New York to Philadelphia than five minutes in a car with Will, I quickly say, "That would be wonderful," without giving my mother the opportunity to object.

As if he knows we must move quickly, Will leads us from the church. When he opens the car door, my mother makes her own move. Blocking me, she holds out her hand for Will to assist her up to the running board. Then she slides right into the front seat.

Will and I share a quiet chuckle as he helps me squeeze into the rear. When the motorcar spits and sputters from the curb, I cannot think of a single thing to say that will interest my mother *and* Will. Their silence shows they feel the same.

In the days that he's been away, my attention has been on my work alone, especially after my discussion with Miss Ovington. But now, seeing him again . . . it's what I told my sister.

Whenever I'm close to Will, I remember.

I remember the last time we were together in August, and God help me on this Sunday morning, I more than yearn for this man; I crave him.

Will edges the car to the curb and helps Maman before assisting me.

Just as my foot hits the pavement, Will says, "Miss Fauset, would you have time this afternoon to review the progress of the *Brownies' Book*?"

Had he heard my thoughts? "Yes!"

Maman's eyebrows lift to the top of her forehead, so I explain what she already knows. "Will has been away. We must review my work."

"That shouldn't be done today." Her tone makes it a command. "This is the Lord's day. Meet with Dr. Du Bois during proper hours."

I take a deep breath and turn to Will. "I'm going to escort my mother inside. Will you wait for me?"

He nods, and I follow Maman as she stomps up the steps. She says nothing as I open the front door, but once inside, she tosses her coat, pocketbook, and even her Bible onto the sofa with fury. "If you want to be a respected woman," she begins, her voice sounding two octaves deeper, "you must behave as one."

"How is this not respectable, Maman? I'm giving the man I work for a report. We're working against an aggressive timetable. I've already worked a couple of Sundays, and I'm certain this will not be the last one."

"There is a time for everything, and a Sunday afternoon is not when you should be doing this work with that man!"

"Those are your rules," I say, keeping my voice steady.

"My rules are the same rules a man with any integrity would honor."

"Maman! That's rude. There is nothing wrong with Will wanting a meeting to discuss the *Brownies' Book*."

"A meeting is not what that man wants from you."

I want to tell her she's wrong. I want to tell her there's no need to question Will's integrity or my virtue. But all I can do is say "I'll return as soon as I can," then rush out the door.

Will stands at the curb, holding the door of his motorcar open. Without a word, I slip inside, and when the car jerks from the sidewalk, I keep my eyes straight ahead. The streets whir by before Will reaches for my hand. "Is everything all right?"

"Yes." Now I am the one spinning lies on a Sunday.

CHAPTER 10

SUNDAY, NOVEMBER 9, 1919

E verything is new in the Hotel Olga. The mahogany headboard. The wardrobe and matching dressing table. The writing desk and the heavy burgundy drapes. It is all brand new since the hotel opened just a month before.

Only Will and I are familiar.

Balancing on my elbow, I stare down at him, his mouth agape, as if, even in his sleep, he is prepared to leap from this bed and deliver a rousing oratory. After a moment, I roll over, tightening the sheet around me. From the shadows cast across the room, I can see the late-afternoon sun has begun its bow to dusk.

A singular thought comes to my mind: God is not pleased.

At times like these, remorse weighs heavy on me. My singular defense is that being with Will this way was never my intention. For ten years, Will was truly only an inspiring mentor who'd taken a special interest in my education. We were correspondents, connecting primarily through letters.

But then came that day in 1914.

smiled as one of my favorite students, Sadie Tanner Mossell, prattled on as we moved from my office into the school's hallway.

"I only have two more years," Sadie said, "but it's difficult to decide whether I want to be an economist to study the economic effects of racism in this country or a lawyer so that I can fight said racism here in America." She sighed. "There's so much to consider."

"Sadie, you just turned sixteen. You have time, and so much will change between now and when you're seventeen."

Sadie continued as if time were slipping away. "I must make a decision."

At the exit, I turned my full attention to my student. "You're so intelligent, you could be both an economist *and* a lawyer."

Sadie's eyes brightened. "Miss Fauset, that is brilliant. I'll become an economist and a lawyer. The only decision I'll have to make is which should come first," she said before scuttling out the door and down the school steps.

I laughed, then proceeded to exit the building myself. At the bottom stair, a gentleman called out, "Miss Fauset."

I didn't recognize the voice, but then the medium-height, sharply dressed man in a dark gray sack suit edged closer. Later, I pondered what made me so certain he was Dr. Du Bois. Was it the way he strode with a commanding confidence befitting arguably the most educated Negro in the country? Or had it been his meticulously groomed mustache and beard? Or his eyes, focused and piercing as if he knew me beyond our many missives and sporadic telephone calls? "Dr. Du Bois!" I exclaimed.

He reached for my hand. "We finally meet."

"Yes." There was a bit of bewilderment in my tone. "I had no idea you were coming to Washington."

"I'm here for a meeting with Alain Locke. He's an assistant professor at Howard University."

"Yes, I know of Mr. Locke. We've attended several of the same social events over the last year."

"Our appointment ended early, and I thought I'd venture here hoping you hadn't yet left for the day."

"I certainly wish you'd written so that I would have been properly prepared for your visit."

"Well, if I'd done that, this wouldn't have been a surprise." His smile warmed me so, I readily accepted his invitation to dinner.

It was not yet five when we settled at our table at Gray & Costley's on U Street. Dr. Du Bois wasn't anything like the staunch, stiff man I envisaged through his letters and his books. While my first assessment of him ten years ago was correct—he was similar to my father in his belief in the importance of being educated, well read, and upstanding at all times—meeting him showed me that he and Papa were poles apart.

He was younger, of course, and more ebullient. We shared many of the same interests: books, certainly, and our passion for languages. While I was teaching French and Latin at M Street, Dr. Du Bois had taught Greek and Latin at Wilberforce University. And he loved music and the theater as much as I did. Both of us wanted to attend the musical revue *Darktown Follies* at the Lafayette Theatre in Harlem.

"Perhaps I'll arrange for you to come to New York, and we'll attend the performance together."

"Yes," I agreed, thrilled at that thought.

As our conversation continued, I discovered that while I was awestruck by Dr. Du Bois's intellect, what I loved most was his wit.

"I bought more than two dozen boxes of Cracker Jack," he said, sounding as if he was still bewildered over that. "I told my daughter all the treats were for her. But I was in search of that new prize they said they'd added to every box. I didn't even take off my jacket, I just pushed up my sleeves and dove into the candy."

I almost keeled over with laughter as I pictured this distinguished man with his hands stuffed inside those candy boxes. "Did you find the prizes?"

"I did," he said proudly as he held up his hands and wiggled his fingers. "Sticky fingers and all."

Before I had the opportunity to wipe the tears from my laughter away, Will began enthralling me with tales of his adventures throughout Europe while he was a graduate student in Berlin.

But then we shared a moment of sorrow when I said, "I will always be grateful to you for answering my letter, Dr. Du Bois. If you hadn't responded that first time, we wouldn't be here today."

He nodded. "When you mentioned that your father had recommended my book, but had just passed away, I needed to reply. I've experienced that deep desolation, and no one should go through that grief alone." He reached for my hand. "Are you all right?"

"Yes. It's been many years now, and I still miss him. But I've learned to live, believing that somehow, he's still with me."

It was astounding when the waiter came to our table and said, "Dr. Du Bois, my apologies, but we must clear the restaurant."

Both of us glanced around, astonished that every table, save ours, was empty. "We're the last ones? How is that possible?" Will asked before we scurried out of there.

I didn't live far from the restaurant, and even though I shuddered against the March chill, I wanted to stroll around the neighborhood so we could continue our conversation.

At the front door of the home where I was living, Dr. Du Bois said, "It was wonderful to finally meet you, Jessie. I hope we'll do this again." He kissed the back of my hand and then trotted down the darkened street.

I watched him, wondering how to call him back. Just so I could spend another hour, or just another minute, with him. It had only taken one evening; I was smitten.

A month later, Dr. Du Bois returned and met me at my front door with a single rose in hand, then took me to dinner, this time at the Whitelaw Hotel's restaurant. We began the evening dining, and ended the night three stories up in one of its luxurious rooms.

Before that night, I had lived thirty-one years following the religious tenets on which I'd been raised. Staying that spiritual course had been less challenging for me than some, I suppose. It wasn't so much that I was a prude, although I had been raised to believe that virginity was the greatest virtue. But rather, I didn't want to echo the life of Maman, ladened with children, abandoning my dreams.

I'd been content with my choices. And then, I had that one night with Dr. Du Bois.

Will's arms fold over me, drawing me back from my memories. I roll onto my back to face him.

"Juliet," he whispers.

If we are nothing else, we are creatures of routine. While my first thought after being with Will this way is always of God, he always awakens calling me Juliet. It is my sobriquet, I suppose. Only when we're alone like this. However, it isn't a term of endearment that I treasure. I'm not fond of being addressed as the heroine from that Shakespearean tragedy.

My response to Will is always the same: "Juliet dies, *mon cher.*"

"But we are not unlike those star-crossed lovers." He sighs. "Jess. My Jess . . . my Juliet . . . another time, a different place." He kisses my fingers. "With you and me, you would have remained very much alive."

I only smile, because there is no need to tell him what he already knows. I am not his Juliet. I am not his Jess.

"But it is probably for the best." Will pushes himself up and swings his legs over the side of the bed. With the sheet slipping away, I join him and take his hand in mine.

"We are back here again." I nod and he continues, "Why do you keep coming back to me?"

I think of how many times I've asked myself that question. Then, I tell him the truth: "Because I love when we're together this way."

His eyes rove over my nakedness. "I wish." The tips of his fingers trace a trail from my jaw to my clavicle before his fingers settle between my breasts. His voice is thick. "One of the things I love about you is that you don't know how beautiful you are. But it is not your beauty I admire."

I accept that Will speaks the truth. I've been blessed through the years to have had my fair share of hopeful suitors. I've been called comely and lovely and winsome. However, it has always been apparent that my appearance is not what's most attractive to Will.

He is very impressed with my scholarly achievements, but he is most affected by my family. While my father wasn't a man of wealth, his lineage dates back to the 1700s in Philadelphia. The Fausets are "Old Philadelphia," so of course this would impress the man who conceptualized the talented tenth.

As he caresses me, he says again, "I wish." From his low voice and solemn tone, I know his thoughts are beyond this bed. He is often this way when we are together: pensive and wistful. "If I had been born later or if we had met sooner."

"But then, we wouldn't be who we are today or where we are now."

"True, but we could have been in a better place."

"Where we are now is good because . . ." I stop. There's no reason for me to repeat what I've told Will. He's very aware that I don't desire anything beyond this.

He nods, understanding what I don't say. "This is good for what it is." He lies back and pulls me with him, resting my head on his chest.

I hear his heartbeat, rhythmic and steady. And I feel his soul stirring. "*Parle-moi.* What's bothering you?"

He squeezes me closer. "No one ever asks me that."

"That's not true." I fondle the hair on his chest. "I've asked you before."

"I stand corrected. You're the only one who asks after me. The only person in my life."

Lifting my head, I say, "I hope you know you can always talk to me."

"Jess." He repeats my name over again. "You're so kind, so generous. I don't know what I did to deserve a gift such as you."

"*De quoi parles-tu?* It's because of you that I have the position I've dreamed of. *You* are *my* gift."

His fingers thread through my hair. "You call me a gift, but if you knew me, 'gift' wouldn't be the word you'd choose."

Now I sit up. "Of course I know you."

He shakes his head. "The world sees only the man I allow them to see."

"Ah, but I am not the world. And few have ever seen you this way." I press my lips against his, wanting to bear some of his burden. "I know you because I've read all of your works." I hold up my fingers and begin counting: "Your books, all of your studies, and every article published in *The Crisis* and elsewhere. And *Darkwater*, of course," I say, referring to his latest book, which will be released in a few months. "How many hours have we put in on that book together? There may be few who know you, but as for me, Dr. Du Bois, I know you well."

My attempt works. He rolls me over so fast, I fly into a fit of giggles. I am pinned beneath him when he says, "So if you know me, then I want to know all about you."

"Dr. Du Bois." I glance down at our nakedness. We're pressed so close, there is no air between us. "I believe you know everything about me."

"Not in this way." His hand moves to my temple. "In this way." He taps his finger gently against my skin. "Unless I get into here, I won't know you. So tell me something, Jess, that only I will know." He nuzzles my neck, and I can scarcely breathe. How am I supposed to think?

"There is something only my family knows . . ." His eyes gleam with anticipation, and I battle to keep a lid on my smile. "My middle name isn't Redmon . . . it's Redmona."

"Redmona?"

"I was named for my father, but my parents added an 'a.' I suppose to make certain people would know I was a girl."

"All right." He nods as if he's trying to determine whether this information is valuable. "I'll have to change the masthead to read Jessie Redmona Fauset."

Playfully, I slap his arm. "Don't you dare. This is our secret. Now, tell me something new about you."

His eyes darken. "You don't want to know more about me."

I cup his face with the palm of my hand. "I do, *mon cher.*"

"If I shared any more with you, then you'd bear my burden, too." He stands and, without modesty, moves to the window.

On many occasions, he has called me beautiful, but the shadows cast across his body make him appear as if he'd been chiseled from stone. I soak in every inch of this *beautiful* man. I've known many women who told tales about their age; I am among them. But there are moments when I wonder if Will has lied about his. One would be forgiven for believing Will is ten, fifteen, even twenty years younger than his fifty-one years.

Staring at him makes me want him more, but I will myself to remain still. He needs a little room to breathe, a little space to think.

Minutes pass, until: "Sometimes, this is an oppressive load to bear."

"What is?" I whisper.

"All the battles that must be fought, all the wars that must be waged. This fight for equality. It's eternal, never-ending."

"But you're not alone. So many are fighting beside you."

Now he faces me. "Who? The NAACP?" He is incredulous. "They're white folks, Jess. Well-meaning and hardworking white folks who will never walk a day in a Negro's shoes."

I accept his words, even as I do not agree. My white stepmother's fight for equality is as righteous as mine.

"That's what makes this burden so heavy. I often feel as if I'm alone. Everyone always wants, always needs, something from *me*. The world wants Dr. Du Bois, the polemic professor, lecturer, and author. The leader of all Negro men.

"Even my friends will not allow me a weak moment. To them, I must be their adviser, counselor, confidant. I am the one on whom they lay all their burdens.

"And when I go home, I'm the husband who provides and the father who grants. Everybody wants something from me. Everyone except for you." Again, he faces me. "You're the only person who doesn't see me as anyone greater than Will. Some days, most days, that is all I want to be." He strides across the room and pulls me from the bed. It isn't the cool air against my nakedness that makes me shiver. His lips tickle my ear when he whispers, "Do you have to leave tonight?"

"Yes," I say, although I wonder why he asks. Doesn't he have to go home to his wife? "I've already missed dinner. I know my mother is not pleased."

"I need more time with you."

I kiss him, a long, lingering kiss that I hope will lessen his troubles. "I don't have to leave at this moment." This time, I am the one to draw him down to the bed. *"Viens à moi, mon cher."*

CHAPTER 11

MONDAY, NOVEMBER 10, 1919

Growing up in Philadelphia, I hated when the lights were turned off at night. In the dark, our five-bedroom house stirred with squeaks and creaks and pops and knocks. Often I slept with the blanket yanked over my head. Until my father explained that the creaking floorboards and knocking radiators were signs of an old house settling.

In this midnight hour, I recall those conversations as I tiptoe through the brownstone's hallway. Since we've moved in, I've noticed how sound travels through these walls, and I pray to the Lord almighty that Maman is having a restful sleep.

I turn the key slowly. Still, the lock clicks so loudly, I expect half of Harlem to be startled out of their sleep. Pressing the door forward, I cringe with every creak, and then I slip inside into the darkness. I wait a moment before I push the squeaky door shut.

The aroma of Maman's yeast rolls lingers in the air. Inhaling makes me *almost* sorry I missed Sunday dinner. When my heartbeat steadies, I take my first step.

And then . . . there is light!

I squint against the sudden brightness. "Maman!"

My mother sits on the sofa in her cobalt-blue dressing gown. Her lips are pressed so tightly, I worry that in minutes they'll match the color of her nightclothes. I stand frozen from shock; she sits, her glare ice-shard sharp. The tick-tick-tick of the mantel's clock is the only sound.

"I cannot believe you are sneaking into our home at this hour."

I scan my mind for something to say, but no lie will suffice. My mother will never believe Will and I worked past midnight. So I only say, "I'm sorry I missed Sunday dinner."

She holds her hand against her chest, stunned at my response. "This isn't about Sunday dinner. This is about it being past the appropriate hour when any respectable young woman should be returning home."

There isn't a way for this conversation to end well. "I'm sorry, Maman. But I have to rise early for work. Can we discuss this tomorrow?"

She slams her fist onto the sofa's cushions. "You gave no thought about sleep when you were with that man! We will talk about this now! What you're doing with him goes against everything your father and I have taught you."

"I don't know what you think—"

"Please, Jessie!" she shouts. "You've insulted me by coming home at this hour. Do not insult me with a lie." When I say nothing, she nods as if claiming a small victory. "You were taught good from evil."

My mouth opens wide. "Maman! There is a difference between something being wrong and something that is evil."

"In this situation, that is a distinction without a difference," she says. "Jessie, that man is not only old enough to be your father, that man has a wife."

I will myself to stay silent and not tell Maman that her words are absurd. Will is not old enough to be my father; yes, he is married, but . . . I will never be able to provide my mother with a satisfying explanation.

Her voice softens. "What are you doing, *ma fille*? And why?"

"Because . . ." My voice trails off.

"Do you know what people will whisper about you? You have been given this incredible opportunity—"

"By the man you detest."

Her eyes narrow. "Is that why he gave you this job? Because you lay with him whenever he demands, like a common . . ."

Her voice trails off, but I am already so offended, I'm trembling. "It's not like that at all."

"That's exactly the way it is. You have no rights with that man, he gives you no respectability."

"I'm not looking for him to give me anything," I shout. And then, only because I've been wounded, I lash out. "Is that the only reason you married my father? Because of respectability? Did you marry him for nothing more than that?"

A flame ignites in her eyes. "That is one reason I married my husband." She speaks through clenched teeth. "For respectability . . . and for love. That Du Bois fellow can give you neither."

"You don't know what he gives me, Maman. You've never asked me, and now you're just attacking me and—"

"This is not an attack. This is me guiding you. This is me being your mother."

"But I don't need your guidance, because you are not my mother!"

Her eyes glisten with the pain I meant to inflict. An apology soars within me, but Maman's words: *evil . . . respectability . . .* and the worst, the one she never uttered . . . swirl in my mind, leaving me so irate, my remorse remains lodged in my throat.

"If I am not your mother," Maman begins slowly, "then why have I cared about and for you? Why have I cared about your well-being and your schooling and where you would work and live?" She pauses. "And if I am not your mother, then why am I here?"

She moves toward me, and I shudder. I have no fear of her striking me. My mother has never raised her hand to any of her children. But her eyes are aflame with fury, and I feel her heat. "A mother is more than someone who births you. A mother is someone who loves you . . . especially at those times when you are most unlovable."

She slices my heart when a single tear seeps from her eye. Then she pivots and rushes away. I want to apologize and beg for forgiveness. But the pain of these last few minutes has left me dazed. So I stand there until Maman disappears behind her bedroom door.

Only then do I collapse onto the sofa and cry.

CHAPTER 12

MONDAY, NOVEMBER 10, 1919

I cover my mouth, hoping to suppress my yawn. But still, a soft moan escapes through my lips. From the other side of his desk, Will chuckles and puffs out his chest. "We did have quite an evening."

I only nod, not wanting to discuss this in the office.

"You know what you need?" Will asks before he stands. "A good cup of coffee. I'll dash over to the Automat," he says, referring to the Horn & Hardart just blocks away.

"No," I protest. "I cannot have W. E. B. Du Bois fetching coffee for me."

He rounds his desk. "I want to do this for you. Moreover, this will give me an opportunity to walk."

I agree only because walking is part of Will's serious exercise routine.

"Don't fall asleep while I'm gone." He laughs.

I wait until he closes the door, then slouch in the chair. Will is right; I am bushed. However, he is not the cause. It is Maman.

After our row, I'd tried to rest, but my mother's words repeated in my mind like a record jammed on a Victrola. It was only after the sun gave light to the new day that I finally closed my eyes. However, just minutes passed before I was awakened by Maman's knock on my door. She entered before I could invite her in.

scooted up in the bed, and Maman began speaking without preamble. "You are correct." The fire that was in her eyes had been extinguished. Now her eyes were soft, sad. "You are thirty-seven, and old enough to make your own decisions. From this point forward, I will not discuss Dr. Du Bois with you. All I will do is pray that God will touch your heart and reach your mind."

I wasn't sure if I should thank her, so all I did was nod.

"But there are two things you must know. First, I do not condone this in any way, Jessie, and I do not wish to be part of this foolishness. I do not wish to be in the presence of you and Dr. Du Bois as you carry on. And you certainly cannot do this in our home." She braced herself before she said, "Therefore, he is not welcome here."

That took my breath away. How could Maman tell me who was welcome in my home?

As if she already knew my thoughts, she added, "I realize that I am here at your pleasure and it is not my decision alone to determine who may enter this apartment. If this request presents any difficulty for you, please let me know, and I will pack my belongings this afternoon and return to Philadelphia."

"No, Maman!" I wanted my mother here, regardless of the rules that she set. "I understand."

She whispered, "Thank you." Then, with her chin jutted, she finished with, "My second point is that you were mistaken last night. I *am* your mother. I have been your mother since I walked into our home with your father. From that day, until this moment, and as long as I walk this earth, that is who I am, and it will serve you well never to forget that."

She stood waiting for me to speak, and finally the words crawled up and slipped past the stone in my throat. "Yes, Maman."

When she turned away, I longed to rush after her, hug her, and have her hold me. I wanted to call her Maman again and again and apologize over and over until this whole dreadful affair was forgiven and then forgotten.

I decided I would do all of that at breakfast. However, by the time I bathed and dressed, my mother was gone. To Mary-Helen's, I supposed . . .

T his should help." Will's voice shakes me from this morning's memory. "Two cups." He places one in front of me.

Will's office is antithetical to mine. Mine is stark, with few trinkets, because I've had little time to think about enhancing my space. Will's office is teeming with personal possessions that reflect him: three bookshelves crammed with hundreds of volumes; the sideboard covered with paper-filled bins, correspondence awaiting his attention. Even the surfaces atop the file cabinets hold framed certificates and distinctions honoring W. E. B. Du Bois.

He takes a sip of his coffee. "Augustus is out of the office, so this morning, it will be just the two of us."

"Very well," I say.

For the next few hours, we review the progress I've made with the *Brownies' Book*. We discuss every topic, from the illustrator I've chosen for the first cover, to the column I want him to write and the content I've already selected: the poems, short stories, and photographs.

It is almost noon when Will reclines in his chair. "Jess, what you've accomplished in such a short time is remarkable."

This morning, I'd walked into this office feeling weary and beaten. But now I am ebullient, with enough vigor to climb all sixty stories of the Woolworth Building. I'm proving my capability to Will.

I say, "Now I will take your vision from this paper and put it into the hands of the children of the sun."

The knock on the closed door makes us both turn, and I am not surprised to see Miss Ovington when it opens. Whenever Will and I are in closed meetings, Miss Ovington finds a way to open that door.

"I thought you two were in here," she says with such glee that I frown.

Yes, Miss Ovington has been more agreeable, but now her smile is brighter than one hundred harvest moons.

She continues, "You will not believe whom I saw entering the Civic Club right as I was exiting."

In the next second, a young woman, about seventeen or eighteen, with bright eyes and thick hair styled in an ear-length bob, bounces inside. "Papa, when did you return from your trip? Miss Ovington told Mother and me you were here."

On cue, an older woman full of elegance, in a chic blue polka-dot day dress, follows her. In seconds, I assess the sight before me—the young girl: Will's daughter, Yolande. The woman: Will's wife, Nina. Miss Ovington, still by the door, her smile even more radiant.

Will kisses his daughter. When he turns to his wife, she offers her cheek.

Mrs. Du Bois says, "I was so surprised when Mary said you were in the office." Her voice is soft, no more than a decibel above a whisper. "I thought you weren't returning until this evening."

Will didn't go home last night?

"I came into the office early this morning," he says. His words are true; what he omitted is the lie. "I had to prepare for this meeting with Miss Fauset."

I'd been standing bewildered, and as frozen as an iceberg, but now, with Mrs. Du Bois's eyes trained on me, I begin to thaw. It takes me a second to compose myself, but I move with the aplomb that Will just displayed.

"Hello, Mrs. Du Bois." I give her a curt nod. "I'm Jessie Fauset, the new literary editor for *The Crisis*. It's a pleasure to meet you."

She studies me, her glance rising slowly from the tips of my T-strap shoes to the top strands of my hair. To Will, she says, "I didn't know you were hiring a literary editor." Then she turns back to me. "Please excuse my manners. It's a pleasure to meet you, Miss . . ."

"Fauset," I say.

"Hi, I'm Yolande," his daughter jumps in. "I'm a writer and an illustrator, too."

My smile is strained and I am bewildered—how had I not prepared for this inevitable moment?

"Papa, are you going to join Mother and me for lunch?"

"I cannot." He shakes his head. "Meetings all day."

"I told Yolande that would be the case when Mary insisted she escort us here to see you," Mrs. Du Bois says.

My glance shifts to Miss Ovington, and I realize two things. With the way Mrs. Du Bois has addressed her twice—as Mary, something Will never does—Mrs. Du Bois and Miss Ovington are more than acquaintances; they're friends. My second realization is that friends is something Miss Ovington and I will never be.

However, that is not my present concern. I only want to excuse myself from this family reunion.

But then Will's wife faces me. "Miss Fauset, do you have time for lunch?" I only hesitate because I am astonished, and that gives Mrs. Du Bois the opportunity to continue, "I'd love to get to know William's new literary editor. I'm sure there's much we have in common."

What?

When Will adds, "That's a good idea," I have to steady myself. Has someone spiked his coffee with whiskey?

"I . . . I . . . I have so much to do . . . I'm sorry . . ." I try to muster a coherent thought. "My work."

"You certainly have to eat, Miss Fauset."

"Yes, but . . ."

"It's settled," she says as if she's heard something I didn't say. "I'll wait outside as you finish this meeting. I haven't been here in months, and I'd like to say hello to everyone."

"Oh, no, Miss Fauset and I are done," Will says. "The three of you can go to lunch."

Yes, there was whiskey in his coffee, or else he's gone mad! At least there is a saving grace; their daughter will accompany us.

But then Yolande says, "Well, now that Mother has someone to join her for lunch, I'm going home. Please take no offense, Miss Fauset. I was feeling ill this morning, and I only came along so my mother wouldn't eat alone."

"No offense taken." I speak what feels like my first cogent sentence.

"Then it will just be the two of us." Mrs. Du Bois glances at her wristwatch. "We'll be a bit late, but I am W. E. B. Du Bois's wife, after all."

What am I to say? "I'll just need a few moments to return all of this to my office."

"There's no need to hurry. I want us to have a leisurely lunch."

She spins around, and everyone follows—Yolande, Will, and finally Miss Ovington—but not before she gives me a parting grin. I've never had a single violent thought toward anyone. Not until this moment.

CHAPTER 13

MONDAY, NOVEMBER 10, 1919

Are you sure the soup will be sufficient?" Mrs. Du Bois asks before the waiter moves away.

"Yes, I'm not very hungry."

"I understand. There are days when I have no appetite at all. However, this isn't one of those days." She laughs. "So, Miss Fauset, I'm sure my husband has told you all about me, but he hasn't shared anything with me about you. Please tell me about yourself."

It is surreal to be sitting here in front of Will's wife. How will I get through this? "There's not much to tell," I say. "I'm simply a woman interested in languages and literature."

"Oh, Miss Fauset, you're being modest. The literary editor of *The Crisis* magazine is a lofty position, and my husband isn't inclined to share such limelight. Yet he asked you to join him and you readily left your life in Washington, DC, behind."

I lower my hands from the table. Mrs. Du Bois has only pretended to know nothing about me, and it is clear that she wants me to be aware of that. But why? Does she harbor suspicions? Is this lunch merely a guise for her to determine whether she should discuss my employment and possible termination with Will?

Then another thought chills my soul: Is Miss Ovington behind all of this? Through my thoughts, Mrs. Du Bois says, "Really, Jessie. May I call you Jessie?"

"Of course."

"And please call me Nina. I really would like to get to know you," she says in earnest. "I'm already impressed. There aren't many colored women, or white women for that matter, who have positions like yours in any company."

I exhale. Perhaps my thoughts are unfounded. "Thank you. But truly, there's not much to tell beyond my teaching in Washington. While I enjoyed that for many years, it was time to move on to what I truly loved. And I love everything about words and writing."

"I'm so impressed with writers," Nina says. "Writing has never appealed to me, but it was one of the things I found most attractive about my husband. He's a prolific writer." She waves her hand with a chuckle. "Of course, you already know that. How did you become interested in writing?"

This feels like a safe space to begin. "I love to read, an affection passed down by my parents. As a child, I read everything—books, newspapers, and I especially loved magazines. That led to my love of writing. However, after graduation, I quickly learned that teaching was a more suitable and secure vocation."

"Certainly. And now you've moved from your profession to your passion."

"Teaching remains a passion. Now I'll do that at *The Crisis*." The waiter approaches with my soup and Nina's chicken and vegetable casserole.

As Nina chatters away, I'm surprised by her loquaciousness. There is, however, only one subject that interests her—me. She asks about my education, and when I tell her that I graduated from Cornell, she says, "I'm surprised you didn't mention graduating Phi Beta Kappa. It's such an accomplishment."

Nina's words continue to contradict her claim of knowing nothing of me.

"What about your family?" she asks.

As I tell her about my mother and sister, my mind races ahead. What will she ask next?

"I'm always envious of those who have so many who love them," Nina says. "That is a blessing from God."

I almost crumple with relief when our plates are cleared away.

"So where are you living?" Nina asks. "In Harlem, I suppose."

I give her my Seventh Avenue address, and her eyebrows rise. "That's very close to our home." Her eyes are set on mine when she says, "Of course, you already know that."

"No." I shake my head, then tell her honestly, "I haven't a clue where Dr. Du Bois lives."

Her eyes crinkle at the edges as if my words amuse her. "Dr. Du Bois?"

"Yes, I've never asked where he lives, and he's never told me."

"I'm surprised you call my husband Dr. Du Bois."

"Nina"—I place my arms on the table and lean forward—"what else would I call your husband?" I say with as much innocence as I can feign.

Her gaze is intense. "Most of his friends call him W. E. B." She pauses for me to speak, and when I say nothing, she adds, "Although I'm certain you're aware that's reserved for his Negro friends only."

I nod. "Yes. And while I consider Dr. Du Bois a friend, most of all, he is my employer."

Moments pass, and then joy fills her smile, as if my words are sweet music to her ears. "Well, I have certainly enjoyed our time together. I'm afraid, however, that I have another engagement."

The next minutes blur by as we settle the check and then say our goodbyes at the club's entrance. I dash down Fifth Avenue, certain that Will is pacing in his office.

The bullpen is swarming with the usual bustle, but as I rush toward Will's office, he calls out to me as he exits the meeting room.

"Miss Fauset, will you join me in your office?"

The moment he closes my door, I let out, "Will, why did you—"

"Look at this!" he interrupts me. He holds up his book. *Darkwater.* "These are the first copies."

His ardor makes me pause. Taking the book, I flip through the pages. His face shines with satisfaction, and I don't want to snatch this moment from him. "*C'est merveilleux*. Congratulations," I say.

"That's your copy, because this would have never been completed without you, Jess. I'm so grateful."

I am astonished when he hugs me, but then flabbergasted when he just walks away. I want to drag him back. But with a sigh, I think it best to allow some time to pass.

Studying the book's cover, I must smile. It is thrilling to be holding this long-awaited continuation of *The Souls of Black Folk*. Over the last year, Will and I have worked diligently on this, compiling poems, short stories, and essays. I was his editor, spending hours reading, editing, and then rereading what Will had rewritten. For the final weeks before his deadline, I'd spent more hours working on Will's manuscript than I spent eating or sleeping or working.

So I should celebrate this moment, this book, *our* achievement, too.

I turn past the first pages and pause at the dedication:

To my wife, Nina. Without you, none of this would be possible.

I stare at those words, then slowly close the book.

CHAPTER 14

SATURDAY, MAY 22, 1920

The hotel attendant sets the tea service on the table. "Will there be anything else, Miss Fauset?" the young woman asks.

"No, thank you."

Alone, I sip the tea and wonder how this orange pekoe would taste with a little whiskey. If I were not a teetotaler and if it were not ten in the morning, some liquor would have been appropriate for this celebratory moment.

Setting my teacup aside, I lay the June issue of the *Brownies' Book* on the table. This is the reason for my joy. Six issues. Each prepared for the children of the sun.

Like every month before, I savor this fresh-from-the-presses edition, pausing to study the masthead. First: **W. E. BURGHARDT DU BOIS, CONDUCTOR.** Then: **JESSIE FAUSET, LITERARY EDITOR.**

I relish each poem, every story. I pause at the photo of the little girls in the Puerto Rican school. Another geography lesson. Over these months, we've taken the readers to the Philippines through folklore. To Africa through riddles. This month, one of my favorites, we took the kiddies to Scandinavia through games.

I turn past my column to get to the Jury. Although I'd made all the selections, I enjoy reading the letters from the children again:

Dear Mr. Editor: I like the Brownies' Book. If I write a story, will you publish it?

I chuckle. Indeed!

Dear Sir: I learn so much from your magazine. Can you include stories of what I can be when I grow up?

This, I love—receiving questions from the children, then publishing the answers.

At the last letter, I pause, even as the words are already marked into my memory:

Dear Dr. Du Bois:

I love school and every subject, except geography. My teacher shows photographs of people from all over the world. They are all beautiful, except for Africans. Why are Africans so ugly? It's because I'm from Africa that I'm ugly, too.

If this letter had stood alone, it would have been heartrending enough. But over the months, I've read dozens of these self-denigrating missives, in particular from girls, who hate their reflections in the mirror—because of America.

This will change with the *Brownies' Book.*

Although this is a role I've always wanted, I hadn't been certain about my transition from teacher to literary editor. The orderliness of the classroom is quite different from the chaos of the office. Yet it has been a sheer delight adjusting to the business and facing the unpredictability of each day.

In six months, I've learned to manage a magazine, although the course hasn't been smooth. The twenty-four hours we are blessed with each day are scarcely enough to accomplish all the tasks at hand. There are times when the work feels like hard labor. However, I labor in love for the children. And for Will's dream.

Will.

With my teacup in hand, I make my way to the window. Below, Lenox Avenue is pulsing with beginning-of-summer energy, even as men and women rush off on this Saturday morning, the last day of the workweek. This sight is familiar now. Harlem is home because of Will.

Will.

Our world is so very different now, and I think back to the day when the change first began.

The dedication in *Darkwater*, written to his wife, convinced me what Maman, Mary-Helen, and even my own conscience could not—I had no rightful place in Will's life.

So without discussion, I ended our relations and centered my energy on the success of the *Brownies' Book*. Through Thanksgiving, Christmas, and the dawning of the new decade, Will asked no questions. He made no overtures. We moved through our days as a man and woman without history.

While the break seemed astonishingly simple for him, for me it was not. My heart fluttered whenever we stood close. My stomach lurched when I inhaled a whiff of his Yardley's English Lavender cologne. Every interaction with him tested my fortitude. My only saving grace was the days when he traveled, first lecturing at colored colleges and then on a tour for *Darkwater*.

Then, three months ago, there was another shift when Will burst into my office.

Jess!"

I glanced up from my desk.

Will said, "Do you know what today is?" My blank stare prompted him to add, "It's Valentine's Day."

"So?" The February issue had long ago been delivered to our subscribers.

He frowned, then closed my door. "What's wrong?" He took my hand
in his, and I wrenched myself from his grasp.

"For a moment, I thought you were talking about us."

Again he reached for me, and this time, I didn't pull away. "Who else
would I be talking about?" His tone was laced with the kindness and
concern I'd almost forgotten.

I pushed my chair back. This could not happen. I'd faced this situation squarely and accomplished what I never thought I'd be able to—I
was living without Will.

"Jess, talk to me."

"There's nothing to say. We're not together anymore."

His frown was deep. "Why would you say that?"

"All of these weeks, three months now, and you haven't noticed?"

He shook his head, befuddled. "Noticed what? Two of the last three
months, I've been away. What did I miss?"

Now I was confused—yes, Will had traveled, but had it been two of
the last three months? Why had it felt like we'd been in each other's
company almost daily?

Will continued, "And during this time, my attention has been only
on two things—my travel and the *Brownies' Book*. And I was only able
to travel for all of those weeks because you have capably managed the
magazine.

"But whenever I was home, you and I have stood side by side, achieving every goal for this magazine. So tell me, Jess, what haven't I noticed?"

I closed my eyes. I didn't want to become muddled. "I don't want to
go back to how we were."

"Why are you saying this? Please, Jess. I need you."

It was a moment of vulnerability that stole my breath and a bit of my
resolve as well.

"I can't let you go, Jess. Not without us talking."

"There's no reason for us to talk."

"We have sixteen years of reasons." He held out his hand. "But this is not the place. Come with me."

I had a million reasons to deny his request. He alone was the singular reason to say yes, and I followed him from the office to his car. As Will drove north, my mind warred with my heart: What am I doing . . . Nothing . . . I'm just going to talk . . . Don't be gullible.

When Will parked across from the Hotel Olga, I was already shaking my head. He said, "We can have an early dinner in the restaurant, or I can get a room."

"No room. We'll talk in the restaurant."

Will held up his hands. "I'm only suggesting a room because we shouldn't have this conversation in public."

I sighed. He was right. What I needed to say could not be overheard.

Thirty minutes after Will had walked into my office, we entered the same hotel room where we'd last been intimate. By design?

Will sat on the edge of the bed and patted the space next to him. I moved to the chair across from the bed. My single act of defiance.

"We can speak just as well with you over there." When I didn't even grant him a smile, he continued. "So, please tell me what's going on."

"It's maddening that you haven't even noticed we have not been together."

"I've been away, Jess. And yes, perhaps when I was home, I was distracted and distant. Since we used to live miles apart, you've never had the opportunity to see what happens when I become focused and obsessed. Some may even say I'm possessed." He paused as if expecting laughter. I folded my arms. "But we've been working hard, and I've been looking forward to Valentine's Day being our reward."

"So you never realized that I had pulled away?"

"Why would you?"

Lifting my chin, I said, "Because of your wife." Those words didn't jolt him the way I intended; Will stared at me without emotion, as if I'd just told him the time. "You sent me to a lunch that I didn't want to attend with your wife, and then you never asked a single question. Did you discuss it with her?"

"No," he said. "Why would I do that? Your lunch wasn't about me."

"How can you say that? Your wife and your . . ." I paused. What was I? "Your wife and I had lunch, and you believe we never mentioned you?"

He raised an eyebrow. "Okay, Jess. Then tell me what you discussed about me."

"We talked about how . . ." I stopped. I couldn't recall a single word of consequence about Will.

He held out his hand as if I'd made his point. "And I would venture to say that if my wife mentioned me at all, she said no more than that I was a prolific writer and loved *The Crisis.*"

I pressed my lips together.

He continued, "So why would I have any concern about your conversation?"

This was maddening . . . and he was correct.

"Well, that is of no matter. Nina and I have met, and now you and I can never be the same."

He shook his head. "That's not true." He came to me and held my face with both of his hands. "There is so much you do not understand, so much I must explain. But first, you must know, Jess, you and I are no casual dalliance. I've told you before—another time, a different place."

Until this moment, I'd thought those words were no more than sweet talk.

"But that life was not to be for you and me." He turned toward the window. "Because I met Nina first. She was one of my students when I was teaching at Wilberforce, and she came into my life when I needed someone to believe in me. She believed, she nurtured, she gave me the attention I craved, and we married." Will kept on. "It didn't take long to realize marriage was not the judicious choice for me. I cannot tell you whether the error was in my choice of wife, my youth, or if I should have married at all." He sighed. "But just as I began to ask those questions, I became a father. To a son."

I breathed in deeply. I knew of his son from reading his book. He'd mentioned his daughter to me. But never his wife, never his son.

"With the birth of Burghardt . . . I had new questions about life,"

Will said. "I had confusion and doubt and anxiety. How was I to be the guardian of this tiny, perfect person? My son deserved so much more than me." He faced me. "At the same time, with the birth of my son, my heart swelled with love I never believed possible. For my son, and for my wife. She'd given me the most precious gift. All questions I had about marriage were answered. I knew my purpose. To be the best father to a colored boy in America."

My lips trembled. I knew the ending before Will began.

"Then, when he was just a toddler, diphtheria claimed my son, ripping him from my heart and my life. I nearly drowned in a cesspool of questions and grief. Why had my son died, yet I still breathed? Why hadn't God taken me?"

When he paused this time, I finally said, "Will, if this is too much . . ."

He shook his head. "I want you to know, because that loss is the reason for who I am today. It took years for the fog to clear, but once the light returned, my purpose became clear, too.

"I always knew I had a greater calling, and at its core was my overwhelming love for my race. The sense of responsibility I felt for our people increased tenfold after I lost my son. I began to see him not as dead, but free. Free from a world that considered his skin a problem, that would see his ambition as impudence and would view him always with suspicion at best, but more likely with enmity. I understood I had to create a world where colored boys didn't have to die to be free."

I was bereft of speech. What he had just shared was so painful, so wrenching.

"That became my duty—to create a world for colored boys where life, and not death, is freedom. Burghardt is why I fight." So much sorrow was infused in his tone. "But my desire to fight is in conflict with what most believe a marriage should be. Instead of having a family dinner, I'd rather be standing in front of a hundred men, rousing them to go to war against the Ku Klux Klan. Instead of being home, I'd rather be in a classroom with young Negro men, equipping them with the tools they must have to navigate life in this country. Instead of sitting with my wife, I'd rather be in front of influential white men, imploring them to push Congress to pass the Dyer anti-lynching bill so not another colored boy will swing from a tree.

"My heart beats for these fights and for my people." There were tears in his voice when he added, "Much more than my heart beats for my wife.

"Even if I made the decision in my head to abandon this fight, my heart would never follow. I must fight until racism is effaced. Or perhaps it will be my end that comes first. That, I do not know. All that is clear is that only my death will bring an end to my war against white supremacy." He exhaled a long breath. "So how am I to have an acceptable marriage when being at the forefront of this struggle is my greatest love?"

In a whisper, I asked, "Have you ever spoken to Nina as honestly as you've just spoken to me?"

"There's no need. She's an excellent woman, a very good wife. And she gave me another beautiful gift—our daughter, who helped bring me back to life."

I knew Will spoke the truth about his daughter. It was in his smile that rose from his soul the few times he'd mentioned her to me. But it was most in the profound dedication he'd written in *The Souls of Black Folk: To Burghardt and Yolande: The lost and the found.*

"Nina's done everything right. I am the one who is misplaced, who has too many obligations outside of my home." He stared at me. "Too many obligations, and too many desires."

My eyes stayed on him. "Shouldn't your desires be inside your home?"

His lips curved upward. "White folks still have us bound. The chains that shackled us were beyond physical."

His words felt offensive, and I crossed my arms.

"Negroes are bound by rules and regulations and societal norms that are based on nothing more than white folks' religion and opinion. I don't subscribe to any of that. Perhaps it's because I've had the privilege of traveling the world and that very act has freed me from the spurious bounds of America. If an omnipresent God is love, then our love should be without limit as well."

This was how he justified us. His love without limits allowed me to be in his life. "Does Nina believe in love the same way?"

He shrugged. "Again, this is not a conversation we've had. If I had to guess, I'd say men and women approach love differently."

"Is this fair to Nina?"

"My wife is very aware of who I am. She could have left me years ago, but she's made the decision that even with my shortcomings, we serve a purpose for each other. I give her the respectability of a husband. And she cherishes her roles as a wife and mother."

"And . . . what does she give you?"

"She accepts that I am a weak man who seeks more than what one woman can provide."

I shook my head. "I don't know how your wife can accept this."

"She's not the only woman who has done this, Jess. Nina and I have been married for a long time and she understands marriage is a compromise. She knows who I am and what I need, just as I know who she is and what she needs."

To some, Will's words may have been startling, perhaps even shameful. However, I understood. Just like Will believed every Negro had two souls, he had two hearts, as he'd so often tried to tell me. And it was his two hearts that made him complete.

"I take care of my home, and in turn, my wife wants me to be the best I can be. And I am best when I'm with you." He crossed the room and, with his palm, caressed my cheek. "There are times when I become distracted and distant, for days, for weeks, even months. What you must know is that my desire for you never wavers.

"However, what I've just shared may be burdensome. And although my heart will suffer, I will understand if you decide that I, as I am, will not be enough for you. The choice, the decision, is yours, Jess. Do you choose me?"

I prayed that somehow the God I loved would understand this love I had for Will. I didn't want to be Will's wife, but against all that I was raised to be, I wanted what he was offering me.

I pressed my lips against his fingers. When he kissed me, what I felt eclipsed the familiar frisson between us. With this revelation, we now shared a bond that was far stronger than when we had entered this room. He shared his heart with me, and now I was willing to give him mine completely.

J ess."

Will's voice draws me from the past, and I turn from the same window where he'd stood three months before, baring his soul. He'd left this morning for his breakfast meeting before I'd awakened.

"I'm sorry it's taken me so long to return. The meeting lasted longer than expected." When he presses his palms together as if he's about to pray, I frown, until I see his grin peeking beneath his mustache.

"What did your editor want to discuss?"

"Harcourt, Brace, and Howe is releasing a second printing by the end of the summer."

"Good heavens. Already?"

"*Oui!*" he says, and we laugh. "*Darkwater* is doing well here, but it's a success in Great Britain, too."

This is an enormous accomplishment, although I am not surprised. *The Souls of Black Folk* is considered one of the most important books of the past decade. The follow-up has been awaited eagerly.

I wrap my arms around him. "*Je suis si fière de toi.* So very proud. This calls for a celebration."

"Yes," he says. "And the festivities will begin right here." He loosens the tie on my peignoir.

I fall into the kiss, knowing what the remaining languorous hours of this Saturday afternoon and night will bring. My only question is, Will I make it to church in the morning?

CHAPTER 15

MONDAY, MAY 24, 1920

stand in front of the two-story brick building and frown. The words above the door read **Eloh Tibbar Eht Nwod**. As I descend the rickety metal staircase, the steps rattle beneath my feet. The heavy door moans when I push it open. *What on earth?*

I enter a small smoke-filled cellar. My instinct is to spin around, but Nella Larsen Imes is practically standing in front of me.

"Jessie!" She waves both arms as if somehow I will miss seeing her in this room the size of my parlor.

"Goodness gracious." I hug my friend, and then we sit at a small table. Scanning the room, I take in the space filled with about a dozen round tables, all occupied with colored and white women chatting and sipping tea. My expression makes Nella chuckle.

"I guess you've never been to the Mad Hatter."

"No." My eyes are still adjusting to the dim cellar's light, made more obscure by the cigarette smoke that hovers in the room like a cloud. "It's rather . . ." I search for the appropriate word.

Nella laughs. "Charming?"

"I was going to say cozy. The sign above the door didn't say the Mad Hatter."

"I always forget to mention that the proprietress is an *Alice in Wonderland* aficionada."

"Thus the Mad Hatter."

"And the words above the door—'down the rabbit hole' spelled backward."

"C'est merveilleux!"

"It is marvelous." She laughs. Since the first time we had lunch after Nella responded to my letter asking whether she'd become a contributor for the magazine, we have spent hours together talking and laughing.

Ours was an instant friendship, and my mother, who is now a volunteer working beside Nella at the library, adores her.

"There aren't waiters here," Nella says. "We have to serve ourselves, but the tea and biscuits are just swell."

I follow Nella into the even smaller back room, where we gather teacups and biscuits. When we return to our table, I wait until we're settled before I say, "I wanted to see you for our usual get-together. But also for this." I pull the folded magazine from my satchel and lay it before us.

Nella squeals. "The *Brownies' Book*?"

"Fresh off the presses."

Nella turns the pages, hastening past all the advertising and poetry and stories until she stops and stares. When she looks up, her eyes are glassy.

"Jessie . . . this is me. Nella Larsen Imes. My name in print. For the first time ever."

I smile. "The first of many."

She presses her hands against her chest. "I've always wanted to be a writer." She reads the title—"Three Scandinavian Games"—then studies each game she shared.

Nella had been apprehensive about writing for the *Brownies' Book*. It wasn't until over lunch one day when we shared our experiences of being raised by white mothers, and she told me about her time in Denmark, that I convinced her she had something to contribute.

Finally, she glances up. "Do you realize the important work you're doing for Negro children?"

I nod. "But I wouldn't be able to do it without writers like you."

"No, Jessie. This is all you. I've been there as you've put in the long hours writing articles and stories and poetry to fill the pages. Then poring over submissions. You've done so much, I think W. E. B. needs to step aside and allow you to be the editor."

Her words make me smile again. "Nella, I used to dream of a position like that. From the first time I saw *Vogue* magazine when I was in high school, and one of my teachers allowed me to read her issue. I devoured those pages. But do you know what I envisaged when I saw those fancy women inside?" Nella shakes her head. "I saw colored faces. I would pretend the women in the pictures were Negroes because I wanted to see women in there who looked like me."

"Oh, Jessie, colored children will look at this and see what you imagined. When history is written about the *Brownies' Book*, it will be your name that is lifted high."

I place my hand over hers. "Thank you for saying this, but I am not alone. I have all the contributors to thank for this. From James Weldon Johnson to you. And have you seen all the poems written by Georgia Douglas Johnson? Goodness gracious. She's one of the most important Negro poets of our time, and yet she's been so kind."

Nella's lips curl into a smirk before she takes a long sip of tea, peeking at me over the rim of her cup.

"What's wrong?"

"Is Mrs. Johnson being kind to you or W. E. B.?"

I shake my head. "W. E. B. has nothing to do with the content. I'm managing the *Brownies' Book*."

"And I'll repeat my question: Is she writing for you or W. E. B.?"

I feel heat rising, warming first my neck, then my cheeks. "What are you saying?"

"Well." She makes a show of placing her teacup on the table. "There's a rumor that Mrs. Johnson and W. E. B. are fooling around."

"No! She's married."

"That's why it's called fooling around, Jessie. And when has marriage ever mattered?"

Her words feel like an indictment against me.

Nella continues, "Mrs. Johnson's husband is much older. Perhaps that's the reason for their affair." She shrugs. "Anyway, that's what Elmer and I think."

"Your husband believes there's something going on with Georgia and W. E. B.?"

She nods. "Although, you may find this amusing." She rolls her eyes to the heavens. "At first, he thought you were the one stepping out with the great W. E. B." She laughs as if that is outlandish.

My laughter is camouflage. I'm not certain which of Nella's revelations has shaken me more—Will having an affair with Georgia . . . or Dr. Imes thinking I am.

"Anyway"—she turns her attention back to the magazine—"I will never be able to thank you enough for this opportunity. I know how important status and lineage and college degrees from certain universities are to the Harlem elite. But none of that matters to you."

"Nella, I've told you before. The gift you have comes from God. And that alone is the reason you can stand alongside every Negro in Harlem."

"Seeing my name this way, Jessie, makes me believe that. And now that I know I can do this, perhaps it's time for me to work on that novel I really want to write."

"I must find a way to do that myself." Nella and I have discussed our novels. She's intrigued me with her story of a young biracial woman who struggles with her identity. Nella hasn't written much, but how can I admonish her when I've made so little progress myself? Nella, at least, has a title—*Quicksand.*

I ask, "Would it help if we were to meet regularly to discuss our novels?"

"A writing partner," Nella says. "That would be wonderful motivation for me. Yes, let's do that."

As Nella sips her tea and peruses the pages of the *Brownies' Book,* my thoughts wander back: *There's a rumor that Mrs. Johnson and W. E. B. are fooling around.*

That cannot possibly be true.

CHAPTER 16

FRIDAY, MAY 28, 1920

t's still hard to believe you won't be with me in Atlanta." Will sounds as incredulous as he was three days ago when I told him I wouldn't be attending the NAACP convention. "You won't see me receive the Spingarn Medal. And not only that, you won't hear my speech."

"Your speech will be outstanding."

He nods. "Yes, because of your meticulous editing."

"And there will be thousands cheering you on. I'll just be doing it from afar." I glance at the cabbie; his eyes are straight ahead. Still, I lower my voice. "Atlanta is not a good place for us to be together."

"I don't care what people think."

"I do. It wouldn't be respectable for us to be staying in a rooming house together."

"Are we any more respectable in a hotel?" He sounds truly perplexed.

A hotel is more inconspicuous. No one knows who's behind all of those closed doors. But the Jim Crow laws of the South don't allow colored and white folks to sleep under the same roof. With so few hotel options for Negroes, we would have been left with a rooming house—an unsuitable choice.

Will takes my hand. "I want to be the one who decides how I live my life, but I will always give the utmost respect to you."

We are crossing Fourteenth Street and have little time. "Do you have your train ticket?"

He pats his jacket pocket.

"All right. You'll be arriving in Atlanta tomorrow evening."

"You've forgotten I've taken this trip many times."

"I have not. I just want to remind you of the details. The conference ends on Wednesday, should I schedule your return ticket for Thursday?"

He shakes his head. "I'll get my ticket when I get to Atlanta. I'll be going to Washington."

I don't want to pry into business that is not mine. Still, I say, "I didn't see anything on your schedule for Washington. Should I have Pocahontas block off those days for you?"

"Just one or two. I'm going to spend some time with Alain Locke, and perhaps a few other writers in Washington."

Georgia Douglas Johnson lives in Washington, DC.

With her husband, I quickly remind myself. It's just a rumor.

Will and I have drawn closer since our conversation in February. When he isn't traveling, we spend almost every minute of our waking hours together. How would he have time to keep company with another woman?

I pretend to peruse my notes. "Let me know if you'll need me to make your return reservations." When he says nothing, I add, "I want to review the July issues of both magazines, which will be going to press soon after you return. Nella Larsen Imes is submitting another piece for Playtime."

"Let's keep publishing her. She's a Fisk graduate, correct?"

I know a little of my friend's history at Fisk. How she matriculated there but was expelled (for reasons she's never disclosed) after her first year. However, I also know Will's unspoken but unmistakable antagonism toward Negroes who lack a college education—particularly those he believes had the opportunity to pursue one. I do not want him to think less of Nella. "She attended Fisk" is all I say.

"Good. And the July cover—I loved it. Who's the illustrator?"

"Albert Smith."

"A new name," Will says. "I like that, Jess. New talent may help push sales."

"Are you concerned about sales?"

"Nothing for you to worry about." He pats my hand as if reassuring a child. "The quandary is not editorial, it's financial. You keep building the magazine, and I will manage the rest."

I draw in a breath. I want to demand that Will speak to me with respect. I've grasped the nuances of publishing; I've taken charge of every aspect of this magazine with little input from Will. I am far more than the literary editor, so it defies logic that Will won't share the financial status of the *Brownies' Book* with me.

However, these are our final minutes together, and I don't wish to squander this time with a confrontation.

"We're receiving a barrage of submissions for both magazines."

"Of course. You've opened the doors for Negro writers. Everywhere I go, people are excited about the new literary editor at *The Crisis*."

That is pleasing news.

"I was speaking with Georgia Johnson just the other day."

His words sweep my smile away.

"She's excited about what we're doing with the *Brownies' Book*. I told her it is only possible because of you."

I have questions, but each one is based on rumors.

Making another shift in subject, I say, "Will you have time to write an opinion piece about the conference upon your return?"

He shakes his head. "I'm afraid my schedule won't allow it."

"Write the rough draft," I say, "and I'll have it ready for July."

"How are you going to do that, Jess? Have you completed the novelette you're writing for the next three issues?"

"I haven't finished that, but I will. I've told you, I can manage it all."

He shifts and, with his fingertips, he traces the side of my face. "Every day I discover new ways in which I need you and appreciate you."

His words make me giddy, but there is one final piece of business I must complete. "I've gathered the numbers you requested for the phonograph industry." I hand him the folder. "Record sales may approach one hundred million this year."

He whistles as he peruses the numbers. "My friend Harry is onto something."

Harry Pace, one of Will's former students from Atlanta University, has set his mind to founding the first Negro phonograph company. "Harry *is* onto something, considering that OkeH has announced they will record their first Negro artist."

"I have no faith in OkeH, or any other white company, presenting Negro performers in a positive light. However, the possibilities of what can be achieved with a Negro recording company are infinite." He pauses, in awe of this notion. "Harry's company will be writing, producing, and recording *our* music with *our* performers. This is an exciting time, Jess."

When the taxicab rolls to a stop in front of Pennsylvania Station, I slip out, while Will pays the cabbie and tips him extra to wait a few moments to take me back to the office. Stepping outside of the car, Will gathers his valise, then discreetly intertwines his fingers with mine.

As the hubbub of the city billows around us, we stand as if we are alone.

"I have a favor to ask." I squeeze his hand.

"What kind of favor?" He wiggles his eyebrows, but I don't crack a smile.

"Promise you won't make a ruckus when you have to move to the colored car on the train." Will bristles, but I keep on, "You cannot get arrested before you arrive in Georgia."

"All right," he says.

"And in Georgia . . ." Now Will sighs. "Those white folks would like nothing more than to lock up every colored man attending this convention and . . ."

It is unnerving that the organization founded on the principles of advancing the rights of colored people is actually having its national convention in the South, in a state that abhors colored people and has a very active Ku Klux Klan.

"There won't be any tomfoolery. The mayor himself invited us."

"I will worry until you return. Promise me you'll be careful."

"I'll make all of those promises if you make one for me—write while I'm away."

For the first time since we exited the car, I smile. "Haven't you noticed all the writing I've been doing?"

"I'm speaking about your novel, Jess. I'm speaking about Joanna, Maggie, and Peter." It always delights me when he speaks of my characters with such familiarity. "I appreciate all the writing you're doing for *The Crisis* and the *Brownies' Book,* but another year mustn't pass without your protagonist blazing a trail of success for women . . . just like you."

He lifts my hand to his lips, and his kiss lingers on my fingers.

I whisper, "*Sois bien, mon amour,*" and slide back into the taxicab.

There is but a singular thought in my mind. Professionally and personally, I have never been so happy.

In front of the office, I slide out of the car and take in the crowd of approaching faces. One stands out—a man in a light wool suit and skimmer hat. He hastens past, and I am staring at his back when the memory washes over me.

"Eugene Pinchback," I call out.

The man stops, then spins around.

"It *is* you," I say as he approaches.

He passes me a polite smile. "I apologize, but you have me at a disadvantage."

"I'm Miss Fauset. Jessie Fauset. I was your—"

"French teacher. At M Street High School. I cannot believe I didn't recognize you, because you look exactly the same."

"It's good to see you. I didn't realize you were in New York."

"I came here to continue my education."

"Oh," I say. "I thought you'd gone to the Midwest. I was so impressed that you were going to the University of Wisconsin."

He chuckles. "I couldn't survive those midwestern winters. So I came here to New York, attended New York University and then City College for a while."

"Impressive, but I'm not surprised. You were always a good student. What are you doing now?"

"A lot of different things." He sighs but becomes animated when he adds, "Recently, I've turned my attention to writing."

"Really? Do you have a few minutes, Eugene? I'm the literary editor right here at *The Crisis*. Perhaps we can work together."

"At *The Crisis*." He glances at the building as if he's weighing my invitation. "All right. But first you should know, I've been writing under the name Jean Toomer. That's how I'm now known."

"Your nom de plume. Well, Jean Toomer, I'd love for you to join me for a few minutes."

"Certainly, Miss Fauset."

Minutes later, Jean shares some of the writing he's published in the *New York Call*.

"I'm looking forward to reading your work, but I'd be even more delighted if you'd consider submitting something for *The Crisis*." Jean hesitates and I ask, "Is something wrong?"

"Nothing's wrong. I just wonder . . . isn't *The Crisis* part of the NAACP?"

"Yes, it's the official publication for the organization."

"Miss Fauset, I don't want to slam you or *The Crisis* and the work the NAACP is doing, but I don't consider myself a Negro writer."

I'm not certain I understand. I'm sure Jean, with his pale complexion and wavy hair, is often mistaken for being white. However, that mistake would have been made only by white folks. With one glance, every Negro in America would surmise that Jean is colored.

There must be something beyond his words. "You may not be aware that while the NAACP was founded for the advancement of colored people and *The Crisis* is primarily designed to uplift Negroes, most of the founders of the NAACP were white, most of the board members today are white, and many of our contributors to the magazine are white as well."

His eyes widen with surprise. "I wasn't aware of that."

"I'm looking only for talented writers. I have no cares about race or ethnicity. The stories told are what matter to me." He sits, still grappling with this. I say, "Just consider it. I would love the possibility of working with you."

That makes him smile. But then he studies his shoes. "I don't know if I should say this, Miss Fauset, but there wasn't a boy at M Street High School who didn't have a crush on you."

"I heard something about that," I say with a laugh, hoping to get Jean to kick back. "And I also heard the names you young men called me."

"Oh, no." His tone is serious again. "We never said anything disrespectful. Only that you were the most comely, sophisticated teacher we'd ever had."

"And fashionable," I tease. "I heard you young men thought I was rather stylish."

"Yes, that, too," he says with his head once again bowed.

When I laugh again, he does as well. Exactly as I wished. As our laughter abates, I tell him, "Think about what I've said, Jean, but *sans souci.*" His face brightens. "Whether we work together or not, I hope this won't be the last time I'll see you."

He reaches for my hand when he stands. "You'll be hearing from me."

I give him the "you're dismissed" nod, and he skedaddles away. In the bullpen, I hear the whispers and giggles following him. Just like high school. The girls still swoon over Eugene Pinchback. *Plus ça change, plus c'est la même chose.*

However, my smile fades. Jean's words have left me concerned. When in the last six years had he determined he no longer wanted to be seen as a Negro?

CHAPTER 17

SATURDAY, AUGUST 21, 1920

peruse the pages of Howard University's *Stylus* and then A. Philip Randolph's political and literary magazine, *The Messenger*. I scour the pages in search of writers. After reading through both publications, I set them aside.

Turning to the pile of the *Brownies' Book*, I flip through each issue until the graduation pictures make me pause. I study the young man who first sent us his photograph.

Langston Hughes. This young man is a writer, even if he doesn't yet see himself that way.

Grabbing my fountain pen, I begin:

My dear Mr. Hughes:

Recently, I came across your graduation picture again, and like before, I am impressed with your academic achievements, especially your supplemental school activities.

As the literary editor for the Brownies' Book, I invite you to submit a poem or short story for our consideration. You were correct

*when you said children would be inspired by your graduating
photograph. They will be even more heartened by your words.*

*Sincerely,
Jessie R. Fauset*

Mr. Hughes has graduated, but I'm certain the administrators will
forward my letter.

The knock on my door draws my attention away.

"Miss Ovington," I say, unable to hide my displeasure.

In the nine months or so that have passed since she brought Nina
and Yolande into the office, Miss Ovington has treated me like a ghost,
except when Will and I are together. Only then does she acknowledge
my existence, just so she can make her contempt for me apparent. From
making quite a hullabaloo over several articles she disagreed with to
informing Will she believes I'm not a fitting editor, she wants me out of
The Crisis.

"Miss Fauset, do you have any idea when Dr. Du Bois will be returning?"

I arch an eyebrow. For the last three weeks, Will has been on an
extensive lecture circuit throughout the South. Miss Ovington is aware
of this, not only because of all the applauding coverage Will has received, but because he's speaking on behalf of the NAACP.

Miss Ovington, however, is not aware that Will returned last night.
Before we parted at the Hotel Olga this morning, he'd asked me to tell
Pocahontas he would be taking a few more days at home with Yolande.

My inclination is not to respond to Miss Ovington's inquiry, but I
do say, "I believe he's spending time with his daughter as she prepares
for college."

"Ah yes," she says. "Nina did tell me they were making plans for
their trip to Fisk University. Do you expect him in the office this week?"

I'd answered one question that should have been addressed to Pocahontas. I wasn't going to answer another. "Miss Foster has Dr. Du Bois's
complete schedule."

"I don't believe anyone in this office has a better understanding of Dr. Du Bois's comings and goings than you, Miss Fauset."

I restrain the urge to snap at Miss Ovington. Will and I have given her no further cause to suspect any impropriety between us. Our conduct in the office has remained beyond reproach. Yet . . . how can I be righteously indignant when her insinuation is true?

It is God's hand that leads Countee into my office at that very moment. I leap from my chair and welcome him.

He glances from me to Miss Ovington. "My apologies, Miss Fauset. My father said you wanted to see me today."

"Yes, and you arrived at just the right moment." I force my smile when I turn to Miss Ovington. "We're done here, aren't we?"

"Yes," she grumbles before she marches away.

Countee says, "I hope I didn't interrupt anything."

"You absolutely did not."

I am always pleased to see this young man, who remains as soft-spoken and shy as the day we met. There is a single exception to his meekness. Whenever he speaks of his poetry, his eyes shine as bright as the sun at high noon.

Today, Countee is as dapper and dashing as if he's on his way to Sunday morning services at his father's church. Although his light gray cotton suit can be considered casual, his matching bow tie cannot.

"I wanted to speak with you about your poem." I have the paper he'd given me at church last Sunday on my desk. However, before I hand him the page covered with deletions, insertions, and margin notes, I say, "I'm in awe of you, Countee."

He beams as if I've already said enough.

"You're only seventeen, yet you write with the soul and wisdom of one much older. You write about love as if you've already experienced it."

His blush is largely hidden by his chestnut complexion. Now I wonder—what high school girl has won his affection?

"Your opening, 'Love, leave me like the light'—those words have stayed with me. That being said, there are a few things I want us to work on together."

He sits up straight, as if he's ready to take on the world—and my every word.

"Each line alone is beautifully written. I can see the influence of the Latin and French classes you're taking."

"*Merci, Mademoiselle Fauset.*"

"*De rien, Monsieur Cullen.* I'm impressed with your expressions of the inverse emotions of joy and sorrow and your use of imagery. However, with all of that, I want you to forget what you've written and ask yourself— What message do I want to convey through this poem?" He cocks his head like he doesn't understand. "What you have here are beautifully written lines. Yet you are capable of writing a beautifully written poetic *story*. Poetry is no different from prose, in that sense. It's—"

"Miss Fauset!" Countee interrupts as if he cannot wait another second to speak. "Please forgive me, but I know what you mean. When I read Keats, in a dozen lines, I feel like I've read an entire book."

"Yes," I say.

"I love all of his poems and have read each dozens of times, but my favorite will always be 'To Autumn,' because with his first line, I'm immediately drawn in. Not only can I see the mist, I can feel it. I can see the sun and feel its heat. By the end, I not only feel as if I've lived through an entire season, I am looking forward to living through autumn again. I've always marveled at his ability to make me feel that with so few words."

"I love that poem as well. The interconnectivity of each word and each line is exquisite."

"Yes, yes!" Countee says. "By the time I finish one of his poems, I'm completely satiated."

It is amusing listening to Countee, and watching as he comes to his own understanding.

"I knew there was something missing with my writing."

"Not missing," I correct him. "However, is there more we can add? Not in terms of the number of words, but in your choice of words to paint a panorama for the reader." I reach for the poem. In his eagerness, Countee almost wrenches it from my hand. "I'm sorry, Miss Fauset."

I laugh. "Your enthusiasm is wondrous. As is your receptivity."

"I want to be a good poet so that perhaps someday, people outside of Harlem will know my name. Like John Keats. Everyone knows him, and he only lived to be twenty-five."

"I have a feeling you will be very well known. Because not only have you been given a gift by God, but you're nurturing that gift."

He springs from the chair. "Thank you for taking the time to work with me when I know you have so many important poets."

"*You* are one of my important poets."

His grin is so wide when I say that, it's a wonder his cheeks don't crack. He says, "I mean, poets who've been published."

"Countee, work on what we talked about today, and you will be one of my published poets."

CHAPTER 18

SATURDAY, AUGUST 21, 1920

I push open the front door to our apartment, then freeze.

I can't sleep at night . . . I can't eat a bite.

Even though Maman's back is to me, I can tell she is already dressed for our party. As she sets a platter of deviled eggs atop the table, she sways to the music. She doesn't notice me until I kiss her cheek.

"Oh! I didn't hear you come in."

"I should have called out, but you were having such a good time. I didn't even know we had this in the house," I say, picking up the record sleeve.

Maman's complexion flushes crimson. She waves her hand as if she wants to expunge the sight and the sound of what I'd just seen and heard. Crossing to the Victrola, she sets the player's needle to the side. "It was just . . . I needed . . . some sound."

With a smile, I turn away. Even after all these years, Maman still fancies herself a reverend's wife and presents herself according to the pious principles she learned from Papa. Before my father passed away, the only music in our home was hymns and old spirituals.

In the months since we've arrived in Harlem, my mother has begun to shed some of those convictions. The hems of her skirts have risen with the fashions, her ankles now clearly in view. She sometimes uses the city's slang, just the other day telling me she plans to catch "the first thing smoking" home to Philadelphia next week. And this isn't the first time I've caught her *almost* doing a little jig to the blues.

This is the gift of Harlem—the dress, the music, the language. It isn't possible to live here and not begin to breathe and bleed this place.

"Maman, this looks splendid." The table is covered with white linen, and white balloons are in all four corners of the parlor. "And the banner is even better than I thought it would be."

The purple, white, and gold banner stretches across the width of the parlor with my favorite suffragist quote: **Votes for Women—Equality Is the Sacred Law of Humanity.**

"Nathan hung that banner for me. It is just the adornment we needed."

"It is. And, Maman, you look beautiful." My mother wears a lovely white ankle-length dress with chiffon sleeves. A purple sash completes her ensemble. "You look like the cat's pajamas," I razz her, and she laughs. "I'm sorry I wasn't here to help you prepare."

"I know you had work to do. How was your meeting with Countee?"

Each day, Maman continues to request a review of my accomplishments. In fact, she'd read Countee's poem and studied the edits I'd prepared for him.

"He's so delightful, and he took my suggestions well."

"As he should. You're a good editor."

I rush to give her a hug; I never tire of my mother's praise. "I'll change my clothes and then help with whatever you need."

This morning, I'd set out my dress, and as I lift it from the bed, I feel more delight than anxiety. This marks our first time entertaining in our home, and I've selected my guests with great consideration. I've invited women who are of like mind and ready to celebrate this momentous occasion. And one additional guest, whom I want to know better for different reasons.

I slip on the dress that I purchased from Hecht's last time I was home. The white sequined sheath glitters with every move, and the long fringe swings just above my ankles, concealing the dress's true hem, which ends at my knees. I add the ostrich-feathered purple beaded head-piece, and now I am ready.

When I step into the kitchen, Maman's eyebrows rise. "That's an interesting dress for this evening."

"Maman, this"—I sweep my hand from my head to my toes—"is what this evening is about. We're celebrating this country finally rec-ognizing that women can do everything men can do. We can be who we want, we can dress however we wish, and now, Maman, we can vote."

When I grab her hand and twirl her, she giggles and then slaps my hand away. "Stop all of that," she scolds. "Our guests will be arriving soon."

Her words are like a prompt, and the front door swings open. "Hello." Mary-Helen sweeps inside. "I bring you greetings and guests."

My sister's dress is similar to mine: white, of course. I've asked all the women to wear the color of the suffragist movement. Although Mary-Helen's dress has fringe, too, her hemline is a bit more modest than mine. Nella follows, and then Ernestine Rose, whom I hug first. Ernestine is closer to my age, but she's become quite a friend to Maman, as my mother's work as a volunteer has her in the library several days a week. Many evenings, I've returned home to find Maman and Ernestine huddled at the kitchen table sharing tea and conversation.

Nella says, "You didn't tell us, Jessie, we were to come as showgirls."

I laugh with my friend. "I told you to come dressed up."

As Maman greets the three, I attend to the door when there is an-other knock.

"Sadie!" I pull one of my favorite students into an embrace. "I'm so very glad you were able to make it."

"I'm so glad this party coincided with business I have here in New York. It's good to see you, Miss Fauset."

"I thought we'd agreed you would call me Jessie."

She laughs. "I'll try. It will be difficult since I will always see you as my favorite teacher."

I lead Sadie into the kitchen. "This is Sadie Tanner Mossell. One of my students from Dunbar High School."

My friends surround Sadie with warm greetings. Then Maman asks, "Is this the first time you two are seeing each other since then?"

"Oh, no," I say. "We went from student and teacher to being students together at the University of Pennsylvania. But I asked Sadie to join us today, not only because I adore her, but because she recently became the first national president of Delta Sigma Theta Sorority."

"Oh, the colored women who marched in the suffrage parade," my mother says, and I hear her admiration.

"Maman, how did *you* know that?" While my mother prides herself on staying abreast of matters of equality, I'm intrigued that these women and their accomplishments had captured her attention.

She glances at me as if she's the one astonished. "I thought everyone was aware of what those young colored women did that day. Were you there?" she asks Sadie.

"I was still in high school, or else I absolutely would have been in that procession."

As they all continue to chat about the march, I rush to the door to greet another good friend.

"Laura!" I exclaim as I hug Laura Wheeling, the artist extraordinaire who has illustrated more than a few beautiful magazine covers and articles for *The Crisis*, while at the same time becoming quite well known for her Negro portraitures. "I cannot believe this is the first time I'm seeing you."

"I apologize, Jessie. Those students at Columbia have kept me busier than any past summer." Then she adds, "Even busier than our summer in France!"

We laugh, recalling when we met in Paris in 1914. I was taking classes at the Sorbonne, while Laura was studying at the Académie de la Grande Chaumière. We attended a reception my first evening in Paris, and from that time forward, when we weren't in class, we were inseparable. Laura lives in Philadelphia, which makes it easy for us to visit whenever I'm home.

I lead Laura to the kitchen with the others, and after another round of introductions, Maman tells us to serve ourselves before we settle in the parlor.

"Before we do that," I say, "we must have a toast."

When the glasses are filled with grape juice, I begin, "Here's to men finally realizing that the most valuable assets in this country are women."

"Hear! Hear!" Nella calls out.

More seriously, I continue, "When we received the telegram that Congress had ratified the amendment, I sat in my office, absorbing what it meant to have equal participation in this democracy. Our voices will be heard, our concerns will be addressed. Soon, there will be women in government, perhaps even running for office. This country will be better for this. Tonight, I want to salute all the women *and* men who fought so hard to secure our right to vote."

"Finally!" Nella exclaims.

We follow Maman into the parlor, and once we sit, Ernestine says, "I was on tenterhooks until the amendment was actually ratified."

Nella raises her hand as if she's in a classroom and seeking permission to speak. "But do we think this amendment will make a difference? For you, perhaps, Miss Ernestine, and you, Mrs. Fauset. But for those who look like me"—she glances pointedly at the colored women in the room: Mary-Helen, Laura, Sadie, and me—"nothing will change. This amendment isn't for any colored woman. For us, it will be another law that excludes our participation."

The truth of Nella's words weighs heavy.

For those who look like me.

There is little contrast between the porcelain complexions of Ernestine and my mother, and the sandpaper-colored tones of ours. It is impossible to regard us as Negroes by our skin alone. Yes, our complexions are a bit duskier, and our hair coarser. Our noses and lips a bit fuller, though it is scarcely noticeable. Truly, the differences are minimal—except for what this country has placed upon us. At least one drop of our blood is considered Negro, and even if the other ninety-nine percent is from generations of white ancestors, we are colored—as defined by America. We are less than—as defined by Americans.

"You may be right, Nella," Laura says, her voice as soft as always. "All we have to do is look at how colored men have been treated in the fifty years since they were granted the right to vote."

"Exactly. They have a *constitutional* right, yet white folks," Nella continues with a bit of insolence in her tone, "don't care." She glances at my mother and Ernestine. "Please, no offense intended."

"No offense taken. You can speak freely here," Maman says. "I agree with your point. But progress happens in phases. First we had to get the right to vote, and now we must be diligent to ensure it happens for all."

Nella shakes her head. "The forces are too strong against us. Did you hear about that senator from South Carolina who railed on the floor of Congress, opposing giving the other half of those *unfit Negroes* the right to vote?"

Moans and groans fill the room, none louder than Maman and Ernestine.

Nella continues, "That man spoke of us as if we weren't created by the same God."

"Nothing we've ever accomplished as women has been easy," Maman says.

"Then add being colored," Laura interjects. "This will be a fight."

Sadie speaks up, and we all sit up at the force in her voice. "Yes, the fight will continue. It will just be a different battle now. We must get out and vote. Let them turn us away at the polling precincts. I believe colored and white women will rise up and stand in solidarity on this."

Nella says, "I'm not certain there will be a united front of women. There are just as many women who didn't want the right to vote."

"I'm astonished whenever I hear that!" Ernestine says. "I was at an event where women were the ones who spoke against women's rights."

"A woman actually said to me"—Mary-Helen transforms herself into a Southern belle—"'I don't have time to worry about all of that political speech. My goodness, how am I supposed to discern the difference between a senator and a congressman when I'm busy taking care of my husband and my home?'"

Nella laughs at my sister's antics, but I quickly jump in. "Although I want every woman to know she is worthy of equality, I don't want to disparage or discard women who think they shouldn't vote."

"Why not?" Nella says. "It's silly."

"It's not silly if a woman believes that. And isn't this what we've been fighting for? To be equal so that we can have our own opinions and make our own decisions? If we don't respect women who have differing thoughts, we are no better than the men who tell us we are not worthy of thoughts at all."

"I agree, Jessie," Sadie says. "We must support all women, regardless of their beliefs. However, if we aim to change minds, education is the key, as so much of what someone believes is based on knowledge. Women, especially Negro women, have been denied the same access to education as men."

"That's one reason why I love what I'm doing at *The Crisis*. I'm dedicated to bringing these issues before more women and educating them at the same time."

"If their husbands allow them to read magazines, that is. Especially one published by Negroes." Nella shrugs.

I nod. Although *The Crisis* has many white subscribers, it is a Negro publication. However, one of my goals is to use the magazine as a bridge, bringing colored and white readers together. I want white readers to come to understand the many challenges facing Negroes, and offer white Americans the opportunity to join the struggle.

This is a plan I've already charted in my mind. All that remains is to convince Will.

"That sounds grand, but I have another solution," Nella says. "Perhaps those anti-suffragists should enlarge their social circle and spend time with women like us. Jessie, you should have invited a few." Nella raises her glass. "Although, you would have needed something stronger than this grape juice. A few bottles of beer, or I could have shared some of the whiskey in my flask." She pats her pocketbook.

Everyone laughs, although I'm not certain Nella is joshing. She glances at my mother once again. "Please, no offense intended," she repeats to more laughter.

"No offense taken," my mother reiterates. "Just know I am a woman who stays on the right side of the law. Keep that flask tucked away."

"Yes, ma'am." Nella giggles, and we all glance up at the knock on the door.

"Were you expecting another guest?" my mother asks as I stand.

Nella says, "Maybe it's one of those anti-suffragists."

While the others titter, I take a deep breath. Then, with a smile as wide as I can muster, I open the door. "Mrs. Johnson, welcome to my home."

Although we'd met only once, she embraces me as if we are already friends. "Thank you for inviting me."

Turning to everyone, I announce, "I'd like all of you to meet Mrs. Georgia Douglas Johnson."

Her accomplishments are widely known, as her first published collection of poetry was critically acclaimed. The women stand to welcome her, and when she greets Nella, Mrs. Johnson says, "I've enjoyed reading your pieces in the *Brownies' Book*. Did you grow up in Denmark?"

"I grew up a few miles outside of Denmark—in Chicago."

The room echoes with more laughter.

"But I do have wonderful memories of my time in Denmark with my mother."

As the chitchat continues among the others, Nella sidles up to me. "Did you invite Mrs. Johnson to find out about her and Dr. Du Bois?" she whispers.

"I would do no such thing," I say with such conviction, I almost believe my own lie.

"Well, I would." Nella rushes into the kitchen, fills an empty glass with juice, and then hands the drink to Mrs. Johnson. "So, Mrs. Johnson, do you get the opportunity to travel to New York often?"

"First, please call me Georgia. Mrs. Johnson seems so formal, and I already feel as if I'm among friends."

"You certainly are," Nella says with a bit too much cheer.

Georgia continues, "I come to New York as often as I can arrange. Of course, I love Washington, DC, but there's a certain energy in New York, Harlem especially, that is unmatched."

"Does your husband travel with you?" Nella questions.

"Oh, no. My husband is no fan of the work I do." When eyebrows rise, Georgia waves her hand. "He's very busy with his law practice as well as all the work he does with the Republican Party. So, of course, he'd like me to be home more and travel less." She sighs. "But we've arrived at an agreement."

Before Nella can ask another question, I interject, "Let me tell you why I asked us all to gather here today. Of course, I wanted to celebrate with friends this pivotal point that will be remembered in history. But I also wanted the women I care about to come to know each other. Laura"—I turn to my friend—"should we share some of our stories about our time in Paris together?"

"Oh yes!"

Nella turns to me with a smirk. My friend is annoyed that I've stopped her interrogation, but I want everyone who comes to my home to feel comfortable. And truly, I would like Georgia and me to become friends.

I just hope I will not discover anything that will hinder that from happening.

CHAPTER 19

TUESDAY, OCTOBER 12, 1920

The moment Augustus and I settle into our seats inside Will's office, he addresses Augustus.

"I'd like to make an offer to our subscribers—any reader who brings in five new subscriptions will receive their own annual subscription for free." Will's voice bears an unfamiliar note of concern.

"That's a sound strategy," Augustus says. "Let me look at those numbers."

Glancing between the two men, I ask, "Is everything all right with the *Brownies' Book*?"

"The magazine is doing well because of you; however, we need more colored folks to support us. But"—Will holds up his hand—"don't worry your pretty little head about this, Jessie. Augustus and I will manage the numbers."

I will my voice to remain steady, even as I push back. "Perhaps, W. E. B., you should remember that you have another capable problem solver on this team."

Augustus exhales. "It certainly wouldn't do any harm to see what Jessie thinks. We must find a way to increase the number of subscribers. This month, we'll be short by—"

"Augustus!" Will exclaims. "We'll manage this."

I say, "I believe I can—"

"Jessie!" Now he's aggravated with me. But his annoyance cannot possibly match mine. "You are managing the content and so much more on both magazines. I want you to continue, because the quality of each issue is of paramount importance, especially now. As I said, Augustus and I will manage the financial side of the business."

It is a battle to refrain from telling him what my "pretty little head" thinks of the patriarchal one that wobbles atop his neck. However, being contentious will not serve a single purpose.

For now, I hold my rebuke. "Very well. Have you had the opportunity to review my edits for your column?"

He nods, pleased that I've relented. "I made the changes you suggested, and I agree with your note here." He hands me a page. "We need to say more about the upcoming election."

"That's a good point, Jessie," Augustus says. "Especially since, for many colored folks, this will be their first time voting."

"I am one of those first timers," I say. "I fear that for so many women, voting will be intimidating. We must do all we can to educate our readers."

Augustus adds, "I agree, and speaking of educating, perhaps we should tell our readers about this." He opens the folder he holds, and passes both Will and me a pamphlet.

On the front is a picture of Warren Harding, the Republican presidential candidate. Underneath in bold type are the words *Is This Man a Negro?*

"What is this?" Will and I say in unison.

"It's what it says. A research study was conducted, and the conclusion: Warren Harding may have a little bit of Negro in him."

Augustus chuckles as I scan the pamphlet. According to residents from Harding's hometown in Ohio, Harding's great-grandmother was a Negro. "Who wrote this?"

"No one has claimed authorship," Augustus says. "Although I spoke with Henry Johnson, and the Harding camp believes it was written by a professor from the College of Wooster. A Woodrow Wilson supporter."

I believe Augustus's source. Although I have never met Georgia's husband, Henry Lincoln Johnson is a prominent Republican, one of the few Negroes appointed to a federal position under President Taft.

"I'm thinking we should print something about this," Augustus says.

When Will nods, I am incredulous. "Absolutely not." Both men stare at me. I toss the pamphlet onto Will's desk wondering how they, and especially Will, could consider such a thing. "This is nothing but rumor. It has no basis in truth."

"We could report it that way," Augustus says. "There is unsubstantiated information floating around and—"

"This isn't information, this is malicious gossip."

"Being a Negro is malicious?" Will asks.

"This pamphlet is being distributed by Harding's opponents. What better way to turn white voters against a candidate than to have everyone believing he's colored?"

When Augustus says, "This may get Harding more of the colored vote," the men chuckle, but I find nothing amusing. Rising, I say, "*The Crisis* magazine stands as the foremost Negro publication in this country, and we must never spread gossip as if we are no more than a common rag." My glance goes from Augustus to Will. "These allegations cannot be published. Yes, you are the editor, but my name is on the masthead as well, and I will not allow this."

Will arches an eyebrow, and then his lips spread into a slow smile. "I feel as if I've just been chastised." To Augustus, he says, "The literary editor has spoken."

Augustus tucks the pamphlets back into his folder. "In all honesty, I believe Jessie is right. I guess this meeting is over."

"It is." Then Will turns to me. "I have a few items to review with you."

I settle back into my seat, and when we are alone, he says, "About that Harding information, thank you for considering our reputation." I wonder if, without me, Will would have allowed such nonsense into the magazine. There are times when it seems as if the magazine he loves is no longer at the top of his mind.

Through my musing, he continues, "Remember, we have tickets tomorrow evening to see Fletcher Henderson with the Harlem Symphony."

I shift my thoughts from our professional life to the time we share personally. "At eight, correct?"

When he nods, I say, "I spoke to the tailor. Your suit will be delivered to your home before you leave for your trip in two days."

"Thank you."

Anyone overhearing our exchange could very well assume that Will and I are married. We have settled into a life where, when Will is in the city, I am by his side for everything—from helping him select proper suits, to attending important events like fundraisers at the Harlem Symphony Orchestra or social gatherings at Reverend Cullen's brownstone. Whatever the occasion, we are together.

In the beginning, being with Will continually was unnerving. I wondered if our constant companionship raised suspicions. However, Miss Ovington aside, no one in our coterie seems wary of our coupling. It makes sense that as *The Crisis*'s literary editor, I would assume that place beside Will. It's well known that Mrs. Du Bois is extremely busy tending to their household and caring for their daughter, who, at times, is quite sickly. It is also understood that Mrs. Du Bois isn't fond of attending the numerous social events to which Will receives invitations.

He says, "I'll have the finished version of the Opinion column for you before we leave for dinner this evening."

As I move to stand, I say, "Oh, I almost forgot. Did you see *The Emperor Jones* is opening on the first of November? I've requested tickets for—"

"I won't be attending."

His words astonish me. "Why not?" For the first time, not only will a major production feature an integrated cast, but a Negro will be in the lead.

Will says, "I am not interested in another well-meaning white man deciding he is brilliant enough to write the words and know the thoughts of a colored man."

"You're upset because the play was written by a white man?" I don't give him space to respond. "But the words of a Negro will be spoken by a Negro. For the first time."

Will shakes his head. "This isn't the first time a Negro has stood in the lead."

"This is the first time a colored man will have the lead in a white theatrical performance. The most important role isn't being played by a white man in blackface."

He shrugs. "I'm only interested in the stories written for us by us."

Of course, I understand and agree with his argument. Nonetheless, I am pleased that progress has been made, and I tell him that. For a time, Will and I debate, something I relish, as it reminds me of the challenging discussions I used to have with Papa.

However, Will remains resolute, and when he says, "When a colored man writes a stage play that stars a colored man, I will be the first one to purchase tickets for you and me to sit in the front row," I acquiesce.

"D'accord."

It seems I will be attending the premiere of *The Emperor Jones* without Will. This may be rather fortuitous. Maman enjoys theatrical performances as much as I; however, in the year since we arrived in New York, we haven't attended any such event together. I am always in the company of Will.

Now Maman and I will have this time together. And perhaps Mary-Helen and Nathan will join us. The evening will be a fine family affair.

CHAPTER 20

MONDAY, NOVEMBER 1, 1920

The center aisle of the Provincetown Playhouse is packed with patrons. Men, donning elegant suits with wide cuffed trousers, and women, every bit as modish in sleeveless cocktail dresses with plunging necklines and daring hemlines, greet each other with hugs, kisses, and expectant chatter. Everyone in this crowd, colored and white, knows that something singular is about to occur.

I push through the crowd, smiling at familiar faces, until I reach the second row. "We're sitting here, Maman."

My mother enters first, followed by my sister. However, before Mary-Helen can take her seat, I grab her hand. "Maman, I'm going to . . . introduce Mary-Helen to someone." I scurry up the aisle with Mary-Helen in tow.

At another time, I would have taken a moment to appreciate this Greenwich Village staple of the arts that once housed horses and still has a hitching post on the left wall as proof. At another time, I would have stopped to greet Nella and her husband, and James Weldon Johnson and his wife, properly. However, my focus is finding a place where my sister and I can speak privately.

"Jessie," my sister shouts above the din as I yank her along. "What is going on?"

When I finally stop, my breath is labored. "I wanted to let you know Will is going to be here tonight."

Her frown is deep. "I thought he didn't want to see *The Emperor Jones*."

"He didn't. Suddenly this morning he asked Pocahontas to add a ticket to my group. Before I could question him, he left to attend a board meeting outside of the office. He'll be here at any moment, sitting right beside us."

Mary-Helen blows out a long breath, but then shrugs. "Such is life. This is a public theater, not a private affair. And of course, Dr. Du Bois should be here. This is an important event. He and Maman need never exchange a glance or a word."

"Do you think it will be that simple?"

"Of course. Maman told you he wasn't invited into her home. Surely she didn't expect that to extend to public places. She'll be fine." She pauses as if she has a new consideration. "He won't confront her, will he?"

"No, certainly not. He hasn't a notion of how she really feels."

"Then all will be well."

She spins away from me, but before she can take a step, I say, "Please tell Maman that he will be here." I feel like a child once again, imploring my big sister to intervene with our parents on my behalf.

As in those days, Mary-Helen says, "No! This is your predicament, not mine."

My sister is right. My concern is utterly preposterous. There will never be a confrontation with my mother. Not here. Proper decorum at all times.

Yet my apprehension lingers, and then I hear, "Jessie!" Will calls to me as he enters the playhouse. He is accompanied by Joel Spingarn and his wife. In the last year, Mr. Spingarn has become one of my favorite officers of the NAACP, always ready with a kind word.

After I greet the Spingarns, Mr. Spingarn says, "We were just discussing you at our board meeting, Jessie. Everyone has taken notice of the work you're doing at *The Crisis*, especially your own writing for the magazine. We're impressed and pleased."

"Thank you." Glancing at Will, I add, "I have a great mentor."

As the Spingarns make their way into the crowd, I pull Will aside. He says, "My apologies for being a little late. The meeting ran much longer than expected."

"Did everything go as planned?" I always ask about his concerns first.

He nods. "I made my presentation to the board. Either they'll finance my study on the effects of the war on Negroes, or they'll support a second Pan-African Congress. They won't do both."

I want to ask Will his thoughts and give him mine, but other words spill from me. "My mother is here."

A moment's pause. "It will be good to see her again," he says with studied nonchalance. Then, sensing my apprehension, he shrugs. "We're adults, Jess." He places his hand on the small of my back and leads me down the aisle still crammed with patrons.

My mother and Mary-Helen are sitting close, deep in conversation. Then, Maman glances up with a smile that quickly fades.

"Mrs. Fauset, it is a pleasure to see you again." Will holds out his hand, and just for a second, my mother leaves him hanging in the air. Then, when she takes his hand, I breathe.

But in the next moment, my mother gathers her wrap. "I'll be leaving." Her tone is terse. "I'll hail a taxicab."

"Maman!"

I rush behind her, but she moves quickly, zigging then zagging through the crowd, and I cannot catch up until we are in the vestibule. "Maman, there's no reason for you to leave."

Slowly, she pivots and faces me. A sprinkling of theater patrons remain in the entrance hall, so she whispers, "I will not sit next to you and that man in this theater."

"Maman," I say with tears brimming in my voice. "It's just a play. I'm not asking you to share a meal or even a conversation with Will."

"I may not be breaking bread with him, but sitting next to you and that married man would be equal to me condoning my daughter being that man's—"

"Maman!"

This is the second time her words have slashed me so. She closes her eyes and holds up her hand as if she's reprimanding herself for the words she'd once again almost spoken. Her voice is gentler now. "You may not respect yourself, Jessie, and that tears my heart in two. But I will not allow you to disrespect me."

"I apologize. I didn't think you'd feel disrespected. I thought . . ."

"You thought I'd agree to accompany you while you're out with a married man?"

"Will and I are both here in our professional roles."

"Is that the lie you whisper to yourself? Is that the lie behind which you always hide?"

I shake my head, having no answers. I say, "Let me get my coat."

"No."

Mary-Helen's voice comes from behind us. "I'll take Bella home with me. Nathan won't be returning until tomorrow. So she can stay the night."

"Thank you, Helen. Now, come." Maman turns from me without saying goodbye.

"Go back and enjoy the play," Mary-Helen whispers. "This is a big night, and you'll have to report on it for *The Crisis*. Bella will be fine by morning." She gives me a final squeeze before she rushes Maman out the door.

The crowd in the aisle thins as the theatergoers find their seats. As we sit, Will discreetly lays his hand over mine and threads our fingers. Will never has any concern about public affection, but I do, and my natural instinct is to pull away.

Usually, he will let go, but this time, he holds me tighter. As if he knows I need his touch at this moment.

"Good evening, Dr. Du Bois."

Will drops my hand before he stands. "Mr. and Mrs. Johnson." As

Will greets Georgia and her husband, I stand beside him, and then Georgia turns her attention to me.

Glancing at her husband, Georgia says, "This is Miss Jessie Fauset, the literary editor of *The Crisis.*"

"Oh." He nods. "You're the one who keeps my wife away from home so often," he says with a smile that doesn't travel beyond his lips.

My glance darts between Georgia, her husband . . . and Will. It is Georgia who saves the moment.

"Now, darling, I'm not in New York all that often. And you were the one who said you didn't want to miss the play."

Will says, "Well, I'm certainly glad you wanted to make this trip, Mr. Johnson. It's important for a man in your position to be here."

I'm not surprised by Will's words. Georgia's husband is everything that impresses him: He is an Atlanta University graduate, who, because he was colored, couldn't attend law school in the South. He studied at the University of Michigan and is now a very successful corporate attorney. However, what is most pleasing to Will is Mr. Johnson's standing with the Republican Party. Although Will himself is not attracted to what he calls the perniciousness of politics, he admires anyone in proximity to that power.

The two men chitchat about tomorrow's election, and as they speak, I study the interactions between the three. Georgia stands by her husband's side, her eyes on Mr. Johnson. Not once does she glance at Will, not even when he speaks.

I shake my head. Despite my efforts to resist, I've squandered time lamenting over Nella's rumors.

When Mr. Johnson says, "Excuse us. We must find our seats," Will shakes his head.

"Why don't you join us here?" He points toward the bench where my mother and Mary-Helen had been sitting.

"Those seats are empty?" Mr. Johnson asks.

"Yes"—Will glances at me—"there was a last-minute change of plans."

The Johnsons scoot past me, just as the theater darkens and the stage curtain separates, revealing a set decorated in purple and gold, a royal parlor of sorts. After the opening dialogue between a maid and a military officer, Charles S. Gilpin steps onto the stage.

Time and the performance freeze. There is perfect silence, as if everyone wants to immerse themselves in this moment that history will remember. Then the playhouse explodes in applause. Mr. Gilpin stands in his regal uniform: a light blue jacket over bright red pants, accentuated with gleaming gold buttons. Throughout the ovation, he never breaks character.

Once the applause abates and Mr. Gilpin begins to speak, I am drawn into this story of Brutus Jones, a colored man who had been imprisoned for murder but escaped. He fled the country to a Caribbean island where, for the past two years, through some persuasion but mainly manipulation, he installed himself as the emperor.

But now, unrest has seized the land, and once again, Brutus Jones is forced to flee.

The entire play is in Mr. Gilpin's hands. Although there are others on the stage, the play is basically a monologue, and I am spellbound by Mr. Gilpin's performance. Between his words, the beating drums that intensify in volume and rhythm with each scene, and the light that fades with each passing moment, I feel the emperor's advancing angst, then fear, and finally his descent into madness, which leads to his demise.

Eighty minutes later, the stage darkens again. I am completely drained and have been thoroughly entertained.

I stand with everyone else, giving this integrated cast the honor of an ovation. The applause continues for minutes. My eyes are riveted to the stage, where colored and white actors stand shoulder to shoulder taking their bows.

It is difficult for me to look away, which is why it takes a few minutes for me to notice that Will is the only person in the theater who remains in his seat.

CHAPTER 21

MONDAY, NOVEMBER 1, 1920

The wooden steps creak under our weight as we climb the stairs to the second-floor landing of the brownstone. Will opens the door, and when I follow, I squint, giving my eyes a moment to adjust to the curls of dense cigarette smoke spiraling throughout the duskily lit room.

"You can't keep a good man down," Mamie Smith's contralto vibrates throughout, *"no matter how hard you try . . ."*

I can scarcely see Mamie or the band through the thick crowd of men and women who've taken to the dance floor. White couples sway on the right side, while Negroes dance on the left.

Standing on my toes, I get a fleeting glance of the statuesque Mamie Smith, glammed up in a gold sequined gown with a plunging neckline that, in the dim light of the club, makes her sparkle like the North Star in a blackened sky. Her lips are the color of rubies, and as she sings the blues, her gloved hands glide through the air, punctuating each note.

I'm glad I decided to accompany Will and the others to Happy Rhone's, although, when the actors had taken their final bow, I'd gathered my coat, prepared to rush outside and hail a cab to Mary-Helen's.

It had been Will who suggested that my mother needed some space tonight and I should speak with her in the morning.

"Dr. Du Bois," the black-suited maître d' greets Will, then nods at me. "Welcome."

"There will be eight of us." Will glances over his shoulder at the Johnsons, the Imeses, and Walter White with his sister, Madeline, visiting New York.

I am certain we'll have to wait. But then, the gentleman says, "Follow me," and once again, I am reminded that I am with Dr. W. E. B. Du Bois.

We angle through the black-clothed tables, passing men sipping brown liquor from low ball glasses and women clutching silver cigarette holders held high in the air. The maître d' stops at a large round table with a **Reserved** sign, and we ease into the white-upholstered chairs.

He will always win in the end . . . so girl, take my advice . . .

Mamie's voice is an instrument, synthesizing with the clarinet, trumpet, and trombone played by the trio behind her. There isn't an empty seat in the club, although that's no surprise. Even without Mamie performing, Happy Rhone's is always hopping.

While Harlem is the hub of the city's nightlife, this is not how Will and I usually spend our evenings, preferring poetry readings at the library, literary salons at the homes of our friends, or performances at the Opera House or Harlem Symphony. However, as this is the perfect place to gather with friends after dinner or the theater, I've always enjoyed being here.

Mamie holds that final note in her famous vibrato, and the club erupts in applause. "Thank you," she says through the clapping and the whistles. "I'm going to take a little break. I'll return with another set."

The din rises, even as the lights stay low. Chatter and laughter mix with ice clinking inside glasses.

"So what are you gentlemen and ladies drinking tonight?"

Here, the waitresses take orders for drinks as if it isn't against the law. I've never heard of Happy Rhone's being raided; I suspect this establishment shares its profits with the police.

The woman smiles through the red rouge that stains her lips. Her heavy makeup, finger-waved hair, and the loose-fitting black sleeveless dress with dark stockings that hide her knee-length hem make her appear older than what I guess is her twenty years of age.

"I'll have a gin rickey," Georgia's husband says. Georgia orders a Bee's Knees.

The rest of us are teetotalers, at least in public, while the country is dry. Will and I order strawberry sodas, and everyone else orders juices.

As the waitress sashays away, Mr. Johnson says to Will, "I hope my wife and I having a drink doesn't offend you, Dr. Du Bois."

He shakes his head. "Not offended at all. Adults have the right to make adult decisions."

"I am aware of your position on temperance and Prohibition and how Negroes should never indulge in liquor."

"I am not a pietistic man, Mr. Johnson. So 'never' is not the word I would use. In fact, my support of Prohibition is not directed at the individual at all. Instead, I am against the capitalistic greed that is so prevalent in this nation. I believe the greed of the powerful will lead to the addiction of the weak."

"I appreciate that." Mr. Johnson nods. "I was a very young man when I attended a Frederick Douglass rally, and he shared similar sentiments."

"And yet . . . you were not moved by Mr. Douglass's words. He was the one who helped me understand how liquor has been used for purely evil purposes."

Mr. Johnson chortles. "Evil? Perhaps *that's* the word you shouldn't use."

"There is no better word. How else would you describe anything that was used by slave owners to maintain absolute control over the men they enslaved, knowing that an inebriated man would no longer need physical chains? His bondage came in a bottle. That brown liquid became a long-reaching whip, beating men into submission, removing the threat of that man ever having the desire to be free." Will peers at Mr.

Johnson. "While slave owners held back food, they allowed enslaved men to have unbridled access to liquor. That knowledge alone should make every colored man put down his glass and encourage others to do the same."

As if she'd received a stage cue, the young woman returns with glasses balanced on a serving tray. The gaiety carries on around us, but at our table, we are silent as the waitress sets down each glass. When she places the last one in front of Mr. Johnson, it lands like a boulder.

I am certain the others share my question: Will Mr. Johnson now push his drink aside?

Mr. Johnson slowly spins the glass in his hand. "I appreciate your wisdom, Dr. Du Bois." He lifts the glass high as if he wants to make a toast . . . or as if he's baiting Will.

Will hesitates, but after a moment, he holds up his strawberry soda, and I exhale. "To temperance," Mr. Johnson begins, without a smile. "May we all be temperate and learn to exercise self-control in whatever area of our lives it's needed."

Will clinks his glass against Mr. Johnson's. And I notice how Georgia has drawn back in her chair.

My eyes narrow. What is the meaning behind Mr. Johnson's toast?

I'm saved from the discomfort of the moment when Walter White says, "I never thought I'd see the day when a colored man would have the lead in a white theatrical production such as what we witnessed tonight."

"You say that as if you've lived a long life," I tease. "You're not even thirty years old."

"For a colored man, thirty is a long life," he says, then grins to lighten the weight of his words.

"The play was outstanding," Nella says, and her husband nods alongside her. "The acting was splendid, but there were so many thrilling aspects."

"Yes," I join in. "The use of darkness showing the emperor slipping into madness."

"It was the darkness and the drums for me," Georgia says.

I say, "Every seat was taken tonight, and the word will spread. I expect soon, they will need a larger venue."

The conversation carries on with Walter, Nella, Georgia, and me—the writers among us—sharing more observations about the play. The others occasionally offer a word as we deconstruct every facet of each performance.

Minutes pass before I notice Will hasn't spoken. Georgia has taken note as well, because she asks, "W. E. B., did you enjoy the play?"

Without hesitation, Will says, "No, I did not. And frankly, I'm astonished at how you've spent the last thirty minutes examining a white man's meaning behind words he wrote for a colored man."

The others shift in their seats. I am the only one not surprised by Will's words.

"Everyone is applauding that a Negro had the lead, but it was just another performance in blackface; however, tonight, no makeup was needed. This play has nothing to do with us."

I say, "I agree with you. However, I'm still grateful for the play, because it's progress."

"You call this progress?" He sounds as if my words surprise him, even though we've had this very debate.

"I do. While I agree that we must get to the place where we are the ones telling our stories, I applaud tonight as a beginning."

"Hear! Hear!" Walter raises his glass, and the others join in.

I continue, "Let every white theater company in the nation know that it's time to allow Negro men and women to play the parts of Negro men and women. Blackface be gone!"

We laugh, but the merriment stops when Will says, "Blackface is not gone! If the words are written by a white man, then it doesn't matter if it's a colored man on that stage or a white man in blackface. The words are still written by men who've never lived a moment without privilege, telling stories of men who cannot even purchase access to privilege."

"Again, I agree." I nod to make certain he knows the two of us are in unanimity. "However, you're speaking as if a white man writing our words is new. White folks have been delivering our messages in all

forms of art because their words, their poems, their stories, their performances, their paintings, their music . . . all of it is considered valuable
when our art is not. But we must recognize what is different—that a
colored man stood in a colored man's place on that stage."

"Your reaction is the very thing that gives me fear." Will taps his
finger on the table. "A white man put that colored man on the stage, and
now Negroes across the county will laud this as some great achievement. 'Look at that Negro up there, the world is a changin'!'"

"It's not enough change," I say. "But it would be disingenuous to not
call this progress. And I'm surprised you don't see it, because progress
is what you fight for every day."

"No," he says through clenched teeth. "I have never fought for enti-
tled men to become the experts of our thoughts. To write without
knowing our pains or without appreciating our few gains. Any art about
Negroes must reveal all of that. Something a white man can never do."

"Everything you say is true," I agree again. "But art doesn't always
have to be propaganda." I expect the writers to join me in this perspective, but no one speaks up. So, I continue alone, "Sometimes art can just
be art and we can enjoy its beauty."

Will's glare is so intense, I press back in my seat. "Perhaps art
doesn't have to be propaganda," he says so softly, we all strain to hear
him. "Although if it's not, it has no purpose.

"However, what art must always be is truthful. And a white man will
never, as long as this earth spins, be able to tell the truth of the Negro.
And if one cannot tell the truth, then he is unworthy of telling our stories." He pauses. "And anyone who doesn't understand that may be unworthy of telling our stories, too."

I am confounded. We've had debates before, but he's never rebuked
me, and never in such a public manner. How should I respond? I can get
up and walk out, but I've never been one for such histrionics. Yet sitting
back and saying nothing to his rudeness is not acceptable at all.

Before I can decide how to proceed, Georgia speaks up. "One thing
you must admit, W. E. B. At least this play didn't have a colored man
shucking and jiving."

"Or women just showing off their legs," Walter offers.

Around the table, everyone nods and says, "That's right," and even Nella's husband offers an "amen."

"You're right," Will says to Georgia. "Thank you for helping me see the little bit of light that can be gleaned from that performance."

With those words, the tension lifts. However, now I am the quiet one, still sitting in stunned silence. How many times have we had this discussion, with Will telling me that a white man can never be our messenger and me retorting that every journey begins with a single step? Each time, we've disagreed, but the final word was always followed by a squeeze of the hand or a kiss on the forehead.

Nella's lips turn downward when she glances at me. I force a smile. Then, Mamie Smith grants me a respite when she returns to the stage. The room darkens, and I no longer have to pretend.

That thing called love will make you sit and sigh . . . will make you sad . . .

I feel the sting of hot tears behind my eyes. Fury threatens to overtake me, so why do I want to cry?

After two more songs, Will stands and gives his regrets. "I have an early morning meeting."

We arrived together, so I stand with him. After I say my goodbyes, he assists me with my coat.

Outside, Will remains silent, and in his car, he cranks up the engine, then eases into the midnight-quiet street. As the car bounces down Seventh Avenue, I ponder what to say. By the time Will's car stops in front of my brownstone, I am ready. But before I can speak, he says, "You must never speak to me in that way again."

I am flabbergasted. He's spoken the words I'd determined to say to him. "What did I say to offend *you*?"

He stares straight ahead, as if the answer is hidden in the darkness of the night. "It was more than your words. Georgia asked a question, and you used that opportunity to belittle my opinion."

"*C'est ridicule! Je n'ai pas fait ça!*" I am so upset, I must remind myself to continue in English. "I didn't do anything of the sort. We've had these discussions before."

For the first time, he looks at me. "In private. But at that table, you criticized me, and I will not allow that."

"Everything you're saying, I can say about you. You belittled my opinion and you criticized me. Yet I had no objection, because I know you are passionate about this. My only objection is how you spoke to me at the end. How you chastised me. That is something I won't tolerate."

"On that, we can agree." After glaring at me for a long moment, he turns away. "I'm leaving now." He dismisses me.

I wait for him to do what he always does—open my door. He sits like a block of ice, and finally, I slide out. Then the motorcar splutters away, and I stand on the curb, alone, seething, and completely in the dark.

CHAPTER 22

TUESDAY, NOVEMBER 2, 1920

t is a bit before noon when I step into Frank's. Although almost all
the tables are occupied in this popular 125th Street restaurant, I spot
Maman at a booth against the rear wall. Her eyes are cast downward
as she peruses the bill of fare; she doesn't see me approach.

I take a deep breath before I say a shaky "Good morning" and slide
onto the vinyl seat across from her.

Her lips are pressed tightly until she looks up. Then her brown eyes
soften. "Jessie! Are you all right?"

With my fingertips, I massage my temples. No, I am not well. The
two people I care most about are incensed with me. Hence the dark
circles framing my reddened eyes, the evidence of a sleepless night. "I'm
fine. I was just up very late."

Maman's lips purse once again, and I realize my faux pas. She as-
sumes my late night involved a passionate evening with Will. There is
no need to tell her the truth. Not only am I not certain where Will and
I stand, but sharing what happened at the nightclub will only deepen
her disdain for him.

"I see," she says, her eyes returning to the bill of fare. After another moment, she sets the card down. "Thank you for meeting me this morning."

"Of course, Maman. I wanted to speak with you last night. However, by the time the play ended, the hour was so late, I was certain Mary-Helen would turn me away."

She nods. "Have you voted yet?"

I shake my head. "I was hoping we'd go to the precinct together, like we planned." Before she speaks another word, I say, "I'm sorry about last night. Will was never supposed to attend, and I'm horrified that I placed you in such a predicament."

"I was certainly uncomfortable."

"It will never happen again."

"You're correct. It won't." She glances down at her hands. "It may be time for me to return to Philadelphia."

"For the weekend," I state, because I cannot consider the alternative.

"No." Her eyes are steady on me. "It may be time for me to leave New York permanently."

"But I don't want you to leave."

A semblance of a smile curves her lips. "A year ago, you were telling me all the reasons why I shouldn't come to New York with you."

"I didn't want a chaperone. But that's not what you've been." I pause. "I've loved having my mother here."

Those words are true. Although I treasure my time with Will, my most cherished evenings are the ones when, after a long day, Maman and I sit at the kitchen table assessing my daily accomplishments.

"I have enjoyed my time with you, too." Melancholy is laced through her tone. "But I cannot stand by and watch you destroy not only your life, but another woman's as well."

Our voices are low, yet I still peer around. The restaurant is bustling. Lively conversations mix with clinking cutlery as waiters weave through the tables. No one takes notice of us.

When our waiter steps to the table, we place our orders quickly: Hungarian beef goulash for Maman, while I ask for only a boiled egg.

The moment we are alone, I tell my mother, "I'm not destroying my life or anyone's. I have this all in hand."

She shakes her head. "When you're with a married man, you haven't any control."

"I have control if I have no desire to muddle his marriage. Maman, I want Will to be with his wife. I want him to be happy with her, just as I'm happy with him. Marriage is not my goal."

"Then why, *ma fille*? What is the purpose of you and that man?"

I wish I could explain how much I enjoy being with Will—our conversations, our laughter, the way he challenges me, and, before last night, the way I challenged him. Will has taken such interest and care in what's important to me. He created an entire role at *The Crisis*, which will of course benefit him, the magazine, and the NAACP. But when Will tailored the position of literary editor for *The Crisis*, I was on his mind. Until last night, I've loved every moment that I've spent with him.

When I say nothing, Maman sighs. "Perhaps I should take some responsibility for what has happened. Perhaps when you were younger and spoke of how you were going to master the world, I should have guided you in a different direction. I should have encouraged you to do what was right and proper."

"And what is right and proper, Maman? To be married? To have children? To live a life just for a husband and give up all that I want to do like—"

Her eyes narrow when I stop. "Like . . . me? Are you insinuating that's what I've done?"

"No, I didn't mean—"

She holds up her hand. "I know exactly what you mean." She sighs. "Yes, I did give up a lot to be a wife and a mother. But I have no regrets. Not in the way you believe. Would I have loved the opportunity to attend a university, to spend a summer studying in France, and then live the life of a writer? Of course. However, would I give up what I have now for the dream I once had? No. I don't regret marrying and bearing six children, then becoming a stepmother to all of you. It's the life God granted me, and anything from Him is a gift."

Not only are her words earnest, but they astound me. "I always thought you had regrets. I thought that was why you pushed me so."

"No, *ma chérie*. How can I regret all the love I have?" She reaches for my hand. "The only regret I've had is not guiding you to a respectable life."

"My life is respectable."

"No matter what you've said to convince yourself, being involved with a married man is never respectable. Are you so blinded by your love for him that this, you cannot see?"

"I can see clearly. I understand that no more will come of Will and me."

"Then I'm the one who doesn't understand. Why are you settling for less when you can have more?"

My sigh is filled with exasperation. "There are many ways to love, and there are countless ways to be fulfilled. I am overjoyed with my life."

"Even if you are now, you must think of your future. Where will this lead? If you want no future with this man, then why are you here?"

"I'm here because of my career. I'm here because this is what I want to do."

"Your career is tied too much to this man." She's clearly given great thought to her next words. "You've worked so hard, *ma chérie*, but if you cannot end this with Dr. Du Bois, then perhaps you should leave."

I bounce back against the booth. "Leave? *The Crisis?*"

She nods. "You've done wonderful work there, you've made your mark. But now, it is prudent and wise for you to walk away."

"That's preposterous!" I say, then lower my voice. "I will not walk away from the work that I love."

"Sometimes, there are things more important than work. Sometimes, you must save your soul."

"I can't leave *The Crisis*."

"You are very good, but they can find another literary editor."

"But I'm more than the literary editor, Maman. In all practicality, I am the editor. And you ask about my future? Well, that's my future. My future is that I want to be the *editor* of *The Crisis!*"

The shock on Maman's face matches the astonishment that I feel. But then I repeat those words in my mind—I want to be the editor of *The Crisis*—and I allow that thought to settle. Yes! For a year, I've been fulfilling all the editor's responsibilities for both magazines. I've enjoyed every moment of that work, and now I want the recognition of that title as well.

I am grateful when the waiter sets our dishes in front of us, giving me a respite to consider my words. It was Papa who taught me that out of the abundance of one's heart, the mouth speaks. That was one of his favorite scriptures, and apparently, it is my truth.

Even once the waiter walks away, Maman's mouth is still agape; she and I push our plates aside. "You want to be the editor of *The Crisis*?"

This time, I speak with a bold strength. "Yes, I've been acting as the editor, and I want to be appointed to that position."

"How will this happen?" There is considerable confusion in her tone. "Is Dr. Du Bois leaving?"

"No," I say. While this idea has obviously been sitting in my heart, I don't have a plan. But I continue speaking with my mother as if I do. "Will isn't leaving *The Crisis*, but I've been demonstrating to him—and I will continue to do so—that he can. Not leave completely, of course. He can hold an emeritus position, I'm certain."

She shakes her head. "He founded that magazine. Why would he leave?"

"He wouldn't be walking away from it. But, Maman, my becoming the editor has to happen for Will to fulfill his purpose. Since founding *The Crisis*, in these last nine years, he's become the voice of ten million American Negroes. Many believe him to be the leader of colored people throughout the world. He's constantly traveling. He just returned from a two-week trip to eight cities, where he lectured about the election to-day. And he'll spend the month of January traveling throughout Europe and Africa.

"He's writing, he's lecturing, he represents the NAACP at all conferences. People listen to him; they want to follow him, and all of that draws him away from *The Crisis*. His attention is too divided."

"Does Dr. Du Bois agree with this?"

I shake my head. "I haven't mentioned this to him yet, but it's so clear to me. He loves *The Crisis* and will always want what's best for his magazine. And what would be best is me becoming the editor."

Her eyes fill with her skepticism.

"I'm not saying this will happen tomorrow. There is still so much for me to learn. But this is what I want. That is why I must stay in New York. No matter what happens between Will and me, I want to be the editor of *The Crisis*."

"Jessie?"

Maman and I look up.

"It *is* you. I thought I recognized your voice."

A lump rises, then swells in my throat. My mother glances at me curiously, then holds out her hand.

"Hello, I'm Mrs. Bella Fauset, Jessie's mother."

"Oh, so nice to meet you, Mrs. Fauset. I'm Mrs. Nina Du Bois, W. E. B. Du Bois's wife."

As Nina stands at the edge of our table, as regal as ever in a raspberry-red coat with a fur collar and matching fur band at the hem, I wish that, like Houdini, I had learned the art of disappearing. My mother, however, holds her bearing. "It is nice to meet you as well."

"Jessie told me you had come to New York with her. Are you enjoying the city?"

"Oh." My mother seems as dumbfounded by those words as I am by Nina's presence. I'd never told my mother that Nina and I had met, since until today, the Du Boises were never mentioned in any of our discussions.

"Yes, I like living in New York. At least for now."

"Oh, are you planning on leaving soon?"

Again, my mother glances at me. "No, I had considered returning to Philadelphia, but I'll be staying." Returning her gaze to Nina, she adds, "My daughter needs me."

"I understand. My husband and my daughter are my anchors, so I know how wonderful it is for Jessie to have you here with her. Well, I don't want to interrupt you any longer." To me, Nina says, "I hope we'll have the opportunity to lunch together again soon."

"Yes," I reply, squeaking out my first word.

Our eyes follow her as she and another woman navigate through the diner and walk out the door.

When we turn back to each other, I know our thoughts are the same. If Nina recognized my voice, what had she heard?

CHAPTER 23

FRIDAY, NOVEMBER 12, 1920

Are you ready?"

I glance at Will standing in the threshold of my office, fedora atop his head, his overcoat draped over his arm. His stance is as stiff as his tone. I respond in kind. "Yes."

He assists me with my coat, and then our footsteps echo through the empty office. At the elevator, the operator greets us with a "Hello," and we reply with only a nod.

Outside, the wind whips around us, and I tighten my coat. Even with the evening's chill, I am glad we are walking to the Civic Club rather than driving uptown. It is easier to brave the forty degrees and wind gusts than endure the frost of Will's silence inside the comfort of his car.

Eleven days have passed, and I am still as aghast as I'd been when Will spoke to me with such disdain.

The silence has continued, though not literally. We work together, attend meetings, and have spent hours planning for the upcoming Pan-African Congress, an international gathering of Africans from all over the world, a project so dear to Will's heart.

Professionally, nothing has changed. Personally, we have not shared a lunch or a dinner. And certainly not a bed.

I'm not certain whether Will's aloofness stems from what happened at Happy Rhone's, or if his wife has reported the conversation she overheard, *if* she'd heard anything.

While I have doubts about whether Will and I will personally weather this storm, professionally, my confidence has not wavered. Between the magazine and now, all the work I'm doing for the Pan-African Congress, I've become indispensable to Will, and my desire to become the editor has strengthened.

Finally, we round the corner of Twelfth Street and enter the club. "Dr. Du Bois!" a young man calls out.

"Harry, my boy." Will's tone is filled with joy and laughter when he greets the man who is many years from being a boy. Without an introduction, I already know the gentleman is Mr. Harry Pace, the reason for this gathering.

Harry covers my hand with his. "You must be Miss Fauset. After all of our correspondence, it is a pleasure to meet you." His skin is so pale, I wonder if I'd be able to readily identify him as Negro if he chose to pass. But his smile is so warm, I forget that thought and just take in the handsome man with his wavy hair parted down the middle and eyes that hold his smile.

"I share that sentiment, Mr. Pace."

"Please, call me Harry. Mr. Pace is my father."

I laugh. "Only if you call me Jessie."

With a smile, Will says to me, "All of these years later, Harry still remains at the top of my Atlanta University favorite students list." He speaks to me with the familiarity and warmth that he always has—before the last eleven days.

Harry gestures toward the staircase. "I've reserved the back parlor rather than us taking our meal in the dining room. For privacy."

He leads the way, and once again Will surprises me when he places his hand on the small of my back. Another familiar gesture that has been missing. Inside the small private room, which is just as elegant as the rest of this mansion with its gilded mirrors and wainscoting, a round table, draped in white linen with a gold candelabra atop it, has been set with service for seven.

"Ethlynde!" Will greets a petite woman, à la mode in a gold-beaded chemise that is scandalously short, barely touching her knees. Her rolled-down silk stockings complete her look and make me feel downright dowdy in my tweed suit.

Will introduces me to Ethlynde—Harry's wife—and then the greetings continue: John Nail, whom I've met before, is just as dapper (in his navy pinstripe suit and gleaming black patent leather shoes) as all the other times I've seen him. He is the real estate mogul who owns many properties in Harlem, including the brownstone where I live. I greet the pianist Fletcher Henderson, whom Will and I have seen perform many times. And William Grant Still, another young man who will be working with Harry.

Finally, Harry says, "Before we sit down to dinner, I'd like to begin with a toast." He motions toward seven crystal goblets atop a sideboard, and we each take one.

"First, thank you to the men who have counseled me." He glances at Will and Mr. Nail. Then, to Fletcher and William, he says, "Thank you to the men who accepted my offer to join me to make certain . . . Black Swan Records will be a success."

"Black Swan Records?" Ethlynde places her hand on her husband's shoulder. "Sweetheart, you didn't tell me you'd settled on a name."

"It was Dr. Du Bois's idea," Harry says. "We discussed it and I love it."

"I do, too," Mr. Nail says, and the others agree.

"Yes," I add. "It reminds me of the singer Elizabeth Taylor Greenfield."

"Of course you would know who I was thinking of when the name came to mind." Will's tone shares his pleasure that we are, once again, in synchrony. "Miss Greenfield, a woman rising from the humblest beginnings, and doing so while colored people were still in chains, became an internationally acclaimed star and, most importantly, a credit to her race."

Harry says, "All that Miss Greenfield represented is what I hope to accomplish with Black Swan Records. We will use this opportunity to showcase the best of who we are through the artists we choose and the music we record. I will build this company into an enterprise everyone here will be proud to call their own."

"Hear! Hear!" Will and Mr. Nail say together.

"Something you taught me, Dr. Du Bois," Harry continues, "is that art must be used as propaganda, or what's its purpose? I'm committed to ensuring that everything we record will change the way this country sees its Negro citizens."

Harry speaks as if his soul is one with W. E. B. Du Bois's, and he holds his goblet high. "To Black Swan Records."

"To Black Swan Records," we repeat.

Will adds, "The only genuine colored recording company." He pauses. "The others are only *passing* for colored."

Everyone laughs at the twist of that irony. After Mamie Smith's massive recording success with OkeH records, suddenly white recording companies are scrambling, each in search of their own Negro sensation.

While the laughing continues, I repeat Will's words: "'The others are only passing for colored'—that's the beginning of an excellent marketing campaign."

More grins, and then, as that idea settles among us, nods of agreement.

"Jessie . . . you're brilliant," Harry says.

Will laughs. "I could have told you that, my boy!"

We clink our glasses in a salute before we settle at the table. As the first course of parsnip and celery bisque is served, the conversation shifts from the politics of business to the business of politics.

"I, for one, am pleased that Harding won the election," Mr. Nail says.

"He won because so many Americans related to his call for a return to normalcy," Harry adds. "Let's hope he can deliver on that promise after Woodrow Wilson."

Will glances around the table. "I think everyone knows I withdrew from the Socialist Party to support Wilson, and it was with the vote of colored men who followed me that he won." There is a sigh in his tone when he continues, "But his betrayal . . . he says he isn't a racist, but he awakened every racist in this country. Supporting him was the greatest political mistake I've made."

Before these last eleven days, I would've taken Will's hand beneath the table. Tonight, I do not.

"You rallied quickly," Harry says, defending Will. "There hasn't been anyone more outspoken against his administration. He never would have won a third term because of the way you raised your voice."

In the silence, the jubilance of earlier is gone. Until Mr. Nail says, "I finally had the opportunity to see *The Emperor Jones*. It was first rate. Charles Gilpin is a star."

Everyone nods; I stiffen. Mr. Nail is only attempting to enliven the conversation. He has no understanding where his words will lead.

Mr. Nail adds, "Just eleven days in, and there's already talk of the play possibly moving to Broadway."

"I can understand why," Ethlynde says. "Harry and I saw it a few days ago, and it's fabulous."

While others around the table agree, I turn my attention to my soup. Then Fletcher asks the wrong question. "Have you had the opportunity to see it, Dr. Du Bois?"

In the silence that follows, I inhale. Although I will not chime in first, if I am asked my opinion, I will speak the truth. Setting my spoon down, I prepare myself for battle.

Finally, Will says, "While I am not a fan of the writer, I admire Mr. Gilpin and his performance."

I stare at Will while the others at the table agree.

He continues, "I've read the reviews, and it seems that I'm not the only one who admires Mr. Gilpin. But I am among the few who respect him."

My eyes widen with my astonishment. Where is his indignation?

Mr. Nail frowns. "The critics have been effusive with their praise."

"True, however, those who give critical acclaim to his acting don't respect him as a man. The *New York Times*, for instance, said he was powerful and imaginative—great praise for an actor. Then they ended the review by saying Mr. Gilpin is a negro."

I sense everyone's confusion, although I am clear. Will and I have had this discussion, too.

Fletcher says, "Dr. Du Bois . . . Mr. Gilpin is—"

Before Fletcher can continue, Will says, "Whenever Mr. Gilpin or anyone of our race is addressed in the newspapers as a Negro, the 'n' is never capitalized. This *New York Times* review is lauding Mr. Gilpin and, at the same time, disrespecting him. If Caucasian is capitalized, Negro must be as well."

"That's a very good point, Dr. Du Bois," Harry says.

Mr. Nail nods. "I'm sure you're going to do something about that."

There are chuckles around the table, although every eye remains on Will.

"I have a few ideas." He glances at me. "Jessie and I will spend some time considering this."

When the attention turns to me, I say, "We should begin with a letter-writing campaign from our readers to the newspapers. Perhaps they will respond to a public outcry."

There are nods around the table. I look directly at Will. "W. E. B. is correct. You cannot respect that man as an actor yet disrespect him as a Negro."

Harry says, "Please let us know what we can do to assist."

"You manage that recording company," Will tells Harry. "Jessie and I will steer this ship."

Will smiles at me. He probably thinks I am atoning for the words I'd spoken at Happy Rhone's. But I am merely speaking my truth tonight, the way I'd spoken it then.

After dinner, topped with pineapple upside-down cake, the men move to the corner of the room for a smoke to accompany their after-dinner conversation, while Ethlynde and I chitchat at the table.

It is around ten when everyone gathers to leave, and outside, we say quick goodbyes, as the wind is more biting than before. Will is still jovial as he walks close to me.

When we arrive at his car, Will takes my hands in his. "It's not very late, we should go somewhere and talk . . . about the planning for the Pan-African Congress, perhaps."

I know that by "somewhere," Will means the Hotel Olga, and by "talk," he means we'd share a bed.

The cutting wind circles us, yet now I feel warm, practically hot, the heat rising from my ire. "I'm going to hail a cab and go home."

His face stretches with his surprise. "You don't need to do that. I'll take you home."

After a moment's thought, I nod. But this time, when Will helps me up on the running board of his car and then it sputters into traffic, I am the one who keeps my eyes straight ahead and remains silent.

CHAPTER 24

TUESDAY, FEBRUARY 8, 1921

I glance at Will seated across from me in my office before I continue reading the letter aloud: "Dr. Du Bois, you are doing a disservice to Negro Americans with your commitment to this Pan-African Congress. Please turn your attention to the more important issues affecting us here in the United States."

Will bows his head and presses the tips of his fingers together. "I'm not concerned about our readers. I cannot expect average Negroes to envisage what educated white folks cannot see," he says, referring to the NAACP board, which has refused to assist Will financially with the second Pan-African Congress.

It has been twenty years since the first Pan-American Conference, and to Will, not only has too much time passed, but it is more imperative than ever that this congress happen. European colonization has led to egregious oppression in Africa, and Will wants the darker races of the world to band together to support our African brothers and sisters.

Finally, Will says, "Jess, few understand that this is my greater purpose. I'm not meant to be confined to the spaces within these walls. I must advocate for the rights of those who cannot fight for themselves."

He adds, "We will continue with our planning for the congress. Our readers and the NAACP will come to see the light."

"Very well." This is what I've been saying. Will's calling is beyond the publishing of *The Crisis*. "Where should we begin?"

Will gives me a list of tasks: contacting Mr. Blaise Diagne, the Senegalese politician, one of the organizers of the first conference; selecting locations throughout Europe; preparing agendas for the program.

By the time an hour has passed, Will reclines in his chair. "This is yet another goal I wouldn't achieve without you. Thank you." He glances at his wristwatch. "I have a quick meeting with Augustus and then an overflow of correspondence that I must get through this morning. You and I can finish this later. Over dinner. Or after."

Long after Will leaves my office, my mind is still on his words: *Or after.*

I always feel a bit of schoolgirlish glee in anticipation of when we'll be together. However, there are moments when thinking of Will makes me sigh.

Months have passed, and the memory of those eleven dreadful days in November linger. Whenever I remember the words he uttered that night, I have remnants of the rage I'd felt.

And then there are instances when I envisage him bursting into my office with a monstrous fury, shouting that he'd spoken to his wife. "You're fired!" I imagined him screaming. "From *The Crisis* and from my life."

However, there has never been any mention of Nina, and after the dinner for Black Swan Records, Will has tried to mend the breach between us. From gifting me with a sample bottle of a new perfume—Chanel No. 5—which is still a few months away from mass production, to, days later, surprising me with a lovely sable-collared opera coat, Will has asked for forgiveness in many ways.

But the best times in these last three months were the few days when Will arranged for us to sneak away to our room at the Hotel Olga, where we worked together for hours on my novel.

Will gave me the gift of time and feedback so that I could journey through the lives of my characters. It was during one of these after-noons when I began to shift my thoughts about my protagonist, singularly focused on her desire to be a singer and dancer. As the story progressed, she'd mounted small victories, traveling outside of New York to places like Princeton, New Jersey, and Hampton, Virginia, to perform at churches and holiday events.

However, one afternoon, as Will and I tarried in bed, I wondered how to give Joanna more. And it came to me in an instant—instead of my novel being the story of three childhood friends, what if two of the friends—Joanna and Peter—fell in love?

"What do you think of that?" I asked Will when I told him the idea. "Give Joanna a real love interest?"

"Yes, to raise the stakes. If Joanna falls in love, readers will wonder if she'll remain true to her convictions. Naturally, she will stay her course. She will toss away love for her greater gain."

"Hmm . . . it may make for a more interesting story. Yes, do it."

Just thinking of those discussions with Will makes me smile. While Will often speaks of how I've helped him achieve his dreams, he is cer-tainly assisting me with mine.

I shake my head to bring myself back to all the tasks I have before me. I cannot fancy the day away, and I turn my attention to the pile of submissions on my desk. I begin to scan through each.

After reading for almost thirty minutes, the first lines of one poem arrest my attention:

> I've known rivers:
> I've known rivers ancient as the world and older than the
> flow of human blood in human veins.

I sit up straight as I read the rest and travel with the poet through time, back to the beginning of civilization, and then forward through the centuries. In ten lines, I traverse the world. From the Euphrates to the Mississippi River.

Then I come to the last line:

My soul has grown deep like the rivers.

There is only one thing to do—I return to the beginning. This time I read aloud, and I'm filled with emotions: pride, sadness, then hope, and finally a profound peace and joy I cannot explain. Through this poem, I've lived Negro history.

Who is the author of such brilliance?

First, I notice the title: "The Negro Speaks of Rivers." Then, the name of the poet: Langston Hughes.

Langston Hughes?

We'd corresponded a few times after he received my letter: He thanked me for my interest and shared that after graduation, he moved to Mexico with his father. I urged him to use the time and the experience to write.

Right before Thanksgiving, I heard from Langston again—three submissions, if I recall correctly. And I published them all.

Pulling out the file with past editions of the *Brownies' Book*, I set aside last month's, then flip through the pages to Langston's first submission—three Mexican games.

Continuing, I find the second of Langston's submissions:

> The little house is sugar,
> Its roof with snow is piled.
> And from its tiny window,
> Peeps a maple-sugar child.

Like the first time, the imagery of "Winter Sweetness" transports me to the center of a field with the house before me. I feel the frigidness and taste the sugar.

Toward the back of the issue is the third of Langston's submissions, "Fairies."

My prayer has been to discover writers who can change this world with words.

Leaping up, I rush to Will's office. I knock, but enter before I'm invited inside. Will and Augustus are seated with a stack of the *Brownies' Book* piled before them. Their faces are drawn—they must be meeting about the financial state of the magazine. Once again, I've been excluded.

But how can I be troubled when I hold such glorious words in my hand?

"You must read this." I thrust the paper at Will. Then I cross my arms and tap my foot, willing him to read those ten lines quickly. I watch the movement of his eyes. Then he does what I did—he starts at the beginning. Again.

He glances up. "Who is this?" He passes the page to Augustus.

"Can you believe there is a colored man who has been given this gift to stir souls, yet no one knows his name? Everyone must come to know Mr. Langston Hughes."

"Langston Hughes," Will repeats. "This must be published."

"Oh, it will be. I've published him three times in the *Brownies' Book*. This will be his first submission for *The Crisis*."

Augustus nods his approval. "This is really good."

I step out of Will's office and exhale a breath of delight. This is why I came to New York. I am elated, and now I must meet this young man.

CHAPTER 25

MONDAY, MAY 23, 1921

As the sun begins its ascent over the horizon, I click off my desk lamp. I've been here for an hour, approving the proofs for the magazines to go to the printer.

After scanning the final page of the *Brownies' Book,* I turn to *The Crisis.* I pore over the pages line by line until I stop on page seventy-one. I'd placed Langston Hughes's poem at the bottom, following the article on Negroes in the Kentucky mountains.

I am brimming with anticipation for the world to read "The Negro Speaks of Rivers" and to meet Langston Hughes.

Langston is still in Mexico, but he is considering returning to the country in the fall to enroll at Columbia University. I'd asked him to inform me the moment his foot touched American soil.

The rapping on the door interrupts my reverie. "I thought I'd be the first one arriving this morning." Will sounds weary.

"I wanted to approve the proofs before our meeting."

He nods. "I just need a few minutes." However, instead of going to his office, he slumps in the chair beside my desk.

I wonder what has Will so fatigued, but I never intrude on his life outside of our time together. He shares what he wants, always about Yolande, never about Nina.

He says, "Yolande will be coming home in a few weeks."

"Is she all right?"

When he nods, I sigh with relief. A few months prior, Yolande had been confined to an extended hospital stay, while at Fisk, for an abscessed tooth . . . this time. Will's daughter is so often beset with illnesses. She'd been diagnosed with inadequate levels of lime, which leads to excruciating joint pain and muscle spasms, sometimes so severe, she's hospitalized for weeks.

"This summer will be better for her," he proclaims as if he can make it so. He stands. "Come to my office when you're ready."

I review the last pages of *The Crisis*, and just as I set aside the proofs, the outer office door opens once more. When Miss Ovington stomps by, I hold my breath, and my heart follows suit. She strides straight toward Will's office, no doubt harboring some new grievance about me. As time has passed, her quibbles have become more frequent and much sharper.

As soon as I hear Miss Ovington say, "Dr. Du Bois, may I have a word with you?" I grab my notepad and folder I prepared for the meeting before I rush into Will's office.

"Oh, Miss Fauset, I didn't realize you were here. It's just as well." She turns her attention to Will. "Dr. Du Bois, I hope next month's issue of *The Crisis* hasn't yet gone to print."

"And why is that, Miss Ovington?" he asks with a weary patience.

"I discovered several typographical errors."

"I'm sure there are. We work diligently; however, like every publication, we experience human error. There are times when mistakes get past us."

"Then explain to me the purpose of having a literary editor." She turns her disdain toward me. "There were four mistakes, Miss Fauset." She flips open the magazine she holds. "That is unacceptable."

"Four?" I am astounded. "Miss Ovington, there are fifty-two pages in that issue, and you're fussing over four errors?"

There is an air of superiority in her tone when she says, "As the official publication of the NAACP, *The Crisis* has to reflect the excellence of this organization."

"We'll get on it," Will cuts in, as if he understands that I'm prepared to go to war with Miss Ovington over those four errors.

"Thank you, Dr. Du Bois. I'm glad *you* wish to maintain the highest standards."

She tromps away, and I want to slam the door behind her. "Good grief. What does she think I am? A machine that can automatically correct spelling or typographical errors?"

Will chuckles. "Ignore Miss Ovington."

I fold my arms. That is an impossible request. Miss Ovington has but one objective—to see me terminated from *The Crisis*.

Will asks if I'm ready, and I nod, even though I'm still fired up with fury. But I settle my thoughts and hand several letters to Will. "All of the venues I recommended for the Pan-African Congress have been approved. The Methodist Central Hall in London, the Palais Mondial in Brussels, and one of my favorite places in Paris: the Salles des Ingénieurs."

"Excellent." He scans the letters of commitment.

"The dates and now the venues have been finalized and—"

"All that's left are the agenda and speakers," Will finishes for me.

For the next hours, Will and I deliberate on how each session will proceed. Pocahontas brings us sandwiches as we work through lunch. It is almost three when Will and I sit back, satisfied with the pages of notes I've taken.

"Every element of the congress is beginning to align," he says, sounding well pleased, but his brows have dipped into a frown. I remain silent as he sorts through his thoughts.

"One challenge remains." His eyes are still lowered. "I'm concerned about—"

"The expenses." This time, I finish for him. Without support from the NAACP, raising funds for this congress has been an arduous task.

"The money is coming slowly. We're operating from a deficit, particularly concerning our travel expenses."

"Don't be concerned about my expenses," I say.

He shakes his head. "I want you in Europe with me. You've done most of the planning; your presence is vital for the congress's success. And . . ."

He stops as if *and* is a complete sentence. To me, it is.

Will and I have never experienced the luxury of spending a week's worth of nights together. And while the congress will be demanding, there will be other hours and many nights that I am eagerly anticipating.

"I will be there."

He leans forward and studies me. "Do you own a bank you haven't told me about?"

I laugh. "Nothing like that." I stop, not certain how much I should share. I have an idea I'm considering, but I haven't pursued it. "I will find a way to raise the money for my expenses. I'll find a sponsor, of sorts."

His eyes narrow as if he's contemplating questioning me more.

"I will be there, Will. We'll be in Europe. Together."

CHAPTER 26

THURSDAY, JUNE 2, 1921

This isn't my first visit to this Hudson Street building. I'd been at *The Crisis* just a few weeks when Augustus brought me here for a tour of the printing facility where *The Crisis*, the *Amsterdam News*, and the *New York Age* are printed.

However, the press manager, Mr. Brown, had not received me well. Throughout the entire thirty minutes, he'd addressed only Augustus, as if I were invisible. On subsequent trips, I'd only met with Mr. Brown's assistant.

As I step into the large freight elevator, I think today will be different for Mr. Brown and me.

Even before the elevator begins its ascent, I hear the rhythmic churning of the presses, and a moment later, the pungent scent of the ink assails my nostrils. By the time the elevator jerks to a wobbly stop and the gate is yanked open, the overwhelming odor leaves me woozy.

I step into a swarm of activity. The cavernous room, at least five times the size of *The Crisis*'s bullpen, holds a half dozen printing presses. The cylinders whir as four or five men, some hoisted up on high platforms, surround each machine. Everyone, it seems, has a post.

The machinery's din is so deafening, my footsteps fail to echo on the concrete floor as I move toward the offices. I approach the first open door, check the nameplate, and then rap lightly. "Mr. Brown."

It is ironic that this gentleman's name is Brown when something closer to Crimson would be more fitting. His face is flushed and ruddy as if he has just scaled the side of this building—twice.

He peers at me through his squinty eyes. "Are you with the cleaning crew?"

"Pardon me?" I ask, startled.

I'm wearing a suit! I wonder if that disparaging comment is meant as an affront to me as a woman or a Negro. But I answer my own thoughts. My race enters the room before I do.

Before he can offend me further, I say, "I'm Jessie Redmon Fauset, the literary editor for *The Crisis*. We've met before."

His bushy eyebrows furrow. "I have an appointment with Augustus."

"Mr. Dill sends his apologies," I lie. "However, I can speak to you about this since I manage the magazine."

He smirks. "What do you want to speak to me about, doll?"

Two minutes, two affronts. I don't wince. "We're looking to lower some of our expenses with the *Brownies' Book*, and I have a few suggestions."

"You have suggestions?" His laughter is almost loud enough to drown out the machines. "What do *you* know about printing?"

I smile. "Oh, Mr. Brown, there is little I know." When I shrug, he chuckles. "I only know the first printing press was invented by Johannes Gutenberg, although that was in Germany. The first American presses didn't arrive here until the 1600s, primarily because of the large demand for Bibles—you see, my father was a preacher." I continue, without a single breath, telling what I know about how the Gutenberg presses gave way to the Stanhope presses, the first made of iron, and then the Columbian presses that incorporated the rotating cylinders. I tell him about the steam-powered presses that printed over one thousand sheets every hour.

His eyes widen with each word, and after minutes, I finally say,

"That's all. However, I know much more about ink and paper. Shall I . . ."

He holds up his hands. "No, that's fine." He sits up straighter. "So how can I help you?" His gruff tone remains; however, he's dropped the *doll.*

"As I said, I've been studying our expenses. We can cut costs in the choice of paper we're using."

He scoffs. "I have *The Crisis* and the *Brownies' Book* using the best!"

"That is true. We're currently printing on uncoated paper."

"Like I said, the best."

"And the most expensive."

He growls. "How far did you get in school?"

"Pardon me?" This time, I am more stunned than offended.

"I'm attempting to make this simple for you," he says. "The best costs money."

There are a dozen ways for me to respond, but two reasons why I cannot voice my true thoughts—I am colored and I am a woman. "I understand the best costs money, Mr. Brown." I'm astounded I've kept my smile. "However, the best doesn't necessarily always mean a higher cost. Are you aware the less expensive coated paper is actually better for printing magazines?"

His Adam's apple crawls up and then down his throat.

I continue, "The coated paper allows for much better image quality. And better durability, which is important for the *Brownies' Book*, as I'm sure you know."

The blood drains from his face so quickly, now his last name could have been White. However, he collects himself. "I don't need to talk to you about these kinds of decisions. I'll speak to Augustus."

"You can certainly do that," I say as I stand. "And while you're speaking to him, I'll speak to Dr. Du Bois and others at the NAACP. I'll let everyone know that you were aware of the cost savings and benefits of the coated paper, yet you chose to charge us for the more expensive paper because, to paraphrase, 'you have to pay for the best'—regardless of what was actually best for our magazine." As I move toward the door, I add, "After my meeting with Dr. Du Bois, there won't be any reason for you to speak with Mr. Dill."

Before I cross the threshold, Mr. Brown calls, "Miss Fauset." He clears his throat. "There's no need to get all of those other folks involved."

I slide back into the chair. "Well, Mr. Brown," I say. "Where should we begin? I have all the numbers right here."

walk out of Mr. Brown's office with an approximate twenty-five percent cut in our printing costs. I'm not certain how much this will help the *Brownies' Book* numbers; Will still has not included me in those meetings. After this, however, I'm certain he will. The sooner he sees me as capable of managing the financials, the sooner he will see me as the editor. The letter he'll receive from Mr. Brown, with the revised printing quotes *and* a two-hundred-dollar rebate, will certainly help with that.

It is the rebate I'm most eager to share with Will. However, when I step inside the NAACP offices, all thoughts of Mr. Brown disappear. The bullpen is swarming with twice the number of people as usual. Some faces I recognize as NAACP members, but most I do not.

I search for Pocahontas, but none of the stenographers are at their appointed desks. Everyone's attention is on one place—the meeting room. At the threshold, seven or eight people cram the doorjamb. I peer over the shoulders of men I do not know.

"This happened over the last two days." James Weldon Johnson is in the front of the overflowing room of colored and white men, Miss Ovington, and the stenographers. "We don't have a branch in Tulsa, only in Oklahoma City. It will be difficult to gather specific information quickly."

Miss Ovington says, "The *New York Times* is reporting eighty-five Negroes and whites were killed and—"

"I don't believe that," Walter White jumps in. His voice quivers with rage as he leaps from his chair and joins James at the front. "For two days, white mobs went into that Negro quarter and burned down every building they could find and attacked every Negro they could see. So there are *more* than eighty-five Negroes dead. It'll be hundreds, perhaps even thousands dead at the end."

Thousands? I press my fingertips over my lips, praying my gasp will remain inside. I've only heard a minute of this, and yet I know the story. There was vigilante violence against Negroes. In Tulsa, Oklahoma. What is the supposed offense *this* time?

"How did this begin?" Will asks, as if he heard the question in my mind.

James shakes his head. "Like I said, reports are still coming in. Some say a colored man stepped on a white woman's shoe."

"But most," Walter interjects again, "say that colored man assaulted that woman. Now, tell me, how did he do that in the middle of the day in an office building in downtown Tulsa?" Walter's ire is raging. "It's a lie. Just like every other accusation they've ever made. Lynching has become a sport, with advertising in newspapers, inviting folks to bring their children to watch. They'll make up any lie to play this murderous game."

"So what is the plan?" Will's voice is absent of the anger that roils within Walter. Will's rage is in his countenance: his rigid jaw, his crossed arms, his wide stance. He is prepared for this battle.

Walter says, "The plan is I'm going down there."

"It's too volatile." Moorfield Storey shakes his head. "According to the *New York Times*, this riot is not like the others. This riot was devastating to Negroes."

Will's eyes blaze with incredulity when he faces the president of the NAACP. "*This* riot was devastating? Every riot, every lynching, every time a white man takes the life of a colored man just because he can, is devastating, is disastrous, is destructive. One is not better than another. Walter *should* go there the same way he has for all the others."

"I'm just suggesting that this time, it may be too dangerous," Mr. Storey insists. "Whether this one is like all the others or not, an entire section of the city where Negroes lived is no more than rubble. I don't want this organization to put one of our own in that peril."

Arthur Spingarn, the chairman of the Legal Committee (and Joel Spingarn's brother), speaks up. "I agree. You aren't an investigator any-more, Walter," he says, referring to Walter's recent promotion to assistant secretary, which came at the same time that the NAACP board moved James into the role of executive secretary. "That's no longer your role."

"Let me tell you my role . . . I am a colored man! And I'm going to use my pale skin, blue eyes, and blond hair to trick those racists, and hopefully for once, we'll bring the leaders of the mob to justice!"

The applause that erupts startles me, and as James tells everyone that a plan must be developed before Walter hops onto the train to Oklahoma, I back away.

Inside my office, I close the door, although I cannot completely shut out the raised voices and continuing applause.

It is difficult to erase the vivid picture of the mob Walter painted. In my mind, I see those men, their faces contorted with seething enmity circling the Negro section of Tulsa. It is frightening enough to envisage what happened; it is utterly terrifying when I think about Walter racing into that inferno.

For three years, Walter has investigated lynchings by going into cities, pretending to be a white supremacist to glean information that would bring the murderers to justice. It has been arduous and danger-ous, and he'd come close to discovery more than once. But God never blinked! Walter was always saved.

I snatch the *New York Times* I'd bought this morning from my satchel. I hadn't taken a moment to read it on my way to the printer, wanting to study the notes I'd prepared for that meeting.

But there it is—the headline: *85 Whites and Negroes Die in Tulsa Riots* . . .

As I read the article, I'm filled with overpowering dread for the very existence of every colored man, woman, and child in this country. When I read, *Fires continued to rage all morning in the negro section*, the lump in my throat threatens to strangle me.

I toss the newspaper aside. This is not a time for emotions. This is a time for all of us to fight.

But what can I do? I cannot infiltrate racist mobs like Walter, nor can I rouse an audience like Will.

Change this world with words.

I reach for the current issue of *The Crisis* and hasten through the pages until I arrive at page 71:

> I've known rivers:
> I've known rivers ancient as the world and older than the
> 　　flow of human blood in human veins.
> My soul has grown deep like the rivers.
> I bathed in the Euphrates when dawns were young.
> I built my hut near the Congo and it lulled me to sleep.
> I looked upon the Nile and raised the pyramids above it.
> I heard the singing of the Mississippi when Abe Lincoln
> 　　went down to New Orleans, and I've seen its muddy
> 　　bosom turn all golden in the sunset.
> I've known rivers:
> Ancient, dusky rivers.
> My soul has grown deep like the rivers.

There is not a better moment for America to meet Langston Hughes.

As Tulsa burns, *The Crisis* magazine is right now being delivered to one hundred thousand homes, where those who need these words will read them.

As Tulsa burns, Langston reminds us that whatever we've endured, we are an indomitable race, with a legacy of perseverance, resilience, and fortitude.

As Tulsa burns, this poet declares that as a race, we will not die. Even in the face of injustice, generations of Negroes will continue to rise!

Neither Langston nor I had any notion of this timing. But as Will and James and Walter and the others are needed in this moment, so is Langston Hughes.

And so am I.

My role in this fight is right here at *The Crisis.*

I reach for my pen.

CHAPTER 27

SATURDAY, AUGUST 27, 1921

My English breakfast tea is slightly sweet, very robust. Perfect. During the six days' transatlantic journey, I have adjusted to the time change. I'm totally prepared, albeit a bit anxious. What will the first day of the Pan-African Congress bring?

It is just after seven as I settle back in the velvet cushions of the chair. Through my hotel window, my gaze settles on one of London's favorite sights—the University of Westminster stretches across the avenue, standing almost as grand as this hotel.

Twelve hours ago, I stepped into the opulence of the Langham, and bellhops in emerald-green double-breasted jackets, matching pillbox hats, and white gloves hastened to assist me.

I have traveled to Europe but have not visited Great Britain. Yet London, even this hotel, feels familiar because of Arthur Conan Doyle's novels. Maman and I read his books together when I was in high school, and my love of Mr. Doyle is something I recently discovered I also share with my former student Sadie. Thinking of her makes me move to the window. I have Sadie to thank for attending this congress. Sadie and the Delta Sigma Theta Sorority.

Sadie and her sorority had been on my mind when I told Will I'd find a sponsor. That afternoon, I sent Sadie a letter, and she at once responded, informing me that she and Delta Sigma Theta were interested in learning more.

I hopped on a train to Philadelphia wanting to sit vis-à-vis with my former student to discuss more than just the congress.

After welcoming me, then spending a few somber moments speaking about the news in Tulsa, Sadie led me to her kitchen table for lunch.

When I told her that I was so proud of her, she laughed. "You've been saying that since I was sixteen years old."

"Can you imagine having so many accomplishments that I've been able to say that for all these years? Your PhD." I pressed my hand against my chest. "You earned your PhD in economics, just like you said you would when you were in high school."

"It's been exciting. The only thing . . ."

Reaching across the table, I covered her hand with mine. "What's wrong?"

"Being colored outweighs my PhD." There was such a sad sigh in her tone. "I haven't been able to find a professorship here in Philadelphia."

I was taken aback. "But you have a PhD. Is there another colored woman in this country with a PhD in economics?"

"No, but that is of no consequence."

I'd traveled here expecting to celebrate, but now I felt only distress. "Sadie, I am so sorry."

"You have no reason to apologize. Although"—she tilted her head—"as I recall, you experienced the same when you graduated from Cornell."

I nodded. My hope had been that with my degree, along with my Phi Beta Kappa key, I'd gain entry into a publishing company. I knew the daunting odds and had been willing to accept a junior post. Yet despite my education and achievements, I was unable to secure even a modest position as a stenographer. I'd had to redirect my attention to teaching, although quickly I discovered those opportunities were just as grim.

"That was a difficult time," I admitted. "Equality should be our right, but it seems impossible for us to even earn it. Instead of squandering too much time lamenting, though, I left Philadelphia. Once I made that decision, the world opened for me."

Her face brightened. "It really did," she said. "Please tell me more about the Pan-African Congress and how Delta Sigma Theta Sorority can help."

It hadn't taken too much time or too many words before Sadie was convinced. She was certain Delta Sigma Theta would not only want to sponsor my trip but participate and support me in any way.

The knock on my hotel door pulls me from that memory. I tighten my peignoir before I open the door slightly.

The young woman who'd brought my tea to the room says, "Miss Fauset, you have a telegram."

"Thank you." I close the door, then study the envelope before I scan the telegram quickly:

JESSIE WILL HASN'T RESPONDED TO MY TELEGRAMS STOP I
BELIEVE HE'S WITH YOU STOP PLEASE TELL HIM TO CONTACT
ME STOP NINA DU BOIS

I drop onto the bed. A telegram from Nina. Twenty or so words that leave me with so many questions: She must know that Will is staying at the Savoy, yet she sent this telegram here? To my hotel? That is enough to make my heart stop, but there are greater questions. Why is she so desperate to contact Will? Is Yolande sick? Is Nina?

I toss the telegram onto the desk. I have to get to Will.

My plan had been to arrive here at Central Hall an hour before the start of the ten o'clock meeting. I'd wanted to bask in the shadows of Westminster Abbey, which stands right across the street and has hosted British monarchs' weddings and funerals for almost a thousand years. However, after receiving Nina's telegram, I'd spent the next hours attempting to contact Will. The Savoy's attendants had been unable to locate him, and I realized he was likely in a last-minute breakfast meeting outside of the hotel.

My thoughts are heavy, but still, I gasp when I step inside Central Hall's vast entry. A cascade of morning light floods through the tall windows, but it is the ceiling dome with its gold etchings that captivates me.

Again, I wish I could tarry, but I follow the directions the events manager sent to me and make my way through the long hallways.

"Miss Fauset?"

A stout gentleman, with wispy blond hair and dressed in a light wool three-piece suit, calls out to me.

"You must be Mr. Addington."

"It is a pleasure to make your acquaintance." He speaks with a thick accent—clear and very British—which I adore. He steps aside, and I enter the room before him. We circle the space, which is just as exquisite, with elegant wainscoting and chandeliers, as the other parts of this hall. He asks if the tables and chairs, set up for one hundred and fifty, are arranged to my satisfaction.

When I tell him all is well, Mr. Addington goes on his way just as I hear the echo of heavy footsteps. Seconds later, Will enters, along with another gentleman, and while I hold back my smile, he doesn't.

"It's good to see you, Miss Fauset," Will says.

Will arrived in London five days before to meet with the congress's leaders. The planning and then the journey to Europe have kept us apart for almost two weeks.

"Dr. Du Bois," I say, then turn my attention to the gentleman with him. "You must be Dr. Alcindor," I say to the dark and dashing physician, a Trinidadian who has made London his home.

"Miss Fauset, I hope your travel to our country was satisfactory."

"It certainly was. Thank you for agreeing to assist Dr. Du Bois in today's session."

He nods at Will. "As I was telling Dr. Du Bois, I've been looking forward to this gathering since our first Conference in 1900. We are ready for a time such as this. With the escalation of colonization and imperialism, we must unite the colored people of the world."

I ask Will if I can have a private word, then slip him the telegram. I am desperate to know his thoughts; however, while he steps out of the room, I hasten to the door as the delegates and attendees begin to arrive. I welcome men from the United States, like the Reverend William Henry Jernagin, from Washington, DC, and then delegates from the Gold Coast, Sierra Leone, Liberia, and Martinique. Mrs. Davis, from South Africa, is the first woman I greet, and I compliment the exquisite red and purple shweshwe dress with matching head wrap she wears.

Not all of the attendees are Negroes or Africans.

"I bring you greetings from East Africa," a white man with a British accent says, then introduces himself as Dr. Norman Leys, the British Africanist who is a strong proponent in the fight against imperialism.

As the last attendees file in, Will returns. But before I can rush to him, he's surrounded by admirers, each eager to have the opportunity to shake the hand of the most famous Pan-Africanist. Even when Reverend Jernigan asks everyone to take their seats, I'm not able to get a moment with Will before he joins the reverend in front.

As the meeting commences, I study Will's face, searching for a trace of a clue about Nina's message. But his focus is fixed on the subject at hand. Dr. Jernigan introduces Will, and the audience rises to give him a standing ovation.

How am I to keep my attention on the congress when questions about Nina's telegram burn in my mind?

My attention remains divided as Will begins speaking about the purpose of the congress and the unity that must be gained if we are to help our African brothers and sisters. We designed this first day as a get-acquainted session, knowing that in the beginning, the men and women would be wary. While we share skin tones, we are strangers, separated by land and sea, traditions and customs, languages and convictions.

However, Will deftly moves through the audience, speaking personally to participants, asking questions, joshing with a few. It doesn't take an hour before the delegates and attendees are speaking freely. Thoughts of Nina and the telegram are swept away as men and women from Africa share their native experiences.

The West Africans tell us how devastating colonialism has been in their countries. African citizens have no representation in government, and all political power has been stripped away from them. The West Africans are forced, through segregation, to live in substandard housing, with few educational resources, and are allowed to have only the most menial jobs with no opportunity for advancement.

East Africans are in a similar crisis—again without vestige of political power. However, their trials are even more debilitating. These brothers and sisters suffer from the government despoiling their land, completely stripping away their wealth. There is no means of retaliation, no opportunity for people to reclaim their property from European colonizers who entered their countries with a singular purpose—to pillage and plunder.

The stories are horrific and heartrending—and not dissimilar to the Negro experience in America.

As the hours pass, it becomes apparent that we live kindred lives, weeping over similar tragedies and celebrating our limited triumphs.

By the end of the first day, we are bound beyond our complexions. We are united by blood . . . we are all children of Africa.

After Will gives the closing remarks, the room explodes with applause and the attendees rush to the front; everyone wants to congratulate Dr. W. E. B. Du Bois.

Through the crowd, Will searches for me and then gives me a smile.

Our first day is not only complete, but a success.

CHAPTER 28

FRIDAY, SEPTEMBER 2, 1921

Each dawn has offered me the gift of a first experience. The first time I visited Great Britain, the first time I had the opportunity to commune with brethren from a dozen different countries. And the first time Will and I were together in a foreign land.

In London, Will and I returned to my room at the Langham. My hotel had been chosen by design, fifteen minutes away from the other attendees.

Being alone afforded me the first opportunity to question Will about Nina's telegram. He told me he'd responded, but he wasn't troubled.

"And you needn't worry," he said. "Yolande just returned to school. There's probably something pressing she believes she needs. Nina will respond with any concerns."

"So you're not anxious at all?"

He shook his head. "I know Nina. There was nothing urgent in her message. But I, on the other hand, am experiencing a pressing need." When I frowned, he said, "You. I need you. All I want to think about now is making love to you in French."

Thoughts of the telegram and Nina were gone! "You mean in *France*, but we are in London."

"I mean"—he pulled me into his arms—"I want to make love to you *in French*. When *you* speak French, it's more than a language. French is music and art . . . and love. And you, *chérie*, are the embodiment of it all."

His words were so lovely that for the rest of that night (and the next), I'd spoken to Will (and had done much more) in French.

Then, yesterday afternoon, we took flight. Again, a first . . . my first time in an aeroplane. The two-hundred-mile journey that would have taken as many as ten hours by rail and ferry had taken only three by air. I was astonished I had little fear climbing into a machine that would lift us thousands of feet above land. Will held my hand, and I smartly averted my eyes from the window as we soared into the clouds.

We landed in Brussels yesterday evening—another first. Again, we were in separate hotels, but this time, we slept apart as Will's attention turned to this congress.

Brussels would be different from London. Mr. Blaise Diagne, the Senegalese politician who had been a leader at the first conference, was now a French official. While Mr. Diagne had been a great supporter of African nationalism twenty years ago, his allegiances and alliances had shifted. Now Mr. Diagne believed Africans should be more *amenable* to colonialism.

It was a disturbing change that Will noted too late. We had already left much of the planning in Mr. Diagne's hands, and evidence that his objectives differed from ours was notable just minutes after we stepped into the Palais Mondial.

"Bonjour, Dr. Du Bois and Miss Fauset. Welcome to Brussels," Mr. Diagne greets us.

He looks exactly as I envisaged, wearing the features of his native Senegal: dark eyes, a broad nose, thin lips that seem on the verge of breaking into a smile.

After greetings, Mr. Diagne explains the agenda. "Rather than complaining about the problems, I want this congress to focus on progress. The emphasis will be on the advances that Belgium has made in the Congo. Several government officials will be joining us." Will and I exchange quick glances. "Dr. Du Bois, you, of course, will do the welcome.

However, I will lead it from there." He turns to me. "Miss Fauset, are you prepared to speak about the progress that's been made in America?"

"Yes," I say. "Thank you for inviting me to speak. My address will be on the advances of Negro women in our country."

"Very well." He excuses himself to greet arriving delegates.

Will and I stand to the side as the room fills. We notice the first difference from London—here the attendees are primarily white, rather than the Africans who are most affected by colonialism. And here, no one rushes to greet or meet Will.

There are more than one hundred people in the room when Mr. Diagne introduces Will. After welcoming the attendees, Will speaks of the success of our London meeting, and then he challenges this congress.

"My hope today is that as we speak in lofty terms of the progress of colonialism, we are most mindful of the true plight of our African brethren who are suffering under the imperialistic governance of European countries. Thank you very much."

I applaud; I am the only one.

Following Will, there is a litany of speakers, unlike in London, where there was open discussion and a free exchange of ideas. Here, there are speeches only, and the message—whether from a young man who'd been born in the Congo, or a Belgian general donning the splendor of his uniform displaying a rainbow of ribbons and polished medals—is the same: colonialism has been a benefit and a blessing to Africans.

There is no mention of the truth—that violence and degradation are the pervasive outcomes of what these European countries have done to the nations of Africa.

Then Madame Saroléa, the first woman and another Belgian dignitary, speaks of the efforts to support Congolese women. I am to follow Madame Saroléa, and because I am certain she will repeat the same prepared message, I turn to my notes.

As the attendees applaud Madame Saroléa, I stand, giving myself time to smooth my off-white linen suit. Mr. Diagne introduces me, and I step to the lectern to polite and disinterested applause.

Looking out into the grand room, I begin: "I bring you greetings from the United States, from New York and the neighborhood of Harlem, which is where I live. I bring you greetings from the ten million American Negroes, half of which are women. It is this latter group of which I will speak today.

"There is much for me to share on our plight as Negro women in America. Starting from our arrival on American soil. For the enslavers, colored women's wombs held a pecuniary value. Without Negro women and our bodies and our babies, America would not be what it is today.

"I share this with you because any discussion of Negro women in America must begin with that fact—the *labor force* that built the country was born from our wombs. However, this is not where I want our attention to be. I, too, wish to speak of progress, and how today, American Negro women are using our power to be a momentous force in this struggle for complete emancipation.

"We have never been silent in this fight. From raising money for the Union during the Civil War, to assisting the colored troops as they traveled and battled, we have served as aides, as cooks, and as nurses. Negro women even worked as spies inside the Confederacy.

"Finally, there was victory. In December of 1865, the Thirteenth Amendment to our Constitution was ratified. Equality was a right granted to all.

"Except . . . that was not the case. While Negroes in America have some freedoms our brethren around the world are still fighting for, we are in a perpetual war against codified racism, and once again, Negro women are leaders in this fight."

Glancing into the audience, I'm pleased that every eye remains trained on me. I continue, showcasing Negro women's participation in the fight for freedom, including forming an alliance with white women in the battle for the right to vote.

Then I move to the crux of my speech. "Negro women are keenly cognizant that the most crucial step in this fight toward equality is education.

"From freedmen's schools to the more than forty colored colleges that have been established, Negro women have made great strides in education, earning college degrees as well as master's. With these degrees, we are now employed in every field, from social work and nursing to education and business.

"I would be here speaking every hour for the next two days to acknowledge all the Negro women who have achieved these goals. However, I want to highlight three who have attained the highest academic achievement in our country—these Negro women have earned the doctor of philosophy."

I pause to gather the photographs from my folder, and the audience stirs. Men and women turn to each other with questions in their eyes.

One murmur stands above the others: "Did she say Negro women . . . doctor of philosophy?"

The words I've just uttered are a thunderclap inside this room. Negro women with PhDs?

I say, "In just a little over fifty years since emancipation, and while racism remains pervasive, three Negro women have defied all that has been set against them and have received the highest academic degree awarded in our country."

Now I am the one surprised when the room applauds. Holding up the first photograph, I say, "Let me introduce Miss Georgiana Simpson, who just received her PhD in German philology." I pause as I glance at the next picture, another one of my former students. "Next is Miss Eva B. Dykes, who received her PhD in English language. And finally." Again, I take a moment as Sadie's photograph smiles up at me. "Miss Sadie Tanner Mossell, who received her PhD in economics."

Again, applause. Everyone in the room, colored and white, recognizes the importance and impact of what I've shared.

"Every obstacle has been placed in front of these women. However, they have learned that obstacles hinder, but cannot halt, fortitude.

"I've often heard people say education is the great equalizer. I disagree." I pause for the astonished mumbles in the audience. "I say that because these women with PhDs have still been denied rightful employment.

"So education has *yet* to provide equality. However, this is where we must begin. Because while we can be denied employment, we will still have our education. While we can be turned away at every door, we will still have our degrees. We will continue to graduate, to graduate with honors, to receive Phi Beta Kappa keys. And we will continue to earn PhDs."

The applause has already started again, but I continue, my voice soaring above the ovation. "Negro women in America will continue to reach the highest levels, continue to be the best and the brightest, and then force others to tell us that with these qualifications, we are disqualified. We will force others to tell us that our credentials are fine; our complexions are what's offensive.

"We will force these conversations until all realize these arguments are nonsensical and have no place in our world!" I take a deep breath before I conclude with, "So to all of you, I pray that you will carry this message of hope to the women of your nations. Please tell them that across the ocean, Negro women in America extend our hearts, praying that our achievements are encouragement to all. Thank you for your time and attention."

When the assembly stands, I am astounded. And no one applauds with more enthusiasm for me than Will.

CHAPTER 29

TUESDAY, SEPTEMBER 20, 1921

I cannot insert my key into the lock fast enough, so eager am I to share (almost) everything about Europe with Maman. I'd sent a telegram letting her know that I was arriving in the early hours of this morning. I'd expected her to be sitting in the window, watching and waiting.

Before I can turn the key, the door opens, and I reach, ready to pull my mother into the tightest embrace. But hers is not the face I see.

"What are you doing here, little brother?" I ask Arthur.

"Is that a proper greeting for your favorite Fauset?" He gives me the hug I had planned for our mother.

"We can never allow anyone else with that name to hear those words."

He laughs as he carries my valise inside.

"So," I say, taking off my gloves and glancing around the parlor. I'm surprised the aroma of cinnamon porridge isn't lingering in the air. "Where's Maman?"

"Mother and I traded places," he says. "She went to Philadelphia to be with Earl and his wife."

My concern is instant when I hear our brother's name. Over the years, I've lost five of my siblings, some earlier in their lives than others, all to only two diseases: diphtheria and the measles.

More than a decade has passed since one of my siblings has died. Still, I worry when someone in my family sneezes. "Is everything all right?"

"Earl's son has influenza"—I gasp—"but he will recover."

"Are you sure?" I ask. Although the great influenza pandemic, which began in 1918, has passed, there are still serious outbreaks that continue to take lives, adding to the already fifty million souls that have been lost to what many call the Spanish flu.

"He's already out of the hospital, home and resting," my brother says, trying to calm me. "He's a bit fussy. At two years old, he doesn't understand. Which is why Mother went to Philadelphia—to shower him with the love that only a grandmother can give." The doubt in my eyes makes my brother add, "Our nephew will be fine."

"Thank God. I'll call Maman, perhaps later this evening," I say, finally relaxing. "So, what brings you to New York?"

"I'm working on a project with Alain, and he's here this week," he says, referring to Alain Locke, whom he considers his mentor. "We're having breakfast this morning."

"I hope you have a few minutes for your big sister." I sit on the sofa and pat the space next to me. "Since Maman isn't here, you'll have to be her stand-in and hear all about my European adventures." I'm eager to get into the office, but I'm still bursting with excitement.

Arthur stares at me for a long moment before he sits beside me. "I've heard so much already from some of the delegates."

Ah yes. My brother is active with the local NAACP and has probably been introduced to many by Alain.

He says, "Most of my friends returned to the States ten days ago."

"Well, yes. They left at the end of the congress," I say, as if that should have been obvious. "I stayed for the League of Nations."

"You stayed . . . and Dr. Du Bois stayed as well."

His words are simple, but his accusation echoes in my ears. My brother and I have never discussed Will in this manner.

"We often attend events together."

"Oh, I know." Again, there is an indictment in his tone.

"And he didn't want to go to Geneva alone."

"Dr. Du Bois travels all over the world. He is most often alone."

"Perhaps that's why he didn't want to be alone this time."

When Arthur glances away, I am relieved. But then my brother says, "There's a lot of talk, Jessie, about you and Dr. Du Bois."

"From Maman?" I sigh.

"I wish it was just Mother and her weekly harangues. Before the congress, I was already hearing murmurs about how much time you and Dr. Du Bois spend together."

I shake my head, not wanting to give credence to any of this.

"But since the congress," Arthur continues, "the rumors have escalated to blatant insinuations."

"I cannot believe you would listen to groundless gossip."

"This is not idle chatter. You were seen in Paris quite a few times by quite a few people in quite a few places."

Although my heart quickens, I muster nonchalance. "Of course we were seen in Paris. That was the third city for the congress."

"And when the conference was over?"

My brother's question takes me back. To those three days and three nights between the end of the congress and the beginning of the League of Nations. When Will and I were alone in the City of Love. Where we spoke to each other in French by day and by night.

We'd tried to be cautious, seldom venturing out, and when we did, always in our roles as the literary editor of *The Crisis* and the leader of the Pan-African Congress. But we were in Paris, for goodness' sake. And there were moments when, as we strolled down those narrow cobblestoned streets, passing corner cafés and dodging sidecar bicycles, we'd hold hands or steal a kiss. How could we not? No one was supposed to know us or see us or care.

"Jessie, you have done so much for *The Crisis* and the *Brownies' Book*, and now you're receiving resounding acclaim for your speech in Brussels. You've been a good representative for the NAACP."

Those words snap me from my memories. "All of that remains true."

Arthur still pushes. "But it will come to an end if you and Dr. Du Bois continue this way." His sigh is steeped with sadness. "Jessie, you have to stop."

I open my mouth to deny once again, but my brother stands, grabs his jacket, and walks out the front door.

What a welcome home.

The tap on my office door makes me glance up. "Welcome home. I have a few gifts for you." Moorfield Storey lays a stack of newspapers on my desk. "I passed Pocahontas as she was bringing these in, and I asked if I could do the honors." He glances at the newspapers already piled in front of me. "It appears you have quite a few to go through."

"I do," I say to the NAACP president. "Thank you for bringing me these."

"You created quite a stir with your speech in Brussels. You continue to make the NAACP very proud."

Again, I thank him.

"Joel and I were speaking yesterday," he says, referring to Joel Spingarn. "We may need to talk to Dr. Du Bois about expanding your role here." I hold my gasp inside. Have the board members shared my thoughts on who should be the editor of *The Crisis*? "You ought to be traveling the country delivering your message on behalf of the NAACP."

I exhale. It is not the expansion of responsibilities that I desire, but this conversation pleases me, nonetheless. The board members must continue to take notice and see me favorably.

Once Mr. Storey leaves me alone, I sit, absorbing his words and those I've read since I arrived at the office this morning. Pocahontas had the newspapers waiting for me—dozens of articles had been written about the Pan-African Congress from around the world: the *African World* (London), *Petit Parisien, Glasgow Herald, Belgian Star, West Africa* (London). In each edition, the journalists were effusive with their praise:

> Remarkable convention . . . speakers were im-
> pressive, eloquent and persuasive.

> Few whites are aware of this group of educated,
> deliberate and powerful colored men and women,
> who refuse to be considered the inferior race.

What has been most surprising are the articles that were written about my speech. I return to the Paris edition of the *New York Herald*:

> Few could imagine colored women rising above
> their domestic roles. Yet, Jessie Fauset shared
> the achievements of negro women, particularly
> three, and she inspired us to believe that more
> PhDs for negro women are coming. She should
> carry her message around the world.

I've been the subject of at least three dozen such articles. Yet I cannot revel in the wonder of this recognition, because a pall has hung over me since my conversation with my brother this morning. If it had been Arthur alone, I may have tossed his words aside. But his warnings come atop the concern I've carried since Nina responded to Will's telegram our last night in Paris.

After the attendant delivered the telegram to our room, I'd held my breath while Will read Nina's message. Then, without a word, he'd tucked the telegram into his jacket.

"Is everything all right with Yolande?" I'd asked.

"Yolande is fine," he'd told me.

I'd hesitated before I'd continued, "And Nina?"

"You needn't be concerned."

That reply rattled me. I knew I had much to be concerned about. My anxiety only grew when we traveled to Geneva and telegrams traveled back and forth between the two.

Now I wonder, had Nina heard the rumors that Arthur shared with me? Was that the message she was sending to Will in all those telegrams?

Before I left for Europe, I'd been trying to determine how to manage Miss Ovington. Now I faced a greater threat—Nina.

CHAPTER 30

FRIDAY, SEPTEMBER 30, 1921

The moment the young man and the woman step over the threshold of the Civic Club dining room, Will and I both stand. Langston's mother spots us and navigates past the tables, leading her son our way.

I reach out to the woman with an oval face and wide eyes. "Mrs. . . ." Then I pause. She is divorced from Langston's father; is she still Mrs. Hughes?

She answers my unspoken question. "Please call me Carrie, and this is my son, James Mercer Langston Hughes." Her voice resonates with pride as she introduces him, as though he isn't the one with whom I arranged this dinner.

Langston is his mother's child, same face shape, same wide-open eyes. "Langston, I cannot fully express my pleasure at meeting the young man behind such profound words."

"Thank you."

His voice is soft, his hand clammy, and his eyes wander as if he cannot quite believe the grandeur of this room. Until now, I hadn't considered how awestruck this nineteen-year-old might feel meeting W. E. B.

Du Bois, as well as the literary editor of *The Crisis*, inside the famed Civic Club.

Langston almost trembles when he shakes Will's hand. When we settle, I say, "I have waited months for this meeting."

Will nods. "She's been excited since reading your poem back in February. And I as well. You're gifted, young man."

"Thank you," Langston says, then glances away.

His mother says, "I want to thank you for inviting me this evening. It is an honor to sit here with both of you."

"It's our pleasure," I say, without mentioning it was Langston who asked if his mother could accompany him. "Why don't we order dinner and then we can talk." I raise my hand for the waiter, who's been hovering close by.

As we study our bills of fare, I surreptitiously glance at Langston. The young man is shaking. Isn't he aware that we are the ones privileged to be in his presence?

We choose our meals, and I turn back to Langston. "James Mercer Langston Hughes. I love your name. Sounds like a writer."

Carrie jumps in with a laugh. "I guess I'm responsible for that. It is a big name for a young man, but it's a family name. John Mercer Langston was my uncle."

"John Mercer Langston." Will repeats the name as if it's familiar to him.

She nods. "He was the founding dean of Howard University's law school."

"Yes!" Will exclaims. "He came to Cambridge during my time at Harvard and gave a speech about his role in composing the legislation that became the Civil Rights Act back in 1875. He was proud, but he also told us about his overwhelming despair when it was overturned by the Supreme Court." Will gazes at Langston. "So, John Mercer Langston is your uncle."

"My great-uncle, sir."

In Will's eyes, I see his thoughts. The talented tenth bears the talented tenth.

"I'm impressed, young man."

"Thank you, but those accomplishments belong to my uncle."

"I'm speaking about you," he says, although I know he's alluding to Langston's pedigree as well.

"Thank you, Dr. Du Bois," Carrie interjects once again. "I am so proud, and we are so pleased that his work is now published in *The Crisis*." She shakes her head as if that fact is still staggering.

To Langston, I say, "You're at Columbia; I graduated from Cornell."

"I didn't know that. Did you study English or literature?"

"My concentration was languages. What are you studying?"

His shoulders slump. "Engineering. At the request of my father. He called it a compromise, but it was more an edict. Either I study engineering or I am never to contact him again."

"His father"—Carrie's voice is thick with her disdain—"made such an iniquitous request. My son had to shake hands with the devil to attend Columbia."

Langston shifts uneasily at his mother's words, and I'm grateful he receives a reprieve when our dinners are set before us.

As I cut into my chicken a la king, I say, "Langston, 'The Negro Speaks of Rivers' is one of the best poems I've read. Where did that come from?"

I'm certain my question will make Langston smile. Instead, he casts his eyes downward. "I was on the train with my father when we passed a field filled with bands of colored laborers, and my father . . ." Langston loosens his tie, as if he needs more air before he can speak. "Made some derogatory statements about those men."

His voice is so sad, I wish I'd never asked.

"Every time since, when I've passed that field, I've thought of those men. Last year, I decided to give those men new words."

Even in that sadness, there is beauty in Langston's framing of his story.

Carrie says, "His father despises his own race. Even though Langston has shared that story with me, he's never told me exactly what James said. I'm sure it was degrading and demeaning and all baloney."

I will not engage in a discussion disparaging Langston's father. So I shift back. "I love how you used that experience to write such beautiful poetry."

"That poem flowed from me."

"Like a river," I say.

For the first time, Langston smiles.

"My son often writes from a place of pain. In fact, what is it that you always say, Langston?" she asks, then answers the question. "He writes because he's sad."

Langston quickly interjects, "'Sad' may not be the correct word. It's more melancholy. I'm just a pensive person."

"You're so young for that," I say.

"He may be young chronologically, but my boy's soul is older than his years." There is nothing but joy in her eyes. "Langston is so wise."

"I don't know if I'm wise. I've just lived a lot of places and seen a lot of things."

"I've lived many places myself," Will says. "Where have you lived, son?"

Langston's face brightens. "Most of my childhood was in Kansas with my grandmother."

"My mother." Carrie beams. "The first colored woman to attend the preparatory of Oberlin College."

Will puts down his fork. "Really?"

Langston nods. "She's the reason I'm a writer. Growing up, she mes-merized me with stories of the fight for freedom before emancipation. When she wasn't telling stories, she was reading to me. Everything from the Bible to *The Crisis*, both of which were mandatory reading once I came of age.

"I'm so grateful to her for encouraging me to read. The characters inside books became my friends. I loved every story, even the tragic ones. Because even in tragedy, the words can make a pitiable life beyond beautiful."

"Such a lovely way to say that. I felt that with your poem 'Aunt Sue's Stories,'" I say, referring to the second work of Langston's that we pub-lished in July.

"That was inspired by my grandmother. It was a way to celebrate her inside the magazine she loved. It's because of her that I'm here with the editor and the literary editor of *The Crisis*. There isn't a colored writer who isn't hoping to see their name inside those pages."

"Well, your name is there," I say. "And if you continue writing, I believe everyone will not only see your name, but one day, people will be sitting in this very room saying, 'Have you read Langston Hughes's newest poem?'"

My words fill Langston with delight. He rears back and laughs, a rapturous, glorious sound that makes us all join in. Even patrons at surrounding tables glance at us with grins.

It takes some moments for Langston to gather himself. "I hope that's true, Miss Fauset. I hope one day everyone will come to know me and you."

CHAPTER 31

THURSDAY, OCTOBER 13, 1921

I read through Will's speech once and then pick up my pen. This is the first time he's prepared so early for an occasion—President Lincoln's birthday in February.

Just as I start reading again, Pocahontas says, "Miss Fauset, you have a visitor." She steps into my office and lowers her voice. "I didn't want to turn her away because she says she's a friend. Sadie Tanner—"

Before she can finish, I leap from my chair. Sadie stands by the door, immaculate in a smart crimson suit with a cream-colored blouse. Her hair, so perfectly coiffed in waves, seems like an accoutrement.

"It is wonderful to see you." I pull her into an embrace. "What are you doing here?"

"I came to speak with you. I hope I'm not interrupting." She glances around the bustling bullpen. "It feels rather exciting here . . . and quite busy."

"It's the work of fighting for equality." I lead her into my office. "I wish Dr. Du Bois was in today. I'd love to introduce you. He's in Tennessee speaking at his alma mater. His daughter is attending Fisk University."

"How wonderful it must be for her to have her father return while she's a student."

I laugh as we settle into our chairs. "I'm not certain of that. I remember how my father could be, especially around my friends."

Sadie laughs with me. "Fair enough."

"How's your job search coming along?"

"I'm taking your advice and leaving Philadelphia. I won't be working in education as I would like." There is profound resignation in her voice. "I've accepted a job as an actuary with a colored company in Durham."

I'm joyful that Sadie has found employment. However, I'm still astounded that only a colored company will hire her.

"That's wonderful."

"Well, it's my turn to speak about all the wonderful things you've done. I should have been here a month ago, but my schedule has kept me from traveling. I wanted to say thank you, Jessie. Not only did you represent Delta Sigma Theta well at the Pan-African Congress, but you stood for all Negro women."

"Ah . . . you heard about my speech."

"Of course. My friends and ladies in my sorority are still sending me newspaper clippings. I'm so grateful that you included me in your speech as well as the other women. I don't know if you're aware that Eva Dykes is also a member of Delta Sigma Theta."

"I wasn't aware of that," I say, delighted to know that fact. "She was one of my students as well, although she was a few years before you."

Sadie nods. "I've spoken with Eva, and she, like everyone, is so proud of you. You've become an international star!"

This is not the first time I've heard those words. Over the last month, I have received letters of congratulation and appreciation not only from the NAACP board and other members, but from the editors of the *Chicago Defender* and *Pittsburgh Courier*, as well as Mr. Eugene Kinckle Jones, the president of the National Urban League, and Miss Hallie Q. Brown, the president of the National Association of Colored Women. "I will always be grateful to you and the women of Delta Sigma Theta. I wouldn't have been able to attend without you."

"And because of you, Negro women had a voice on an international stage."

"There are not many places where Negro women are asked to speak, so whenever I'm given that opportunity, I will stand for all of us."

She nods. "You did that at the congress, you've done that with *The Crisis*. Standing against the prejudices of Negroes, especially women, is what we do at Delta Sigma Theta. Which is why I'm here." She pauses. "The members of Delta Sigma Theta would be elated if you would join us as an honorary member of our esteemed sorority."

More than an hour has passed since Sadie departed, yet her invitation to become a member of her sorority lingers in my mind. What a privilege! Between my work here at *The Crisis*, my speech in Brussels, and now having the opportunity to become a member of Delta Sigma Theta, I should be walking among the clouds.

However, my personal affairs are a stark contrast. Thoughts of my conversation with my brother persist. What is being whispered about me behind closed doors?

"Hey, Jessie."

I glance up at the tap on my door, and my smile is instant.

I stand to hug Langston. "I'm always so pleased to see my favorite poet." I take in his brown shawled cardigan over his white shirt, tie, and black pants. With his textbooks strapped over his shoulder, he looks like such a college student. When he sits, his books hit the floor with a thud.

"I wanted to give you this."

Every time Langston hands me new poetry, I feel as if I'm receiving a blessed gift. His words more than delight me; he tests my skills as an editor, challenging me to delve beyond the words on the page. "The Negro," I read. "The title alone . . . I love this already." I continue: "I am a Negro: Black as the night is black, Black like the depths of my Africa."

In six stanzas, Langston tells the Negro's story: the struggle and the perseverance, the defeats and the victories. From slavery to today's segregation.

"This is beautiful. I can see how you're stretching the way we discussed."

"You said to go inside, to dig deeper. I'm trying." His voice is without energy or enthusiasm, a tone I have not heard from him since the first days after we met.

Over this last month, Langston and I have spent countless hours together. Between his classes, we've had lunch at the Automat, dinners in Harlem diners, and root beer floats at the drugstore near my apartment. We've attended poetry readings at the 135th Street library, where I introduced him to Ernestine and Countee. On Saturdays, we've hung out at rib joints, and on Sundays, he's had dinner with my family twice.

Our conversations are always full, sometimes with moments of joviality; other times, we're pensive and reflective. And then there are the times when we open our hearts—I told Langston about the despair I felt growing up, surrounded by so much death. He told me about the sadness that shrouded his life—growing up in Kansas while his father lived in Mexico, leaving the country before Langston even started school. And how his mother was often absent as she lived and worked in other cities. Without brothers or sisters, he felt separated and alone.

I've vowed that Langston will never experience that isolation again.

I push his poem aside. "What's troubling you?" When he remains silent, I say, "Langston, I pray you know that you can always talk to me."

"That's why I came by." He combs his fingers through the waves in his hair. "I'm thinking about leaving Columbia."

"You haven't been there for two months!"

"It didn't take long to discover all the problems." He stands; he paces. "I'm wasting time studying calculus and mechanical drawing when all I want to do is write."

"You *are* writing. You have three poems in next month's issue of the *Brownies' Book*. And this"—I hold up the paper he'd just given to me—"will certainly be published. You've been prolific, and with each poem, you're growing. That engineering degree will never preclude you from being a writer." Some of the luster is gone from my voice when I say, "You must remember the agreement with your father."

"That deal with him is one reason why I want to blow that joint." He shakes his head. "I haven't heard from my father since I arrived in New

York. I've written letters and sent telegrams. I'm not even certain where I stand with him. But I'm clear about Columbia, starting with the dormitory situation."

I am as perturbed as Langston about that. He'd been denied a room on campus solely because he's colored. "As racist as that was, let's celebrate the silver lining. The YMCA is better for you," I reason. "You're around men of like mind."

"Perhaps, but the racism hasn't ended there. I'm ignored in the lecture halls—only my French professor will set up office hours with me. I'm not wanted there, so why should I stay? It's time to just breeze out of there. I'd be better off in one of the colored colleges."

"Colored colleges are just fine. But you're enrolled at Columbia, and you cannot allow anyone to push you out. You belong inside those buildings as much as any of those white students. Perhaps even more, because you're there on merit and not because of your last name." I shake my head and command, "You're not leaving," as if I have any say in this.

He stares at me, then with a shrug, says, "All right." He holds up his finger as if giving me a warning. "But I'm not going to take being brushed off too much longer. And as far as my father, if he never contacts me, I've already received what I needed from him. I'm in New York, I'm living in Harlem . . . and I'm writing."

I feel the weight of Langston's troubles, an ever-present millstone around his neck. He says, "I've got to get to the library."

I hug him tightly before he trudges from my office.

CHAPTER 32

MONDAY, OCTOBER 24, 1921

Y ou want to do what?" Mary-Helen's eyes shine with amazement as she gazes at me from across her kitchen table.

I repeat, "I want to give Will and Nina a twenty-fifth wedding anniversary party."

"Jessie," she shouts as if I'm not sitting close to her, "you've gone utterly batty."

I stay composed, hoping Mary-Helen will do the same. "You told me you were concerned about all the rumors after Paris."

"Yes, but—"

"And didn't you say I had to put the rumors to rest?"

"Yes, but the best way to end a rumor is to stop the behavior that started it."

"I've given this a lot of thought, Mary-Helen, and—"

"And *this* is your solution *after* a lot of thought? You need to go back to the beginning and think again."

I ignore her mockery. "This will not only end those rumors, it will free me from the concerns I have about Nina. I've been able to think of little else since my conversation with Arthur."

"Has anything happened since Europe?"

I shake my head. It's only been a month since we returned to the States, and for a significant portion of that time, Will has been traveling, giving speeches around the country about the Pan-African Congress. "Nothing's happened, but that doesn't mean she doesn't know. Either I host this party or accept living with this unending anxiety, waiting for that moment when Will, at the behest of his wife, terminates me."

"First of all, if Mrs. Du Bois was aware of your relationship with her husband, your position with *The Crisis* would already be in the history books."

Mary-Helen's words give me a small measure of solace. Of course, if Nina knew, I would have been swiftly dismissed.

"Still, I cannot sit by and wait. The stakes are so much higher now."

"Why? What's changed?"

A year has passed since I mentioned this to Maman, and although I have always shared everything with my sister, this has been the single time I've remained quiet, not wanting to tempt fate. But now seems like the right moment to confide in Mary-Helen, especially as my ambition to become the editor has only deepened in the last year. I say, "There's more at stake because I'm working to become the editor of *The Crisis.*"

"Why?" Her frown is deep. "You're not happy being the literary editor?"

"I'm very happy, but I want to advance."

"But what about your work with the writers?"

"I'll continue to do that and much more. My responsibilities will expand." The mere thought of this sets my heart racing with excitement. "I'll have a larger role in determining the direction of the magazine, giving women a greater voice, and influencing readers by educating and entertaining. This has been my passion since I read through my first magazine."

"I know this is something you've loved for a long time, but now you're actually thinking about being the editor—is there another female editor of a magazine? I'm not even going to ask if there's a Negro woman in that position."

"When have I ever set my goals based on other people's accomplishments? How many times have I been the first and the only?"

In her silence, I know my sister is considering my achievements. "So how is this going to happen? Is W. E. B. leaving?"

"No, and I don't want him to. But he no longer has room for *The Crisis* in his life. Mary-Helen, you should have seen his reception in London and Paris. And when we arrived in Geneva for the League of Nations, I felt like I was traveling with a government official. We had not one meeting scheduled, but once attendees heard that Dr. Du Bois was in the city, everyone clamored to see him. Will's purpose extends beyond the borders of this country now. He can no longer be confined to an office. That's his problem, and I'm his solution."

After a moment, she says, "I've always been so concerned about you, Sissy. As a woman, you must admit that your ambition is troublesome. And, I'm afraid, so many find it unbecoming."

I want to tell my sister my ambition is not at all unbecoming to Will. But I only say, "If I were a man, would you say such things? Are you concerned at all about our brothers' ambitions?"

"All right, your question is fair. But you're introducing a new complication into your life. No one, not even W. E. B., will make this easy for you. You know how difficult it will be for you as a woman."

"Correction—as a Negro woman, nothing has ever been easy for me."

She sighs. "Well, you are correct, the stakes are higher."

"Which is precisely why I thought of the party."

"No, that notion . . . utterly batty," she mutters again, but this time, her voice is soft and tinged with a touch of sorrow.

"It may seem like the most harebrained scheme, but this is my only recourse. I'm certain once I host this celebration, no one will ever suspect that Will and I are involved."

When she gazes at me, her eyes are brimming not with anger but something worse—disappointment.

Mary-Helen says "Pardon me" and pushes back from the table. "I'm meeting a few friends for lunch."

Her words shock me. Lunch? I resist glancing at my wristwatch, but I know it's not yet ten o'clock.

"Mary-Helen, please understand."

She stares down at me. "I truly want to, but I never will."

I stand and follow her through the parlor. But when my big sister sends me on my way without a hug or another word, I feel like I am broken.

CHAPTER 33

FRIDAY, OCTOBER 28, 1921

I step over the threshold of my brownstone and frown at the sight before me. Will stands with his arms crossed, leaning against his motorcar. He is without an overcoat, as the fall temperatures feel more like spring.

I hasten down the steps. "Welcome home," I say. "How was your trip to Fisk?"

He smiles, but the mirth doesn't reach his eyes. "It was good. Clarifying."

I wait for Will to say more. "What's wrong?"

He opens the car's door. "We need to talk."

This isn't the first time Will has shown up at my home this way. One Saturday morning, he'd taken me on a surprise excursion to Coney Island, and another time he'd picked me up before work for breakfast in Morningside Park. However, this is the first time he's greeted me without glee and laughter. Today, it feels as if he's in mourning.

Before he cranks the engine, he squeezes my hand, to reassure me, I suppose. But he stays silent as he maneuvers into the street.

I'm flummoxed. Why does Will need to speak to me with so much urgency that he couldn't wait to meet in the office? Or perhaps it's what he has to say that cannot be spoken in front of others.

Nina.

This has to be about Nina, which means my notion to host a wedding anniversary celebration has come too late.

As Will angles through the streets, my thoughts are jumbled—is this the end of our relationship? What about my employment?

Finally, Will edges his car in front of Morningside Park. He grabs a paper bag from the back seat before he helps me out. When he holds my hand as we walk away from the car, I don't pull away.

My heart pounds to the rhythm of our footsteps. Have we returned to this place, where we once shared conversation and laughter, just so Will can tell me we cannot see each other anymore? The thought of living without him now feels intolerable. The thought of being forced to leave *The Crisis* has me reeling.

We settle on the bench facing the statues of Washington and Lafayette, and he opens the paper bag. "I brought tea for you and coffee for me."

No bacon muffins like the last time.

As he hands me the tea, he says, "Take it easy, Jess," as if he feels my angst. "We're going to be fine."

His words give me permission to breathe. When Will reclines on the bench, I do the same.

The tension remains, but I try to appreciate the beauty of this day: the parade of young men and a smattering of women who traipse by with books strapped over their shoulders as they cross the park to Columbia University; the morning birdsong that blends with the breeze; all of the sights and sounds; and the way Will and I sit, quiescent, able to enjoy each other's presence without a spoken word.

"It's almost blasphemous to speak of business when surrounded by all of this," he says.

"It's so peaceful."

"That's what I needed this morning. A modicum of peace." A pause. "I want to talk to you about Langston's poem 'The Negro.'"

Is all of this about Langston?

Whenever Will travels, I leave folders on his desk with papers that need either his approval or his review. Although he's left the literary content to me, I enjoy sharing Langston's poetry. "You've read his poem already?"

He nods. "I always search for Langston's poetry first because I enjoy his writings so much. But not this one."

"This poem is as good as his others."

"It is, but . . ." Will looks straight at me. "This isn't the kind of poetry I want to publish in *The Crisis*."

"I thought we wanted to publish the best writers and their best works. Perhaps you should read that poem again."

"It's well written, that is not the question. But we must focus on writing that is more uplifting, less disheartening."

"We uplift every time we present an intelligent and gifted writer. Langston, if he isn't already, will be one of the best writers *The Crisis* will have. That poem is insightful, it's brilliant."

"I concur, but *The Crisis* is a lifeline for Negroes. We teach, we entertain, we motivate. What's most important is that we elevate."

"I agree. However, there is more than one way to elevate. Sometimes words like the ones in Langston's poem can be uplifting because a colored man or woman will feel seen. That poem validates the slaves and the laborers and the entertainers . . . and the victims of white violence. I don't know what can be more inspiring than having your circumstances acknowledged."

"I've traveled this country, and I understand the trials and tribulations of our people. I know what the writers should be writing because I know what colored folks need to be reading."

"Will, Langston just turned nineteen. He's finding his voice. He has to write from his heart, not yours."

After a moment of silence, he says, "Perhaps I'm being a bit circumspect, as we now have to consider every article, every story, every poem we publish."

"Now? We've always done that."

And then I see and hear something so unfamiliar to me—a crack in Will's veneer. His voice quivers. "The December issue will be the last issue of the *Brownies' Book.*"

His words catch me unawares. "What? *Non, ça ne peut pas être vrai!* Why?"

Grief is chiseled into every crease of Will's face. "Colored folks say they want a magazine for their children, but when it came to supporting, many talked, but few sent in the dollar-fifty annual subscription."

There is so much I want to say: we have to keep fighting . . . we can do more promotions . . . we can go door to door and sell the *Brownies' Book* like the insurance men in Harlem.

But I say, "We cannot stop. What about the children?"

He doesn't look at me.

"Are we relinquishing our responsibility to give our children positive reflections of themselves? Are we sending our children back to reading poems like 'Ten Little Niggers'?"

My words are meant to shock him into the action I want him to take. When he slowly turns toward me, I see in his eyes the battle he still wants to wage, but this time, he knows we cannot fight alone.

"I didn't come to this decision lightly, Jess. It just isn't possible to survive on only four thousand subscriptions."

I blink back tears as I try to understand not Will, but the thousands of Negroes who read *The Crisis.* How could the readers allow the only magazine for colored children to fail?

His voice is soft when he says, "I'd wanted the *Brownies' Book* for so many years, and it didn't become possible until you joined me. But now we must shutter the magazine, which brings me back to Langston's poem. Each piece we publish must convey the messages I want."

I nod, not because I agree. I will publish Langston's poem; however, that is a fight for another day. I only say "I'm sorry" because my concern is for Will. "This was your dream."

His smile is small. "*The Crisis* is my dream that I birthed alone. But the *Brownies' Book* was my dream that I birthed with you." He reaches for my hand. "We still have work to do, Jess. The *Brownies' Book* may be drawing to a close, but with *The Crisis*, our possibilities are boundless."

"Yes," I say, astounded by Will's words. Boundless possibilities. For both of us. Will's vision for the future of *The Crisis* is aligning even more with mine.

He stands, then pulls me from the bench. "It's time for us to get into the office. Let's make this final edition of the *Brownies' Book* the best we've ever published."

CHAPTER 34

WEDNESDAY, NOVEMBER 9, 1921

glance at my wristwatch as I stand on the steps of the 135th Street library. Just as I turn to go back inside, I hear, "Miss Fauset!"

I am relieved to see Jean Toomer finally approaching, his long strides making it appear as if he's almost running.

"I'm sorry I'm a little late." He sounds out of breath. "The subway train."

"The IRT isn't the most reliable."

As we enter the library, my mother welcomes us. Maman has fully embraced her volunteer assignment, understanding her importance. So many of the Harlem residents who migrated to New York had never been allowed to enter Southern public libraries. Maman is here to ensure the community understands that in this place, all are welcome.

After I introduce the two, Jean follows me down the paneled hallway to a room with a desk, two round tables, and a bookcase stacked with volumes. "Thank you for meeting me today."

He glances around. "I was surprised when you asked to meet here."

"Why? We're writers, and writers love books, correct?" He laughs. "If there is one thing that Miss Rose, the librarian, loves more than books, it's the people who write them. She's set aside this office, this writers' room, for writers to write, have meetings, or just sit and think. Have you ever been to this library?"

"I have, although not as often as I'd like. But I love libraries. Growing up, my library was my refuge on many days."

"For me as well," I say before I continue. "Jean, the reason I asked to meet you is I've read more of your work and I'm hoping you'll reconsider writing for *The Crisis*."

"I figured this was the reason for our meeting. I appreciate you thinking of me again." His eyes are on the window when he says, "My concern about writing for *The Crisis* hasn't changed. I don't want to be seen as a Negro writer."

"May I ask you something?" He faces me. "I can understand not wanting to be seen that way because of the limitations put on us. However, the fact remains that you *are* a Negro writer. Wouldn't it be better to accept that and find a way to—"

"No, I'm not," he interrupts me. "I'm not a Negro writer, because I don't consider myself a Negro. But neither do I see myself as white. I am a man who is both, and perhaps if there is any color in between, I'm that as well. I'm like so many men and women in this country." He peers at me. "Probably even you, Miss Fauset. It's evident you're not one hundred percent Negro."

"I'm not," I say. "However, it is also clear that I have more than one drop of Negro blood." I pause, wanting to be sure he hears my next words. "As do you. And in this country, we're not defined by what we believe ourselves to be. We're defined by America. America says we're Negroes."

"I don't accept that. That one-drop definition comes from white supremacists. I've never understood why anyone would abide by the rules and rantings of madmen. How can men who hate me, without knowing me, define me?

"My father was the son of a woman who was enslaved and the man who was her enslaver. And on my mother's side . . . both of her parents were of mixed race. I have far more white ancestry than Negro in my blood, yet white folks can tell me who I am?" He leans toward me. "I'm everything, Miss Fauset. I'm Negro and I'm white. But what I am most is American. That's who this country should want me to be."

That is a noble ideal. However, by now Jean, at twenty-six or twenty-seven, has surely encountered many white people—madmen or not—who've told him a different truth.

Yet, I say, "If you ever decide writing no longer interests you, you must consider the legal profession. You make quite an argument." There isn't anything more to say. "I do thank you for giving me your time. If you ever reconsider, I would love to work with you."

He removes a folded paper from his jacket, then smooths out the creases before he slides it across the table to me. "I've been working on this."

I peruse the typed words. At the top: *Song of Son*. I begin to read:

"Pour, O pour, that parting soul in song . . ."

I read the rest of the poem, and once I finish, I gaze at Jean. We'd just spent ten minutes discussing how he doesn't consider himself a Negro. Yet this poem speaks so beautifully of the relevance of our experiences in slavery. In his writing, he urges us to remember all that our ancestors had endured.

"Jean . . ."

His eyes glow with expectation.

"This is quite lovely."

He exhales. "Thank you, Miss Fauset."

"I'm just a bit perplexed."

"I never said I didn't want to write about these kinds of experiences. I just want to do it from the perspective of all that I am. I don't want anyone to read my writings and say, 'Those words are from a colored man.' Characterizing my words that way not only forfeits the value of my work, but that depiction is inaccurate. I didn't write this poem with just my five Negro fingers, and the words didn't come only from the white side of my brain. Ten fingers and every thought and emotion I've had went into writing this. I want everyone to accept that."

His words are profound, and one day, I hope to convince him to write a piece on this subject for *The Crisis*. However, my attention is now on his poem. "As the literary editor of *The Crisis*, I will speak of you only as a great writer, a great American writer."

Jean grins. "Well then, Miss Fauset, I would love to work with you. I've never been seriously edited, and I'm looking forward to it."

"Have you ever heard the expression 'Be careful what you wish for, lest it come true'?"

"High school. First year. *Aesop's Fables.*"

I pick up my pen. "I'd love to have a week with this poem. However, I may have a few comments after a first look. Would you mind if I take a moment?"

"Please do." He pushes his chair back. "I'm going to take a swift lap around the library."

"Give me about fifteen minutes."

Once alone, I read the entire poem again. Like I'd told Jean, it is very good, but it is a tad bit flowery; there are parts that can be reworded for clarity. I begin jotting notes. When Jean returns, the page is covered with my comments and edits.

"This is light editing, but first, this poem is outstanding."

"Really?" He sits on the edge of his chair. "Miss Fauset, one of the reasons I decided to do this is because I know you will pull the best from me."

"Well, let me begin with all the wonderful—"

He holds up his hand. "Even as a teacher, you always told us the good parts first. I know my poem is good. What I want to hear is how I can make it better."

"Very well. This beginning is beautiful. There's nothing I would do with the opening stanza. However, in the second stanza, while I understand what you're saying, it feels a bit cumbersome. I had to read these lines several times to get your meaning. It's overwritten. Do you know what I mean?"

He nods slowly. "Even when writing, I felt as if I was overreaching. I was searching for the words to pull the reader into the same place as those parting souls."

"I knew exactly what you were doing, and I have a suggestion. I know you've studied French . . ."

"Only what I learned in your class."

"Why don't you study French a bit more? Exploring and analyzing other languages will help you become more cognizant of your own words. You'll begin to understand the rhythm of language, and the pulse and the pace of whatever style of poetry you choose."

"That's a good idea, but . . . where would I begin? You're no longer teaching French, are you?"

"No, but you can begin here in the library. One of the best ways to learn a language is to read it. I fell in love with French reading the English translation of *Les Misérables*, and then reading the French version. You can start with French poems."

His eyes are bright and eager. "I will definitely do that. I've loved writing for a while, but I've never felt this excited. Thank you, Miss Fauset."

"You're welcome, but may I ask you a favor? Now that we're working together, don't you think it's time you called me Jessie?"

He shakes his head and smiles. "You'll always be the comely Miss Fauset to me," he says before he walks out of the room, leaving me laughing.

CHAPTER 35

TUESDAY, DECEMBER 27, 1921

This is the night of my utterly batty idea.

How I accomplished this feat, I will never know. Between juggling the end of the *Brownies' Book* and the dawning of a new era with *The Crisis* where the literary section has an even more prominent position, I have scarcely had a moment to draw a single breath. Yet I've brought this harebrained scheme to life.

I'd decided Will and Nina's party would be better as a surprise celebration, and arranging this had been simple enough. I waited until Will and I were together at the Hotel Olga, and I became the distraction as I asked Will to join two of my professors from Cornell for a special dinner after Christmas. When I casually told him they'd asked to meet his wife as well, Will agreed, his attention centered on what I was doing rather than what I was saying.

"Yes," he said over and over again. "We'll be there."

Now I slide out of the taxicab and shiver as I make my way into the Civic Club. It is bitingly cold, and I pray this weather won't deter guests. Inside, Pocahontas greets me in the foyer, where the entryway is still very merry with Christmas. The twelve-foot tree sparkles with tinsel and garlands and what appear to be hundreds of white lights.

"You've timed your arrival perfectly, Miss Fauset. More than half the guests have arrived."

I sigh in relief, then check my coat. As I follow Pocahontas up the staircase, she says, "The headwaiter confirmed that dinner service will begin at seven twenty."

I calculate the time in my mind. I'd asked Will to arrive promptly at seven, and then I added about fifteen minutes for Nina and him to quickly greet guests. Dinner first; the celebration will follow.

At the threshold of the room, I pause to study the arrangement. Every room in this mansion is as elegant as the next with the gilded mirrored walls and glittering chandeliers. Unlike the dining room, this one features large windows, each framed by burgundy-velvet draperies.

Ten tables with ten settings at each are arranged throughout the room. Even from where I stand, the silver gleams and the crystal flutes shine.

Draped across the front of the room is the silver banner: CONGRATULATIONS—25 Happy Years of Marriage.

I read those words again and inhale deeply. I need oxygen.

The room is already festive as waiters zig and zag throughout with canapés and stuffed mushrooms, while others offer glasses of water, iced tea, and juices. I'm greeted first by Nella and her husband.

"It's been so long since we've had the opportunity to lunch." She kisses my cheek. "You've canceled on me twice."

"I'm sorry. I didn't know ending a publication would take as much effort as starting one."

When I spot Moorfield Storey and Joel Spingarn across the room, I excuse myself. "We're sorry about the *Brownies' Book*," Mr. Storey says after we greet each other. "The work you did with that magazine was most impressive. However, the silver lining is that you can now turn your full effort to *The Crisis*."

Mr. Spingarn agrees. "With your attention no longer divided, all of us are looking forward to what you will do with the magazine."

As I move through the crowd, it begins to feel like a reunion with all the writers and publishing associates. I stop once again when I hear

"Hello, Jessie," from behind me, and I recognize the baritone of James Weldon Johnson, with his wife on his arm.

I've adored the vivacious Mrs. Grace Nail Johnson ever since I met her at a dinner party she and her husband hosted. Grace is as much of an activist as James, and being the sister of John Nail, the wealthy real estate developer and my landlord, she dabbles a bit in the family business, too.

"This is so wonderful," Grace says. "W. E. B. and Nina never take any time for themselves. I'm so glad they will have this celebration because of you."

"Everyone here will make this night special. So thank you for coming. And, James, we have something else to celebrate tonight. You have the publication date for your book, correct? This spring?"

"*Our* book, Jessie. I'm just one of the thirty-two who contributed to this poetry collection. I'm grateful you agreed to be part of it."

Carving out the time to write for *The Book of American Negro Poetry* had been quite a feat. Yet the opportunity to contribute to this first compilation featuring so many Negro poets was too significant to allow to pass. "Perhaps tonight we'll have a toast. A number of the poets are here, Anne Spencer and Georgia Johnson. And when W. E. B. arrives, that will make five of us."

"Actually, six," James says. "I hope you don't mind that I brought an additional guest. Jessie, I'd like you to meet Mr. Claude McKay."

I turn to the gentleman standing next to him and smile. I'm very familiar with Mr. McKay's work. Like many, I was first introduced to him through his sonnet "If We Must Die," which I read in the summer of 1919. While his writing impressed me, it was his call to arms for all to rise up against the violence that beset Negroes that moved me. In his words, I felt his fury, respected his absence of fear, and by the end of the sonnet, I wanted to rally and fight, too. I've been enthralled by this man's words since.

"It is a pleasure to meet you," I say as Mr. McKay takes my hand. "You're an artist with words."

"I've been told that before," he says, his tone a bit pompous. "And it is a pleasure to meet the esteemed editor of *The Crisis*."

I'm certain Mr. McKay is aware that I am not the editor, so why has he chosen to address me this way? I only say, "At *The Crisis*, we're always looking for great poets. I would love to work with you."

He throws his head back and laughs. I stand there, not at all puzzled as to why he's so amused. Mr. McKay is the co–executive editor of the very political socialist monthly journal *The Liberator.* Surely, he isn't interested in writing for *The Crisis*.

But then he says, "You know, Miss Fauset, I don't believe any writer can have too much exposure. I would very much consider writing a piece for *The Crisis*. You'll be hearing from me."

I'm sure Mr. McKay is just being polite. Before I can ponder his words more, Langston taps me on my shoulder.

"I'm glad to see you." I hook my arm through his. "Are you prepared to say a few words?"

"That's why I was looking for you." He stops moving. "Jessie, I don't know Dr. Du Bois and his wife very well, and I don't want to get up there and just bump my gums. So, I wrote a poem."

"That's wonderful," I say as Reverend and Mrs. Cullen and Countee approach us.

After the greetings, I say to Countee, "I haven't had an opportunity to congratulate you on your win."

"What did you win?" Langston asks, glancing between Countee and me.

"This young man just won the Douglas Fairbanks Oratorical Contest."

"That's solid!"

"And the big day is approaching," I say.

Countee grins. "Next week. I'll be a high school graduate and on my way to college, just like you, Langston."

"You have a long way before you catch me, kid."

We all laugh, since Langston is just barely a year older than Countee.

"Please," I say to the Cullens and Langston, "enjoy yourselves. I'm going to make certain everything is in place."

As I search for Pocahontas, someone else taps me. When I spin around, I wrap Mary-Helen in a tight embrace. "Thank you for coming."

"I'm here because you asked me to be," she says. "And to make sure you'll be all right." She glances around the room, with now close to eighty people milling about—freezing temperatures and all. "This is quite impressive."

I glance at my wristwatch. "It's time for me to greet the guests of honor."

I ignore my sister when she rolls her eyes, and I hasten to the door where Pocahontas waits. "As soon as you see Dr. Du Bois enter, please let everyone know."

Downstairs, the foyer remains crammed with patrons, meandering in front of the Christmas tree. At exactly seven, I edge closer to the door. But then, the minutes tick by . . . and soon twenty minutes have passed. Has Will changed his mind? No! It is probably Nina who doesn't want to break bread with me.

Just as I begin to believe that my harebrained scheme has flopped, the front door opens and a gust of cold air whips around me as Will and Nina hurry inside.

"I'm sorry we're late, Jessie," Will says. "But my car doesn't like this frigid weather."

"Neither do I." I take a deep breath and face Nina.

After all the planning for this party, how am I not prepared for this moment?

"Jessie, how lovely to see you again," she greets me with such grace. "How's your mother?"

Will frowns. "You've met her mother?"

"Oh yes, I didn't tell you, dear. A few months back. We were all having lunch at Frank's."

So Nina *hadn't* told Will anything. Which meant she'd heard nothing. Knowing that makes our chitchat less awkward as Will checks their coats.

"You look lovely," I tell her. She really is resplendent in a sleeveless, lace-shouldered, white-beaded dress.

"Thank you. I was moved when Will said your professors wanted to meet me as well."

They follow me up the stairs, and then, at the room, I wait a moment before I open the door. When I step aside so Will and Nina enter first, the guests shout, "Surprise!"

Cheers ring out so loud, it is shocking, even to me. But to Will and Nina, the surprise leaves them standing like stone statues.

They don't move until people rush to greet the two. Will's and Nina's faces glow as they hug and kiss their friends and colleagues.

Since we are behind schedule, Pocahontas assists me as I encourage all to be seated for dinner: consommé, lamb chops, duchesse potatoes, and creamed spinach. Dessert will follow as guests offer formal congratulations.

I sit at the table with Will and Nina and others from the NAACP as Reverend Cullen blesses the food. When our soups are set before us, it is Moorfield Storey who begins the conversation. "Dr. Du Bois, twenty-five years! Do you even recall how you met your wife?"

As everyone chuckles and Will and Nina gaze into each other's eyes, I push my seat away from the table. "Pardon me. I'm going to check on the other guests."

I speak to no one in particular, and the conversation continues as if I hadn't spoken at all.

At each table, I linger, stretching out the conversations through the soup and then the serving of the second course. When the waiters begin clearing the tables, I move to the lectern.

I begin, "This is a special occasion. Dr. and Mrs. Du Bois observed their twenty-fifth wedding anniversary in May. However, because of Dr. Du Bois's schedule, they weren't able to celebrate this milestone. While we were all at the Pan-African Congress, Dr. Du Bois lamented how he'd wanted to do something special for his wife, but time had prohibited him."

I glance directly at Will. He had said no such thing, but it is a line that I pray will help to silence every rumor.

"I knew we had to do something for this wonderful couple. For Dr. Du Bois, who unselfishly gives of himself fighting for all of us. And to his wife, Nina, who stands by his side loving him and supporting him so that he is able to continue his great work."

Will kisses Nina's hand, and I take a deep breath.

"So to the Du Boises . . . this is your night. And there are a few people who wish to share this occasion with you."

Applause fills the room as I finally return to my seat. I'm pleased my plate has been cleared away. It is impossible to eat when jitters utterly consume me.

Reverend Cullen steps up first. He congratulates Will and Nina, then speaks to Nina directly. "For a minister, a good part of God's work is beyond the walls of the church. For a man like W. E. B., his work is beyond his home, beyond his city, and ofttimes beyond his country. And God has blessed him beyond measure with you as his understanding wife."

The congratulatory speeches continue, with several from the NAACP members. Miss Ovington, of course, gushes over Nina. James Weldon Johnson and Countee speak before Langston closes this part of the program with his poem.

Once again, I stand before all the guests. "We will begin the real celebration with music and dancing, but first, I must take a moment of personal privilege. I'm grateful I have this opportunity to celebrate the two of you," I say, staring straight at Will and Nina. "W. E. B., you've given me so much in terms of my career. I love what I do, and I'm doing it only because of you.

"Beyond my career, however, is what you mean to the world. You're challenging America to rise to its ideals, and when history is written, your name will be among those of the giants of this struggle.

"And, Nina, every success W. E. B. achieves is because you are not only behind him but beside him. I have the greatest respect for both of you."

Will glances at his wife, and then they kiss.

My breath quickens, but still I raise my glass high. "May you have another twenty-five years of wedded bliss."

As "Hear! hear!" rings throughout, Mary-Helen catches my eye. She raises her glass, then gives me a begrudging nod.

Without a word, my sister conveys this was a job well done. I hope so, I think, as I take a sip of juice and wish that it were wine.

CHAPTER 36

WEDNESDAY, MARCH 29, 1922

I t is not even ten in the morning, yet as I hasten along Seventh Avenue, I am weary. Three months of fifteen-hour workdays have left me spent. It has been this way since Will left New York days after the anniversary party, traveling, once again, throughout Europe. His lecture this time: how democratic governments must live up to their democratic creeds.

From the day Will boarded the ship until now, I have managed every aspect of *The Crisis*, including all the financials.

Of course, my work has continued with the writers, and they have been the salve to my bushed bones. Lunches with Countee, who'd graduated from high school. Dinners with Langston, who still struggles with Columbia. And Jean Toomer, who may be my greatest achievement— the man who didn't want his words to appear in a Negro magazine delivered a glorious poem.

It has been a three-month whirlwind of excitement and exhaustion.

I round the corner of 135th Street, then push open the storefront's door. Although stepping inside Lucille's isn't like entering a storefront at all. Rather, Lucille's is a swanky parlor, with plush purple-velvet chrome-armed chairs circling a low octagon-shaped glass table. A chandelier even hangs from high above.

Lucille Campbell Randolph is one of the first graduates of Madam C. J. Walker's Lelia College of Beauty Culture. Now she owns one of the most exclusive beauty salons in Harlem.

"Hi, Miss Jessie," Lucille calls out.

I return her greeting, then nod my hello to the woman sitting in Lucille's chair. I recognize Mrs. Blunt, the wife of one of the top Negro insurance agents in Harlem.

Lucille says, "I'll be with you in a few minutes."

I am quite content to bide my time, relishing the absence of the echoes of typewriters. Here, there is only low chatter and Ethel Waters singing from the Victrola in the corner.

As Ethel sings about coming changes, I settle back into the chair's plush cushions and surrender to the song's melody. It feels as if a tidal wave of changes is approaching in my own life. First, Will's return. I expect him sometime this week, and the anticipation of seeing him has become more insufferable with each passing day.

When I sigh, Lucille says, "Miss Jessie, you all right?"

"Oh yes." I sit up straight. Clearing my throat and my thoughts, I pick up a copy of *The Messenger* from the stack on the table. I haven't read this current month's edition, but Lucille keeps copies of the magazine published by her husband, A. Philip Randolph, out for her customers.

When the front door opens, I leap from my seat. "Mrs. Terrell!"

"Jessie Fauset! You are a balm for my eyes, my dear."

I'd first met Mary Church Terrell in 1906 when she hosted a new teacher reception at her home. Even though neither she nor her husband worked at M Street High School at that time, they were still very much connected because of their long history there. Over the years, Mrs. Terrell was my angel, keeping watch, counseling me on lessons, guiding me with the students, even offering advice when one of the other teachers began to court me.

"What are you doing in New York?"

"My husband has meetings, and I thought this would be a good time to do a little shopping." After greeting everyone, Mrs. Terrell sits beside me. "Congratulations on all that you've accomplished. I'm in touch with several of the NAACP board members, and everyone is impressed with the work you're doing."

"Thank you."

"You're making your mark, Jessie. Your speech in Brussels, and"— her smile is wide when she continues—"becoming an honorary member of Delta Sigma Theta. Enjoy it all. The successes, the lessons, each are only moments on your journey."

We sit back and chitchat about my time at the Delta Sigma Theta National Convention in Philadelphia, which she wasn't able to attend. It isn't long before Lucille interrupts us, letting me know she's ready.

As she begins to wash my hair, Lucille asks, "Any special occasion I should know about as I'm styling you today?"

I think of Will's imminent return, but all I say is, "No, it was just time for me to see you."

As Lucille moves me to her chair, the salon's door opens again, and this time, Grace Nail Johnson saunters in.

Grace greets everyone, then shrugs off her full-length mink. In her carmine drop-waist dress and several long strands of pearls, James Weldon Johnson's wife appears to be on her way to a political event with her husband rather than sitting for a salon appointment.

As Grace settles into her chair, a young woman working in Lucille's shop pipes in, "Has anyone heard what's going on with Marcus Garvey and his wife?"

Lucille says, "We've all heard. It's just scandalous."

Actually, I hadn't heard anything. However, I don't ask because I don't care to participate in this conversation. I'm certain this is how the whispers began about Will and me—in beauty salons.

So as Lucille styles my hair and the women share their stories about Marcus Garvey, I close my eyes and center my attention on Ethel's singing. But the music cannot blot out the conversation:

"Well, she says he was cheating, but he says she was the one who cheated."

"And now he's divorcing Amy to marry Amy."

"What?"

"That's right!"

"So let me see if I have this straight . . . Marcus Garvey was cheating on his first wife, Amy, with the woman who will soon be his second wife, Amy."

"Yes, dear. And what's worst—the Amys were best friends. The second Amy was the maid of honor in the wedding of the first Amy and Marcus."

"Goodness gracious. I need a ledger to keep track of it all. Can it possibly get any more shameful than that?"

Is this the best conversation we can have about Marcus Garvey? I am no admirer of the founder of the Universal Negro Improvement Association, whose advocacy for racial separatism and leadership in the back-to-Africa movement is the antithesis of Will's (and my) belief of integration. Still, Mr. Garvey warrants greater respect than this.

I search my mind for something more uplifting to discuss. Then Lucille asks, "Has anyone read that new book *Birthright*?"

My eyes snap open when Grace says, "James and I were just talking about that book. He's read it; I have not, but I don't know what to make of it."

"I can't say much, either," Mrs. Terrell adds. "I haven't read it, but on the train, I scanned the review in the *New York World*."

"I haven't heard about this book," I say.

"Really?" Grace sounds surprised. "I often look to your column for my reading choices."

"I make an effort to stay abreast of new releases, but I've been so busy."

Mrs. Terrell hands the newspaper to me. "The novel is about a young Negro man, a graduate of Harvard, who returns home to some small town in the South. He faces challenges from not just white folks but colored folks as well."

"Good heavens! It's a novel?" I am flabbergasted. "About an educated

Negro? Everyone should be talking about a book like this and a Negro author like that."

"Oh, no," all the women in the shop sing together.

"The author isn't colored," Grace tells me.

My mouth is agape. "A white man wrote a book about an educated Negro?" I snatch open the newspaper, read the synopsis, and scan the review:

> **Birthright is an educated study of the mulatto . . .**
> **Stribling has masterfully written a story that**
> **needs to be read . . . his literary skill . . . this**
> **novel will be celebrated . . . one of the best books**
> **of the decade.**

Mrs. Terrell says, "Well, I for one am glad to see a novel like this. We don't need any more stories of slaves and servants. I'm eager to read it, even if it's from the perspective of a white man."

The others nod and hum their assent, but I do not agree. We do not need the perspective of a white man about a Negro.

As I have this thought, Will's words rush back to me. About Eugene O'Neill and *The Emperor Jones*. The night he berated me because I didn't agree with his view that a white man shouldn't be writing the thoughts and words of a Negro.

All this time later, I am the one seething. I am distraught because T. S. Stribling has completed the novel I've talked about for so long.

He has written my story.

CHAPTER 37

WEDNESDAY, MARCH 29, 1922

My intention had been to rush straight to the office once I left Lucille's. However, now I hurry to the 135th Street library.

Maman greets me, and then, after I explain that I want to see Nella, she sends me on my way. I navigate through the paneled hallway, then pause in front of the Children's Reading Room. I listen for the sound of chattering, but hearing nothing, I push open the wooden door. The five round tables set up for children are empty.

Nella is alone behind the desk, a stack of children's books piled high in front of her. She glances up and smiles. "Jessie!" But just as quickly, the ends of her lips curve downward. "What's wrong?"

I settle into one of the chairs meant for someone decades younger. "I didn't mean to alarm you. I need to talk. About a book."

"A book?" She frowns, clearly bemused. "We could have sent the book to your office as we always do."

"I must read this now. Have you heard about the novel *Birthright?*"

"That's interesting," she says. "Walter White checked out a copy this morning."

"Evidently, I'm the only one who hadn't heard of it. I just came from Lucille's . . ." Then I share everything I learned about *Birthright*—the author, the story, and how he'd written what Nella and I have been talking about for over two years.

When I take a breath, Nella jumps from her chair. "I'll get the book." Within minutes, she returns, and I follow her into the writers' room.

As I sit at one of the tables, Nella asks, "Are you going to read the entire book today?"

"Yes, it's less than two hundred pages. I'm not leaving until I'm finished."

"All right. I'll return to look in on you."

I glance at my wristwatch. I have almost five hours before the library closes. First, I scan the table of contents, determining how to pace myself.

Then I turn to chapter one:

At Cairo, Illinois, the Pullman-car conductor asked . . .

After a few pages, I can say the writing is colorful. I feel as if I'm on that Southern rail with the protagonist, Peter Siner. Moving through the chapters, I find the book to be well written. The pacing flows and the story is engrossing.

However, I flinch after the tenth time I read the words *nigger* or *negress*, as if that is the only descriptor for Negroes. Then the author named a part of the city Niggertown. By chapter five, I've lost count of how many times he's gratuitously used these offensive words.

Two hours in, the oak chair has hardened, and I stand to stretch. Nella opens the door as if she anticipated my taking a break. "I'm going to make a run to the diner. Would you like a sandwich?"

"Yes! Thank you."

I am once again engaged in the story when Nella returns with a corned beef and pickle on rye. I don't pause—I eat and read about Peter's struggles and his grappling with the revelation that he is of mixed race. I read as the sun's shadows shift across the floorboards and the day's light dims.

Finally, I come to the last words and slowly close the book. I sit still, absorbing it all. If I had to describe this book in one word, it would be *amazing*. It is amazing just how horrible this novel is . . . amazing in its excess use of stereotypes and amazing in its contradictions. I wonder if T. S. Stribling cares about the fallacies he's perpetuated in this novel.

The knock on the door drags me from tumbling deeper into my reverie. "Do you need anything?" Nella asks.

"Do you have time to talk about this?"

"I do. You finished?"

I nod. "Nella, this is worse than I thought. It's a good story . . . except for the characters and the plot."

"Good heavens!" She is aghast. "What else is there?"

"The story moves. It wasn't difficult to continue reading, because I did want to know what would happen next. With every turn of the page, I hoped it would get better. It never did. The author wrote about an educated colored man, and it is apparent he's never met one. He only knows Negroes as subservient, and he thought because *he's* educated, he could put a black face on someone like him."

Nella squints, trying to understand. "So the colored character is really white?"

"It's worse than that. The character is neither an educated colored man nor an educated white man." I begin counting off on my fingers. "First, the protagonist derides himself! Every positive characteristic, he attributes to his white blood, and then the story is filled with comments about the natural indolence of Negroes." I continue, explaining the stereotypes: the whiskey-drinking, shiftless colored men; the *negresses* who all turn their heads in a certain degrading manner; and of course, most of the characters are inarticulate. "By the end, he used the words 'nigger' and 'negress' in almost every sentence," I say, only slightly exaggerating. "Nella, these characters are unrecognizable to me. We should have written our novels."

Nella responds with a one-shoulder shrug.

"Well, there's nothing we can do about the past, but now we must complete the work we've started. Like W. E. B. has told me so many times, and now I completely agree, we must tell our stories." The doubt in Nella's eyes and the crease in her brow make me add, "We can do it. We'll do it together, the way we've planned."

"Yes . . . we can do it . . . together . . ."

My eyes narrow as I study Nella. "I thought you wanted us to work together."

"Oh, yes. From the moment you suggested that, I've been excited knowing that's what I've always needed—a writing partner."

"So let's get started."

She throws up her hands. "Really, Jessie? You've been saying we'll write together for the last two years, yet do you know how many times I've seen you in that time?"

"What are you talking about? I just saw you at the Du Boises' anniversary party a few months ago."

"Oh, certainly we see each other at social events. I'm talking about how you suggested we meet for breakfast or lunch and take an hour or so, just the two of us, to work together. You've talked about it often, but it's never happened. You have little time for your friends."

"That's not true. I care so much about you."

"That's indisputable. You definitely care, you just don't have time."

I fold my arms, feeling a sharp sting from Nella's words. She is wrong; I do carve out time for my friends. I meet with Langston and Countee and all the other writers as much as my schedule allows. But then I pause. While Langston and Countee are friends, our gatherings center on work. And truth be told, I can't recall when last I spent time with Nella outside a social event.

I'm more than hurt; now I'm saddened.

As if she knows I need comfort, Nella says, "The blame is not completely yours, Jessie. It's W. E. B."

"What? No!"

"The reason you don't have time for anyone is because you're not just the literary editor. W. E. B. has you working as if you're *the* editor. He's working you to the bone, exploiting you and your good nature."

"Goodness gracious, it's not like that at all."

"You may be too close to see it, but how many hours are you in the

office? And while you're working so hard, he's free to travel the world."
She shakes her head. "As your friend, I should have said something a
while ago. But I'm telling you now, it must stop!"

"You don't understand."

"I have eyes. I can see. W. E. B. is using you for his own gain."

"He's not. This is my gain. I *want* to be the editor!"

Nella's mouth opens as wide as mine, both of us shocked by my words.

"What are you talking about?" Nella whispers.

I hadn't wanted to tell another soul, understanding that the more
who know a secret can tell a secret. "You cannot say a word."

"All right."

"I've been working hard, but it's because I *want* W. E. B.'s position."
When she moans, I add quickly, "I don't want him removed." Then I
explain to Nella what I've told Mary-Helen and Maman. As I lay out my
thoughts, after a few minutes, instead of shaking her head she begins to
nod, although doubt lingers in her eyes.

At the end, she says, "It makes sense. You've assumed the duties of
the editor, and this would allow W. E. B. to rise to even greater prominence."

I exhale, relieved. Nella is the first person who hasn't sent me away
with dire words of warning.

But then she says, "Have you spoken to W. E. B. about this?"

"No. Not until I'm totally prepared. Nella, when I take this idea to
him, I want him to wonder why he didn't think about it. I want him to
see the greater advantage is for him."

She contemplates my words. "Have you considered that he won't agree
with you, only because of how much he loves *The Crisis*?"

I reflected too soon. Nella's words *are* very much like Maman's and
Mary-Helen's. "I loved teaching, yet I willingly turned from teaching so
I could pursue my true passion. The same will happen for Will. He will
transition from *The Crisis* to his greater calling of serving his people.
It's already happening, and it will be his love for *The Crisis* that makes
him decide that I should be the editor."

"When you say it that way, it seems so apparent." She smiles, though uncertainty remains in her tone. "If this works out the way you wish, I'll be so happy for you." Then, with a sigh, she adds, "I guess our novels will be on hold for a little longer."

"No! I'm really sorry I've neglected you, our friendship, and our agreement. But writing our novels is even more imperative now, especially after *Birthright*. So will you grant me a second chance?"

"I don't want your burden to become heavier because of me."

"I'm asking you." Reaching across the table, I say, "I want to do this with you."

She grasps my hand. "I want to do this with you. And, Jessie, I'm behind you with *The Crisis*. Just be careful."

My smile tells her there's no reason for her caution. I will just have to show her. I will show everyone.

CHAPTER 38

SATURDAY, APRIL 1, 1922

The taxicab eases to a stop in front of the Civic Club. I am more than a little tardy, almost twenty minutes late—a rarity, since I hold punctuality as a virtue.

Yet this morning, I have to give myself grace. Time slipped by during my first writing session with Nella. Over tea and toast, we wove through the threads of Nella's plot, and then Nella and I debated how far I would take Joanna and Peter's relationship. Should my protagonist and her love interest become engaged, just to have Joanna break Peter's heart?

It's thrilling to return my attention to the story that has lingered in my mind. I'm eager to share this news with Will as soon as he returns.

When I spring from the car, I see Claude McKay standing in front of the club.

"Mr. McKay, I'm so sorry. I'm not usually—"

He holds up his hands, interrupting my regrets. "Miss Fauset, no apology is necessary."

I continue anyway. "And you waited outside."

"By choice," he says. "Spring has sprung, and I was so delighted to see this resplendent weather that I decided to stand here so the sun could bask in all of my glory."

"Your glory?"

When he grins, I laugh, although I'm unconvinced Mr. McKay is joshing.

He gestures toward the door. "Shall we?"

The dining room is full, as expected at noon. However, as a club member and W. E. B. Du Bois's associate, I'm seated at once. When I thank Mr. McKay again for agreeing to this meeting, he says, "Please call me Claude."

I pause to observe this man who holds such a royal bearing. He sits with squared shoulders and his head held high, as if he is glancing down on his court from a throne. "I will call you Claude, if you call me Jessie."

"I've already begun. I told you, Jessie, you'd be hearing from me."

When the waiter hands us each a bill of fare, I study the daily selections. As I consider the soup, I hear familiar laughter behind me. Will? At once, I am excited. Has Will returned?

Glancing over my shoulder, I sit stock-still. My mind doesn't understand the sight before me: Will seated with Georgia Douglas Johnson?

When had Will returned to New York? Why hadn't he come to me directly? Didn't he miss me as much as I'd missed him?

"Jessie?"

My name echoes in my ears. For a moment, it seems, I've forgotten where I am.

"Is something wrong?" The creases in Claude's forehead are deep. "I've called you several times."

"What?"

"This young man has been asking if we are ready to order."

"My apologies." I blink to bring the waiter into focus. "I'll have the vegetable soup, please."

"Are you all right?" Claude's tone still bears concern.

"Yes. I was distracted for a moment."

"Well, it doesn't seem as if you're very hungry, but I hope you won't mind if I have the veal cutlets."

"Of course not. The veal . . ." Behind us, more laughter. "Is excellent."

When the waiter moves away, I use every muscle within me to focus on Claude. "I was surprised to hear from you."

"Why? Was your offer for us to work together not sincere?"

"I was definitely sincere." Again, laughter behind me. "I have admired your writing for some time."

When Georgia's laughter reverberates throughout the room, I can bear it no longer. Placing my napkin on the table, I say, "I apologize, but will you excuse me for a moment?"

"Of course."

I inhale a deep breath of courage before I maneuver through the tables. My eyes are trained on Will and Georgia, although they do not see me. Their heads are bowed, and so close the two are almost pressed together. "Will?" I say his name as if I'm still uncertain that he is here. As if he and Georgia may possibly be an apparition.

When they glance up, I am struck by the fact that one of them is startled—and it is not Will.

"Jessie." He stops, as if my name alone is sufficient.

"When . . . did you get home?"

He glances at Georgia, then says, "I haven't been in the office yet."

That was not what I asked, but I only say, "I didn't know you had returned."

"We'll talk, Jessie. I'll be in the office, perhaps tomorrow. I'm eager to speak with you."

It is more than his words, it is his caustic tone that dismisses me.

Qu'est-ce qui se passe? I want to stand there and demand answers. However, proper decorum—so I spin and waddle on wooden legs back to my table. As I approach, I see Claude peering at me. I pretend not to be dying and smile.

When I slip into the chair, Claude says, "I hate to ask again—are you all right? You seem somewhat disoriented."

"Oh, no." I'm grateful my tone gives no hint of my thumping heart. "I just—"

"I saw you speaking with Dr. Du Bois," he interrupts.

"Yes." Again, I am thankful for a steady voice, when my heart is not. "He's been traveling, and I welcomed him home."

He passes me a sardonic smile, and my eyebrows lift. Without moving his lips, is he calling me a liar? "It looks like he's having quite the lunch with Mrs. Johnson."

What does he mean by that? Although that isn't the question I ask. "Oh, do you know Mrs. Johnson?"

"Who doesn't know Georgia Douglas Johnson? Many consider her the most renowned poet of today."

I lean toward him. "I'm surprised you don't see yourself that way."

"Oh, Jessie." He mimics my posture. "I didn't say *I* believed that. I said 'many,' and I am not among them."

For the first time since I realized I was in the room with Will and Georgia, I laugh. "Well, that's why I would love to work with you. Because I agree with your assessment of your talent."

"Do you? Why? Tell me, Jessie, what do you know about me?"

I will forever be beholden to this man for centering my attention on him. "I know you were born in Jamaica and had already published two books of poetry before you enrolled at Tuskegee. Then, eventually, you moved here to Harlem. And you did all of that before the war."

As the waiter sets our plates in front of us, Claude chuckles. "I'm charmed. Most people know nothing of me beyond my poem 'If We Must Die.'"

"Surely you cannot hold that against anyone. What you wrote went beyond the bounds of poetry. It was one of the best political statements I've ever read."

"It was," he agrees with a nod.

"And I've admired your work with *The Liberator.*"

"Well, if I've accomplished all of that, why would I want to work with you?"

I've yet to take a spoonful of my soup; still, I push the bowl aside. "I know you have a new book releasing soon. And while your accomplishments are impressive, being published in *The Crisis* will give you even greater prominence."

Again, he nods, although this time, he seems to be impressed with *me*.

"It's no secret *The Crisis* has the highest circulation among the magazines where you can be published." Now he laughs, knowing that I'm speaking about his magazine, which had been founded only four years before. "And I believe a good writer is always challenged by a new editor, a good editor."

"Are you a good editor, Jessie?"

"I am," I say with the same hubris he's shown. "I am also a writer, which gives me special insight into being an editor. And I'm tough. I only want the writer's best on the pages. My writers and I work together to deliver their finest work."

I believe he is considering my words, until he says, "Honestly, I can't envisage how much editing I'd need from you. However, if I decide to submit something to *The Crisis*, I will take your edits under advisement."

Before I can tell Claude that I'm only interested in working with writers who desire to work with me, we hear, "Jessie," and Claude and I look up.

My heart thuds once again.

"I didn't realize you were here with Mr. McKay." Will gives him a nod. "How are you?"

"At the moment," Claude glances at me with a grin, "I'm as good as can be."

Will's jaw clenches. "The two of you are having lunch?"

His question is directed to me, but it is Claude who responds, "That is quite evident."

Before this moment, I had not been aware of any animosity between these two. Will stands as if waiting for an explanation, and I return to him what he had given to me—nothing. The silence becomes prolonged and awkward, but I remain resolute.

Finally, without saying goodbye, Will leads Georgia from the dining room. My eyes follow them, and I notice the way Will protectively presses his hand against the small of Georgia's back—an intimate touch so familiar to me.

My heart no longer thuds. It has stopped altogether.

"That was strange," Claude says, shattering the silence.

"It seems as if you and Dr. Du Bois . . . have some challenges."

"Indeed. When I was in college, I read Dr. Du Bois's *Souls of Black Folk*. Never before had I read anything like the words he'd written. He stirred my soul." Claude lays his hand against his chest as if he's about to make a pledge. "Reading that book was the beginning of me wanting to be a reformer and bring change to this country."

"Then I don't understand. The way you spoke to each other, I would have presumed you'd never had a cordial conversation."

"Oh, we haven't," he says. "After our first meeting, I wondered how such a pompous and intellectually disingenuous man had penned such important and moving words. I've heard him speak about art being propaganda, and that's pure nonsense. Art must be about art. Art must be about truth."

I nod, but I will go no further in speaking against Will.

"And now today, I've discovered something else about Dr. Du Bois."

"What?" I ask before I can consider my question. I'm certain whatever he's discovered, Claude will not be kind.

"I'd heard about his reputation, but now I see that what's whispered in the dark is the truth in the light."

Beneath the table, I clench my hands. "I've never heard those whispers, but I'm surprised you would now believe what you've heard based simply on a man and woman having lunch."

He laughs. "You sound so naive, Jessie. That wasn't merely a lunch. And it would also explain Mrs. Johnson's great rise."

My eyes narrow. "You're edging dangerously close to slander."

Now he laughs. "Are you saying you haven't heard that the sofa in Dr. Du Bois's office has often been used as a stepping stone for many women poets?"

Heat warms my cheeks. "Not only are you smearing two people's reputations, but I can assure you of two things. Georgia Douglas Johnson is talented in her own right. She needed no assistance from anyone to achieve her success. And second, there is no sofa in Dr. Du Bois's office."

"You're not much of an editor, Jessie, if you don't understand I'm be-ing metaphorical." He raises his hand for the check.

I sit and seethe as Claude pays the bill, although I'm not certain whom my ire is directed toward—Will or Claude.

Once the check is settled, we stand to leave. I must be gracious, even if he has rattled me. However, before I can thank Claude, he says, "My apologies if I offended you."

"Why would you think you offended me?"

"This entire conversation . . . I'm sure you're distressed since we were all here at this very club, not that long ago, at your beckoning to celebrate Dr. Du Bois and his wife. What he's doing is an affront to his wife." He pauses and gives me a pointed stare. "And to you as well."

CHAPTER 39

SATURDAY, APRIL 1, 1922

Hours have passed since I saw Will in the Civic Club, and I remain in a state of incredulity.

Upon his return, Will arranged to be with Georgia before he came to me.

I feel betrayed!

Then, my next thought—how preposterous! Who am I to be hurt? What right do I have to be dismayed? On what grounds do I stand?

There is only one woman who has a claim on Will—which is the way I've always wanted it. This arrangement between us has worked. Nina is his wife, and I am the woman who . . .

The woman who what?

The light knock on the door wrenches me away from my reverie. "Yes."

I fully expect Pocahontas to step inside, but when the door opens, I stiffen.

"I was hoping you would be here," Will says before he enters.

"Where else would I be? I have work to do." He nods and I add, "I'm surprised to see you."

"Where else would I be?" When he smiles, I realize his words are meant in jest. He closes my door, then sits beside me, the way he has a thousand times. Although today feels like the first. "While I was away, I received reports of your excellent management of *The Crisis*. I owe you a thank-you."

This is what he says to me? Thank you? I don't want his gratitude. I want an explanation.

"Even Miss Ovington begrudgingly mentioned that you had everything in hand."

This world has turned topsy-turvy, and I can bear it no longer. "When did you return?" My tone is curt, absent of all the emotion that rankles within me.

"Last night," he responds in kind.

At least he's answered this time. "I thought you would have informed me that you had returned." Like you always have, I think but do not say.

"I was astonished to see you as well."

Now this conversation has become a game of hide-and-seek, and I don't wish to play. Although this is not an exchange I want to have in the office, where a dozen people are outside my door, I lack the fortitude to hold back.

"Are you involved with Georgia?"

He leans back as if my words have both offended and shocked him. Had he not expected my question?

"I don't discuss my personal life with anyone."

I push back. "I'm not *anyone*, Will."

"That's true."

"And I deserve to know."

"Deserve?" he says, as if he's surprised by my audacity. "You're asking me questions my wife would never ask."

I should back down, but I do not because I cannot. "Perhaps she doesn't want to know. I do."

"Beyond me not understanding what business this is of yours, I have to ask: What difference do you think it will make?"

"Is that a yes?"

His shoulders slack. "Jess." He says my name so softly, with such compassion, I inhale hope. "I've given you a part of me that I've shared with no one. I've told you things I've never told my wife or any woman. And I will repeat some of that now. I'm a different man. With different needs."

"I understood that to be the reason why you and I were together. I was unaware that meant . . ." I pause because it is torturous to say. "There . . . are other women."

His response: he presses his lips together, and then, after a moment, he lowers his eyes.

Still, I force it. "You have not answered my question."

Now he looks straight at me. "I answered, Jess."

I ask nothing else and move to stand. I want to snatch the door open and thrust him into the bullpen. But then Will holds up his hand.

"I have a question for you. It's business."

From this day forward, this is how it will be. Will and I will work together, having hundreds of meetings and thousands of conversations. In my professional role, I will have to forget all that we've been.

I am prepared for this shift . . . just not today. Perhaps after tomorrow, and then all the days, weeks, and months that follow, I will be able to perform like the editor I want to be.

However, now I need space to piece my heart back together. I will live through this; I endured losing my mother, my father, and my siblings. So, of course, I will survive . . . and thrive. I just need time.

But I cannot say any of this to Will.

He says, "I was surprised to see you with Claude McKay. Was that a business lunch, or was it personal?"

Will has never questioned my meetings with men. Perhaps he's always assumed it was business. But after the conversation we just had, *he* has *no right* to make any such inquiry of me.

I am inclined not to respond. However, I am mindful that despite the end of our involvement, we must remain amicable if I am to receive his support and blessing to attain the position of editor.

"It was a business lunch. I'd spoken to Mr. McKay a few months ago about working with him."

"That's not a good idea."

My eyebrows climb all the way to the top of my forehead. "Why not?"

"He writes for *The Liberator.*"

"I am aware of that."

"We don't need him writing for *The Crisis.* There are enough writers who want to see their names inside the pages of my magazine." He stands, putting a period on our conversation. But then he says, "I want to go through my mail. How long will you be here?"

"I'm leaving right now."

"Right now? I thought you had work to do."

"I did. But I don't anymore." His frown deepens, but I refuse to explain.

"Oh well . . ." He pauses, as if there is more he wants to say, but then he walks out my door.

And, that simply, my eight-year relationship with Will has come to an astounding end.

CHAPTER 40

FRIDAY, APRIL 7, 1922

This is remarkable." Pocahontas stands over my desk. "Has anyone ever had their poetry displayed on a full page like this?"

My eyes remain on the poem, "Song of the Son," penned by Jean Toomer. "No, but this is so glorious, it deserved its own space."

Pocahontas begins to read:

> Pour O pour that parting soul in song,
> O pour it in the sawdust glow of the night
> Into the velvet pine-smoke air tonight,
> And let the valley carry it along.
> And let the valley carry it along.
>
> O land and soil, red soil and sweet-gum tree,
> So scant of grass, so profligate of pines,
> Now just before an epoch's sun declines
> Thy son, in time, I have returned to thee,
> Thy son, I have in time returned to thee.

As Pocahontas continues reading the next three stanzas, which I've already committed to my memory, I think about the effort Jean put into writing this piece. He'd taken my critiques and read French poetry like "Demain dès l'aube" by Victor Hugo and "Le corbeau et le renard" by Jean de la Fontaine. Then he rewrote and I edited and he rewrote and I edited, until he delivered this treasure that reads like a folk song.

From where Jean and I began, to these words on this page, where he pays tribute to those who'd been enslaved and implores the generations who follow to never forget, reveals the complexity of the relationship between Negroes and America.

Pocahontas reads the last line. "'All that they were, and that they are to me . . . caroling softly souls of slavery.' Miss Fauset, that's so lovely." She sighs. "I wish I could write like that."

I close the magazine and gesture for her to sit down. "Pocahontas, you're a beautiful writer."

"But I don't write like Mr. Toomer or Mr. Hughes. Mr. Hughes can tell an entire story in two stanzas."

"I've learned something simple about writing." Her eyes are wide; she is eager to hear. "The more you write, the better you become. You already have two published pieces in a major national magazine," I say, referring to the poetry and stories she submitted for the *Brownies' Book*. "How many young women can say that? You keep writing, and I'll keep editing you."

"I appreciate that, Miss Fauset. I'm getting better because of you."

"You're getting better because you're gifted."

When she bolts from her chair and hugs me, I am both surprised and delighted. But she pulls back quickly, as if suddenly realizing what she's done. "Thank you, Miss Fauset," she says, and scurries from the room.

What a rewarding week this has been. First, on Monday—seeing Jean's face and his eyes fill with tears (which he will always deny) when I gave him a copy of *The Crisis* with his poem. Then, Tuesday—my luncheon with Langston began in its customary fashion . . . I had to persuade him to remain at Columbia. And it concluded the way our lunches often did . . . he bestowed upon me another literary gift, this time titled "Mother to Son," with opening lines that I know will echo throughout history:

> Well, son, I'll tell you:
> Life for me ain't been no crystal stair.

Even now, I can scarcely breathe thinking of every line of that poem. Now today—another blessing to see the desire and determination in Pocahontas's eyes.

This is why I am here. This is why I will stay.

What will happen now, however, will be determined by Will.

Will.

Every thought begins a journey that leads me back to him.

Always.

However, although Will remains on my mind, the greatest gift in the last week has been that we haven't shared the same space. Each day, I've seen him for no longer than a moment as he dashed from one meeting to the next. He's been amiable, but it is evident that he agrees with my conclusion—our relationship is over.

Five days have passed, yet time has not served as a salve. My sadness lingers; however, work is my distraction, and my ambition is my saving grace.

Then . . .

"Jess."

My head snaps up as fast as my heart leaps.

From my thoughts to the threshold of my office—there he is.

"Do you have a moment?"

"I . . . I do."

When he sits beside me, I notice his mustache has been trimmed. I wonder who scheduled his appointment, since this is something I've always done.

He settles back as if this is an ordinary day. As if his next words won't be the first words beyond *good morning* that he's uttered to me in a week. "I hope you're well."

"I am?" It is meant to be a statement, but these last thirty seconds have me bemused.

"I'm trying to readjust and return to my usual routine. It's been difficult, especially with so much happening at home."

My question is instant because I still care. "Is it Yolande?"

He nods. "She's fine. Just her normal aches and pains." His glance crosses my desk and settles on my manuscript piled on the corner. "Is that your novel?"

Thoughts from a week ago rush to me. How excited I'd been to be working on my novel, how eager I'd been to share that with Will.

He reaches for the stack of pages. "You're making progress. I'm happy about that."

If our life were not askew, I would have told Will about *Birthright*, and we would have been off somewhere laughing and lambasting that book—together.

"Finally, I'll discover how Joanna's story unfolds. I hope Peter isn't destroyed when she chooses her career over him." He flips through the typed pages. "I'm really proud of you, Jess, and I'm here to support you in whatever way you need." His voice is gravelly when he says, "I mean it."

I swallow and nod.

"Perhaps we should have Pocahontas take some responsibilities from you. Or even hire another stenographer to give you more support."

His kindness has me reeling. "I appreciate you thinking of that. I will let you know . . . if I need anything . . . from you."

"From the moment we met, I knew you would one day write that great American novel. I believe in you, Jess."

Those. Words.

Like my father, Will always believed.

Then he says, "Oh," as if he has a sudden recall. "I actually came to speak with you about this." He holds up a book that I hadn't noticed resting on his lap. "I have something for you to read." The way he caresses the book's cover makes me frown. Then it dawns on me—Will has written another book and has waited until now to surprise me. But how? Without me knowing? Without me editing?

I am so eager that I almost snatch the book from his grasp. My grin is wider than his when I read the title: *Bronze: A Book of Verse.* But then the next words reach from the cover and slap me:

GEORGIA DOUGLAS JOHNSON.

"Georgia's new book will be published in a few months. We must review it."

I have to push the words past the stone that has closed my throat. "We? You mean you want *me* to review it?"

"Yes," he says, as if he's proud that he's asked me. "You're the best at reviews."

"Yes. I am the best." I am profoundly grateful for the rap on my door that gives me time to steady myself. But the respite lasts for only a moment when Nina peeks inside.

"I didn't want to walk in on anything," Will's wife says with what sounds like a sardonic chuckle. "Darling, Pocahontas told me you were in here with Jessie." Once Will stands to greet her, she turns her attention to me. "How are you?"

I nod because I cannot yet speak.

"I've never had the opportunity to thank you for the wonderful anniversary celebration you gave for Will and me. It was splendid."

"You thanked me that night."

"Yes, but I haven't seen you since, and I wanted you to know how much that evening meant to me." She loops her arm around her husband's. "I will always be grateful for you acknowledging Will and me that way."

Will says, "Let me know when we'll publish the review of Georgia's book."

As they amble toward my door, Nina says, "Georgia has a new book?"

Will closes the door behind them before I can hear his response.

I sit for a few minutes in confounded silence.

Nina and Georgia. Will and me.

This is beyond peculiar; this is utter madness!

I sit and think, sit and wonder. And because I don't want to sit and cry, I reach for my pen and journal. Without thought, I begin:

> On summer afternoons, I sit . . . Quiescent by you in the
>   park . . .

My pen moves feverishly across the page, my emotions unleashed with every stroke. The words pour from me, line by line, stanza by stanza, and in less than an hour, I lift my pen. Five stanzas, pulsing with our story—Will and me.

I scratch out a few lines, begin again, and another thirty minutes later, I am content.

Usually, I set my poem aside, to return the next day and read with fresh eyes. Today, I do not wait. This poem, like Will and me, has to be finished.

I need a beginning—a title. And I need words that will bring the story to an end—the last lines.

Reading it again, the title comes to me. One of my favorite French phrases: *La vie c'est la vie.*

Now I ponder the ending, and after a while, I wrench the final lines from the storm of anger and sadness that thunders inside. I lift my pen once more:

> The world is full of jests like these.
> I wish that I were dead.

CHAPTER 41

SATURDAY, MAY 20, 1922

rap on the double-leaf decorated wooden door of the Cullens' brownstone, then glance at my watch. I still have ample time.

"Miss Fauset," Countee's high-pitched tone greets me. "I was hoping you'd be joining my parents this evening."

"Hello, Countee." I smile at the only reason I ventured to this gathering.

When I step inside, I peep into the front parlor. Just a few guests are milling about. "Can I speak with you privately?"

His eyebrows dip into a frown. "Certainly."

I follow Countee down the mahogany-paneled hall of this massive home. While the brownstone where I live has been divided into apartments, Reverend Cullen owns this entire fourteen-room house, which stretches over four stories. We pass the back parlor, then step down the stairs to the library.

Countee motions for me to sit on the chesterfield sofa, and he settles on the other end. "Is everything all right, Miss Fauset?" He clenches and then unclenches his fists.

"Remember when I said I'd consider your poem for publication?"

He nods slowly. "I understand why you haven't published it yet. There are so many great poets submitting to *The Crisis.*"

"There are." I hand him the June issue, which I've already folded to the page I want him to see. The title of the poem, "If You Should Go," followed by the poet's name, Countee P. Cullen, is centered at the bottom.

His hands tremble, and for a moment, he's bereft of speech. Then he begins to read:

> Love, leave me like the light,
> The gently passing day;
> We would not know, but for the night,
> When it has slipped away.
>
> So many hopes have fled,
> Have left me but the name
> Of what they were. When love is dead,
> Go thou, beloved, the same.
>
> Go quietly; a dream
> When done, should leave no trace
> That it has lived, except a gleam
> Across the dreamer's face.

Countee sounds like he's singing a song. So beautiful. His recitations are as lovely as his poetry.

"Miss Fauset, I didn't know you were publishing this now."

"I wanted to surprise you. And you will be paid."

"That's fine, but I don't write for money. This is what I've been waiting for my entire life."

His entire life? In a few days, Countee will be nineteen. Suddenly he shifts, and before I can blink, he grabs me, hugs me, holds me for a few heartbeats. "Thank you, thank you, thank you."

Then, just as quickly, he pushes away and his hands fly to his face. "I'm so sorry, Miss Fauset. Please forgive me."

When I frown, he lowers his eyes. "We're going to have to do something about this."

"I didn't mean to offend you in any way."

"Well"—my voice is stern—"I wouldn't say I was offended, but we must change a few things. You're a high school graduate, an award-winning and published poet. I think it's appropriate for you to call me Jessie."

After a moment of astonishment, his lips spread into the widest smile. "Miss Fauset! I mean, I know all of your poets call you Jessie."

"Now you're one of my poets."

"Would you mind if I showed my parents?" Before I can respond, Countee bolts from the sofa.

"Countee, I have copies for your parents."

He is already halfway up the staircase. "I'll be back with them."

I laugh and think never have I felt such contentment. This June issue of *The Crisis* is a sublime reminder of what I've achieved in the last two and a half years. The pages are filled with artistic brilliance: the cover illustration is sketched by a woman, and many other ladies are found throughout the pages with their poetry and short stories. And this month, my three favorite poets: Langston, Jean, and now Countee.

This is a splendid time, although it has been hard fought arriving here. For the last six weeks, I've had to conduct business with Will as if we'd never had a personal connection. But I'd learned as a child how to set my heart aside, each time one of my siblings passed away. The lesson: weep, rise, and carry on—and my childhood lessons have allowed me to arrive at a place where Will and I coexist and collaborate in harmony.

My heart, however, still bears the scars of our relationship, and there are moments when my yearning for him seems boundless. I've controlled those times of longing, especially by maintaining my distance from Will outside of the office. We haven't attended the same social event in all these weeks. Now I glance at my wristwatch, because I want the same for tonight.

"Jessie!"

Reverend Cullen's voice reaches the library before he does. "What are you doing down here when the party is upstairs?"

"I wanted to speak to Countee in private and give you and Mrs. Cullen this." I hand him the magazine.

"This is a very proud moment for us." He leafs through the pages, and when he finds Countee's poem, he stands silently, basking in this moment. Finally, he says, "Let's get upstairs to the party."

Then, as if he has a sudden recall, the reverend says, "Where's W. E. B.?" This is a question I've answered often in these past weeks, primarily because of the reverend's next words: "You two are always together."

"He's running late" is what I tell Reverend Cullen as I follow him up the staircase.

At the landing, I'm astonished to see both the front and rear parlors teeming with guests.

When Reverend Cullen calls out "Adam!" to the pastor of Abyssinian Baptist Church, I see my opportunity to slip away. As I inch down the hallway, I hear familiar laughter. Walter White stands in a small circle with his bride, Gladys, and Grace and James Weldon Johnson. If I weren't pressed against the clock, I would have stopped to say hello, but I continue navigating through the guests until I step over the threshold.

I exhale, and then I glance up.

"Jess!"

"Hello, Will."

"I was hoping to see you here."

When he pauses, I wonder if he's waiting for me to say the same.

"Are you leaving? I'd like to speak to you."

"All right." When he motions toward the door, I say, "It's very crowded inside. Can we talk here?"

He shakes his head. "Too many people coming in and out," he says, just as a man and woman walk past us to enter the Cullens' home.

When he places his hand on the small of my back, I hold my breath and try not to remember. We press through the guests, then down the staircase, and Will and I return to the library.

Will motions toward the sofa, but I say, "If this is quick, I'd prefer to stand. What do you want to discuss?"

"The June issue."

My shoulders had been hunched, but now I relax. Will has to be as proud of this upcoming issue as I am. Perhaps this is his first moment of recognition that I can step into his role.

"Countee and his parents are, of course, very happy."

"His poem is excellent. However—" He paces away from me. "I read your As to Books column."

I cannot recall Will and me ever discussing that column, but then it comes to me. "Are you concerned about my review of *Birthright*?" Before he can respond, I explain, "It's a book everyone is talking about, so we had to write an opinion, and as always, I gave an honest review."

"So you believe everything you wrote in that column?"

"Of course. I would never print anything I didn't believe." I am nonplussed. What part of the review troubled Will? "Yes, it was critical, but it was honest. I focused on what the white reviewers missed."

He sits on the sofa. "So you're fine with what you wrote about *Harlem Shadows*?"

Harlem Shadows? Again, I scan my memory to recall the exact words I'd written about Claude McKay's latest book of poetry.

"That's the review that's troubling you?"

He nods. "I asked you not to work with him."

"I didn't work with him; I reviewed an upcoming book release."

"Although you shouldn't have done that, it's what you've written that concerns me." I'm astonished when he pulls out a clipping of my review, then begins to read: "This book is pure poetry . . . his writing is extraordinary . . . he writes with such vividness and passion about his race." With each word, I hear the derision in Will's tone.

I ask, "Have you read *Harlem Shadows*?"

"No, and I don't plan to."

I truly don't understand Will's animosity.

"And then, you wrote, 'Mr. McKay has accomplished what few writers have the ability to do. He fills the pages with his passion, absent of propaganda.'" Will clenches his teeth before he adds, "And I don't want to neglect the part where you call him a genius."

I peer at Will, trying to discern whether this is jealousy or antagonism. "Every word is true."

"No, it's not."

As I've done over these last weeks, I consider my words, always mindful that I must have Will's support for what I want to achieve.

Still, I cannot resist asking, "How can you tell me what I've written is not true?"

"Because your review is not about Mr. McKay. Your review is about me."

My mouth opens wide. Oh, the hubris . . . I want to shout. But I only say, "I would never insert my personal feelings into the pages of *The Crisis*. I wrote my true impressions."

His glare is red-hot. "If that is true, then it makes what you wrote even more egregious. You know how I feel about art and propaganda. And the way you contested my beliefs this time is worse than when you challenged me in public. This time, you sought to embarrass me in print."

"How can you believe I would do something like that to you?" I fight to press down my ire. "I wrote this from my perspective, as I have every review I've had in this column."

"Your perspective is of no significance, Jessie. *The Crisis* belongs to me!"

His words, his tone, drip with such rancor, I take a few steps away from him.

"I'm the one on the front lines in this war declared against our race, and you publishing that review goes against all that I'm attempting to accomplish."

I labor to keep the trembling from every part of my being. "I was not going against you, and if you were being reasonable, you would know that. And you would remember I've always shared your vision."

"It is becoming increasingly clear that you have no understanding of *The Crisis*'s mission, and if this continues . . ." He ends his sentence there, stands, and, without uttering another word, marches past me.

Up the staircase.

CHAPTER 42

FRIDAY, JUNE 2, 1922

Mary-Helen blows out a long breath. "And to think I was just stopping by to say hello," my sister says after I finish recounting my confrontation with Will. "This is not the conversation I expected to have with you."

I tuck my feet beneath me on the sofa. "I hope you're not sorry."

"Not sorry. But I do want to speak to W. E. B. and tell him exactly what's on my mind. How have you sat in the same office with that man after that conversation?"

"Thank heaven, he hasn't been in New York. He's traveling, planning for the third Pan-African Congress."

"I suppose you won't be participating in this one."

"Not at all. I don't even know where it will be."

"But he's going to return at some point, Sissy. What are you going to do?"

"What I've always done. Carry myself with composure."

"Yes, proper decorum. However . . ." Mary-Helen hesitates as if she's not certain she should continue. "No one should have to endure such working conditions. Perhaps it's time for you to leave *The Crisis*."

"*Absolument pas!* Why would I leave when I love what I do? How can

I walk away when I relish every moment with Langston and Countee and the others? And why should I, when I've poured everything within me into this, and now I'm so close to having what I want most?"

"Because you're closer to being terminated than you are to gaining the editor's position."

"Will has no suitable replacement for me. I will not be dismissed."

"Sissy, no one is indispensable or irreplaceable."

I give her a long glance, because I believe, in this situation, I am both indispensable and irreplaceable.

"Jessie!" Mary-Helen whines.

I hold up my hand to stop her from a rant. "I'm not depending on that alone. I have a plan." I unfold the paper that Pocahontas had given to me yesterday. "I have the schedules of the NAACP board members, so I know who, over the next several months, will be coming to New York and when they'll arrive."

My sister stares at me blankly.

"The board members are already impressed with my work, and by spending a little time with each of them, when a decision has to be made about *The Crisis* . . ."

"You believe they will push W. E. B. out and put you in," she says before I can finish.

"I will never stand for that. Despite the upheaval in our personal life, I enjoy working with him and love the knowledge that I've gained from him. He brings so much to that magazine, I want him there."

"But your plan . . . it all sounds rather convoluted to me. The only good news about any of this is that you *have* walked away from Will. I just hope . . ." She stops.

"I can assure you this is the end of Will and me. What he said at the Cullens' party did more than the passing of time ever could. He alone has ensconced my heart in steel." I pause, thinking of that evening. "I never want to be with Will again."

The click of the front door's lock makes Mary-Helen and me turn, and Maman exclaims "Oh" when she enters. "Both of my daughters are here. Look who escorted me from the library."

When Langston follows my mother inside, both Mary-Helen and I greet him with a hug.

"Thank you for bringing my mother home."

"I always enjoy my time with Mrs. Fauset." Then he says, "But, now that I'm here, Jessie, would you mind if we spoke for a few minutes?" He glances between my mother and my sister. "I don't want to interrupt any family time."

"You're family," Mary-Helen says as she gathers her pocketbook. "I was just leaving." As she hugs us, she says, "I'll see you at Sunday dinner."

While Mary-Helen exits, Maman retreats to her bedroom.

Langston waits until Maman closes her door before he flops onto the sofa. He seems utterly exhausted, and since he's dressed in his usual cardigan and slacks, I suspect he's had a marathon day of classes. "We can talk or I can listen."

He doesn't open his eyes. "I've tried, Jessie." After a moment, he sits up. "I'm leaving Columbia."

"Langston, no." I lower myself onto the sofa.

"I'm not asking your opinion. I came here to tell you I'm through."

"But if you leave, they'll win."

"They've already won. The weight of being there is too heavy to carry." He stands and moves to the window. His eyes are on Seventh Avenue when he says, "Why should I go through all of that when I don't want to be an engineer?"

"All right. Then study writing or languages. Perhaps your father won't even have to know."

He faces me and squints as if he's bemused. "Why should I study writing at Columbia when I have you?"

"I'm not a professor."

"You're right. You're better than that. And how many of my poems and stories have you published? Eight, maybe nine. I'm a published writer. I don't need to be at Columbia to become one." When I say nothing, he adds, "I know you're disappointed, and maybe in a few years, I'll go back. Not to Columbia, but to one of the colored colleges."

"I'm not disappointed, Langston." I hear my own resignation. "I do want you to go back, because having that college degree is imperative for a Negro man."

"I'll figure it out." His shoulders relax as if, with this declaration alone, the burden has already lifted.

"What are you going to do?"

"I'm going to do what everyone else does—find a job. But what I'm *really* going to do . . ." He rushes back to the sofa. "I'm going to write. I'm going to write more poetry, more short stories, and I'm going to write my novel. And who knows. Perhaps my novel will become an international bestseller and I'll become independently wealthy."

Now I laugh. "Wealthy writers are only white. But I'll admit, this can be a blessing. My only concern is your livelihood. Have you thought about where you might work?"

"As a busboy or dishwasher at the Civic Club. Or in a factory. It doesn't matter. I'm not afraid of hard work. I'm really jazzed about this, Jessie," he says with an enthusiasm I've rarely heard from him. "I'm going to finish this semester, but just making this decision . . . I'm free."

"All right. We'll begin first with finding you employment."

He clasps both of my hands inside his. "Thank you."

When he stands, I say, "Come by my office in the next few days and we'll develop a plan."

"I'll be there." He winks, then walks out the door.

I had prayed he'd be able to endure Columbia, but after having lived through such experiences myself, I understand. No one, especially not a young man who is discovering his place in the world, should have to bear the encumbrance of such racism.

I *am* deeply concerned, though. Can Langston stand on his own here in New York? He's only twenty years old, for God's sake.

"Jessie?"

I hadn't heard my mother's footsteps. "Are you all right?"

"I am," I say. "However, Langston—"

"I know. I didn't mean to eavesdrop, but you two weren't whispering."

"Maman, I'm so worried that Langston will be out there on his own."

"On his own, but never alone." She eases onto the sofa next to me. "He has you, *ma chérie*, and he's an industrious young man."

"This should be a carefree time in his life, and now he has this burden."

She leans her head back, finding my words astounding. "There is never a carefree time for a Negro in this country. He was born with the burden of his race, and now, as a young man, he's learning to survive with it."

My mother, with her pale skin and colored sensibilities. She is often the one to remind me of truths I want to forget.

She pats my hand. "I may have a means to assist him."

"Do you know someone who's hiring college dropouts who once studied engineering but now want to write?" I laugh, but Maman does not.

"As it happens, I do." My smile fades. "I know someone who would love to help Langston. She won't give him a job, but he will have money."

"Someone who doesn't know him, but who will give him money without a job?" I look at my mother sideways. "What will he have to do for the money?"

"I don't want to say anything more until I speak with Charlotte."

"Who?"

"Charlotte Osgood Mason. She and I have been friends for a while, but that's all I will say until I speak with her." She stands. "I'm going to prepare dinner."

My eyes narrow as I watch my mother. Who in the world is Charlotte?

CHAPTER 43

SATURDAY, JUNE 3, 1922

Maman and I enter the elevator chamber, and when the attendant closes the gate, Maman says, "The penthouse, please."

The penthouse? How tall is this building? I glance at the elevator's panel. Twelve stories?

The chamber doesn't shimmer and shake, and I wonder what else is different about these Park Avenue high-rise buildings. Once we step off, I follow Maman, our footfalls silenced by the Oriental rugs covering polished hardwood floors.

"Remember what I told you," Maman whispers with the same warning in her tone that she had this morning. "Charlotte's a bit . . . eccentric. She may say things that will . . . challenge your sensibilities. Just know she means well and will help Langston."

The way Maman navigates through the mazelike hallway makes me ask, "Have you been here before?"

"Yes." Maman stops before a door and presses the buzzer, which echoes into the hallway.

"You never told me you came here."

Maman's brown eyes peer into mine. "*Ma chérie*, are we now sharing our whereabouts? I'm more than happy to tell you where I am every moment of the day. As long as you do the same."

When I say nothing, Maman smirks and faces the door.

The door opens, and a young woman greets Maman with delight. "Mrs. Fauset!"

"Good morning, Miss Chapin. This is my daughter, Miss Jessie Fauset. Charlotte is expecting us."

Inside the entryway, a high-hanging chandelier dazzles with a thousand crystals and reflects off the rose-colored walls.

"Bella!"

I hear the voice, strong and commanding, before I see the woman. Charlotte is in her sixties, perhaps seventies, and she approaches with outstretched arms. "I've been waiting for you." She gathers Maman into a tight hug, then faces me.

"Jessie Redmon Fauset." She says my name with reverence.

I take in the woman with snow-white hair pulled into a severe chignon, and round silver spectacles that match the shape of her blue eyes. She wears a white laced-collared blouse with a blue pleated skirt, although there is nothing simple about her outfit. Diamonds dangle from her ears, while half a dozen strings of pearls adorn her neck. A heavy silk shawl draped over her shoulders completes her ensemble.

She takes my hands into hers. "It is such a pleasure."

"It's nice to meet you, Mrs. Mason."

"Please, you must call me Charlotte."

"All right. Thank you for having my mother and me in your home." I glance around once again at the high ceilings, the paneled-wood wainscoting, and the area rug that feels as if I'm standing on a cloud.

"You don't understand, Jessie. Having you here is my pleasure." She turns to the woman who opened the door. "Cornelia, we'll be served in the drawing room."

"Yes, Godmother."

Charlotte hooks her arm through Maman's. "You don't have the slightest notion how happy I am that you're here."

The drawing room is filled with more opulence. Peach is the color scheme: from the cherrywood-mantel fireplace with peach-colored surround tile, to the walls and empire sofa and two damask armchairs.

But what draws my eye is the art. The room isn't filled with European antiques as I expected, but rather African artifacts.

"I see you're taken with my collection," Charlotte says.

"I'm sorry, I didn't mean to stare . . . but these pieces." I glance at her in amazement, and then I realize why she and Maman are friends. Charlotte has to be an integrationist, too.

"It's all so beautiful, isn't it? These are fetish totem masks from the Ivory Coast." Charlotte points to a set of four masks hanging side by side. "And this is one of my favorites. A Bundu secret society mask."

The tour continues with two African headdresses, a spear, and other small weapons. By the time she explains every piece, I am awestruck.

"I have many more pieces hidden away. You'd have to visit the Motherland to see a collection as extensive and fascinating as what I've amassed."

My brows lift an inch at Charlotte referring to Africa as the Motherland. I've only heard Marcus Garvey use that terminology.

There is a longing in her tone when she says, "I used to dream of Africa as a child."

"Really?" Besides Maman, I've never met a white woman who's taken such an interest in people who do not look like her.

"Yes!" she exclaims. "Didn't you?" Her question is rhetorical, because in the next instant, she directs Maman and me to the sofa while she settles into one of the chairs.

"Let's begin!" Charlotte sounds like she's calling a meeting to order. "Bella, when we spoke last night, I cannot say if I was more surprised or delighted. We'd just seen each other a few days ago, and you never mentioned this."

Maman offers me an explanation. "Charlotte is a frequent visitor to our library."

"Yes, and did your dear mother tell you how we've become so close?"

Again, she doesn't pause for my response. "It's because your mother and I have lived the same life."

Charlotte laughs, and Maman says, "But I lived my life without all of the money."

"Oh, dear Bella," Charlotte says. "I told you money is coming."

The corners of my lips twitch as I battle to hold my smile. "You have money coming, Maman, and you didn't tell me?"

She chuckles. "Charlotte was married to a doctor who studied supernormal psychological phenomena. So she believes things only she can see."

"Supernormal . . . psychological . . . phenomena?"

Charlotte responds, "It's the study of all things supernatural. Not only did my husband research subjects such as telepathy, he was best known for his ability to communicate with those who've gone to the great beyond."

Laughter bubbles inside of me, but before I can throw my head back and release a guffaw, Maman gives me a stern glance. I stifle my laughter and pretend to clear my throat.

Charlotte doesn't notice the exchange between my mother and me, because she continues, unabashed. "My husband was well known for hosting seances and psychic gatherings."

Goodness gracious! *This* is the woman my mother believes can help Langston? Who is she going to raise from the dead for him?

As Charlotte goes on about her husband's channeling sessions, I glance at my mother. A few minutes ago, I believed this woman was just like Maman. Now I know the opposite is true.

"This is the one area in our friendship where your mother and I disagree," Charlotte says with a heavy sigh. "I married a man of science, while your mother chose to wed a man of the cloth. Her religious beliefs hold her back from seeing the truth." The lilt returns to her voice when she hastens to add, "But that is where our differences begin and end. Has she told you all the ways our lives are parallel?"

Again, Charlotte continues without giving me a chance to respond.

"We married much older men; we married widowers with children, so we became mothers, and we became widows in 1903. Isn't that extraordinary?"

"I was already a mother," Maman corrects her.

Charlotte waves her hand. "A minor point of clarification."

Maman adds, "As well as the fact that I married Negro men."

"And that, my dear Bella, is the perfect segue. Because, Jessie, while I never married a Negro, I want to work with Negroes."

Two dark-haired women with their faces set in stone, and wearing white aprons over navy dresses, enter. One carries a platter with cucumber and watercress finger sandwiches, and the other woman sets the tea service in place. Then the two exit the way they entered—silently.

"Please." Charlotte gestures, directing us to serve ourselves.

I am grateful for the reprieve; I need a few moments to reconcile the woman I thought Charlotte was with all of this rising-from-the-dead rubbish. My mother used the word *eccentric*; *zany* better describes what I've just heard.

When we return to the sofa, I prepare myself for more foolish talk. But Charlotte says, "Jessie, Bella tells me you can assist with what I want to do most with my life. I've been a patron of the arts for over twenty years, and I'd like to continue with Negro writers."

Even though I cannot fathom how Charlotte might answer my question, I ask, "Who have you worked with before?" I brace myself for Charlotte to say last week she had lunch with Charles Dickens or tea with Shakespeare. If she says that, I will grab Maman so we will not squander another minute of our time.

Charlotte says, "I've worked with the Indians in the research for *The Indians' Book* by Natalie Curtis. I'm sure you're familiar with the book and the author."

"I apologize. I'm not."

"I'm not surprised. The book didn't sell well, and now I must move on. I've been following what you're doing at *The Crisis*." She lifts a copy of the magazine from the table. "I've enjoyed *The Crisis* for years, always very interested in the political and social issues that Negroes face. But recently, I've noticed the literary section has gained greater prominence. I assume that's because of you."

I nod.

She claps, delighted. "I've savored each poem and every story."

"Thank you. I've had the honor of working with several gifted writers."

"Yes, you have. I met a talented Negro recently. Do you know Alain Locke? He's a wonderful poet, and so smart. He's the first colored man to be a Rhodes Scholar, you know." She doesn't take a breath. "As I've explained to Alain, there is so much talent in the Negro community, but we're not hearing those voices. Money is an impediment for colored writers, and I'm here to make certain that it will no longer be.

"I can help lift Negro voices. And after speaking with Bella, I want to help Langston Hughes. I've read several of Langston's poems, and that young man . . . oh! When I read 'The Negro Speaks of Rivers,' his words gave me great insight into the true primitive nature of Negroes."

Primitive nature?

"That poem was so profound and powerful, I almost felt like a Negro myself. I want to see more writing like that. So that not only I but other white people can come to understand the authentic Negro. I want to understand how Negroes feel. I want to know how all of you think."

I take the deepest breath I've ever taken in my life. "If you want to know that about us, all you have to do is look in the mirror. Negroes feel and think exactly like you. We have the same heart and the same brain and the same blood from the same God."

Mrs. Mason stares at me, and then she leans her head back . . . and laughs. I clench my teeth, but before I can share some very special words with her, Maman touches my arm. "Whatever the cause or the case, Charlotte can *help* Langston," she whispers.

Once again, Charlotte seems unaware of the exchange between Maman and me. "So how soon can I meet this Langston fellow?"

I will need to have a very long talk with Langston before I commit to this introduction. "I will contact him, and in a few days—"

"No, no, no! When I asked how soon, I was speaking of minutes, perhaps an hour, my dear. Where is he? I will have my driver pick him up now."

Again, I glance at Maman, and now she only shrugs. "I haven't spoken to him about this, and I wouldn't want to place him in an awkward situation."

"My dear, what's awkward about money when you need it?"

Now Maman looks away, giving me no hint of what is proper. If a white man approaches Langston and tells him to get inside a car, Langston will dash in the other direction. It isn't safe for a Negro to follow a white man anywhere.

As if she reads my thoughts, Charlotte says, "I have an idea." She pulls stationery from the desk and hands me the linen paper and fountain pen. "Write him a note and tell him to meet you here," she demands.

I stare at her and the paper and the pen. I feel Maman's eyes, pleading with me to do as Charlotte requests.

Even if my note can lure Langston, I don't wish to bring him into a situation where he will feel uneasy. However, this meeting is beyond this moment. This meeting could very well alter the course of Langston's life.

I take the stationery and pen and scratch out:

Langston:

This gentleman will bring you to where my mother and I are having tea with a woman, Charlotte Osgood Mason, at 399 Park Avenue. Mrs. Mason is very eager to meet you and I believe this can, in turn, be for your benefit. I will explain it all when you arrive.

Jessie

Befuddled. That is the best word to describe Langston when he strolls into the drawing room with his satchel slung over his shoulder. I jump up to greet him, hoping to alleviate any doubts or fears he may have had in the time between reading my note and now.

I grab his hand. "I know this is unusual, but thank you for coming."

His glance moves to Maman and Charlotte. "I trust you, Jessie," he says, although his wary tone matches the suspicion in his eyes.

Charlotte beams at Langston as if he is her favorite son. "Langston Hughes. What an honor for me."

He reaches for her outstretched hand, but he glances back at me. "Langston, this is Charlotte Osgood Mason, a friend of my mother's and—"

"A patron of the arts," she finishes before I can. "It would be my greatest honor if you and I worked together." She motions toward the chair, and we all sit.

Langston lowers his satchel onto the floor. "Work together? How so?"

"How shall I explain this?" She raises her glance to the ceiling as if the heavens hold her answer. "I want to be your benefactor."

Langston shifts, and when he glances at me, I nod.

Charlotte continues, "I understand you've left school to write, correct?"

"I won't be leaving until the end of this semester. I want to get the credits for this year."

"I knew you were intelligent. Your brilliance bursts through your poetry. I've read everything you've written, or should I say, I've read everything you've published. If you have unpublished works, I would certainly love to read those as well."

"I have a few works in progress that Jessie is working on with me for publication this summer."

Charlotte says, "Perfect. Langston, what are your plans for the future?"

"Once the semester ends, I'll be looking for a job. In a restaurant or—"

"No, no, no! That's not a future. Those are mere tiny stepping stones that won't take you beyond next year. What I'm speaking of are your hopes and your dreams—your future. What is it that you really want to do?"

This time, when he looks my way, I know his thoughts. He is extricating himself from a situation where no one cares about him. Yet here is this white woman who wants to know the desires of his heart. He slides to the edge of his seat. "Mrs. Mason, I want to be a writer."

His words click something on inside of Charlotte. Her eyes sparkle. "And as a writer, would you consider yourself a poet only?" She holds up her hand. "I'm not making any judgment. I just want to know of your other writing aspirations."

"I've written short stories, but what I want to do most is write a novel. I have a title, *Not Without Laughter*. I haven't written much yet, but it's a story of a Negro family in the Midwest, in Kansas, perhaps." He smiles. "It's not an autobiography; well, maybe it will be semi-autobiographical. But I want to write about issues like race and class and religion that no one has considered with Negro characters." He delves a bit into his idea, highlighting each character, taking us through the arc of every one. "I've written about these themes in my poetry."

His passion is palpable. Maman places her hand on mine, her face aglow with pride. But Charlotte's eyes are no longer twinkling; they shimmer with unshed tears.

When Charlotte stands, Langston does the same. She reaches for his hands. "You haven't written a word, and I know this book will be a massive success. If writing that novel is what you want to do, my boy, you shall do it. You will not work in a restaurant or a mailroom. Your only responsibilities will be to read and write."

"Mrs. Mason . . ."

She continues, "You will have everything you need, from where you shall live to what you shall wear. It will all be provided for you, along with a living stipend, of course."

"Mrs. Mason," he repeats, and once again, he glances toward me as if I have the answers to his myriad of questions.

Now I struggle to stifle my own tears. In the hours I've spent with her, I've found her wacky, sometimes disparaging, and strange. In the end, however, Charlotte is just as Maman said . . . a woman who wants to help.

"I don't . . . know what . . . to say," he stammers.

"You don't have to say anything." She pulls Langston even closer. "You are a brilliant, precious brown boy. The world is waiting for the great Negro writer Langston Hughes."

CHAPTER 44

SATURDAY, JULY 15, 1922

orchestrate this perfectly.

As Mr. Storey slides out of the chauffeured car that picked him up from Pennsylvania Station, I stroll toward the entrance of 70 Fifth Avenue.

Seconds later, Mr. Storey and I reach for the brass door handle at the same time.

"Oh!" we exclaim together, step back, then laugh when we face each other.

"It's good to see you, Mr. Storey."

"And you as well, Miss Fauset."

Graciously, he opens the door, and we enter the lobby. As we await the elevator, we chitchat: I ask him about the weather in Boston; he asks me if I've been home to Philadelphia recently. It's an encouraging omen that the president of the NAACP has taken an interest in my background.

When we enter the elevator, I wait a few moments, wanting to sound spontaneous.

Mr. Storey speaks first. "Miss Fauset, I continue to be impressed with your work for *The Crisis*, especially this past year. Your influence is apparent, not just in the literary section but in the very essence of the magazine. It's been remarkable to watch and wonderful to see, especially with the rise of subscriptions."

"Thank you. I've only been able to do this because of Dr. Du Bois's guidance and the latitude he's given to me."

"As well he should, given his extensive travels."

As we step off on the fifth floor, I say to him, "There is a story I've been considering for the upcoming children's edition. I'd like to write a feature on the founders of the NAACP." Mr. Storey raises his eyebrows, his interest piqued. "Many children know of the NAACP, but not the founding of the organization and its mission."

"That sounds fascinating, Miss Fauset. Please let me know if there is anything I can do to assist you with that." Once we enter the office, he adds, "I hope one of these times when I'm in New York, you will have time to perhaps have lunch with me. I'd like to hear more of your ideas for *The Crisis*."

After I tell him I look forward to that, I thank him and rush into my office.

Next week . . . Joel Spingarn.

t is only three o'clock when I step outside onto Fifth Avenue and pause to soak up a bit of this sun-drenched July day. Pedestrians stroll past the street vendors and peddlers. No one is hurried in this heat.

I linger at the corner of Fourteenth and Fifth. Should I hail a taxicab or take the subway?

And then:

"Jess."

I brace myself, standing as stiff as a flagpole. Only my heart thunders.

When Will says "Jess" once again, I must spin around and face him. My fear is no longer that I'll follow him. He's done more to encase my heart in steel than I could have ever done. Now I only fear that he will draw me into a repeat of our last extended conversation, and at the end of a discussion like that, I'm not certain I'll still have my position. He may not be an ally, but Will cannot become the enemy.

"Hello, Will." I sound as if I'm greeting a stranger. That's how he feels to me, since I've only seen him three, perhaps four times after he'd admonished me so.

"It's good to see you."

"Yes" is all I say at first, and then I add, "Good to see you, too. I didn't realize you were back."

"I returned yesterday and was on my way to the office. Are you leaving for the day?"

"I am." And then, because I'd been used to sharing the details of my life with him, I add, "I'm going home to work on my manuscript."

His smile radiates across his face. "It does my heart good whenever you talk about your novel." He reaches for me, but I step back. "I've always believed you would do it," he continues, not at all miffed by my action. "If you ever want to discuss anything about Joanna, Peter, and Maggie, I'm here. I want to help you achieve this."

The sweetest words.

He asks, "Do you have a moment? There is something I'd like to discuss."

"Certainly."

"Perhaps we can have dinner." I inhale and he says, "A business dinner, Jess."

Before the Cullens' party, Will and I had been working concordantly, and if I want my plan to succeed, we must find a way to do that once again. This is an opportunity to reset our professional relationship.

"All right. The Civic Club is fine."

"They're having a private event tonight. It's closed for the day. We can hail a taxicab up to Harlem since"—I shake my head before he finishes—"we haven't had dinner at the Hotel Olga in a while."

"No, Will."

He holds up his hands. "There aren't many restaurants where we're welcome, Jess, and I'd like to dine someplace where I won't have to organize a protest just to be served."

"No."

He grins and glances away as if my response amuses him. "I want to discuss business over dinner. That's all."

My cheeks flush. Of course he isn't inviting me to his bed, and now I'm utterly embarrassed. "All right," I say, and within minutes, we are in a taxicab, shrouded in silence.

However, this is not at all like the serene moments Will and I once shared. This is awkward, both of us with our eyes on the windows, pressed against opposite sides of the car to keep the utmost distance between us.

When we arrive at the hotel, I pray our dinner won't feel as unsettling, or else the next hour will be wretched. Although, as we walk toward the hotel's doors, it feels so familiar. The way we are side by side, with Will's hand resting easily on my back.

At the door, I step aside for a woman exiting. It is not until a man follows her that I exclaim, "Langston!" and hug him as if I'm reuniting with my missing son.

"Jessie," Charlotte says. "Is that you?"

"Yes, it's good to see you," I say, although all of my attention is on Langston. "I haven't seen you in weeks. Six weeks exactly," I say, sounding like a doting and disappointed mother. "How are you?"

"I'm well." He speaks the truth as I notice his attire: a satin-lapel black dinner jacket over a white waistcoat and white stiff-collared shirt. This is the first time I've seen Langston in a bow tie.

"Mrs. Charlotte Osgood Mason," I say, "I'd like to introduce you to Dr. W. E. B. Du Bois."

"Dr. Du Bois, I'm astonished this is our first meeting. I'm enamored with all of the work you do on behalf of Negroes everywhere."

"Thank you, Mrs. Mason. And, Langston, it's good to see you, son."

Before Langston can respond, Charlotte says, "Langston and I are off to see the last performance of *Shuffle Along*."

Will's eyebrows inch higher, but I'm only surprised to learn that Charlotte has waited this long to see the first all-Negro Broadway musical. "We were at the opening performance," I say. "You will enjoy it."

"So I've been told. Have a good evening."

She holds out her arm, and Langston loops his through hers. Over his shoulder, he says, "I'll come by your office soon."

Then Will and I watch a Packard Twin Six limousine come to a stop in front of the two. Charlotte and Langston wait as a middle-aged white man, dressed in a double-breasted black jacket, hops out and opens the door. Charlotte slides in first, and I don't miss the pure disdain on the chauffeur's face when Langston follows.

The car eases away, and the limo rolls smoothly down Lenox Avenue without a rumble or a sputter.

There are questions in Will's eyes, and I shake my head before we enter the restaurant.

"Dr. Du Bois, Miss Fauset," one of the waiters greets us. "It's been weeks since we've seen the two of you."

Longer than that, I think as Will takes a moment—the way he always does when he has the opportunity to speak with a young colored man.

Once we settle at our table, Will says, "Tell me about Langston and the dowager."

I press my palms against my cheeks. "I hope I did the right thing."

Deep lines are marked in his forehead. "Is there a reason for me to be concerned?"

"Langston isn't going back to Columbia." When Will raises his eyebrows, I quickly continue, "He will be going back to school. He was navigating too much racism at Columbia."

I begin what feels like a recitation, explaining Langston's college experience, which is, of course, familiar to Will. Then I tell him about Charlotte. "I thought it was the perfect pairing. Langston's a restless writer, and she's a wealthy widow who doesn't want to spend her time sipping tea. She wants to make a difference."

"It seems she already has. Langston's tuxedo . . . I don't own a dinner jacket like that."

"It's not just clothes. He now has an apartment on 127th Street. Charlotte has kept her word. I'm glad about that part."

"And the other part?"

"I'm a bit concerned about who she is. My mother calls her eccentric. I say she's as mad as a hatter."

Will's head falls back, and he laughs so loud. I join him, and in that moment, the heaviness lifts. We are the friends we once were. Then I tell Will about Charlotte's infatuation with the dead.

At points, he laughs. Other times, he shakes his head. At the end, his forehead is creased with concern. "Watch Langston closely, Jess. He's one of our gifted ones, and he'll be safe as long as he remains under your guidance."

I nod. "I care about all of the young men and women I'm working with. They all feel like my children, but Langston is special."

"He is." His tone softens. "And are you aware how special you are?" He reaches into his pocket and pulls out a clipping. I freeze. The last time Will did this at the Cullens' home, chaos ensued.

He places the magazine clipping on the table, and at once, I recognize my poem—"La Vie C'est la Vie"—I'd published it in this month's issue of *The Crisis*.

"Jess . . ." I glance up. "Is this . . . about us?"

"It's a poem" is how I choose to respond.

"And it's very good. Except . . ."

"It's just words, Will."

At first he nods, but then he shakes his head. "Nothing a writer writes is just words. There's an intention behind every line."

I suck in air. I cannot debate the truth.

"These words," he begins again, "remind me of us together."

Still, I say nothing.

"It's the last line, Jess."

I don't have to look down to recall my words: *I wish that I were dead.*

I allow a few seconds to pass before I look at Will. "You're correct. Every word has meaning. And this means that I was being very dramatic."

"So this is not about us?"

I shake my head, but that only makes Will sigh. "I never wanted to see words like this pour out of you because of me."

"I'm a poet. I write about all experiences, not only those of my life. And everything I write is not about you."

"This is," he says, as if he knows the truth.

I only shrug.

"Can we talk about it?"

"About what?"

"About us. I miss you, Jess."

No! I scream inside.

"And from what you wrote here, I know you miss me, too."

"I don't, Will," I say, hoping my steel heart won't crack from the way it slams in my chest. "I did miss you in the beginning. But I don't anymore, and I'm grateful for that, just as I'm grateful that we can be friends."

"All right." His tone is filled with resignation. "If that's what you want."

I exhale.

"But first, there are things you must understand. Jess, you've always had a singular place in my heart. And even if you go away, my feelings for you never will."

I can't help myself when I say, "How can you say that when . . ." I draw back the words I'm about to speak.

He frowns. "When what?"

I ponder whether I want to have this conversation, then decide that if Will and I are to have a new beginning as friends, our ending as lovers must be resolved. "When you've been involved with other women."

He nods slowly. "I thought I explained this to you years ago. I told you, I have other desires."

I sense that one day, I will look back on this moment and wish that I'd thanked Will for the dinner invitation and then just walked away. However, I'm not capable of that action in this moment. "You did speak to me about this, but you said you needed your wife . . . and you needed me. I didn't understand there would be others." When he remains silent, I say, "Are you involved with Georgia?" not certain why I ask that question again.

"What would you have wanted me to say if anyone asked about you and me?" Before I can respond, he continues, "I would never confirm or deny my relationship with any woman who is not my wife. I wouldn't do it to you or anyone else."

I'm pained once again by his words. But why? My steel heart should be completely impervious to Will. It matters not who is entangled with whom.

"However," he continues, "you cannot assume the answer is in the affirmative. All you need to know is the depth of my feelings for you is unparalleled. Unlike anything I've ever felt for anyone." He reaches for my hand and, God help me, I don't back away. "I've told you so often, another time, a different place . . . but I cannot change the past, nor can I change who I am. But I can do everything to make life joyful for us in the present."

He threads his fingers through mine, and my mind screeches! My heart . . . which is steel . . . has stopped beating.

"I miss you, Jess," he says softly. "I've never missed anyone the way I miss you."

I shake my head, because I've come so far and today *has to be* the ending.

"And I need you."

No!

I tug my hand away from his, but just as quickly, he pulls me back. "Come with me."

No! is what I want to say. But my heart—I never knew that steel could crack.

"Please."

In my mind, I scream at him to go away, stay away.

"Jess."

"No!" Finally, I find my voice.

He stands, and I remain in my chair. But then, as if I hadn't spoken, he reaches back for me. My cracked steel heart is drawn to him, as if to a magnet. I want to fight, but I am no match for the force that draws me inexorably to this man.

So I do what I've always done—I stand, too. And I follow Will, even as I know it is impossible for this to end well for me.

CHAPTER 45

WEDNESDAY, SEPTEMBER 20, 1922

Days ago, I narrowed the selection down to these three photographs across my desk. Yet I still struggle to choose the sweet baby who will appear on the cover of the first children's issue of *The Crisis* since we shuttered the *Brownies' Book*.

"I've been waiting for you."

I smile before I glance up. Will stands in my doorway. It is his eyes that draw me, wild with lust and longing.

"Waiting for me? I've been in the office since before eight this morning."

He nods. "I know. Meetings have kept me from even stealing a glimpse of you."

The sweetest words.

This is how it's been for the last two months. Will and I have dwelled in our little corner of paradise. He is once again the attentive and loving man I'd given my whole heart to back in 1920.

And God help me, like before, my heart is bare to him. In a single night, he'd stripped any remnants of the steel away. However, although our time together has been glorious, I'm treading lightly. Amid my unending love for him are my persistent doubts. So I remain measured and guarded . . . always.

"Are those the photographs for the children's edition?"

"Yes. I've narrowed it down to three, but I'm grappling with which to choose."

"Would you mind if I looked at them with you?"

It is a curious request, but I guess Will is walking softly, too.

"I would love that," I say. "I'm inclined toward one in particular."

He stands behind me, leaning over my shoulder. Anyone passing my office would believe only that Will and I are studying photographs. No one would notice the way my breath quickens or hear my heart's pulse in my ears.

I strain to center my focus. "Does any one of these babies stand out to you?"

The heat of his breath warms my neck. "They're all so . . . beautiful." That word lingers for a moment. "However . . . I have a preference. Do you want to know which?"

Without glancing back, I say, "Only if you agree with me."

His hand slips to my shoulder. It is becoming beyond my ability to keep my attention on the photographs. "This is what we'll do," he whispers. "On the count of three, we'll point to our choice." He counts. "One . . ." He caresses my shoulder. "Two . . ." His lips graze my ear. "Three . . ."

I am relieved when he snatches his hand away . . . until he points to the same picture and his hand covers mine.

We laugh.

"Who is that?"

"Valdora Turner. I love this picture because she's not even two, yet so proper and confident."

Will steps away, setting me free to breathe. "I imagine you were very much the same at two." He reaches for me once again, but this time, I pull back.

In the last year, the rumors have quieted. The anniversary party,

Will's travels, and of course our estrangement are the reasons for this. I do not wish to stir up new whispers.

The rap on my door catches our attention. "Langston!"

He greets me, then turns to Will. As the two men chitchat, I study Langston. It has been only three months, but he is quite the cultured young man now. Today, he wears another expensive suit with brown suspenders that match the color of his striped necktie. Absent is the book strap he once carried. Now he holds a leather briefcase.

When Will says, "I will leave you two to your meeting," Langston settles in the chair beside me.

"I'm so glad you came by. You must tell me everything that's happening with you."

"Honestly, Jessie, it's been a real jamboree," he says with so much joy. "When Godmother said she wanted to be my patron, she—"

I hold up my hands. "Godmother?"

With an unabashed grin, he shakes his head. "Never repeat that."

"You call her Godmother?"

"That's how she wants to be addressed by all of her godchildren."

"Godmother? Godchildren?" I massage my temples.

"It's not nefarious. Just one of the little idiosyncrasies that Godmother . . . Charlotte has. This is how she expresses her affection and how she wants us to express our affection for her, although we're never to call her Godmother in public. In fact, when we're out without her, she doesn't want her name mentioned."

I reflect on that for a moment. "I respect Charlotte for that. She's not doing this to receive adulation and praise. Although, how can she keep what she's doing hush-hush when the two of you are so very public? Everyone sees you together everywhere."

"That's all she asks of me. To escort her to these events. Although when Alain comes to New York, he takes over that role."

"At least you're not committed to her every night."

"I wouldn't mind if I were. I enjoy Charlotte. Her age aside, we have a lot in common. She loves to read. She loves music and art and the theater—everything that's important to me. And we're not out every night. Sometimes, she serves what feel like ten-course dinners in her penthouse, and afterward, I read her my poetry or excerpts from my novel."

"You give her your time and private readings."

"And for that, I receive an open checkbook." His tone is filled with incredulity. "From my apartment, to shopping at stores like Bergdorf Goodman and a new one just for men—have you heard of Brooks Brothers on Madison Avenue?" I shake my head. "Most of these places wouldn't allow me to peek through their windows. However, when I'm with Charlotte, not only are the doors open, white folks are suddenly interested in my writings."

"That could be very good for you."

"I've never had access to this level of money or influence, but it's more than the cash. Charlotte saved my life." When I gasp, he holds up his hand. "Not literally. She's saved my life in that now, I'm living. I wasn't living before, Jessie. I was performing the daily tasks of life, but now, I'm breathing because I'm writing."

I reach for his hand. "As long as it's working, I'm delighted."

"It's working for me and Alain, and Charlotte wants to help others. She believes she was chosen to lift up the primitives, as she sometimes slips and calls us."

I wince. "You and I never discussed some of her . . . beliefs. Some of her language offended me."

"It's taken some adjustment. Especially when she told me to maintain my primitive purity."

"What does that mean?"

"She says I'm close to the earth." He shrugs. "Perhaps she knows that I love walking around barefoot at home, I don't know. I don't even think Charlotte can define that. She's just fascinated with Negroes, and Harlem is her playground. She wants to dine where Negroes dine. She wants to listen to what she calls Negro music. I indulge her fantasies because I am grateful to her. I'll let it roll until . . ."

He stops, as if he's searching for the right word. But then, when he doesn't continue, I say, "Until?"

He stands and pushes his hands deep into his pockets. The joy wanes from his countenance and his voice. "There will be a time when this bill comes due. And I'm not certain how I'll respond."

I squint, not understanding. "She wants you to repay her the money?"

"Oh, no. It won't be money that she wants." The confident young man who strolled into my office minutes before is gone. In his place is the brooding Langston I'd first met.

"If not money, what do you think she wants?"

He doesn't hesitate. "She wants my soul."

"Langston!" His words send an icy shock through me.

"In the past when I shared my poetry with Charlotte, she'd call me her brilliant precious brown boy." He laughs, but gone is his mirth. "In the last few weeks, she's become more critical. And not in the way you edit or encourage me to think deeper. She believes Negroes are creatively superior to whites because we're closer to the earth. And she wants me to write that way."

This sounds like the same gibberish she shared with Maman and me.

"She wants my writing to celebrate not only being a Negro but my primitive nature. And she's the decider of what that celebration should be."

"She's telling you what to write?"

"Not the exact words, but the themes. The other day I read her a poem I'd written about Africa. I thought it was the essence of the purity and primitiveness that she wanted. But when I finished reading it, Charlotte had quite a bee in her bonnet."

Reaching for his briefcase, he hands me a typed page.

I read aloud:

> So long,
> So far away
> Is Africa.

I read through the twenty-four lines and, as always, my first thought is—what beauty. I feel Langston's angst with the continent—his longing to know, yet his distance because of what he doesn't know. I've felt the same dichotomy, equal measures of pining and hesitancy for this place where my ancestry began, but I feel no connection.

"This is lovely."

"Charlotte didn't appreciate my ambivalence. She only wants to celebrate the Motherland. But, Jessie, I cannot write to other people's hearts. You've taught me to reach inside my own, and I'm still learning to do that."

"Your best work will always come from deep inside. So trust yourself. Write from the heart God has given to you."

"But after all that Charlotte has done . . ." His voice quivers.

"She cannot have your soul. That belongs to God." I allow those words to settle before I continue, "This is what I believe. Charlotte is a gift. However, like most gifts, there may come a day when you will outgrow it. And when that day comes, you will be fine. Because no matter what happens with Charlotte, your *gift* of writing is everlasting."

He takes a deep breath, and when he releases it, his lips curve into a smile.

CHAPTER 46

MONDAY, JANUARY 8, 1923

The aroma of fresh-brewed coffee, the haze of cigarette smoke, the chatter, and the laughter all intermingle in the Greenwich Village diner. The space is already half-filled when I enter, mostly with New York University students, young men, many still in their overcoats and matching caps, several wearing fedoras. More than a few young women are among them, although I am not surprised. NYU has welcomed women.

Pressing through the students, I find a table in the back and choose the chair facing the door. This lunch is meant to be informal, just an editor saying hello to one of her writers. In truth, I want to see Countee here, in this environment. Perhaps if I'd done this with Langston, he'd still be at Columbia.

My satchel is heavy with typed pages of my novel, but I pull out the *New York Times*. I peruse the pages until a headline on page four stops me cold:

LAST NEGRO HOMES RAZED IN ROSEWOOD

It feels like an ax is beating in my chest as I read the story of how twelve homes, the only houses remaining after last week's riot, were burned to the ground.

The first sentence of the third paragraph—*Each home was burned deliberately as the crowd of about 150 men looked on*—makes me close the newspaper. The loathing toward Negroes is staggering. When is this going to stop? Or perhaps the better question isn't when, but whether it will ever end.

"Jessie!"

I glance up and Countee rushes toward me. Joy emanates from beyond his face; his entire being glows. I set aside the newspaper and smile. "Look at you," I say after giving him a hug.

Countee removes his newsboy cap and overcoat. In my mind, he is still the shy sixteen-year-old. However, the young man before me is quite the sophisticated collegian.

"I'm sorry I'm late. I found myself a bit behind the clock when one of my professors stopped me as I was leaving the lecture hall."

"Oh?" Immediately, I envisage a white man accosting Countee in a corner and accusing him of some fabricated infraction.

I brace myself for the story, but when Countee's grin grows wider, I'm nonplussed.

"My professor asked me to submit a piece to the Witter Bynner undergraduate poetry contest."

"Your professor suggested this?"

His smile vanishes. "Yes. Why? You don't think—"

Before he can say more, I hold up my hand. "No. You definitely should. You must. I wish I'd been the one to encourage you to enter." After just two minutes, there is no mistaking that Countee's experience is very different from Langston's, and I scold myself for my negative assumption. "That's a prestigious award."

"I know. Of course, I don't expect to win."

"Don't say that."

"Do you know how many submissions there will be? Hundreds!

College students from all over the country will be competing for this distinction."

"Indeed. And you're one of the best. I'm overjoyed that your professor suggested this."

Countee and I move to the order line, and as we wait, we chitchat about his college experiences—all good—thus far. At the counter, Countee orders a liverwurst sandwich, while I ask for a Cuban. Minutes later, we are back at the table, and I return our conversation to the contest. "Have you decided whether you're going to submit something new or something you've already written?"

"Definitely something new. I have the theme, and walking over here, I've already conjured up a few lines in my head. I'll get working on it tonight to give myself enough time."

"Perfect. We will need extra time for the edits and—"

"Jessie—" He interrupts me and presses his hands together as if he's going to say a prayer. "I don't want you to edit this."

"All right," I say slowly.

"I love working with you. However, what kind of competition will it be if Jessie Redmon Fauset edits my work?" He laughs. "It won't be equitable at all."

"Well, if you change your mind, I am here."

He points his finger at me. "This only applies to this poem. I still need my editor for everything published in *The Crisis.*"

Sitting here with Countee, I feel jubilant, and we turn to his classes. He's made a couple of friends, and his teachers are supportive—for the most part. "There are a few who are ambivalent toward me. But it's going well. That's what I told Langston when we had dinner last week—"

"I didn't know the two of you were getting together."

"We have dinner regularly. He keeps his eyes on me because of what he went through. Just like you're doing today."

"I . . . that's not why . . ."

"Was I supposed to believe you just happened to have a business meeting on this campus?" He laughs, but then, once again, he's serious.

"I appreciate your concern, but my experience is very different from Langston's. I wish he'd stayed at Columbia, or perhaps even transferred here. However, I'm fine."

"Just know, any support you need, I'm here."

"I wish . . . Langston understood he has support, too." He pauses, as if he's considering whether to share his next thought. Finally, "I don't want to reveal any confidences; however, you should know there's a rich lady sponsoring Langston."

"I introduced him to Charlotte."

"Oh!" he exclaims. "I was under the impression he'd met her through Alain Locke. It was Alain who suggested Langston reach out to me about Charlotte. She read my poem in the Christmas issue of *The Crisis* and has requested a meeting. She wants me to turn my attention completely to writing."

"She's not talking about you leaving school, is she?"

He shrugs. "I didn't ask Langston too many questions, because I'm not interested."

"Good, because first and foremost, you must get this degree."

"Leaving NYU is off the table. However, there's more to that woman's offer that I find disconcerting. My father has a saying: 'A man's mouth follows his money.' Everything may be well for now, but, Jessie, she'll want something in return for all she's done."

I recall Langston's words: *She wants my soul.*

"Perhaps you should voice your concerns to Langston."

"I wanted your thoughts first, but I certainly will." He pauses. "Now, can I ask you something?"

"Of course," I say, taking a sip of my Coca-Cola.

"My father and I were talking about you possibly becoming the editor of *The Crisis*."

I almost spew out my soda. "What?"

"I don't mean to upset you."

"No," I wave my hand. "I'm just surprised. Go on."

"I was telling my dad how much I've learned from you, and he said, if Dr. Du Bois was smart, he'd make you the editor of *The Crisis*. And I agree." Countee shrugs. "Everyone thinks of you as the editor anyway. Would you be interested in that?"

I inhale, knowing that whatever I say, Countee will repeat to his father. I take a few moments, then: "What I'm most interested in is the success of *The Crisis*. So wherever I'm needed, I'm prepared to step into that role."

"That sounds like a hard 'Yes, I'm interested' to me." Countee laughs, but I don't utter another word. He says, "I'm going to get another Coca-Cola, do you want one?"

"No." I push my soda aside. "I've had enough." As I watch Countee step to the counter, I can scarcely contain my excitement. It seems I'm not the only one who can see my dream.

CHAPTER 47

WEDNESDAY, MAY 9, 1923

I yawn as the taxicab splutters from the curb at Union Station in Washington, DC.

"Still sleepy?" Will laughs. "You dozed off for the entire train ride."

"We had such an early start." I rest my head on his shoulder. "But I'm glad I'm here." I take in the sight of the Capitol before the car rounds the corner. "And I'm particularly thankful I'm here with you."

Will squeezes my hand. "Having Dunbar High School ask you to return to speak to the students is remarkable. And that they want you to discuss your time at *The Crisis* is excellent. Perhaps I'll even say a word or two, if you'll allow me."

"As long as I speak first, because once you begin, no one will be interested in me."

"That's not true," he says, although the chuckle in his tone tells me he agrees.

As we drive up Seventh Street, passing homes and storefronts that are familiar, it's impossible to believe that only four years have passed since I left the District of Columbia. The thrill of returning to Dunbar is augmented by Will being by my side. As my colleague, of course.

Our car eases to a stop in front of the hotel, and the car door is opened by a young man, who's been awaiting our arrival.

"Mr. James Du Bois," Will says, greeting the young man the way he always did.

"Good morning, Dr. Du Bois. Welcome to the Whitelaw Hotel." Then, James turns to me. "And you, too, Miss Fauset. I hope you're well."

"I am."

As James carries both valises, I follow as he and Will chat, the way they have for all these years. It was about five years ago, while Will and I were attending a conference here, when we first met James and his brother, who'd just started working at the Whitelaw. When Will discovered that he and the boys shared the same surname, he'd taken a special interest in them.

As we approach the front desk, Will asks, "How's your brother?"

James beams. "Chip will be completing his first year at Harvard in just a few weeks."

"I am so very proud of him," Will says. "And you, as well. I understand you're moving up here at the Whitelaw."

"Yes, sir," James says, his chest expanding a bit.

James escorts us through our check-in, then whisks us upstairs. I'm grateful for the efficiency. In just an hour, I'm due to arrive at Dunbar.

"I'm going to freshen up. Then we should leave straightaway."

The sharp knock on the door makes me pause. When Will answers, the young man says, "Dr. Du Bois, you have a call at the front desk."

I gesture for Will to go ahead. But when I return to the bedroom minutes later, Will is pacing.

"What's wrong?" My first thought is the call he received had come from his wife. Yolande recently had an appendectomy.

"Jess, I'm not going to be able to accompany you this afternoon."

"Do you have to return to New York?"

He responds by glancing away, and my heart tumbles to my feet.

Will says, "There's something I must attend to here in Washington."

Georgia! I want to shriek, ask him why he traveled more than two hundred miles just to do this to me.

But I stifle my words and suppress the torrent of my emotions. Even behind a closed door with a married man en route to a rendezvous with a married woman—for me, it must be proper decorum at all times.

"I'll go downstairs with you," he says as I gather my pocketbook.

I say nothing as we exit the room and then stroll through the lobby. When the taxicab arrives, Will escorts me to the curb. "We'll have dinner together."

I stare at him and wish to God my heart didn't ache. I say, "Don't make any promises you can't keep," then hasten into the car.

As the cabbie maneuvers into the street, I keep my eyes straight ahead and blink back every tear. In the months since our reconciliation, Will made me feel as if I were the center of his affection. My weakened resolve led me to forget one crucial truth—I am but one of Will's many desires.

Relief! That is what I feel when I return to the hotel. The discombobulation that has plagued me from the moment Will told me he had another engagement lingers. But I persisted through my presentation and endured the subsequent faculty luncheon.

It is not yet two o'clock, and I haven't the faintest notion when Will will return. However, I have no desire to idle away my time. Instead, I reach for the fifty typed pages of my novel that I brought along. How rare is it for me to find myself away from work and home with so many spare hours before me?

I retreat to the bed and lay the pages on my lap. This is a bright spot in an otherwise dismal day. After a decade of starts and stops, the end of my novel is near. However, my excitement is tempered by anxiety. A story isn't a novel without an ending.

Throughout the book, Joanna has scoffed at the idea of forsaking her ambition for love. Yet now I'm conflicted—should Joanna find success and contentment in the independence she's sought so fiercely? Or should I satisfy the readers and deliver the traditional happy ending, having her choose a life with Peter?

I'm bewildered by this struggle. From the beginning, I've been certain Joanna would continue her quest for success, leaving Peter and all thoughts of love behind.

However, now I wonder—is this tussle in shaping Joanna's fate a creative conflict or a personal one?

Setting the pages aside, I recline and reflect on my question. This isn't the first time that, as I've delved deeper into my novel, it feels as if my life and Joanna's are converging. Like my protagonist, I've found tremendous fulfillment in my career. And I know my finest professional hours are before me. But will I be satisfied if this alone is my happy ending?

Will and I will never settle into a life of bliss, and prior to my arrival in New York, I had no such illusions or desire. But then came that moment when I surrendered my heart. And now I rue that day.

Would this be a struggle if I had forever excluded love from the balance of our relationship?

That is my last thought.

Until . . .

His lips on my forehead make me stir. My eyes flutter open, and it takes a few seconds for my vision to clear—there is Will before me.

He strokes the side of my face, and unwillingly I shudder. I push myself up on the bed. "What time is it?"

"A bit after six."

I'm startled that so much time has passed. "I cannot believe I slept so long."

"You were tired from our early start. How was your day at Dunbar?"

"It was fine." After a pause, I ask, "How was your . . ." I stop, not knowing what to ask.

He draws his hand away, then stands and loosens his tie. "It's been a long day."

I cross my arms as he removes his jacket. I have so many questions. But, I already know, there will be no answers from Will.

"Several students wanted to know what it was like to work with W. E. B. Du Bois."

He faces me with a small smile. "I'm afraid to ask for your response."

"I said working with you fills all my days with joy."

He laughs and returns to the bed. This time, when he kisses my forehead, his lips linger. "Jess, my Jess." He sighs. "Another time, a different place." His eyes search mine before he pulls back and settles on the other side of the bed.

"Were you working on your manuscript?" he asks as he lifts the papers.

"Yes, I'm grappling with the ending."

He grins. "The ending . . . you're so close."

"I just don't know how I want Joanna's storyline to conclude."

He slides closer to me. "Do you want to talk it through?"

"Of course. I've always valued your thoughts. I'm trying to determine if Joanna will make the choice to get married."

He nods, pensive for a moment. "Hasn't she spent the entire novel fighting against that? Pursuing a career and success above all else?" He looks straight at me. "Even above love?"

"She has. But wouldn't it be an interesting development if she were to decide that success alone isn't enough? That perhaps love is the greatest achievement. As long as it is requited love."

"That would be an unpredictable ending." He looks away when he adds, "Not at all what I would have expected."

"What would you expect?"

"I think a fitting conclusion would be Joanna achieving her intended goal. She should find the success she's craved."

"Even success without love?"

He twists his body so he squarely faces me. "Joanna . . ." He pauses as if he wants her name to hover between us. "Made her choice long ago."

The lines in this conversation have blurred—is he speaking of the choice I made to be with him, knowing there would never be anything greater than what we share in this moment, in this bed? And even this will not last.

Another time . . . a different place.

He's more joyful when he says, "Whatever you decide, this will be a wonderful story. Educated colored characters with a strong lineage, striving and achieving."

How effortless it is for him to move away from a discussion of us.

"Thank you for your advice." I set the pages aside on the bedside table.

He says, *"De rien,"* and for the first time since he entered the room, I smile. He pulls me closer, and I rest my head on his chest.

"Oh!" he says suddenly. "Have you decided on a title?"

I have not. But as I lift my head and study Will, a mosaic of all our days together plays like a montage in my mind. I think about all the years and all the love we have shared. I recall our tears of laughter and the ones that ensued from pain.

Suddenly, there it is. A title. One that exquisitely describes this relationship between W. E. B. Du Bois and Jessie Redmon Fauset.

"I may not have the proper ending, but I do have a title."

"Finally!" he exclaims. "What is it?" His eyes shimmer with anticipation.

"There Is Confusion."

CHAPTER 48

FRIDAY, AUGUST 10, 1923

onjour," I say when I open the door to Countee, and right away, I'm astonished to see him standing with a pretty young woman, conservatively dressed in a short-sleeved Peter Pan–collared blouse and navy skirt. More than her ankle socks and loafers, it is the brilliance of her smile that completes her ensemble. "Bienvenue," I welcome them.

"Bonsoir, Jessie. *Merci de nous avoir invités*," Countee responds, then says, "Jessie, this is Gwendolyn Bennett. She's a student at Columbia and also a poet. A very good one." To Gwendolyn, he says, "I'd like to introduce you to Jessie Redmon Fauset, the—"

Before Countee finishes, Gwendolyn stretches her hand toward me. "Miss Fauset, I've been reading *The Crisis* since I was a little girl, and I've been hoping for the opportunity to meet you. The only thing is—" She stops and looks from me to Countee. "I don't speak French. After I say bonjour, don't expect too much more until I bid you au revoir."

We all laugh. "It's fine, Gwendolyn. I'm glad to have you here," I say, just as my mother enters the parlor.

She welcomes Countee, and as he introduces her to Gwendolyn, I return to the door when I hear another knock. This time, I greet the guest I most want to see.

"Georgia," I say with the biggest smile I can manage. "I'm glad you came."

"I love these literary salons, and when I received your lovely note, I couldn't resist my second invitation to your home."

"Georgia," Maman welcomes her, and draws Georgia away from me. I'm glad it's Maman and not my sister who greets Georgia. Since I do not discuss Will with my mother, she isn't aware that Georgia and I may be involved with the same man.

I return my attention to the front door and greet James and his wife, Grace, followed by Walter and his wife, Gladys. Right behind the Whites are several of the female authors (and their husbands) who have published with me time and again in *The Crisis*.

The chatter and laugher are already rising throughout the room when I turn to the door once again.

"Nella!" I hug my friend. "I wasn't certain you'd be able to make it this evening."

"Elmer is on a last-minute trip, so I hope you don't mind a woman attending your salon alone."

I wave her words away. "How silly. You're always welcome, with or without Elmer. It's such a foolish notion to question an unescorted woman. No one ever questions a single man. I'm never concerned when I attend an event alone."

Nella laughs. "Now you're the silly one. When are you ever alone? In fact, where is your ever-present escort?" She makes a show of standing on her toes and glancing over my shoulder. "Is that Georgia?" she whispers.

"Yes, it's always great when we can gather as writers."

"Hmm . . ." she hums. "All these years and I still wonder about her and W. E. B. Let me say hello to her before he arrives."

She saunters away before I can tell her that Will won't be here; he's never received an invitation to my home.

Just as I move to close the door, someone edges their foot over the threshold. I yank the door open, aghast that I may have injured a guest.

"My goodness!" My mouth opens wide in surprise. "Langston!"

I am so delighted to see him—especially sans Charlotte.

"I hope you don't mind me just blowing in, Jessie."

"Pas du tout!"

"I didn't want to miss this first literary gathering at the home of the woman who is making me so well known."

"You're doing that on your own. I would have invited you, but I wasn't certain you could attend without Charlotte. I like her"—I glance around at my guests—"but having her here would have changed the conversation."

He laughs. "She's in Connecticut for the week."

"Then we must have dinner every evening to make up for all of our lost meals. It's been impossible to see you in this last year." I loop my arm through his. "So you're doing well?"

"I'm flying high."

Indeed! Langston looks especially dapper this evening. From the top of his wavy hair to the spit shine of his shoes—Charlotte continues to keep her word. "Still working on your novel?"

"Absolument!" he says, just as Countee and Gwendolyn approach.

I leave the trio to chitchat, and then scan the parlor. Georgia is across the room, still in the hands of Nella. I will bide my time.

I mingle, pausing to join my friends, gathered in small groups, some sitting, others standing.

"*Birthright* continues to sell well," Walter White tells James Weldon Johnson.

I say, "That's impossible to believe." The three of us shake our heads.

James says, "Just shows there's a hunger for these novels."

"Well, I finished mine," Walter offers.

"Really?" After reading *Birthright*, Walter, who has been a prolific writer of political editorials, announced that he was going to try his hand at fiction.

With pride shining on his face, Walter says, "I finished my novel in two weeks."

I take a long sip of my juice, then eke out a smile. "Congratulations!" How can anyone write a novel so quickly? There are times when it takes me two weeks to edit fourteen lines of a poem.

I move to join Langston and Mary-Helen. "That's the name of the play," Langston says. *"All God's Chillun Got Wings."*

Mary-Helen recounts their discussion for me. "Eugene O'Neill's new play is the story of a mixed-race marriage—a colored man and a white woman."

"Oh," I say. "I wonder how that will fare."

"That alone is riveting. However, it's about the couple's marital troubles . . . and it's *not* the husband who's mistreating the wife. He hopes to get Paul Robeson in that role."

When I hear Georgia's laughter, I excuse myself once again. With my eye on Georgia and Nella, I pause to thank Countee for introducing me to Gwendolyn, and I ask her to send me some of her work as soon as she can. Then I am two steps away from Georgia when Maman stops me. "Would you mind setting out the food? I'll be there in a few minutes to help you."

"Of course. You stay here, I can manage."

I smile at Georgia and Nella as I pass the two, deep in conversation.

When I open the icebox, I cannot fathom how Maman has stuffed so many platters inside. I begin with the *gougères*. Balancing the platter, I spin around. "Oh!" I exclaim.

"My apologies," Georgia says. "I saw you come into the kitchen and wondered if you needed help."

"Oh, no. Thank you for offering, but I'm fine."

"Please, Jessie," she whispers conspiratorially. "I enjoy Nella, but I always feel as if I'm being interrogated when I'm with her." She laughs.

"My friend is just curious. About everything and everyone."

"That's how writers should be, I suppose."

"And you're an acclaimed poet. Who wouldn't want to get to know you better?" I set the platter on the table, then return to the icebox, this time handing Georgia the Waldorf salad. "In fact, I was in Washington, DC, recently, and I wished I'd had an opportunity to spend some time with you. We're always discussing work, one new poem or another. We never have a chance to chitchat."

"I wish I'd known. My husband and I would have invited you to our home for dinner. Were you there on business?"

"I was invited to speak at Dunbar High School."

"Oh, yes!" She nods. "W. E. B. did mention that."

My heart flutters.

"That must have been delightful and gratifying for you."

"It was. So . . . Will told you I was speaking there?"

Her voice is soft and sweet when she says, "You call him Will. I've only heard his wife address him that way."

I flinch when I realize my slip. "Sometimes I call him Will. Most of the time, I call him W. E. B., as you do."

Her lips curl into a half smile. "Oh, I don't always call him W. E. B. I have other names for him. I'm certain we all do."

We all do?

"So when did W. E. B. mention my speaking engagement?" I ask as I hand her the platter of deviled eggs. When I take the cucumber and cream cheese finger sandwiches out, I close the icebox.

After setting down the tray, Georgia glances up toward the heavens, as if she is trying to recall. "A few weeks ago, although I can't pinpoint it exactly. Keeping track of where I go and who I speak to daily is quite challenging."

"Were you and W. E. B. at an event when he told you?"

She squints. "Jessie, you're beginning to sound like Nella."

"Like I said, you're a fascinating woman."

"Is it that or . . . is there something you want to know?"

I take a breath. "All right. I trust we can be candid with each other."

"Certainly."

I glance over Georgia's shoulder, wanting to be sure no one is within eavesdropping distance. Still, I whisper. "Are you involved with W. E. B.?"

She laughs. "Now, that isn't a question I expected from *you.*"

There are so many innuendos . . . in her tone, in those words, and in the fact that she hasn't answered. I fold my arms and arch my eyebrows, waiting for her to respond to my question.

"This is a conversation you should be having with W. E. B."

"I'd much prefer to have it with you."

"Oh, Jessie." She titters. "I would never answer that question, not even from a friend. Just like you wouldn't respond if I asked you the same."

My head rears back. She smiles as if delighted by my reaction.

"I will say this, Jessie. Everyone has a role in W. E. B.'s life. His wife, his daughter, his friends, both men and women. We all have our proper roles. We all know our places. And I certainly know mine. Perhaps you have these questions because you aren't certain of yours." When all I do is blink, she asks, "Are we finished?"

"Yes," I say, once again folding my arms, this time to hide my trembling.

"I'm pleased we had this little chat. Now you and I can truly be friends without all the questions between us." She spins around and leaves me alone.

I move to the edge of the kitchen and watch Georgia as she returns to where she'd been sitting next to Nella. I guess after speaking with me, she can manage my friend.

It takes me a few minutes to gather myself, and then, for the rest of the evening, I mingle with my guests as we speak of all things literary. We congratulate Countee on entering the Witter Bynner undergraduate poetry contest, and then both Countee and Gwendolyn recite a poem. Walter reads from his upcoming book, *The Fire in the Flint*, and then Nella stands.

"I've been working on this for a while, and I'd like to share the opening of *Quicksand.*" When she takes a breath, I give her an encouraging nod. "Helga Crane sat alone in her room, which, in that hour, was in soft gloom."

I am so proud as Nella reads the first pages of Helga's story, the mixed-race woman in search of a community.

At the end of the evening, when Georgia stands before me and says, "Jessie, I cannot recall when I've had a lovelier evening," I open my arms and embrace her.

After all, what else am I supposed to do? Georgia has given me invaluable advice.

To find my proper role with Will.

CHAPTER 49

SUNDAY, DECEMBER 23, 1923

The Christmas tree is grand in front of the parlor's windows and illuminates the entirety of our apartment; I am mesmerized by the beauty of this season.

This is the first time Maman and I have had a tree. Our fifth Christmas, so it feels appropriate. This year, we will host my brothers and sisters, their husbands and wives, and my nieces and nephews. They are all making the trek to fill our home with joy.

Stepping back, I sit on the sofa, wanting to take in the splendor of my favorite holiday, my favorite season. And this, with all its milestones, could very well be my favorite year.

Yet, as I reflect, I am overcome with melancholy, even as victories abound in my life.

First, Countee and his second-place prize in the Witter Bynner undergraduate poetry contest. He has been applauded throughout Harlem and beyond. Even the *New York Times* had a front-page story of his win over more than seven hundred entrants. Then, of course, the literary world is still buzzing about Jean's novel *Cane*, a book he decided to finish writing after I published his poem in *The Crisis*. And in 1923 alone, Langston has published more than a dozen poems and stories.

One of the biggest blessings for me has been meeting Gwendolyn Bennett. She'd sent me a lovely poem, "Nocturne," and after just a little editing, I'd published it in the November issue:

> This cool night is strange
> Among midsummer days . . .
> Far frosts are caught
> In the moon's pale light,
> And sounds are distant laughter
> Chilled to crystal tears.

Yes, 1923 has been exceptional for my poets. And monumental for me with the completion of my novel. It had been an arduous task to pen the ending. Yet, once I'd written those last words, I'd been brimming with satisfaction and great expectations. Quickly, however, I discovered there was little hope on the horizon for a Negro novelist.

Despite my being the literary editor of *The Crisis*, the rejections for *There Is Confusion* arrived swiftly and did more than repudiate my work—they were repugnant. The letters didn't critique my writing; it was the characters the editors found offensive:

> *The behaviors and thought processes of your Negro characters are, quite frankly, above the abilities and aptitudes of Negroes.*

> *Our readers will not recognize nor identify with these colored characters who make decisions in a logical manner as if they are white.*

> *It is a stretch for readers to believe that these college-educated Negroes exist.*

I'd been more disgusted than disheartened to discover that the stereotypes of Negroes perpetuated throughout the decades had so damaged society, there was not an editor in New York who could envisage what I'd written.

Then, days before Thanksgiving, my hope soared when a publisher invited me to lunch.

Leaning back, I'm unable to suppress my smile as I recall that magnificent day.

'd just taken my first sip of tea when the gentleman approached.

"Miss Fauset."

I glanced up at the quite tall, very lean man, one of the founders of Boni & Liveright, a publishing company founded not long ago, in 1917. "Mr. Liveright."

He nodded before he sat across from me. "I apologize if I am a little late." He glanced at my teacup.

"Actually, I'm early. I wanted to be certain we had a table." I didn't mention that I wasn't going to chance being a moment late. "The Civic Club can get quite busy during the lunchtime hour."

"I appreciate that, Miss Fauset. And do you know what else I appreciate?" He didn't pause for me to respond. "I appreciated your letter and thoroughly enjoyed your manuscript."

I was pleased that Mr. Liveright had no intention of squandering our time with inconsequential conversation. He didn't even appear to wish to wait for lunch to be served. "Thank you," I said, not daring to hope.

"Before we discuss *There Is Confusion*, I'd like to know more about you."

His request was one I made as an editor at a first meeting. I wanted to know the heart of every writer, wanted to know their life story, which was often at the core of their writings.

I began by telling Mr. Liveright of my childhood, my education in Philadelphia, and my teaching credentials. When I started speaking about my years at *The Crisis*, Mr. Liveright held up his hand. "Like everyone else in New York, I'm aware of your work there. What you've accomplished at *The Crisis* is quite impressive. I'm pleased you're a magazine editor and not at a publishing house, or I might find myself in quite a competition with you."

Both of us laughed at that absurdity. It was almost an impossible feat for me to hold that position at *The Crisis*. Becoming an editor at a white publishing company was as likely as my squeezing a tube of blood from a stone.

"Your work as an editor . . . you brought us Jean Toomer. Are you aware we published him?"

"Of course. It's not often that a colored writer is published, so when it happens, we all rejoice."

He nodded. "We were quite pleased with Mr. Toomer's work. He certainly knows how to paint a picture with his pen." Then his smile faded. "There was one thing, however . . ."

I wasn't aware of any difficulties between Jean and Boni & Liveright.

Mr. Liveright said, "Mr. Toomer and I had quite a row regarding his biographical statement. One of the things I found most impressive about Mr. Toomer's book was that it was, in fact, written by a colored man, and we'd be the first to publish a work of this kind."

"We were all very excited about that."

"So were we . . . until I noticed that Mr. Toomer never mentioned his race. Of course, I assumed it was an oversight, but when I questioned him, he became outraged. So much so that he threatened to pull the book from publication if his race was ever mentioned."

Mr. Liveright sounded astonished; I, of course, was not. However, I would never disclose any conversation I'd had with Jean.

"I'm convinced *Cane* would have been a top seller if readers were aware the author was Negro. It would have been an anomaly and a novelty."

"An anomaly and a novelty only to you, Mr. Liveright," I said with a sharper tone than I intended. However, there was no reason to pause now. It was obvious Mr. Liveright wasn't here to discuss an opportunity for me. He thought I might assist him with Jean. So, I continued, "While you define Mr. Toomer's work as odd, I've been reading and writing those kinds of stories for many years. Perhaps Mr. Toomer's work wouldn't have seemed so unusual to you if, through the years, you'd taken the time to read more Negro writers."

His eyebrows raised an inch, and I expected him to stand, toss his napkin aside, and announce that this lunch—which hadn't yet started—was over. Instead, he smiled. "I only used the words 'anomaly' and 'novelty' because aside from being an editor, I am an innovator. Our company is unconventional. We've published authors that no one else would consider, including the Jewish writer Anzia Yezierska, who became a commercial success. We take pride in being bold. Some call us gamblers, I call us successful. So, my apologies if my words offended you."

I took a moment and a deep breath. "I am the one who must apologize, Mr. Liveright. I was responding to the notion that being a Negro will sell more books. The many rejections I've received made me doubt your words."

"Others have no foresight. I believe—no, rather, I *know* books like *Cane* and *There Is Confusion* are at the forefront of a new era. Once these books are published, more will follow that celebrate Negro life and Negro writers. So my first question for you, Miss Fauset . . . Do you have any concerns with being addressed as a—"

"No, Mr. Liveright," I responded before he finished. "I have always been proud of being the only Negro in my high school class and the valedictorian of my class. I have always been proud of being the first Negro female accepted at Cornell University. I am certainly proud of being the first Negro female to receive a Phi Beta Kappa key. So again, to answer your question, I want the world to know that *There Is Confusion* was written by a Negro woman."

Mr. Liveright's stare was so piercing, I was certain he saw the truth of my words engraved in my soul. "White Americans have never met anyone like you. So, Miss Fauset, how can Boni and Liveright best present you to the world?"

J essie!"

I blink against the sudden brightness in the room and glance up at Maman.

"Why were you sitting in the dark?"

I wipe my eyes and that memory away. "I was enjoying the quiet and the Christmas lights."

"If that is the case . . ." Maman clicks off the lamp, and the room darkens again, aglow with only the tree's lights.

When she sits next to me, I ask, "Did you have a good time with Mary-Helen?"

"I did. Ernestine joined us for dinner. Of course, we missed you, but everyone understood you were writing. We are all infinitely proud of you, Jessie."

When I only smile, Maman covers her hand with mine. "What has you so vexed, *ma chérie*? You've been pensive over the last weeks, when you should be jubilant. To have the opportunity to return to the Sorbonne is quite the achievement."

Ah, yes! Another accomplishment in 1923—an invitation to study at the Sorbonne once again, for six months this time.

"I am thrilled, Maman, even as I won't be able to accept."

"Have you discussed this with . . ." She pauses. "Have you discussed this at work?"

"It's not necessary. I'm managing so much at *The Crisis*, and then there's so much happening with . . ." I stop just before I say his name.

Many silent seconds pass before Maman completes my sentence. "Dr. Du Bois?"

In the last five years, there have been few times when my mother has mentioned Will's name, except in anger, and I wonder why she would do that now. Moreover, I wonder why I respond, "Yes, I'm reconsidering so much, and I've come to understand your disapproval. I've come to realize you were always right."

There is not a hint of triumph in her eyes, only sadness.

"Jessie, I have only wanted what God has planned for you. And Dr. Du Bois was not in His plan."

"I've never managed to adequately explain my feelings for him to anyone. Perhaps not even to myself. But, Maman, I have a bond with him that goes beyond . . ." I pause, then add, "He's helped me in ways that cannot be measured. So much of what I've achieved is because of you . . . and Will."

"You were so young, *ma chérie*. It is not uncommon for an older man to fill the many spaces left hollow by a father's death. He became your emotional crutch."

For the first time, it feels as if my mother understands, and I consider sharing more so that I can ask her advice. But I decide not to squander our time. She will tell me to walk away, and as much as I know that I must, I just cannot.

"I will pray for you," Maman says, already aware there is no more to say.

"I thank you for every time you whisper my name to God." Then I stand and pick up one of the many wrapped boxes already beneath the tree. "I was going to wait until Christmas." I click on the lamp. "But I want to give you this while it's just you and me."

With a huff, she accepts the box wrapped in emerald-green paper. "I always tell you children, Christmas isn't about me." Every year, with every gift, Maman utters the same words. Yet, although she pretends to be peeved, her face always glows with delight.

When she lifts the box's lid, she freezes. *"Ma chérie!"*

She cradles the manuscript—that I'd spent days copying on the mimeograph machine—as if it were a baby. "You finished your novel." She doesn't raise her eyes. "If your father were here, he'd be weeping with joy. He always believed in you."

I can envisage that: Papa on the sofa with Maman and me. Even now, I hear his words: *Little lamb, I'm so proud . . . I always believed.*

Maman says, "I didn't realize you were close to finishing."

"I wanted this to be a surprise."

She glances down at the title page once again. *"There Is Confusion,"* she reads. I exhale when all she says is, "I'm so very happy."

The title of my novel is more than just a perfect depiction of my relationship with Will. It is also a line in one of the poems Maman and I read together when I was sixteen. She'd said delving into "The Lotus-Eaters" by Alfred Lord Tennyson with me made it one of her favorites.

I'm fond of that poem as well, even with the haunting line *There* is *confusion worse than death* . . .

"I cannot wait to read this." Suddenly, Maman's back straightens. "So, what should we do now?" she asks sternly, then quickly answers her own question. "We must send to publishers. Perhaps Ernestine can assist. No, Charlotte."

"Maman, look at that front page." On the cover, not only had I typed the title, but in the bottom right-hand corner, I'd added:

To be published by Boni & Liveright
To be released March 1924

CHAPTER 50

TUESDAY, JANUARY 15, 1924

As we're led to our seats in the new nightclub, it is evident Will is up to some manner of mischief.

"Dr. Du Bois, I hope this table is satisfactory."

"Yes," Will says as we settle at the round table. "Will you let Mr. Henderson know I'd like to say hello?"

"Yes, sir!"

As the tuxedoed maître d' strolls away, I take in the elegance of Club Alabam, with its expansive dance floor in the center. Dozens of waiters amble about, adjusting the red-and-white-checkered cloths at the more than one hundred tables.

The nightclub is a lush oasis with all of its greenery: plush ivy vines that crisscross the ceiling, and a twelve-foot palm tree on the left side of the room. It feels like an Eden, but there is one thing missing—other guests.

"Will, why are we here?"

"I told you. I was invited by the owner for the grand opening."

"I mean, why are we here right now? When the doors haven't opened?"

"I told the club manager I needed privacy before the show, and he suggested we arrive early."

This is utterly bewildering. "This is not private."

"It's private enough to give you this." From his briefcase and with a flourish, he whips out a copy of *The Crisis*. My frown deepens when he says, "This is the February issue."

Now I'm even more nonplussed. "I didn't expect copies until tomorrow."

"You will be getting yours then. This is mine."

Those words make me shudder. Why had copies been delivered to Will? Was he usurping my responsibilities? "Is this a new policy?" I ask, concealing my feelings beneath an air of nonchalance.

"No, I asked for copies earlier, just for this month. I want you to read through it."

"Right here? You want to conduct business in the middle of an empty New York City nightclub?"

He gives me a boyish grin. "My aim is to always surprise you."

I am not amused. "I've read through the proofs, Will. Did you find something that needs correction?"

"Would you mind going through the pages, please?" His grin remains, so whatever error he'd discovered hadn't perturbed him at all.

Still, I sigh.

"Jess." He says my name softly, although now, his tone is tinged with a little impatience. "Just look. You'll know what I'm talking about soon enough."

Not only is this a futile use of time, but it feels especially foolish to be formally dressed with an issue of *The Crisis* spread in front of me.

However, I open the magazine and peruse every page, moving past the ads and Will's Opinion column, and pausing for a moment at Langston's newest genius submission, "Brothers."

Then I turn the page.

It is my practice to remember each article, story, and poem in the upcoming edition. However, this is not an article I approved. I glance at Will—is this what he wanted me to see?

He gestures to me. "Read it."

I begin with the title, "The Younger Literary Movement," and then the first paragraph of this article written by Will:

As is often the case in any profession, the older generation is persistently looking over our shoulders with concern, wondering, Who is behind us, and will they be able to step into our shoes? I am filled with gratitude that there is a younger set of writers who, I believe, will carry on the tradition of Paul Dunbar and Charles Chesnutt.

I continue reading as Will names Jean and Langston and Countee. I am thrilled to see Gwendolyn Bennett . . . and then me!

"Oh my goodness, Will," I say.

Then, in the middle of the column, Will turns it over to another writer . . . A. L. . . . . Alain Locke.

How long has the Negro intelligentsia waited for a novel such as *There Is Confusion*? A novel without slaves or servants or slum living, or equally embarrassing shuckin' and jivin' characters, who are, admittedly, written more for the entertainment of white folks rather than the disparaging of colored folks.

This is not the storyline with *There Is Confusion*. This novel is a thoughtful delve into the Negro middle class. These are real Negroes, not white people in blackface, recognizable by the daily issues and challenges that colored people confront. Joanna, Maggie, Peter, and others in the novel come to solutions with their *Negro* past and *Negro* life experiences in mind.

After I read the last line—"the world will be eagerly expecting Miss Fauset's next great work"—I stare at Will. "I . . . I . . . *Je suis flabbergasté.*"

"Why? I told you this book would be a success."

"Yes, but it's more than that, Will." I am breathless as I continue, "You honored me, holding me up next to Langston and Jean and Countee. Those three young men are literary geniuses."

"Young men who became geniuses after working with you. However, even without those young writers, do you realize all that you've personally accomplished? Are you aware of all that you've written over the last four years and how important your words have been? You've been the most prolific writer at *The Crisis*. And, I would venture to say, the most productive writer in the country.

"You *have* written that great American novel, and this time, I'm not the one saying this. All the reviews will be as effusive as Locke's."

I take in the magazine again; however, before I can reread the article, Will eases it away. "I wanted to do this here because this is not just about the opening of this club and seeing Fletcher. I wanted to celebrate and honor you. Tonight."

Now I understand why Will needed this copy of the magazine. He's leaving for another extensive trip, this time to Liberia. He threads his fingers through mine. "I'm so very proud, but not surprised. I've always believed in you."

I am a medley of emotions—astonishment, joy, pride, and love. After my conversation with Georgia, I'd been trying to be especially measured with Will. But I cannot recall a time when I've loved him more.

In public, I've always made certain to avoid any appearance of impropriety with Will. However, I'm so full at this moment that I lean into him, just as we hear, "Dr. Du Bois, Miss Fauset."

Will's hand slips from mine, and I have to take an extra breath before I glance up at Fletcher Henderson. The last time I saw this young man was a little more than three years ago, at the celebration of Black Swan Records.

Fletcher shakes Will's hand, then greets me before he swings a chair backward, straddles it, and sits. "Thank you for coming tonight."

"Of course, son," Will says. "I was pleased to get the invitation. Fletcher Henderson and His Orchestra . . . the house band for Club Alabam. This is something special."

"I have to admit I was quite dismayed when Black Swan closed down. My hope had been that we'd be a force in the music industry for decades."

"You were a force," Will says. "Because of Black Swan, white companies that never before noticed Negroes could sing are vying for colored artists. That's because of Black Swan and you."

I add, "And in the end, Black Swan became quite a stepping stone for you. Look at where you've landed."

His eyes brighten. "I have to admit, I'm very happy to be here."

"With your own orchestra." Will shakes his head as if he's astonished.

"There will be eleven of us on that stage tonight, although I'm working hard to recruit another young man. A cornet player who's making a name for himself."

It's the excitement in Fletcher's voice that makes Will ask, "Someone local?"

"No. He's out of Chicago. A protégé of King Oliver," he says of the legendary bandleader. "He's only twenty-two, but he's already recorded. It's clear Louis Armstrong is on the up and up, and I'd love to get him as part of my band."

"Louis Armstrong," Will repeats the name. "I'll be on the watch for him."

Suddenly, the club, which has been silent, echoes with chatter. As patrons swarm inside, Fletcher stands. "I'm going to join the guys. We'll be on in about thirty minutes. Maybe we can catch up some more after our first set."

"We'll see." Will gives me a quick glance. "We have an early day tomorrow."

Fletcher thanks us again, and then, a little more than thirty minutes later, the room darkens. When the lights brighten in one corner and Fletcher Henderson and his orchestra appear, no one in that club cheers louder than Will and me. However, by the time the orchestra moves on to the second song, we have dipped out of the nightclub.

We'd celebrated Fletcher, and now we have our own celebrating to do.

When I enter my office ten hours later, I am too exhausted to even breathe. How will I possibly work through the day without resting my head on my desk?

But it is not a cup of coffee that renews my energy. Less than a minute after I arrive, Pocahontas tells me that an operator is patching a telephone call through from Mr. Charles S. Johnson, and my interest is piqued.

I'd met Mr. Johnson and his wife, Marie, several times when they traveled from Chicago to New York for various publishing events. At that time, Mr. Johnson was the director of research and investigation for the Urban League. However, he recently relocated to New York and is now the editor of the Urban League's new magazine, *Opportunity*.

"It is so nice to hear from you, Mr. Johnson."

"Jessie, I thought I'd asked you to call me Charles."

"Yes." I stifle a yawn. "It's nice to hear from you, Charles."

"I wanted to speak with you before your busy day began. I've read an early copy of *There Is Confusion* . . ."

Those words, and the flutters in my chest, awaken me. I am, at once, totally alert.

"Jessie, this is the book that every person in the country, colored and white, needs to read."

Now his words invigorate me.

"I'm pleased to read a story about people who could live in my community. There wasn't a single lynching, wasn't a Mammy shuffling. There were no slaves singing and dancing. Just Negroes striving. Every one of your characters is recognizable and relatable.

"I know this is a novel, but it could very well be called a collective biography of those of us who, to this point, have been ignored in literature. You've brought this truth into the literary world, and I'm very proud."

"This means so much coming from you. I've worked on that novel for many years."

"It shows. And do you know what else you've done for years?" He doesn't pause for my answer. "You've been the center of a movement. Something is happening, Jessie. It's happened on the stage, it's happened in music, and now, this movement has come to literature. We're telling our stories in every form of the arts."

"I'm not the first to write an important book. I'm sure you're familiar with Jean Toomer."

"Of course, and he's a significant part of this. However, Jessie, when I say you've been at the center, I mean beyond your novel. You've been nurturing so many young people. Jean told me you worked with him as well."

"Yes—"

"That's why I'm calling. I want to commemorate this moment and honor you." Now he pauses as if I should speak, but I don't know what to say. "I want to host a luncheon, celebrating the release of *There Is Confusion*."

Comme c'est sensationnel! "That would be so kind."

"It will be small, twenty or so guests, so that the afternoon will be focused on you. I'd like to invite a few other writers," he continues to explain, "but I want editors and publishers to join us as well. With *There Is Confusion* at the center of the discussion, we can begin to build connections between Negro writers and white publishers. It's time for others to follow the example of Boni and Liveright and their publication of two important Negro books."

"Charles"—I'm so astounded, I must make certain I continue in English—"words aren't coming to me right now."

"The only word I need from you is yes." He laughs.

"Well, if yes is all you need, then yes! And thank you."

"Thank *you*, Jessie. I don't believe you realize what you've done to kindle the fire beneath this movement. However, I hope by the time this luncheon is over, you will recognize your role, which has already been set in history."

CHAPTER 51

MONDAY, MARCH 24, 1924

T he taxicab slows to a stop in front of the Civic Club, and I slip out into the spring-has-not-yet-arrived chill of March. I've been inside this mansion close to one hundred times. Yet, for the first time, I enter as a celebrated author.

I shudder as I reflect on this journey—a decade of writing, months of publisher searching, and now, with the release of the book, the reviews. Oh, the reviews that have left me reeling, lifting me so high, my feet may never again touch the ground!

I've been swept up in these last nine weeks since Charles called, scarcely able to manage it all—from the congratulatory correspondence that is piled high on my desk, to the long missives I've received from magazine editors inquiring about my interest in writing an article for their publication.

Then, the telephone calls from Charles. With each, this celebration expanded in scope and grandeur:

"Jessie! We've gone from twenty to one hundred people attending.

"Jessie! This celebration can no longer be just a luncheon; would you mind if we changed the time so we can host a four-course dinner?

"Jessie! The guest list includes the most powerful people in publishing. I cannot fully explain how important this evening will be."

Each conversation left me dizzier than the last, and I will forever be grateful to Charles for his vision.

Inside the foyer, the club is as festive as always, with guests meandering from the front parlor to the dining room and all the spaces in between. I leave my wrap in the cloakroom and then adjust my cloche. Tonight, my black hat, trimmed with pearls, is the accent to my black fringed dress and black silk stockings.

Upstairs, laughter and chatter rise throughout, and it seems as if the celebration for *There Is Confusion* has begun.

The room is grand with its gold-brocade draperies, gold tablecloths, and gold-cushioned chairs. The guests are dressed as exquisitely as the decor. Women in sleeveless pale pink, baby-blue, and mint-green sheaths, some beaded, some sequined, most fringed. And men, just as dapper, in dark wool and tweed suits. This is certainly a gathering of the city's literary elite.

I see familiar faces: James Weldon Johnson, Walter White, and, of course, the authors: Countee, Langston, Nella, and many others.

However, it is the faces of the white guests—Eugene O'Neill, the playwright of *The Emperor Jones*; and Zona Gale, the novelist whose book *Miss Lulu Bett* had been adapted into a play and then won the Pulitzer Prize—that make my heart thump.

I search for Will among the guests and then sigh, although this is not my usual discontent. Will is traveling home from his eight weeks in Liberia. His letters said he hoped to arrive in time to attend this dinner, but he wasn't certain if he would.

"Jessie!" Charles, with his regal bearing and very expensive brown tweed suit—I'd heard he purchased his suits in London—rushes toward me. Even with his short stature, his presence commands the room. "This is the first opportunity I've had to congratulate you in person."

"Thank you for all of this." I gesture around the room.

"You are the one who has provided us with this great opportunity. There are publishers and editors here from every magazine and publishing house. Never has there been an event where so many Negro authors and white publishers have been brought together. Now"—he draws me farther inside—"there have been some program adjustments. When I asked Alain to be the master of ceremonies, he suggested we give others a chance to say a few words."

"Of course. I'll have to thank Alain for thinking of that." I welcome hearing others speak about *There Is Confusion*. Boni & Liveright has done an exceptional job promoting the novel, but having other authors, editors, and publishers speak about my book will be tremendous for sales.

I embrace Nella, Countee, and Langston, and then Gwendolyn Bennett approaches me in the company of a young man with bright brown eyes and a modest mustache.

Gwendolyn says, "Miss Fauset, I just met Arna this evening, and he asked me to introduce you two."

"Arna Bontemps? Oh, my stars. Did you make this trip all the way from Los Angeles?"

"I did. Mr. Johnson suggested that I come." He glances around the room. "I've already met some of the great poets I've been reading for the last few years."

"And next month, they will be reading you."

"Oh!" Gwendolyn exclaims to Arna. "You're going to be published in *The Crisis*?"

He grins. "I've been working with Miss Fauset, but this is our first opportunity to meet." The joy that brightens Arna's face could light the city.

Just as I begin to tell Gwendolyn about Arna's poem, Miss Ovington taps my shoulder.

"Congratulations, Miss Fauset."

My eyebrows rise with my surprise. Of course I expected Miss Ovington to receive an invitation, but what I didn't expect was that she would accept. Especially after she'd given me my most scathing review.

"Thank you." I smile and return my attention to Gwendolyn and Arna.

But Miss Ovington continues as if she and I are the ones in conversation. When she says, "This is quite a turnout," Gwendolyn and Arna back away. In an instant, I am alone with the only person in the room who does not wish me well. Miss Ovington says, "I'm certain you saw my review."

"I did, Miss Ovington," I say, although I'm rather bemused; she could very well have mentioned this to me in the office. "Why would you bring that to my attention tonight?"

"Miss Fauset, if you're going to be a novelist, you must develop thick skin. Yes, you've been lauded in a few reviews, but you must welcome critiques from those of us who are more discerning in our reading and critical in our thinking."

"I was fine with your review, Miss Ovington, but apparently, your readers were not."

Now I am the one smiling. In Miss Ovington's Book Chat column, syndicated in primarily colored newspapers, she wrote that while she understood *There Is Confusion* was a work of fiction, she found no truth in the story or the characters. The inference—Negroes didn't live this way.

It was an astonishing rebuke from a woman whose inner circle included W. E. B. Du Bois, James Weldon Johnson, and others who had attained her status educationally and professionally, if not socially.

However, while she saw no truth in my novel, Miss Ovington had been besieged with letters informing her that not only was my portrayal of middle-class Negroes accurate, but her review was offensive.

When she says nothing more, I thank her for coming and make my way toward my seat.

At my table, Charles is already seated with his wife, and after greeting her, I move to the chair next to Horace Liveright.

"Hello to my newest literary star," Mr. Liveright says.

As I settle, I'm pleased to see with whom I'll be sharing this evening. In addition to Mr. Johnson and his wife and Mr. Liveright, James and Grace Johnson have joined us, along with Carl Van Vechten, the author and photographer, and his wife, Fania Marinoff, an actress.

However, I am most thrilled to be sitting just a chair away from Joel

Spingarn. While I've been able to spend time with Moorfield Storey, this is only my third or so opportunity to engage with the NAACP treasurer. My reconciliation with Will not withstanding, I remain resolute in gaining the support of every board member, with the exception of Miss Ovington, of course.

Once the guests are seated, Reverend Cullen opens the program with a blessing, and the waiters serve the first course: vichyssoise.

Mr. Van Vechten starts the conversation. "Miss Fauset, your book is the talk of New York."

"I wouldn't say New York. Perhaps . . . Harlem."

He shakes his head. "A mention in the *New York Times* makes you the talk of the city."

Mr. Liveright releases a hearty laugh. "It was far more than a mention, buddy. What was written in the *New York Times* for *There Is Confusion* and Miss Fauset was high praise. How exactly did the editor express it?" My eyes stretch with surprise when Mr. Liveright begins reciting, "It is amazing to read a book about Negroes, doing ordinary things and living ordinary lives. And the fact that this book is written by a college-educated Negro woman makes it more extraordinary."

Mr. Liveright recites the review verbatim. I know this because every word is indelibly imprinted in my mind.

Over oysters Rockefeller, the conversation continues, with everyone chiming in about how, to this point, the complete Negro story has been left untold. And as the roasted ducklings are served, we celebrate the white publications that are now rectifying their past misfeasance.

"Miss Fauset!" Mr. Liveright says excitedly, as if he's suddenly had a new thought. "With all of these opportunities opening for Negro writers, what will happen to the Negro publications? We're going to steal away the best, and who will you publish?"

He laughs, and it is not lost on me that all the white guests at our table find Mr. Liveright's statement as amusing as he does, while Charles, James, and I exchange glances.

With my napkin, I dab at the corners of my mouth before I respond, "Publications like *The Crisis* will always be home for colored writers.

After all, our writers must have a place to return when Negroes are no longer in vogue."

This time, it is the colored folks who chuckle, while Messrs. Liveright, Van Vechten, and Spingarn exchange the glances.

"With that said . . ." Charles pushes back his chair and moves to the lectern.

"Good evening. I'm Charles S. Johnson, the editor of *Opportunity*. I'm pleased that so many of you have joined us for this auspicious occasion.

"I do not wish to speak long. There is much for us to discuss. So I'll turn this evening over to Mr. Alain Locke, the master of ceremonies."

I'd only seen Alain from across the room, and I applaud, looking forward to thanking him once this evening is over.

The Howard professor strolls to the stage, as dapper as always in a forest-green pinstripe suit. He echoes Charles's welcome, then adds, "When Mr. Johnson came to me with this idea, I leapt at the opportunity. This is an important night, an awakening. It is the beginning of the New Negro Movement.

"Negro writers are raising their voices unabashedly, acknowledging the issues of the past, unapologetically speaking to the realities of the present, yet finding hope in the future."

The room explodes in applause.

"However, we cannot speak of this new generation without first paying tribute to those who forged this way for us. It is most appropriate to begin with the leader of the old guard of Negro literature, Dr. W. E. B. Du Bois."

Will is here? Once again, there is resounding applause.

When Will struts in and glances at me, I can scarcely hold myself in my seat. I haven't seen him since our night at Club Alabam. How appropriate that he will be the one to introduce me.

After his salutations, Will says, "This is indeed a propitious evening brought about by the publication of *There Is Confusion*." All eyes and the applause turn to me, and I give Will a nod of gratitude. "This novel by Miss Jessie Fauset is the beginning.

"Many in my generation have never been able to write without hesitation. In our never-ending quest to be acknowledged by white companies, we've penned false tales, writing what we believed would be acceptable in subject and verse so that we could receive white validation."

I hold my breath, waiting for Will to say that he is the sole exception, the one who has thrown fire and brimstone at any walls placed before him.

However, he only says, "I am grateful that in my lifetime, I'm witnessing these new voices who are uplifting the Negro race."

As he begins his close, I recall the remarks I've prepared. I don't want to stand at the lectern with a written speech.

Then Will says, "Thank you," and steps back.

I'm puzzled, but at the same time pleased, when Will navigates from the stage and sits in the empty chair beside me. Beneath the table, he squeezes my hand as Alain returns to the stage.

"Thank you, Dr. Du Bois. As part of this new guard, I know I speak for others when I say we will not take this charge lightly. Now, I'd like to introduce someone who has been such an inspiration for many young writers."

I smile at those words, because of all that I've accomplished, what is most important to me are the voices I've discovered and mentored into the literary stars they are today.

Alain says, "Mr. James Weldon Johnson, please come to the stage."

I am bewildered, but applaud with the others. I wonder what is going on—but in the next moment, I realize Alain wants the old guard to speak so that my introduction will be framed as a symbolic transfer of the mantle.

I'm touched by that sentiment, until . . .

Alain asks Carl Van Doren, a Columbia University professor and literary critic, to come up. He says, "The doors of opportunity have been closed to Negroes. While editors may not have specifically closed their doors to colored writers, they never opened those doors, either.

"However, as this new day is dawning, let this be a time of reconciliation. Let us not squander these opportunities with writings that are filled with rage directed toward the white community. Yes, write the truth, but write with unity in mind."

After Mr. Van Doren, a litany of editors and publishers follows, all with the same message: apologies for past transgressions, excitement for what's to come. More than forty-five minutes pass before Alain shifts.

"It is time now to meet this new guard, and I want to begin with one of the best talents in our community."

Enfin! I'm annoyed, but at least it's now my turn.

Alain says, "Countee Cullen is only twenty-one, yet he is already considered one of our best. The second-place winner of the Witter Bynner undergraduate poetry contest will tonight recite his winning entry, 'The Ballad of the Brown Girl.'"

My disappointment does not defuse my enthusiasm for Countee. More writers follow: Langston—who performs what he says is the poem that, because of me, allowed him to fully see himself as a poet.

When he begins, "Well, son, I'll tell you: Life for me ain't been no crystal stair," I think how grateful I am that I will forever be the one who helped Langston gift this poem to the world.

Gwendolyn Bennett and Walter White follow with their readings. I applaud each, but with every writer, I sink deeper into my seat. I do not understand what is unfolding. An evening that was planned to celebrate the release of my novel has transformed into a grand platform for every writer—except for me.

I am beyond insulted; I feel completely disregarded.

More than ninety minutes pass before Alain fixes his gaze on me. "Now I'd like to close this amazing evening with Jessie Redmon Fauset."

Even when the audience begins their rousing applause, I hesitate. Certainly, Alain will say more. But he adds nothing, and that sets off a fire raging in my bones.

Slowly, I move to the lectern and grip both sides. "Thank you for that kind welcome. I was a little concerned. I wondered if I would be invited to speak tonight at all." It is a deliberate departure from my usual decorum, and the laughter is light, as if the audience isn't sure whether to laugh at my words or shrink back from my tone. "Thank you for honoring the publication of my novel," I say, although that has not been the case.

"The spark to write was ignited in me when I was just a child. When I learned how to read, I wanted to write. As an adult, I desired to pen an important novel that would move minds and hearts. As so many have said tonight, I hope *There Is Confusion* will usher in a new era for Negro writers." I have to pause for the applause. "I'm sure you're all aware of the effusive reviews I've received." I center my gaze on Miss Ovington. "I have been honored to have white newspapers throughout the country say the novel is engaging and engrossing, while the international press has said my novel will hold readers spellbound . . . that what I've written is excellent and is art.

"I say this not to boast, but to share that with proper support— support that I have received from Boni and Liveright—not only are Negro writers capable of writing excellent stories, but we can write to entertain beyond our race. Books written by Negro writers can sell, too!"

Even though everyone remains in their seats, the applause feels like an ovation for as long as it continues. There is much more I want to say; however, my time is short. I see it in the guests' countenances—ninety minutes of speeches is too much for anyone to endure.

So I close with, "I can never accept any honor without thanking the young writers who've challenged and stretched me to be the very best. I am here tonight because of all of you. Thank you to everyone."

This time, every guest stands, and I stay on the stage, absorbing this acknowledgment, praying the applause will defuse the ire within me. When I return to the table, both Mr. Liveright and Will stand to greet me. I sit between the two and press my hands together to stop my trembling.

It is a blessing when, minutes later, Alain ends the night and Will speaks to me first. His words, "I am so very proud of you," are the salve I need.

As Joel Spingarn pulls Will away, I'm swarmed with congratula-tions:

"Jessie, do you realize what you've started?"

"Your novel will be celebrated for centuries."

"The impact you've made will never be matched."

I smile, I laugh, I thank everyone. With each conversation, I edge closer to the door. I'm almost at the threshold when Mr. Paul Kellogg calls my name.

"Miss Fauset," the editor of *Survey Graphic* greets me. "I would love to devote an entire issue to the events of this evening. Mr. Locke called it the New Negro Movement, and it would be astounding to have you and Mr. Locke work together on a piece."

I wonder how many muscles it takes for me to maintain my proper decorum. "That is something we can discuss."

After agreeing that he will reach out to me soon, Mr. Kellogg rushes to Charles, to discuss his idea, I'm certain. Most of the guests are still milling about, all understanding that something singular has occurred tonight. It is an evening that will be remembered in history, and no one wants this to end.

No one except for me.

I wonder if anyone will notice when I walk out of the room. Perhaps Will. Perhaps not.

As I grab my wrap from the cloakroom, I have a final thought—a few hours ago, I'd entered the Civic Club floating high.

Now I'm leaving with my feet firmly planted on the ground.

CHAPTER 52

MONDAY, JUNE 30, 1924

I stand the moment Joel Spingarn taps on my door. "It's good to see you, Mr. Spingarn. Dr. Du Bois is ready as well. I'll walk with you to the meeting room."

A few moments later, as we wait for Will to join us, the treasurer of the NAACP and I exchange pleasantries—I ask about his wife, and he inquires about my mother.

Then Mr. Spingarn says, "We haven't spoken since the Civic Club dinner. What an evening."

Three months have passed, and I'm finally at the point where I can breathe when someone mentions that event. For days—honestly, weeks—I winced whenever the dinner was mentioned, wishing that night could be expunged from the collective memory of all.

"Yes, it was quite memorable," I say, my tone sounding rote. "I was honored to be part of that."

"What a joyous journey this has been for you, with the culmination of your recognition and celebration that night."

Will enters, sparing me from a response. After their greetings, the two begin to discuss Will's upcoming trip to Germany, their conversation giving me a reprieve.

I reflect on Mr. Spingarn's words: *What a joyous journey this has been for you.* Both the truth and illusion are mingled together in what he said. Yes, writing and being published have been joyous. However, while everyone saw that dinner as a celebration for me, I'd departed that night feeling as if my honor had been intentionally appropriated by Alain Locke.

'd been so completely desolate when I arrived home that night, fearful that if Maman asked a single question, I'd burst into tears. I will forever be grateful to God that Maman had already retired.

Then, after a night of not a moment of peaceful sleep, I'd bathed and dressed before dawn, but instead of rushing into the office, I purchased a train ticket to Philadelphia. Hours later, I stood in front of the North Philadelphia home where I was raised.

Before I crossed the threshold, I'd already gleaned what I came for— a hug. Standing before the three-story, rust-colored brick row house, I found that embrace in the flood of loving memories, and I wrapped myself in the comfort of being home.

Although I still had a key—we all did—I did not enter. Arthur, while studying for his master's at the University of Pennsylvania, was living back home. So, out of respect, I knocked and wondered if he was already on campus.

When my brother opened the door, his eyes widened. Then, without a single word, Arthur pulled me first into an embrace and then into the warmth of our home.

Papa had been gone for two decades, and Maman hadn't lived here for the last five years, yet the essence of my parents remained. It was more than the same colored walls (which had been refreshed) and the same furniture that remained steadfast in the same arrangement.

It was in the smaller things: every knickknack on the parlor tables, all the metal picture frames that held fading photographs on the mantel. Even the fragrance of Maman's yeast rolls lingered—or was that merely my memory?

I shrugged off my jacket and hung it on the staircase banister, as I had every day when I'd come home from school. Still without speaking, I moved toward the parlor, and my brother followed.

Finally, he said, "Are you going to tell me why you're here?" I only sighed and he continued, "This cannot possibly be about Mother. I know she can be nettlesome, but that doesn't usually require a two-dollar ticket and a two-hour train ride."

Even when I reclined on the sofa, I still struggled for the words. How could I explain all that I was feeling?

Arthur sat next to me. "The dinner was last night."

It was then that I remembered. My brother and Alain Locke were good friends.

"Yes, the dinner Charles Johnson was hosting to honor the release of *There Is Confusion* was supposed to be last night."

"Supposed?" He frowned. "It was canceled?"

"No. It happened, but it had little to do with me." The story spilled from me. I took my brother through every minute of every speech and every affront I'd felt from Alain.

"The whole night was dreadful, Arthur," I concluded.

My brother removed his eyeglasses, and with his handkerchief, he gently buffed the lenses. Then he held his glasses up in the morning light, as if he was checking for smudges. I crossed my arms, wondering why Arthur was dillydallying.

"Arthur." I called his name in the same tone I used when he was six and I was twenty-three. "Did you know the dinner was being changed from celebrating the launch of *There Is Confusion* to something else?"

He replaced his glasses. "No, I didn't. I never asked Alain or anyone about the program. I only knew this was a dinner to honor you."

"*Exactement!*" I said. "And it was all taken away at the whim of Alain, whose only objective seemed to be to exclude me."

My brother only nodded, and it was curious to me that Arthur wasn't as outraged as I was.

"From what you've told me, I don't believe that was Alain's intention," my brother said.

"What else could it be?" I was utterly exasperated. "He slighted me and took away the opportunity to uplift a literary work that celebrated Negroes."

"You know how I feel about *There Is Confusion*. My chest isn't large enough to swell with the pride I feel when I say Jessie Redmon Fauset is my sister. However, again, based on what you've told me, I disagree that anything was taken from you."

"*Qu'est-ce que tu veux dire?*"

"What I mean is exactly what I said. You were honored."

"I was not! *There Is Confusion* was but a mere mention in a night of poets performing and writers speaking about their next projects."

"That's not true," my brother said, as if he'd witnessed the night himself. "You said Dr. Du Bois extolled your novel, and certainly, Mr. Liveright sang your praises. Then you had the opportunity to speak on your behalf. Perhaps it wasn't the celebration you envisaged. However, my dear sister, New York certainly honored you last night. Think about all the writers who were there, only because of you. It sounds like Alain believed that this present moment in this great time demanded a greater mark than the spotlight to be shone on only one."

It pained me that Arthur appeared to be aligned with Alain, but my greater anguish came from the thought that perhaps my brother was right . . .

"The reason I wanted to meet with the two of you," Mr. Spingarn says, snapping me from my reverie, "is that I was so impressed by the dinner in March that I began to wonder how I could participate in this movement."

Will says, "I hope Harcourt, Brace, and Company will be one of the publishers who will now seek out these young Negro writers. You have access to so many through *The Crisis* because of Miss Fauset."

Mr. Spingarn nods. "Although I'm not involved in the day-to-day operations, I have spoken with my partners, and we agree . . . it is time for all publishing companies to be actively supportive of publishing Negro writers.

"However, I've had another thought. What can we do to find even more talent? Yes, we have a plethora of riches, but you, Miss Fauset, are one person. I'm sure you'll agree there is a lot of undiscovered talent."

Will and I glance at each other, then nod.

"So to that end, I want to offer three hundred dollars for *The Crisis* to sponsor a literary contest."

Will inhales deeply, and I am just as astonished. "Three hundred dollars?" I repeat.

Mr. Spingarn nods. "I will not pretend to know how to manage such a contest, especially with that much money. That, I will leave in your very capable hands."

"This is very exciting, Mr. Spingarn. I'm certain Dr. Du Bois and I can design a fitting competition that will attract many new writers."

Will's eyebrows dip into a deep frown, evidence that he isn't as enthusiastic about this idea. He speaks up. "My primary concern, Mr. Spingarn, is that I wouldn't want anything to eclipse the Spingarn Medal. It's crucial for us to recognize the contributions of Negroes who are working toward the betterment of this country."

"Of course. This literary contest will have nothing to do with the Spingarn Medal. The purpose of this three hundred dollars is exactly what I stated, for literary awards. And it's one time, for now. We'll determine if this should be annual at a later date."

Again, Will nods; again, he frowns. "We'll give this our greatest consideration."

"Excellent." When Mr. Spingarn stands, Will and I do the same, but he waves his hand. "I'm not leaving," he says. "I'm meeting with Mr. Johnson."

I wait for Mr. Spingarn to exit before I rush to close the door, then Will and I return to our seats. "I'm thrilled." I can scarcely contain my excitement. "But you don't seem to be."

When he presses the tips of his fingers together, I remain silent, giving him the space to deliberate the conversation. "You believe the contest is a wise plan?"

"I do," I say without hesitation. "In fact, I'm astonished that I didn't think of this. It is only fitting that *The Crisis* should spearhead its own contest for young writers to join the New Negro Movement." If there is anything from the night of March 24 that I appreciate, it is Alain's assessment of this time. "You don't agree?"

"While I believe in publishing writers, I wonder if we need to expend further energy on the literary side when colored men are lynched each week, when colored children are denied educational opportunities and Negro college graduates are still hired only as bellmen or waiters."

"I agree, we're in a perpetual fight. However, we can keep our attention on the struggle while providing hope and opportunities for new writers. And a contest sets us ahead of our competition."

"We have no competition," he says gruffly, but then passes me a slight smile. "Charles Johnson's *Opportunity* magazine."

"Yes, I read that magazine monthly, and in the beginning, Mr. Johnson focused on issues central to the Urban League. However, over the past months, I've noticed more poetry appearing inside those pages."

Will nods. "Including poetry from our poets."

I laugh. "They're not ours. Countee, Langston, and the others should pursue opportunities as we do. However, with *Opportunity* taking that approach, I believe a monetary contest will set us further apart and ensure that *The Crisis* remains the most important publication for Negroes in this country."

He gazes at me for a long moment. "One of the smartest decisions I ever made was bringing you to *The Crisis*. Your affection for what I've built is akin to mine."

"Shouldn't it be? You've always believed in me, and the converse is true. I believe in you and what you've done with this magazine."

"And now, for some of *The Crisis*'s best years, we've been doing it side by side."

When he returns to his pensive stance, I inhale. I know what he's thinking—it's time to pass the editorship to me.

"Jess . . ." He pauses, then shakes his head as if he's clearing away a thought. "You've convinced me. Let's move forward with this competition. What are the next steps?"

Now I must take a moment. What happened to the offer I'm convinced Will was about to make? I clear my throat and my thoughts. "I'll put together a plan and a schedule. I believe the best time to launch this will be at the beginning of next year."

"Should we wait that long?"

"Six months will give us adequate preparation time. However, I will look at the best dates."

He says, "Once we decide the timing, then let's create an early stir. We won't make an official announcement, but we'll hint at this over the next few months."

"That's an excellent idea. If we get people whispering in anticipation, they'll be dashing to get the January issue of *The Crisis*."

"If we're going to do this, let's make it grand and execute it with excellence. I'm agreeing to this for one reason only." He leans toward me. "Because of you, Jess. You've kept *The Crisis* as the foremost magazine, and I know you will continue to do so."

CHAPTER 53

TUESDAY, AUGUST 5, 1924

"Jessie, I need to speak with you."

I glance up at Maman, sitting across from me. Her Bible is closed now; she's pushed it aside on the kitchen table.

"I must finish one of my articles for next month's issue. I'm terribly behind."

"I understand, *ma chérie*. This will only take a moment."

With a sigh, I put down my pen.

"Would you like some more tea?"

Shaking my head, I watch Maman cross the room to refill her cup. Ordinarily, I delight in these mornings with my mother, cherishing this time when I elect to work at home. I do this especially on the days when I know I'll have a late night—with Will. Will and I have plans for this evening . . . a "welcome home" celebration, as he's just returned from Germany.

When Maman sits across from me, she says, "Jessie, you cannot pass up this opportunity to attend the Sorbonne."

"This is what you want to discuss? We've been round and round about this. I cannot leave *The Crisis*. Not at this time." And not when I'm this close, is what I don't say.

"How can you say you can't leave when *you're* often left to manage the magazine alone?"

"It is precisely for that reason. If I'm not there, who will do it?"

"You can entrust those responsibilities to someone for a few months. What about Mr. Dill?"

"He's the business manager. He knows nothing about selecting content or editing or writing. And recently, I've been managing many of his responsibilities, as he's traveled several times to Ohio for a family emergency."

Maman remains resolute. "Then other arrangements will have to be made," she insists. When she takes a deep breath and asks, "Have you spoken to . . . Dr. Du Bois?" I understand how paramount this is to her.

"No, because you know what I want more than attending the Sorbonne again."

Maman opens her mouth, her response ready, but just then, Mary-Helen breezes into our apartment. "Good morning to you!" She hugs Maman before turning to me. "What are you still doing home? I was certain you'd already be in the office handling *Opportunity*'s announcement."

I frown at my sister. "What announcement?"

She tilts her head as if she doesn't understand my question. "You don't know? I received my magazine last night and was astounded when I saw it."

"My magazine is delivered to the office," I say, still not understanding. "It's probably on my desk right now. What was in *Opportunity*?"

"They announced a literary contest."

"What!"

"Yes, and it's so strange because all summer, there's only been whispers about your upcoming contest. No one has mentioned anything about *Opportunity*."

A thousand thoughts meld in my mind: *Opportunity* is hosting a literary contest? When had this decision been made? After we announced ours? But our contest hadn't *officially* been announced—I'd only hinted at it at a literary salon or two in the last weeks to create the stir Will and I discussed.

Then my final thoughts: Had our idea been appropriated? And now preempted?

I rush to my bedroom and grab my satchel, but as soon as I return to the kitchen, Maman actually says to me, "Please, Jessie. Just a few more minutes—"

"I must get to the office. This is urgent."

"Everything with that magazine is always urgent." She sighs as I kiss her cheek, and then I wave goodbye to my sister.

My mother's words are true—it is always urgent. However, today, this isn't urgent. This is a crisis.

In less than an hour, I know just how much of a crisis I am facing. At my desk, all I can do is stare at the magazine before me. It is only a small mention in the editorial section of *Opportunity*, but the words feel as if they are screeching at me from the page.

We're seeking writers, poets, and playwrights—the best among us—for *Opportunity*'s Literary Contest.

Five Hundred Dollars.

How had this happened? Had a writer mentioned this to Charles Johnson and he then said, "That's a fine notion, let us appropriate it and have our own contest"?

Those questions are of no importance now. Decisions have to be made.

Folding the magazine to the article, I think for a moment, formulating what I'll say to Will. When I step into his office, he's absorbed in the mound of correspondence that has accumulated in his absence. I close the door behind me, silencing the office's clamor.

He glances up with a grin, but without preamble, I slide the magazine across his desk. "You'll want to read the announcement in the right column."

As he reads, the lines in his forehead deepen. When his jaw clenches, I'm certain he's studying the mention of five hundred dollars in prize money. "What is this?"

"The latest edition of *Opportunity*."

"I know that," he says gruffly. "They've announced a literary contest?"

"Yes."

"For five hundred dollars."

"Yes."

He tosses the magazine aside, reclines in his chair, and presses his fingertips together. Usually, I remain silent, giving Will time to contemplate the situation. This time, I say, "I know what we must do."

He holds up his hand, stopping me. "How did this happen?"

"I don't know."

"Have you been talking about the contest?"

"Yes," I say, thinking that is an odd question. "Just as we agreed. I've mentioned it at literary salons over the summer, and it was well received. Everyone has been awaiting the details."

"Yet our idea was appropriated by an adversary."

"I've never thought of *Opportunity* that way. Yes, competition; however, I believe we are all working toward the same goal."

He chuckles, although the sound carries no joy. "For someone who's been working here for so long, you're certainly naive."

I bristle, but say nothing.

"Perhaps you shouldn't have been speaking about this contest so freely before we made an official announcement."

I blink at first, bemused. "That is a decision we made together. If you recall, I believe your exact words were 'create a stir.' That's what I've been doing."

"Yes, however, in business, you must know when to pivot." He punctuates each word, jabbing his finger on the desk. "You must know when to adapt and how to adjust."

"Are you blaming me for what *Opportunity* has done?" I am dumbfounded. "How was I to know Charles Johnson would do this?"

"Eyes and ears must always be open, and apparently, yours were not. Now we have this debacle, and my magazine is at risk." He shakes his head. "Obviously, you haven't taken care of *The Crisis* while I've been away."

I can scarcely breathe. "I've worked diligently on this magazine and this contest. I've executed everything based on what you approved. If I'm to blame for our plan, so are you."

"You were here. I was not. If I'd been here, I would've changed the timetable to be ahead of *Opportunity.*"

"This is utter madness," I say, giving no care to the fact that I've raised my voice. "There is not a person in the city who has ever heard of *Opportunity*'s contest. So there is nothing I—or you—could have done."

"Perhaps, then, we should have been like *Opportunity.* Silent!" Before I can protest further, he asks, "So how do we fix this?"

I want to shout and demand that first Will apologize. However, I only take a deep breath. "I have a plan. We weren't going to announce our contest until January. We should announce it in the October edition."

"Why not force it into the September edition?"

Pointing to *Opportunity*'s announcement, I say, "This is just a small mention and looks as if it was rushed into this issue. I'm certain a big announcement will follow in September. I don't want to compete with that." I pause. "That is the first way we can best . . . *adapt* and *adjust.*"

His countenance remains stiff. "Go on."

"We should keep all of the specifics of the contest, like the categories and the ability to have multiple submissions, the same. However, there are two parts we must change. First, we shouldn't compete with *Opportunity*'s time frame. Their deadline is December; we should move ours out to late spring. And finally, we should increase our winnings. From three hundred . . . to six hundred dollars."

He reclines in his chair. "That's doubling the gift we received from Mr. Spingarn."

"Yes, but we cannot follow and offer less."

"Where will we get the funds?"

"I'll prepare a proposal. And I will present it to Mr. Spingarn."

"*You'll* present it?" He smirks.

"Yes." I keep my voice strong, even though I'm shaken. "As the one managing the contest, I should explain this situation. I will also show Mr. Spingarn the benefits of increasing our winnings."

The deep lines remain in his forehead. "All right. Let's get the proposal prepared as soon as possible."

I nod, grateful this meeting is coming to an end. I need to escape just to breathe.

Will says, "It would be best if you were not to mention this to anyone outside of these offices."

I bite my lip, suppressing my scream.

When I turn toward the door, he adds, "One more thing." I face him, and he glances down at his correspondence. He's not even looking at me when he says, "I'm canceling our plans for this evening. There's no time for us to have dinner when you must rectify what you've done."

I am white-hot with fury as I stomp out of his office. His door had been open when I entered, but I slam it shut—proper decorum and my desire to be appointed the editor be damned!

My eyes burn, and I recline in my chair, craving relief from my exhaustion. Since I stormed from Will's office this morning, I've worked—not pausing for a minute—to "rectify," as Will said, what I've done.

As I return to the letter I'm preparing for Mr. Spingarn, a knock on my door surprises me. "Yes," I say, hoping Pocahontas is on the other side.

When the door opens, it is not my stenographer. Of course, it wouldn't be. She's been gone for hours. However, I would have welcomed her, or even Miss Ovington. Anyone besides Will.

"I saw the light under your door," he says, his voice and his countenance softer than when I left him ten hours ago. "Still working?"

"Yes."

When I say nothing more, he enters and sits beside me. I clench my jaw and my hands.

"Anything you're ready to share?"

No, is what I want to say. However, what's next on my task list is preparing papers for Will to review.

So although I do not wish to prolong his presence, I open the folder and slip him a piece of paper. "This will be our announcement."

His eyebrows rise, and I see the question in his eyes. How had I completed this so quickly? If he asks, I will tell him I had a team—Pocahontas and my friend Laura Wheeling, who, thank God, is here for the summer teaching once again, at Columbia. Her illustration skills and commitment to our friendship know no bounds.

"This is very good, Jess."

I do not bother to thank him. "I recommend we publish this in the first pages of the magazine, perhaps under the Opinion section so readers will recognize its importance."

"Let's go with it."

Again, I don't acknowledge his words. "I spoke with Mr. Spingarn. I'm preparing the proposal for him now, but he's agreed to adding funds for our contest."

"You've accomplished so much in a few hours. I didn't expect all of this today." He chuckles uneasily and shifts in the chair. "Jess, I know how hard you've been working, and I appreciate it. Especially with what you've done today." He pauses, as if he's waiting for me to respond to his half-hearted apology.

Not a muscle moves as I stare at him.

He asks, "Have you eaten? It's late, but I'm sure we can get something at the hotel."

"No."

"No, you haven't eaten or—"

"No, I haven't eaten. No, I'm not hungry. And no, because I still have work to do."

I'm not sure if it's my rebuff, my words, or my tone that shocks him most.

"You don't have to finish this all tonight, Jess."

"Yes, I do, because I won't be in the office after tomorrow." Staring straight at him, I say, "I've decided to accept the invitation to study at the Sorbonne, and I'll need time to prepare for the trip."

Will's eyes widen. "I thought you had already declined that offer."

"I had not. And after this *debacle . . .*"

"You didn't cause this," he's quick to say. "I shouldn't have implied that."

"I've decided that perhaps distance will help me," I continue, as if he hasn't spoken.

"Jess, please."

"I have a plan for managing *The Crisis* while I'm away. I will advise the writers that I will still be editing, and I'll post my own articles from Paris. Pocahontas and I will work closely, adhering to strict timelines and constant communication. I will manage *The Crisis* with the same level of efficiency as I always have. Nothing will change."

Will hesitates as if he wants to be certain I've finished. Then he says, "Nothing will change except you won't be here." When I don't respond, he whispers, "For six months, Jess?"

I do not part my lips.

"Is there anything I can do to change your mind?"

"No. Even you said this was a good opportunity."

He gazes at me for another moment before he stands. At my door, he pauses, although he doesn't glance back. And then he's gone.

Will accomplished in one conversation what my mother had been trying to achieve for months. Now thousands of miles and an ocean will separate us, and if I am as brilliant as everyone seems to believe, Paris will become my home.

But although I won't be leaving for a few weeks, I already know I will never stay away. I've not boarded the ship, yet I already feel the pull. The pull to return. To *The Crisis* . . . to Harlem . . . and, God help me . . . to Will.

Perhaps, though, six months away will be the remedy for at least that last desire.

CHAPTER 54

SATURDAY, MARCH 28, 1925

The moment she opens the door, Nella embraces me the way Maman hugged me when I returned to New York from Paris yesterday morning.

"Jessie, it is so good to see you. Six months was too long." Then, as if she suddenly remembers that I'm standing outside, she pulls me into the hallway.

After hanging my coat on the hall tree, she loops her arm through mine and leads me into the parlor. "You must never go away like this again," she scolds me. "Unless you take me with you. Now, how was Paris? What did you eat? What did you wear? Did you go everywhere fabulous? Oh, and the men! Tell me about the Frenchmen."

I laugh as I sit down. "Which question shall I answer first?"

"One that I forgot to ask. Weren't you supposed to return last week?" I nod, and she continues, "Were you delayed by a Frenchman?"

"No. Nothing salacious. I'd made a mistake with my homeward-bound ticket, so I had to remain in Paris a few days."

"How utterly ghastly." Nella laughs. "So tell me everything." She bounces into her chair and tucks her stockinged feet beneath her, settling in for a long story.

"Well, Paris was . . . Paris."

"Yes, but you went at such a divine time."

"It was nice to be there through Christmas and the New Year, but Paris was cold and dreary and gray. Gray at dawn, gray at noon, gray at midnight. Not at all what I remembered from my summer there." I don't mention that it wasn't like when I was in Paris with Will in the autumn of 1921, either. "But it was wonderful. Even better than when I attended the Sorbonne the first time. I learned so much."

"What was there for you to learn? You speak French better than anyone I know."

"I speak French like an American. I want to speak like the French. So this time, I hired a private tutor. Monsieur Beaumont."

"Ooh la la!"

That makes me chuckle. "Rein in your imagination, my friend. Monsieur Beaumont and his wife offer private French lessons to supplement their retirement."

"Darn it all!" She waves her hand in the air. "But was it fun, Jessie?"

"It was. I spent my days in Paris being . . . free."

"Free . . ." Nella sighs as if freedom is something she's never known, yet craves. I understand.

I say, "I've never felt as free as I have these last months. All my life, I've been on someone else's schedule, but in France, even though I was studying and managing *The Crisis*, every day I awakened free."

"I can only imagine the wonder of not doing the usual every day."

I nod, leaving out that my freedom came from not only a break from my routine, but also leaving behind the turmoil that had usurped my life. Instead, I share with Nella all that I loved about my time away, especially the Parisian cafés where I spent hours editing and writing. And then just as much time gazing into the streets, people watching.

Then there were the days when I caught up with new friends, several of the many Americans I'd been introduced to—tourists, students, and expatriates. And we'd sit and chat through the morning, sipping coffee and dining on baguettes. As time drifted to the late afternoon, we'd solve all the problems of the world over aperitifs before we ordered lunch or dinner.

"You indulged in aperitifs?" Nella asks, bewilderment in her tone.

"Once or twice . . . or ten times."

Together, we laugh. "I guess you were set free."

I tell Nella about the nightclubs and cabarets. "It was almost like being here in Harlem. There are so many Negro performers in Paris. I saw a young woman who was in the chorus of *Shuffle Along*. I don't remember her in the play, but at the Théâtre des Champs-Élysées, Josephine Baker is a star. Such a singer, and oh, how she dances. And there was another woman, Bricktop . . ."

"Is that her name?"

"That's how she was introduced. She's not only a singer, but she manages one of the most popular nightclubs in Paris. The night I was at Le Grand Duc, the club was bursting with celebrities. I sat at a table next to F. Scott Fitzgerald!"

"Oh, my stars! Did you introduce yourself as a fellow writer?"

"No." I'm shocked Nella would ask me such a thing. "He's very famous now."

"So are you! I just read *There Is Confusion* is in its third edition, and the book has barely been out a year!"

I'd been so thrilled when Mr. Liveright sent a telegram with that news. "Perhaps when I get to the fifth edition, I'll introduce myself to everyone. Oh, Nella, I had a splendid time. Not just in Paris, but I traveled to Nice and Marseille, and even spent a week in Rome."

She presses her hand against her chest and sighs. "After all that, I can forgive you for leaving me here at home."

"Enough about me; tell me, how have you been? How's your writing?"

"You're not going to believe how much writing I've done. But before we get to that, I've prepared tea. Would you like biscuits?"

"That would be lovely."

She jumps from the chair, and when I ask if I can assist, she tells me to stay. It is not until Nella leaves the room that I notice a large stack of newspapers on the table.

"Are you starting a newspaper company?" I call out to Nella as I shift through the pile of the *Daily News.*

I hear Nella's laughter. "I've been keeping every newspaper that mentions the Rhinelander case," she shouts back. "Did you hear about that in France?"

"Oh yes. I'm certain it was a bigger story here, but it was mentioned in quite a few circles. And everyone in France was trying to understand *quel est le problème.* You know the French are much more liberal than Americans."

If I hadn't been aware of this story, I certainly would have been abreast of it from these headlines alone:

> **BLUEBLOOD WEDS COLORED GIRL . . .**
> **RHINELANDER AND BRIDE VANISH . . .**
> **RHINELANDERS FLEE PUBLICITY . . .**
> **BRIDE OF RHINELANDER ONCE**
> **CALLED MULATTO . . . BLUEBLOOD**
> **CHARGES BRIDE WITH DECEIT OVER**
> **RACE . . . RHINELANDER BRIDE**
> **SCENTS PLOT . . . RHINELANDER SUES**
> **BRIDE, SEEKS ANNULMENT . . .**
> **RHINELANDER CASE GOING TO TRIAL.**

Leonard "Kip" Rhinelander claims Alice Jones never told him she was a Negro. And her side of the story—who said she was colored? And now they were going to court. The Rhinelanders wanted this marriage annulled. They could not have their blue blood tainted by a Negro.

When Nella returns to the parlor with a tea set and plate of biscuits, I say, "I feel sorry for Mrs. Rhinelander."

"I haven't decided." Nella motions for me to serve myself. "Was she passing? Was she not? If she was, did her husband know? Or did he not? This is exactly what I want to explore in my next novel."

"Have you finished *Quicksand?*"

"I'm close to the end. But this theme of passing has been calling to me. That's the title I want for my next novel: *Passing.* After this Rhinelander case, I want to explore what it's like to live a life where you must conceal the very essence of who you are from everyone at all costs."

"There are so many Negroes living that way. I'm considering the same theme for my next novel. I began writing in Paris."

"Oh, everyone is waiting, Jessie." She becomes somber when she says, "May I ask you a question about *There Is Confusion?*"

"Certainly."

"Is it autobiographical?"

I hesitate, then say, "No, why do you ask?"

"There are so many similarities—it's set in New York and Philadelphia, your two homes."

"Yes, but Joanna is a dancer and a singer. And you don't want me to sing."

She laughs. "But you can dance. Seriously, I wondered because Joanna was so determined to build her career. Just like you. And willing to give up love for her ambition. Just like you."

"Ah"—I raise my finger—"but in the end, Joanna didn't."

"No, she chose love with Peter. That was a surprising conclusion." She tilts her head. "Is that how you want your story to end? Was your trip to Paris about abandoning your career to find love?"

My friend is completely unaware of how enmeshed my ambition is with love. "That's not why I went to Paris. I really wanted to attend the Sorbonne, but unquestionably, the timing was fortuitous. Distance gave me room for clarity."

"About being the editor or about love?"

Again, I cannot tell my friend the truth. That while Paris gave me clarity about my ambition—more than ever, I want to be the editor—I remain uncertain of and confounded by Will.

So I only say to Nella, "About being the editor, of course. Even four thousand miles away, I still loved managing *The Crisis.* And I did it well.

Most of the operations remained under my purview. My time away only made me more eager to return."

"Then you must talk to W. E. B. about what you want. You've been at *The Crisis* long enough, and it's time for him to give you your due."

Not yet, I think. We must be on steadier ground. But to Nella, I say, "I will soon."

"Good!" She sighs. "You know what, Jessie, you're right. You're nothing like Joanna. And I admire that. You've kept your steadfast focus on *The Crisis*, not distracted for a moment by love."

I smile at my friend and keep silent. She will never know that I can't have a single reflection about *The Crisis* without thinking about love.

step over the threshold and click on the lights, and when the bullpen becomes illuminated, I exhale with gratitude for this place I've missed so much and love even more now.

I'd waited until this late hour, wanting to ensure everyone was gone. Slowly, I walk toward my office, soaking in all that's familiar: the stenographers' desks, the office machines, and then I notice a new framed photograph on the wall, most likely taken by James Van Der Zee. The picture appears to be at an NAACP meeting of some sort, and Will stands in the center.

I stare at his face, and a tide of emotions engulf me. It's just a photograph, yet it stirs old passions.

This is the reason for my delayed trip home; I'd told Nella that there had been an error with my ticket, but that wasn't true. While I was very eager to return to *The Crisis*, I didn't feel the same about seeing Will.

Then, two weeks ago, Will sent me a telegram with a blessing.

JESS WHEN ARE YOU RETURNING STOP MUST LEAVE FOR
AFRICA ON MARCH 26 STOP MUST SEE YOU BEFORE

He was leaving New York on the twenty-sixth. I changed my ticket to return home on the twenty-seventh.

Moving into my office, I find the folder on my desk with the correspondence Pocahontas has set aside for me. Gathering the papers, I stuff them into my satchel.

But in the front, right before I flip off the lights, the door opens, and my mouth is agape.

"Jess." Will says my name before I'm able to say his.

Then together we say, "What are you doing here?"

He answers first: "I came to get a book I'd forgotten."

"I thought you'd left for Africa."

"I was supposed to leave this past Thursday, but Yolande . . ."

My concern is instant, as always. "Is she all right?"

"She's fine now. What are you doing here? You didn't respond to my telegram, and Pocahontas only said you'd arrive within the next few days."

I'm grateful Pocahontas followed my instructions. "I returned yesterday."

He takes a step closer. "I wish I'd known you were back. It's so good to see you, Jess."

A moment passes. "It's good to be seen."

"I missed you."

I hesitate again, wanting to be careful with my words. Then I tell him the truth. "I missed you, too."

His gaze never wavers from mine. "How was Paris?"

"Delightful."

"I'm happy about that for you. But I hope it wasn't as wonderful as when we were there together."

Is that a statement? A question? I'm unsure, so I just smile.

He takes another step, and now I inhale the lavender of his cologne. "I want to thank you for the job you did while you were away. It was as if you were right here by my side. *The Crisis* didn't falter at all."

"That was my plan."

"I've said it before. The smartest decision I ever made was bringing you here."

I breathe in. Perhaps distance offered Will clarity as well.

He says, "So, where are you going now? Home?"

"Yes, my mother is waiting for me."

He nods, glancing down. "I know it's rather late, but I'd love to go somewhere . . . for dinner. To catch up."

I take another deep breath and pray my heart will not betray me. "It's very late."

"It's been a long time, Jess." When he reaches for my hand, I don't pull away. I should, but I've missed his touch, I've missed him, and I cannot deny or defy the frisson that forever courses between us.

But then . . . I do pull away. "My mother . . . is waiting for me." It is because of the sorrow in his eyes that I add, "But I'll be here when you return from Africa. Travel safely, Will."

I stride through the door, ride down on the elevator, and then hail a cab. It is only when the taxi eases away from the curb that I exhale.

CHAPTER 55

FRIDAY, MAY 1, 1925

Five weeks have passed in a haze of activity. I'd leapt right back into the office routine, sinking into the familiarity of what I loved—spending my mornings reading through dozens of submissions; the afternoons editing, writing, and meeting with authors; and evenings accepting invitations to dine with New York publishers and editors who, before the publication of *There Is Confusion*, didn't know my name.

The days had been joyous—except for my singular concern . . . what would Will's return bring? As the time drew closer, my apprehension heightened. I harbored no doubt that we'd resume our work side by side. It was my heart that I questioned.

Now, as I sit in Will's office on the morning of his return, I know my instincts about working together were correct. As Augustus and I review all that has transpired in Will's absence, this feels like the hundreds of meetings we've had throughout the years.

"This is the kind of good news one wishes to come home to," Will says, his glance still on the ledger sheet Augustus had given to both of us. "It does my heart good to see subscriptions remaining so strong."

Augustus nods. "*The Crisis* has become essential reading for colored folks. You're no longer the only celebrity, W. E. B. Everywhere I go, people ask about Langston and Countee"—he turns to me—"and you, Jessie. You've become a celebrity, too."

That sounds like foolishness to me.

"I've been hearing the same things," Will says. His smile is wide and bright when he glances at me, and my heart flutters. "*The Crisis* is shining because of you."

"Well, that's my report," Augustus says. "If we're done, I have another meeting." When he rises, so do I. "Welcome back, W. E. B."

"Jessie," Will begins, "can you stay behind so we can go through the folder you left for me?"

"Certainly." I sit once again, and when Augustus closes the door, I say, "There isn't much in the folder. Just a new poem from Langston and a few submissions from new poets, I—"

He holds up his hand. "I'm fine with whatever you decide. I wanted us to talk privately."

I shift in my chair. "There is one thing we should discuss . . . the literary contest."

I'm pleased when his smile remains.

Will says, "You did a good job of handling that while you were away. Pocahontas tells me that submissions have been coming in."

"Yes, and within the next two weeks, all submissions will be in the judges' hands."

"Very good. But do you want to know what I'd like to discuss now?" My heart leaps. This is my test.

Will says, "I'd love to have dinner with you this evening. I have a gift for you."

This evening. That is my saving grace. "I won't be able to tonight."

His disappointment is in his tone. "Other plans?" I nod. "Anything you can cancel?" I shake my head.

With his travels, of course, Will has forgotten. "The *Opportunity* dinner is this evening."

His smile vanishes. "The dinner to celebrate their contest?"

I nod. "The winners will be announced tonight."

"And *you're* going?" He crosses his arms. "To the celebration of the man who appropriated the contest from my magazine?"

I pause, wanting to choose my response with utmost care. "I'm not attending this dinner to support *Opportunity*. I'm supporting the writers. The writers who began their careers with us. This is the biggest night for Langston and Countee. They are finalists in the first literary contest that celebrates Negro writers."

His teeth are clenched when he says, "They are first only because . . ."

I brace myself for his chiding.

"They preempted our plan."

"I cannot lay that at the feet of Langston and Countee."

"We can send all the writers congratulatory notes, but we cannot attend that dinner."

"It will be appropriate for you to send notes. But not me." I stand. "I must be there to support them, especially since they supported me when Charles Johnson hosted my dinner."

He drops his hands, and his voice softens. "I know they were there for you, but, Jess, what Charles did with this contest was a personal affront to me and the magazine I created."

"I understand, and if there was any way for me to support Langston and Countee from afar, I would. But both asked me to be there."

"They asked you to attend, and I'm asking you not to."

I think about his words, and then I can only say "I'm sorry" before I step out of his office.

The Fifth Avenue restaurant is only blocks away from the office, and once I walk through the double wooden doors of the massive banquet room, the feeling of foreboding that has hovered over me since my conversation with Will is forgotten. I'm swept into the gaiety of the occasion. The room, arranged with more than thirty tables to accommodate the three hundred attendees, is already crowded with a medley of guests—writers, editors, publishers, critics. Men and women, colored and white.

As elite artists mingle with young writers, it is apparent why a ticket to this dinner is a coveted item. Fannie Hurst, the highest-paid novelist in the country, is chatting with Langston, while just a few feet away, Countee is in conversation with Paul Robeson.

I perambulate the perimeter, searching for table number four, assigned to me with my invitation. I stop when I feel a tap on my shoulder. "Jean Toomer!" I exclaim with glee.

After we embrace, he says, "I'm sorry I wasn't able to attend your dinner last year. Congratulations on the success of *There Is Confusion*."

"I appreciated your note. Congratulations to you as well, on the success of *Cane*."

"Miss Fauset," he says with a wry chuckle, "you're just being kind."

He's alluding to the number of books he's sold in the two years since its release—only five hundred copies.

"There are many ways to measure success," I say, my tone stern. "Book sales are one. Another way is to forge a path and open the door for others. That's what you did for me."

He bows his head in gratitude, and I wonder if he has any remorse about never acknowledging his race. However, I don't ask. It is no concern of mine, and I know the answer: Jean Toomer harbors no regrets.

Jean is pulled away by Eugene Kinckle Jones, the executive secretary for the National Urban League. I continue to walk through the room, and when I see Georgia speaking with the playwright Eugene O'Neill, I wonder if Will asked *her* not to attend this banquet.

"Jessie."

I face Charles Johnson with a forced smile. It has been more than a year since the dinner he hosted for me. Although I did send him a formal thank-you, we have not spoken since. And of course, I never reached out to him after this contest calamity.

Charles says, "I wasn't certain you would grace us here tonight."

"I wouldn't have missed the *first* literary awards banquet."

The ends of his lips twitch. "I understand *The Crisis* will be having a similar dinner in August."

My eyebrows rise high. "Yes, although we haven't made that public announcement."

"This industry is small. If you tell one person, everyone will hear those same words." Then he adds in earnest, "There is space for all of us, Jessie."

"On that, Charles, we can agree."

When I find table number four, I'm pleased to see Langston already seated.

"My favorite poet," I greet him, then turn to my left. "Mr. Robeson, it is an honor to meet you. I'm Jessie—"

"Redmon Fauset," he says, shocking me. He introduces his wife, Eslanda, and continues, "I've enjoyed every issue of *The Crisis*, Miss Fauset, especially since your reign began."

I laugh. "I wouldn't quite call my tenure at the magazine a reign."

"You're being modest. Everyone in the country knows you're the queen of that magazine."

A young woman, about twenty-five or so, wearing a chestnut-colored suit and a matching wide-brimmed fedora cocked slightly, asks Langston, "Is this seat taken?"

He shakes his head, then stands to pull out the chair for her. She introduces herself to Langston, then turns to me.

"I'm Zora Neale Hurston."

"Nice to meet you, Zora. I'm Jessie—"

For the second time in just minutes, I'm interrupted. "Please, Miss Fauset. There isn't a Negro writer in America who doesn't know you. I asked Mr. Johnson to seat me at your table." Then, with such surety and a bit of authority in her tone, she declares, "We must talk."

I like her already.

Charles Johnson moves to the lectern, and after thanking everyone for attending the largest gathering of Negro writers in history, he says, "Tonight, we're here to recognize the winners of *Opportunity*'s first literary prize contest, and I must say, the quality of work we received from the seven hundred and forty-seven submissions was even greater than

I expected. Everyone agreed choosing the winners was going to be an arduous task."

He continues, speaking about his aims for the contest, and he glances at me when he says, "We hope, along with other important magazines, to continue to promote Negro writers. Winners will be announced after the dinner."

As our soups are served, Zora turns to Langston and me. "I've admired both of your work in *The Crisis*."

"Thank you," I say. "And you're a writer as well?"

"I am. I've been in school. At Howard University. I've been writing for *The Stylus*."

Langston snaps his fingers. "That's why your name is familiar to me."

I say, "I'm looking forward to reading some of your work."

"I can have something on your desk in the morning." She laughs, but I'm certain Zora isn't joshing.

The young woman is quite loquacious, and as we chitchat over dinner, I learn as much about Zora as I know of any of my writers:

"I was born in Notasulga, Alabama, although most of my early years were spent in Eatonville, Florida . . . I'm proud of being raised in the first town established by freedmen . . . My father was the mayor for a while."

Then Zora tells us about her high school studies at Morgan College, before she matriculated at Howard.

I'm certain I would have learned about each of Zora's Howard University professors if Mr. Clement Wood, the chairman for the poetry section of the contest, hadn't moved to the lectern. When we applaud the young poet, he shyly combs his fingers through his dark hair and begins, "There are so many writers to celebrate tonight, so I'll get right to it. Poetry was a competitive category, which made determining the winners especially difficult.

"First prize for poetry in the first *Opportunity* literary contest goes to 'The Weary Blues'"—Langston gasps—"by Langston Hughes." The room explodes in applause. I hug him, and his new friend Zora does the same.

Clement says, "I'd like to read this extraordinary lyric poem." He begins:

> Droning a drowsy syncopated tune,
> Rocking back and forth to a mellow croon,
> I heard a Negro play.
> Down on Lenox Avenue the other night.

When Clement finishes, the three hundred guests stand as Langston strolls to the stage to accept the forty-dollar first-place prize.

The second-place winner is Countee, for his poem "The One Who Said Me Nay." As his poem is read, I think this night cannot get any better . . . and then it does. Langston and Countee receive the same number of votes for third place.

The evening continues with judges like Zona Gale, Fannie Hurst, and James Weldon Johnson presenting the cash prizes to winners like Zora Neale Hurston, who wins two prizes herself.

It takes more than two hours for the awards to be announced in all the categories: poetry, short stories, essays, and plays. But even after Charles closes the evening thanking everyone for attending, few exit. The air still crackles with excitement for the monumental three hundred dollars presented to Negro writers tonight.

Just as Langston and I stand, Charles returns to the lectern. "Will all of the Negro poets, writers, and authors, whether you submitted for this contest or not, please join me in the front. I've hired Mr. James Van Der Zee to capture this evening in photographs for posterity."

There is a chorus of excited gasps and cheers. James Van Der Zee continues to rise in popularity, so much so, families now must wait two months to sit for portraits. How thrilling to have the famed photographer here, and I wonder if Charles will allow me to publish the picture in *The Crisis* as well.

I sit as the writers move en masse to the front. Langston and Countee walk side by side, patting each other on the back. On their way, Jean

Toomer joins them, followed by Gwendolyn Bennett and Arna Bontemps, who has recently moved to New York.

From the other side of the room, among the writers moving toward the front are the women I've published. There are only a few here tonight: Nella and Georgia, of course, and Anne Spencer and Carrie Clifford.

The writers gather, laughing and chatting, and Mr. Van Der Zee guides each as he stages the photograph. I take in the men and women before me, and suddenly, I'm submerged in a deluge of memories:

Countee at sixteen, when he couldn't return my gaze as we talked; dinner with nineteen-year-old Langston and his mother, and how terrified he was that evening; debating with Jean as he pondered how he wanted to be acknowledged and addressed as a man in America.

My eyes continue to glance over the men and women: I remember the first poem Georgia submitted, and Nella's eyes as she saw her name in print in the *Brownies' Book*.

Suddenly, emotions sweep aside my memories. These poets and writers came to me so tentative, yet eager. Now they are sophisticated young men and women, self-assured and accomplished, preparing to take center stage in this world.

"Is everyone ready?" Mr. Van Der Zee shouts.

Cheers rise, and my eyes brim with tears at the abundance of brilliance before me.

Just as Mr. Van Der Zee raises his camera, Langston shouts, "Wait!" Everyone freezes. "Jessie! Come up here!"

As if it was rehearsed, every head turns toward me, and now dozens of voices beckon me.

"You most of all must be in this photograph, Jessie," Charles says.

"Yes, you're an author," Zora shouts out.

Countee says, "Jessie Redmon Fauset is more than that."

I gulp down the knot constricting my throat. Then, with the biggest smile I can garner from the emotions overwhelming me, I move toward them.

"Right here in the center," Langston says. "You must stand in the middle of your literary babies."

Laughter echoes throughout, but Langston shakes his head. "I'm se-rious. Jessie, you're the reason we're here. You've birthed most of us. It's like you're a literary midwife."

As he hugs me, the writers around us applaud.

"I love that, Langston," Charles pipes in. "Jessie is the midwife of this movement."

There are more cheers, and I say, "I love it, I embrace it, and I ac-cept it."

Mr. Van Der Zee holds up his hand. "Can I get everyone to look this way?"

I square my shoulders as the words ring in my ears: *the midwife of this movement*. What high praise, I think as Mr. Van Der Zee takes pho-tograph after photograph. I've birthed these writers, and, regardless of the future, this beautiful legacy will remain with me.

Suddenly, Will's voice echoes in my mind: The Crisis *is my dream that I birthed alone.*

I stand there frozen as those words repeat in my head. And then, within seconds, the clarity I've sought for months, perhaps even years, washes over me.

I finally understand, and now I know what I must do.

CHAPTER 56

SATURDAY, MAY 2, 1925

As soon as I hear the click of the doorknob, I take a final glance at the letter and turn it over on the desk. I stand right as Will steps over the threshold.

"I wasn't sure you were going to come," I say.

He stares at me as if my words are absurd. "Of course I was." He glances around the room, our room, in the Hotel Olga. "This is the first time *you've* ever invited *me* here." He sighs, then loosens his tie as he moves toward the bed. "I guess I should ask about the dinner last night."

This is not where I expected our conversation to begin, but I welcome his words. "It was excellent. Very enlightening." When he questions me with just a glance, I add, "Langston and Countee won."

"I'll send them my congratulations." He pauses and softens. "Jess, I apologize for the way we left things yesterday, but I was taken aback. I didn't understand how you could support Charles Johnson after what he'd done to me."

"I understand." Then I repeat what he'd told me years ago: "*The Crisis* is your dream that you birthed alone. It's your baby, and anyone who attacks your baby attacks you."

"I wouldn't have articulated it quite that way, but yes. And it felt as if you were aligning with the man who targeted my baby, as you say."

"I would never hurt you or your baby, Will. I attended the dinner to support *my* babies."

He ponders my words before he smiles. "I guess we both have babies in this literary world." He tosses his jacket and tie onto the bed and then moves toward me. "Thank you for understanding. But more than that, thank you for inviting me here. It's been a long time, Jess. And I cannot put into words how much I've missed you." He cradles my cheek with his palm, and I close my eyes, falling into the feeling. But as he lowers his lips toward mine, I dip back and slip away from him.

He frowns as I move toward the desk. "We have to talk." Gazing over the letter I just completed, I hand it to Will.

Deep lines are carved in his forehead, and his hands remain at his sides as he stares at the paper, then glances at me. He shakes his head, recoiling as if he suspects the words I've written.

I step closer to him. "Please." More seconds pass before he accepts my letter. It takes him a moment to read the first line, and he gasps. He surprises me when he begins to read aloud, as if hearing the words may somehow alter their meaning:

"This letter is to tender my resignation from my position as the literary editor of *The Crisis* magazine."

He flops down onto the bed.

"Effective immediately."

He shakes his head.

"Words cannot express how much I have loved my time at *The Crisis* and the opportunities my position has afforded me." He continues reading, and when he completes the last paragraph, where I thank him for all he's done, he glances up. "No!"

"Yes."

"I cannot accept this."

"You must."

He stands. "I will not accept your resignation when I don't even understand why. Are you that upset that I didn't want you to go to the dinner last night?"

"I'm not upset about that at all," I say, pleased that I'm so calm. "I'm glad I attended, because that's where I gained clarity."

"Clarity about what, Jess? What happened?" His frustration is edging toward ire.

"What happened was that I dreamed, Will. I dreamed so many dreams that led me to you and becoming the literary editor of *The Crisis*. And for these five and a half years, I have lived my dream."

He waves the letter. "So why give me this?"

"Because this is where this dream ends. But I must never stop dreaming. Now I want new dreams."

"What in heaven's name are you talking about?"

"I've come to realize I've accomplished all that I can at *The Crisis*. My position here will never be any greater than what it is now."

"Jess, you're the literary editor, for God's sake."

"But I want more. And I can't have it, because *The Crisis* is your dream, your baby; you birthed it, and you're not giving it up. There's no room for me here."

He holds up his hands as if he's utterly befuddled. "No room? I *gave* you a title, a title of influence that no one has ever had except for you."

I smile, wondering if he hears himself. "You gave me a title, and that is where it will end. Because what I achieve at *The Crisis* will never be based on my accomplishments. What I achieve will only be based on what you're willing to give to me. And a title is not enough."

"So what is it that you want, Jess?"

"What I want, you can't give me. Because it's difficult for anyone to walk away from the dream they've manifested. So if you won't leave, then I must."

He stares, then his eyes widen with understanding. He sinks onto the bed. "Jess, I created *The Crisis*."

"I know."

"The most important periodical in the country for Negroes exists because of me."

"I know."

"I cannot walk away from it."

"I know and have no ill feelings. Working at *The Crisis* has been wonderful and will lead me to my next dream."

"And what is that?"

"To have a greater impact and a greater role." I pause and, with a smile, add, "To be an editor and to one day be as influential as W. E. B. Du Bois and *The Crisis* magazine."

His smile is framed by the sadness in his tone. "You want to become my competition."

"I want to become your equal."

"That's a lovely sentiment, but where will you do that in this country? Do your plans include founding a magazine?"

"I'm hopeful that with the success of *There Is Confusion*, I'll be considered for a position at an existing company."

There is so much skepticism in his eyes, and I understand. It's 1925, yet there are no Negroes—men or women—in New York publishing companies.

"I can do it, Will. I've been the first Negro woman to walk through many doors. I'm determined to do it again. I understand that I won't start at the top, but I'm excited about the opportunity before me.

"And it's not just publishing where the door is now open. I've spent so much time editing and writing for *The Crisis*. Now I'll have the time and the freedom to write what I want, to challenge and change this world with my words." He shakes his head, letting me know he doesn't share my excitement about either of my possibilities. "You've told me that I had many books inside of me, and I believe I do. I've already completed half of my second novel."

His eyebrows rise with surprise, and I continue, "Part of my résumé will be what you and I have accomplished at *The Crisis*. I'm very proud of the work we've done."

He glances at the letter once again. "I don't want you to leave," he begins with a sigh, "but we'll find you a new position. I'll speak to Joel Spingarn and—"

When he glances at me, I shake my head. "I'm leaving *The Crisis*. I'm leaving . . . everything."

When he frowns, I wonder if I should have included another line in the letter: *This also serves to inform you that I will no longer be your . . . I will no longer be your literary editor nor your surrogate wife.*

"Please, allow me a couple of months, and I will be out of the brownstone."

He leans away as if my words are offensive. "Why?"

"We both knew this day would come."

"Why now?"

"Because my career and love for you have become one and the same. It's time to sever both. God help me, I should have done this a long time ago."

He stands, stuffs his hands deep inside his pants pockets, and paces. At least a minute passes, and when he finally faces me, I can see the light has dimmed from his eyes. "I feel like you're taking everything from me at once." He stares at me as if he's never seen me before. "You're *really* leaving me." There is such astonishment in his tone that I wonder— in all his life, has Will always been the one to determine the parameters of every relationship?

I don't ask him, because the answer is of no consequence. When I reach for my jacket on the back of the chair, I will never know how Will crossed the room so quickly. Not even a second passes before he is behind me, his breath burning red-hot on my neck.

"Jess," he whispers, his lips grazing my ear. "Don't do this."

I wait for my heart to regain its rhythm before I slip into my jacket and face him. The sorrow in his eyes matches the grief in mine.

"Jess."

"Will."

"Please."

"Thank you. For everything." I pause to settle the quivering in my voice. "For all that you've given to me."

"I want to give you more."

"There is nothing more that I need. From you." With all my might, I press down the sobs rising within me. "Goodbye, Will."

My steps are unsteady, a mélange of emotions crashing within me. Can I do this? Can I walk away from the only man I've ever loved?

I reach for the doorknob. It is just a split second, but it gives my heart enough time to make me pivot, and I race back to Will. His arms are open as if he knew I would return to him. When our lips touch, love overtakes me, and I kiss Will with zealous passion.

Our kiss goes on and on and on until I find the fortitude to pull away. There is scarcely a breath left within me as I gaze into Will's hopeful eyes. I cup his cheek in my palm. "Another time, a different place. *Je t'aime pour toujours, Will*," I whisper before I walk out of our hotel room for the very last time.

I have found my proper role.

CHAPTER 57

TUESDAY, JUNE 30, 1925

Maman glances around the apartment. "We had such good times here."

"We did," I say, "and there are many wonderful days ahead."

My mother holds my face with both hands. "I'm so very proud of you."

I haven't done anything more than walk away from a married man. But from Maman, I will never tire of hearing those words. "Thank you. But you better skedaddle. You must take your trunk to the railway express before you catch your train."

"When will the messenger be here?"

"In an hour. I'll give him the keys and then I will leave straightaway for Mary-Helen's."

My mother hugs me tightly, and then, with a final glance around the parlor, she exits with my sister in tow.

Once I close the door, I grab my journal and rush to the window seat. I settle on the cushions, wanting to appreciate the final minutes in my favorite place.

I ponder for a moment some of the most important words I will ever write:

Dear Mr. Spingarn:

Thank you for your kind note about my time at The Crisis. I enjoyed my position as the literary editor, and I hope that in my time there, I brought honor to the NAACP.

I am writing to ask you about a possible position with Harcourt, Brace & Company. I realize you are not involved in the day-to-day operations of the publishing company. However, I hope you can direct me to the proper person to speak to, as well as offer a letter of recommendation for me.

I pause, determining how to proceed. Papa taught me that for every problem presented, there must be a solution offered.

I understand the challenges your company may face with a hire such as mine, especially in the position of editor. Although I am certainly qualified, competent, and would welcome such an offer, I would also consider a more modest entry position, where I can work from my home and would not have to enter the office. Perhaps I can begin as a proofreader.

A proofreader is certainly not the literary editor. However, in a bigger—and white—company, this is a great beginning for a new dream . . . if they will consider employing a Phi Beta Kappa graduate with more than five years of editorial experience at one of the preeminent magazines in the country . . . who happens to be a Negro. Even if my hiring can only happen if I work behind the closed doors of my home, it will give me the opportunity to prove my mettle. I will advance from there.

My new dream.

Now I must consider the closing for the letter, and then I will type it this evening at my sister's home.

Leaning against the wall, I can only smile as I consider this opportunity. However, as much as I'm looking forward to a new career in publishing, my greatest joy lies in the time I will now have to write. Even as I'm delving into my next novel, new themes for future stories are already stirring inside of me. Maman is correct—I can change this world with words, and what I want to do most in my novels is impart the lesson that Negroes share the same humanity as white folks.

The knock on the door surprises and disappoints me. The messenger has arrived quite early. I slide from the window and scurry to the door. When I swing it open, my mouth is agape.

"Hello, Jessie."

It takes a moment to find my voice, and once I do, I only say, "Nina."

"May I come in?"

I step aside, then close the door, although I remain where I stand, astonished and curious. My eyes follow Nina as she steps across the room, taking in the space of the home her husband found for me.

She remains silent as she studies the parlor, and I study her in the black-and-ivory day dress with short sleeves that flutter around her arms. The draped collar tie and banded drop waist add to the elegance of her ensemble, as does her black-and-white-striped picture hat. Mrs. Du Bois is always stylish and sophisticated.

Finally, she faces me. "I understand you're moving today."

"Yes," I say, and wonder how she knows. I haven't spoken to Will since the day I left him at the Hotel Olga. Then I consider that Will and Jack Nail, my landlord, are friends.

"I'm sure you're wondering why I'm here." She doesn't pause for me to respond. "I wanted to wish you well."

She sounds as earnest and as gracious as she always has. And I respond in kind. "Thank you."

"One of my greatest regrets is that you and I didn't have the opportunity to spend more time together."

I exhale with relief. I'd considered that Nina was here to confront and accuse me—rightfully so—of all the wrong I'd done. But clearly, that is not the case.

"I never made many friends in the city. *The Crisis* kept me quite busy."

"*The Crisis,*" she says. Then, with a pointed glance, she adds, "And my husband."

My stomach lurches. This *is* a confrontation.

Nina tilts her head as if now she's the curious one. "Did you think I didn't know?"

In my head, I've always wondered. In my heart, I've always known.

"I'm pragmatic, Jessie, not naive. I'm like so many women of my social standing who are neither stupid nor unaware. So of course, I knew of you . . . and all the others." That astounds me, although I don't understand why. If I found out about Georgia, surely Nina knew about me, Georgia . . . and as she just said, the others.

Nina titters. "Jessie, please don't tell me you thought you were the only one."

I stand composed, although I am shaken.

"Yes, there were others," she continues, as if I've responded and we are having a conversation. Her voice becomes softer, sadder. "However, you were the most important woman to Will."

"I don't think that's true." I finally speak. There is no need for further pretense.

"Oh, it's very true. No one has captured his attention the way you have. For God's sake, he created an entire position at the magazine he loves just for you," she says with a chuckle that has no joy. "Of course, he loves me; I gave him his greatest gift. But he saw you as his intellectual and social equal."

My mind is blank of any words that I can speak.

"And because of that, you are the only woman who gave me even a moment of concern."

"I never wanted to muddle your marriage."

"Yes," she nods, "that's what you said to your mother."

She pauses, allowing me another moment to grasp these words. She *had* heard me that day at Frank's. Yet she'd remained silent.

"My husband would never have left me, that was never my concern. But he cared so deeply for you, Jessie. Even now, in the weeks since you ended your affair, he's like a book with missing pages."

I want to stop her, ask her how she knows all of this. But it doesn't seem proper for me to utter more than a few words. And certainly, I have no right to ask *her* questions.

Nina continues, "He'll be fine. I'll make sure of that."

"I want the best for Will." Then I add quickly, "And for you as well, Nina." I'm certain those words don't ring true, but I speak from my heart.

"Will you be returning to Philadelphia?"

"Perhaps." There's no reason to tell her that my greatest desire is to remain in New York, to live here in Harlem.

"I do have to say that, while your position originated only so my husband could have you here, you spun that and built what is now the center of this Negro renaissance. You took something I know Will meant to be nothing, and created a space for Negro writers, especially the women writers. A job well done, Jessie."

Where does this woman get her grace? Under these circumstances, I would never speak with such kindness.

"Thank you for saying that."

"Well, I just wanted to say goodbye. Traveling mercies to you," she says before she steps outside.

I close the door and stand with my back pressed against it, absorbing our conversation. Nina came to give me praise, I'm certain of that. However, I'm just as sure that she came to place a period on my years with her husband.

On that, she and I agree.

The knock on the door startles me, until I remember the messenger. I rush to grab the keys. After greeting the young man, I say, "Can you give me a few minutes?"

"Of course. I'll wait outside. I'll lock up as soon as you leave."

Once alone, I stuff my journal into my satchel, and then I stroll through the apartment. I check each room to ensure we've left nothing behind. And I use the time to say goodbye to this home that gave me so much joy. Just like *The Crisis*. Just like Will.

Standing in the middle of the parlor, I slowly spin, taking in the four corners. Then, without a glance back, I step into the hallway and onto the stoop. I wait for the profound sadness to overtake me, but all I feel is the light shining from my years in Harlem, and the joyful hope for the days ahead.

As when I first arrived all those years ago, I'm enraptured by Harlem's rhapsody. Today, however, it's not Mamie Smith's voice floating through an open window. Nor is it the laughter from the men in front of the barbershop.

Today, Harlem's melody is infused with words:

> Love, leave me like the light.
> Well, son, I'll tell you: Life for me ain't been no crystal
>   stair.
> Pour O pour that parting soul in song.
> This cool night is strange. Among midsummer days.

That's the music that resounds in my mind as I descend the brownstone's steps. Yes, I am bidding farewell to my home and *The Crisis*, but I am leaving behind a gift to the place that has given so much to me. I'm bestowing the words of many to Harlem.

With that thought, I'm almost giddy as I strut past the brownstones and the familiar storefronts. I wave to the little girls playing ring-around-the-rosy and to the women who sit on the stoop chitchatting. I nod at the men shooting the breeze in front of the barbershop, and pause to give the boy hawking the *New York Times* two cents for a copy.

Before I turn the corner, I glance back over my shoulder at the Seventh Avenue block that has been my home.

"J'aime Harlem," I whisper.

And I always will.

AUTHOR'S NOTE

First, I must begin with—this is historical fiction. This is the story of Jessie Redmon Fauset through my eyes, but most of all, through my heart.

I discovered Jessie by listening to an episode from Trymaine Lee's podcast *Into America*, from a series called Harlem on my Mind. As the story of this woman unfolded in the thirty minutes or so of the podcast, I became completely engrossed in her life. As a Black female writer, why hadn't I heard the name of the woman who'd discovered so many Harlem Renaissance writers? Why did I not know Jessie, when she was arguably the most prolific writer during this time?

After that podcast, I found the rabbit hole and jumped all the way in! Like with so many other women who'd been lost in the folds of history, there wasn't a lot of information on Jessie. But by the time I submitted this idea to my editor, I had read dozens of articles, searched through census records, and found out more about Jessie's relationship with W. E. B. Du Bois.

For the next year and a half, Jessie took me on a journey where, at times, she held my hand and guided me. Although I am from New York, I never lived in Harlem, and so twice during my writing, I moved into a Harlem hotel for weeks. I not only walked the streets of Harlem but visited the places central to Jessie's life, from the brownstone where she lived to the church (which is still there) where she worshipped. I went to the addresses of nightclubs and restaurants that are no longer standing, but I was able to imagine what it was like one hundred years ago. (Interesting note: the second time I went to Harlem, I stayed in the new Renaissance hotel . . . the Harlem Renaissance. Get it? How cool!)

What was amazing about writing this story was that I not only delved into the lives of Jessie and W. E. B. but learned so much about the writers I'd known and long admired: Langston Hughes, Countee Cullen, Jean Toomer, and especially Nella Larsen. To this point, this has been one of the highest honors of my career, to portray these literary geniuses and giants. I stand in awe of them.

However, while this has been a wonderful writing journey, every day I was filled with trepidation about one important part of Jessie's life— her affair with W. E. B. I wanted to write this book with care and preserve the legacy of not only Jessie Redmon Fauset but Dr. W. E. B. Du Bois. William Edward Burghardt Du Bois is one of the most important civil rights activists in our history, and that is just one small part of his résumé. The first Black man to receive a PhD from Harvard had a tremendous impact in our society.

Yet W. E. B. Du Bois and Jessie Redmon Fauset did have an affair, and for most people, that is unacceptable. However, I couldn't ignore this part of their story. Their relationship was integral to who the two were, especially together. In fact, I've wondered how history would differ if the two of them had not been involved. Would there have been a literary section of *The Crisis* magazine? Would we have heard the voices of Langston Hughes and Countee Cullen without Jessie and W. E. B. being together?

It was a struggle for me to delve into this part of their lives and write some of their most intimate scenes, but I came to accept that our heroes in history had complicated lives. They, like all of us, were a composite of their flaws and virtues, and I had to present them that way. And, if I was going to write an honest character, which I always strive to do, I had to note W. E. B.'s misogynistic and elitist tendencies.

I hope that inside this story you found Jessie to be the person I wanted you to meet—a brilliant but vulnerable woman who was at the epicenter of the Harlem Renaissance. It was Langston Hughes who first called her the midwife of the literary side of the New Negro Movement.

She was the woman who birthed, nurtured, and then set into the world the literary geniuses we've all come to know.

Besides loving Jessie Redmon Fauset, I am a woman who is beyond grateful to her. As a Black female writer, I stand on her shoulders. Thank you, Jessie Redmon Fauset. Thank you with everything within me.

HISTORICAL NOTE

I loved everything about writing this novel—the time period, the Harlem Renaissance, learning more about writers I'd admired for so long . . . and of course, spending just about every moment of the last year and a half with Jessie Redmon Fauset. I attempted to anchor this story in the historical facts I found inside a wealth of information: biographies, census records, research papers, articles, and podcasts . . . and I read every issue of *The Crisis* magazine from October 1919 through September 1925. Reading *The Crisis* not only showed me what was important to this community but helped me capture the language of the time.

Also, *The Crisis* gave me the details of several events in this novel, especially the Pan-African Congress—the who, what, when, where, and why of the congress, and how Jessie's speech was internationally acclaimed. It was inside *The Crisis* where I learned about all of W. E. B.'s travels, came to understand Jessie's love for French as she translated numerous French poems and stories into English for the magazine, and found the specifics of the literary contests.

It was also inside the pages of *The Crisis* where history intermingled with my personal life. After ending the publication of the *Brownies' Book*, *The Crisis* did a nationwide search for the baby who would appear on the first cover of the return of the children's edition. The baby who was chosen, Valdora Turner, is the mother of my dear friend Jackie Spaulding McCoy, whom I've known for more than fifty years and who brought this picture to my attention. I found her mother's story while researching my book, and I was thrilled to honor my friend's mother this way.

As I researched, I wasn't surprised that I found far more information about W. E. B. Du Bois than Jessie Redmon Fauset; however, often when a source mentioned W. E. B. and his life, Jessie was mentioned. In the Pulitzer Prize–winning *W.E.B. Du Bois: A Biography, 1868–1963*, the author, David Levering Lewis, took great care in describing Jessie and W. E. B.'s relationship, distinguishing Jessie from the many other women in his life. Lewis called the two "star-crossed lovers" and said they had a "parallel marriage." Other sources said that W. E. B. was never seen without Jessie at his side. From that, and from observations in other articles that described their relationship in a similar fashion, I developed the love story between Jessie Redmon Fauset and W. E. B. Du Bois.

Another important source of research was the letters. There weren't many between Jessie and W. E. B. (although there were letters between others about the two), but there were a few between W. E. B. and other women. That's where I discovered his relationship with Georgia Douglas Johnson.

It was also in the letters where I read about the party Jessie hosted for W. E. B. and his wife. Yes, that really happened. In a letter to his daughter, Yolande, W. E. B. described every detail of the party: the date, where it was held, how cold it was that night, what happened to their car in the frigid weather, what they wore, how many people were there—I didn't have to imagine anything about that scene. Without that letter, the party never would have been inside the pages of this novel. How could I ever conceive of a mistress hosting an anniversary party like that? My imagination doesn't run that deep.

I wondered why W. E. B. was so very deliberate and specific in this letter to his daughter about this party. One part of Jessie's story that I didn't include in this novel was her relationship with W. E. B.'s daughter. Yolande was an illustrator and a budding writer whom Jessie took under her wing at *The Crisis*. With the time Yolande spent in the NAACP offices, I'm sure she became suspicious of her father and Jessie. What better way to set aside any concerns Yolande may have had than to tell her about the party hosted by Jessie?

Using the same research sources, I gained insight into the lives of the other Harlem Renaissance writers: Langston Hughes and all of the information about his mother, who was at that first dinner with Jessie and W. E. B., his challenging relationship with his father and how he came to write "The Negro Speaks of Rivers," his other relatives, and his one year at Columbia and his reasons for leaving the university; Countee Cullen and his relationship with his father, all the awards and honors that he won, and his time at New York University; Jean Toomer and his battle with his identity, which was so fascinating to me; Nella Larsen and her husband, her job at the 135th Street library (which is now the Schomburg Center for Research in Black Culture), her struggle with writing that first novel, and being included with, while at the same time often feeling excluded from, the "Harlem elite."

For the narrative and pacing of the story, I took a few liberties as a fiction writer when it came to history and timing. First, when Jessie relocated to New York City, most accounts said she moved there with her sister. However, when I found records showing the sisters with different addresses, I reimagined this story with her stepmother, Bella Huff Fauset, who, for reasons of respectability, never would have allowed Jessie to live alone. Bella—a Jewish woman who married a Black man— was fascinating to me. As an integrationist—I'd never heard that term until writing this novel—she would have been very involved in the New Negro Movement if she had been in Harlem.

I also tinkered a bit with history with regard to Langston Hughes. When Langston left Columbia in 1922, he spent a year in New York, working first on Staten Island on a vegetable farm, and then delivering flowers in Manhattan. The next year, he left the country. Langston worked as a seaman, traveling throughout Europe (living in England and then France for a little while) and Africa for two years. He didn't begin working with Charlotte Osgood Mason until 1927.

However, Langston was such an important part of the Harlem Renaissance that I didn't want to exclude him. He and Jessie developed a very close relationship. So I compacted his story and included his time with Charlotte inside the timeline of this novel.

Charlotte and the many white women like her *had* to be included in any novel about the Harlem Renaissance. I was completely engrossed when I read *Miss Anne in Harlem: The White Women of the Black Renaissance* by Carla Kaplan. Inside those pages, I learned of the various reasons why many white women became part of the New Negro Movement. As patrons, they assisted Black writers financially, giving the writers time and space to write, and socially, helping them make necessary connections with white publishers and others. We can debate the reasons for their assistance; however, their positive impact is unarguable.

While I shifted the timing between Langston and Charlotte much earlier than their actual meeting, the relationship I depicted between them was very close to the reality.

I also adjusted the timing slightly with Nella Larsen Imes's employment at the library. Some records show Nella starting at the 135th Street library in 1921, others in 1922. To move the story forward, I began Nella's employment earlier. However, it is a fact that the 135th Street branch was the first integrated New York Public Library location in the city, and Nella was the second Black person hired, as a junior assistant in the children's section.

Other tinkering I did with the timing: Mamie Smith first sang "Harlem Blues" in 1918. The song was written by Perry Bradford for his revue *Made in Harlem* and was later renamed "Crazy Blues" when OkeH Records released it. However, the song wasn't recorded until 1920. The Hotel Olga actually opened six months later than in the novel. Langston Hughes didn't attend the dinner for Jessie's release of *There Is Confusion* in 1924—he was out of the country—although he did attend the big *Opportunity* literary awards dinner in May 1925, which is where he and Jessie met Zora Neale Hurston.

I did not follow the timeline of magazine production—needing eight weeks for this and twelve weeks for that—at all! So please forgive me for being a better writer than I am a magazine production manager. (Although, I learned everything I could about coated and uncoated paper! Whew!)

It is important that I note two "historical facts" I discovered, which were not facts at all. For her entire life, Jessie believed she was the first

Black woman elected to Phi Beta Kappa. In fact, she was the second. Mary Annette Anderson was elected to Phi Beta Kappa in 1899 from Middlebury College. However, without the internet or even the most basic of research tools available, it appears this wasn't uncovered until the early 2000s. So for the purpose of this story, I stayed with what Jessie, and everyone in her world, believed to be true.

The second "historical fact": Langston Hughes always said he was born in 1902. In 2018, it was discovered he was, in fact, born in 1901. Again, for the purpose of this novel, I used 1902 as his birth year, as that is what Langston believed—or at least that is what he told everyone.

Finally, Jessie left *The Crisis* in 1926, not 1925 as I depicted. While Jessie resigned from the magazine under circumstances a little different from how she departed in the novel, she did leave because W. E. B. had concerns about the financial management of the literary contests. Her departure was not as amicable as I portrayed it, although she and W. E. B. remained in contact. Jessie appeared on the guest list of Yolande and Countee Cullen's wedding in 1928, and there is a letter from W. E. B. to Jessie where he describes passing her home one night and seeing her light on. He wanted to stop, but didn't because she was married. Yes . . . Jessie, who said she would never marry, married Herbert Harris, an insurance broker, in 1929, when she was forty-seven years old.

Upon her resignation from *The Crisis*, Jessie did hope to continue working in publishing. She reached out to Joel Spingarn and suggested "working from home" as a solution to the challenge of her race. However, Jessie was never hired by either Mr. Spingarn or any other publishing company. So she returned to teaching and taught French at DeWitt Clinton High School (the school Countee Cullen attended) from 1927 to 1944. A side note: James Baldwin attended DeWitt from 1938 to 1942. It is very likely that the two met in Jessie's classroom. I can imagine another great poet/writer mentored by Jessie Redmon Fauset.

Although teaching wasn't Jessie's desire at the time, it did afford her the time to write. She published three other novels: *Plum Bun* (1928), *The Chinaberry Tree* (1931), and *Comedy: American Style* (1933). When added to all the other writing Jessie did for *The Crisis* (from 1919 to 1926, she had a poem, story, article, or novelette inside just about every issue) as well as writing for every edition of the *Brownies' Book* for the two years of its existence, it could be said that Jessie Redmon Fauset was the most prolific writer of the Harlem Renaissance.

Yet, despite her achievements, she was unable to find a position in publishing, and eventually this important woman faded into historical obscurity. However, there has recently been renewed interest in Jessie. Articles have appeared in the *New York Times*, the *New Yorker*, and other newspapers and magazines giving her the recognition she deserves. People are discovering this writer, editor, and mentor and sharing her story. A bright light is being shone on this central figure of the Harlem Renaissance, and no one is more deserving of this recognition than Jessie Redmon Fauset.

ACKNOWLEDGMENTS

When I wrote my first novel twenty-five years ago, I realized it had taken an entire village to get my book from a thought in my head to the bookstore shelves. All these years later, that principle remains true. No one can write a good book alone. You were able to read *Harlem Rhapsody* because, while I'm noted as the author, there are so many behind these pages who helped me not only bring this story forward but get this book into your hands.

This journey began, of course, with Marie Benedict, who introduced me to writing historical fiction and the wonderful world of women whose stories must be told. Saying it's been a joy doesn't even describe how much fun I've had working with Marie on our joint novels, but I'll never be able to thank her enough for the tough love she gave me when she edited *Harlem Rhapsody*. This story is so much richer because of her. (Now we must get to work on our third novel together! Get excited, because I certainly am.)

My amazing agent, Liza Dawson, has guided my career for almost fifteen years. And with each year, she presses me to reach higher. Whew! That first editorial letter for *Harlem Rhapsody* almost made me want to find the nearest cliff. But after a deep breath, I went back to work. I'm so grateful that Liza pushed me beyond what I thought was possible.

When I decided to write a solo historical project, I presented three ideas to my executive editor, Kate Seaver. Without hesitation, she chose Jessie's story, and although this wasn't my first choice, I trusted Kate. Best decision I ever made! (Besides agreeing to work with her, of course.) This was the right story, for the right time, and through several rounds of edits, Kate challenged me, never stopping, *always* nudging me further. An editor who believes makes all the difference in a writer's career. I will never be able to express how amazing it is to work with Kate. Each time, I'm better because of her.

For four years now, I've been blessed to work with the most incredible people at Berkley—the team who makes the publishing magic happen: the president of Penguin Publishing Group, Allison Dobson; the CEO of Penguin Random House, Nihar Malaviya; the president of Putnam, Dutton, and Berkley, Ivan Held; the executive vice president and publisher of Berkley, Christine Ball; the senior vice president and editor in chief at Berkley, Claire Zion; the vice president, deputy publisher, and director of marketing at Berkley, Jeanne-Marie Hudson; the vice president, associate publisher, and director of publicity at Berkley, Craig Burke; the senior vice president and executive creative director at PPG, Anthony Ramondo; the director of art and design for Berkley, Emily Osborne; the deputy director of marketing at Berkley, Jin Yu; marketing associate at Berkley, Hillary Tacuri; assistant directors of publicity at Berkley, Lauren Burnstein and Danielle Keir; publicist at Berkley, Dache' Rogers; executive managing editor at Berkley, Christine Legon; associate director of art and design for PPG Interior Design, Kristin del Rosario; associate production manager for PPG, Katheryn Gao; senior production editor at Berkley, Lindsey Tulloch; and editorial assistant at Berkley, Amanda Maurer. And of course, the entire, amazing Penguin Publishing Group sales team. I thank them all for pulling out that publishing magic once again for *Harlem Rhapsody*.

I must shout out my Soror Januela M. Burt, PhD, my "historical editor," who checked the facts about the Harlem Renaissance, Jessie's membership in Delta Sigma Theta Sorority, Inc., and so much more. Without Dr. Burt, Jessie would have been riding around DC looking for a hotel in the wrong section of the district. Yikes!

And speaking of Delta Sigma Theta, what can I say? For years now, whenever the women of my Sorority hear that I have a new book, the support is instantaneous. I cannot possibly begin to shout out the thousands of women who are *always* there for me, but especially because this novel is about one of our esteemed members, I want to recognize Elsie Cooke-Holmes, international president and chair, National Board of Directors, Delta Sigma Theta Sorority, Inc. And I may get into a little trouble here because there are so many I love, but there are a few Sorors who have had my back since the beginning and pushed my career as if it was their own. A million thank-yous to: Stephanie Perry Moore, Denise Dowdy, Marci Butler Holt, Yolanda Rodgers, and Charlene Ayers, and especially all of my Sorors in the Long Beach Alumnae Chapter (my home for over nineteen years), and now my chapter Sorors in the Washington DC Alumnae Chapter of Delta Sigma Theta Sorority, Inc. I think Soror Jessie Redmon Fauset would be so proud of what our Sorority has become and all the work we've accomplished in the one hundred years since she was initiated! I am forever grateful to all of you. AOML.

Finally, the people who are listed here last certainly come first: the booksellers, especially the independent bookstores that hand-sell our novels; the librarians who have constantly championed my books year after year; the book clubs that rush out to buy my novels as soon as they hit the shelves; and all the readers who spread the word—there aren't enough words to express how thankful and blessed I am to have all of you. These last twenty-five years have only happened because of you all. Now, here's to the next twenty-five!